A Place of
Meadows
and Tall Trees

In memory of my brother
Huw Thomas Jenkins
1964–2005

Clare
Dudman

A Place of
Meadows
and Tall Trees

SEREN

Seren is the book imprint of
Poetry Wales Press Ltd
57 Nolton Street, Bridgend, Wales, CF31 3AE
www.seren-books.com

ISBN: 978-1-85411-518-8

A CIP record for this title is available from the British Library.

Cover image: 'Patagonia' Oil canvas by Elisabet d'Epenoux
Typesetting by Lucy Llewellyn
Printed in Plantin by Cromwell Press Group, Wiltshire

The publisher works with the financial assistance of The Welsh Books
Council.

Contents

Prologue

North Wales 1849

Old Hannah Lloyd was roused from sleep by the dogs. Intruder. Their barks should have made her frantic, but she paused for a few seconds to touch the other side of the bed. Of course he wasn't there: a dream, that's all it had been. She shook the impression of his hand from her shoulder and the warmth of him from her back. Gone. Gone for good he was.

A renewed burst of barking made her crawl over the coldness of his side, grip onto the walls of her bed and let herself down. These days it did no good to hurry. The world had become treacherous, with objects obscured by the thickening skin of cataracts.

The dogs were at the door, leaping at it, snarling. When she lifted the latch they were away into the haze of morning light, yapping absurdly at something. Before she could open the door fully there were shouts, one high-pitched scream which could have been animal or human and then the sound of a gun firing, once and then once again, and then silence.

'Gwyn? Anwyn?' She stood at the door peering dimly through the bright air.

'Where are you, *fy mechgyn?*'

She felt for her shawl, pulled it around her and started slowly along the path. She knew each broken slab, each place where she would have to reach out to find a handhold to help her step down. She was still firm on her feet but her near-blindness had made her afraid. In the haze that now afflicted everything, she could hear whimpering.

'Gwyn? Is that you?'

She waited, her head tilted to the side, listening. The whimpering changed pitch. She stepped forward again. 'Who's there? Who is it?'

She had gone beyond the garden now, past the wall and

into the meadow where there was no path. A few paces more and she trod on something soft. She stumbled, her arms out, her knees sinking into warmth.

'Anwyn!' Her favourite dog. Her old friend. The golden fur and the black eyes. She shuffled backwards, caught his head in her hands, and clutched tightly onto his ears even though she could feel something wet, something warm. The animal whimpered again and his eyes closed against her hands. 'Anwyn!'

Behind her the long dry grass snapped and broke. A foot in a boot nudged Anwyn's rump and then a single sudden wrench pulled her to her feet. She could just see the cloth of a jacket: good stuff, too good for anyone she knew. She tried to pull herself away but whoever was holding her had a grip like lockjaw.

'Leave me alone. Let me go.' She lurched forward with her head, her mouth open. Some of her teeth were loose. She left one of them embedded in the hand of the man who held her. He cried out, tried to shove her away but she went for him again, using her nails as well this time. He backed away gaining enough momentum to sweep forward again with his fist, cracking it smartly against her chin so she crumpled immediately onto the carcass of her dog.

'Behave now will you, *gwrach*?'

She moaned softly into Anwyn's fur.

'You had Sir Philip's letter, didn't you?' The boot nudged at her just as it had nudged at the dog, 'You have to be out. Today. *Heddi*. Understand? Your son, the one with big ideas, didn't vote for him. His Lordship didn't like that.'

'Probably can't read, anyway.' Another voice, and then another boot joining the first one, trying to turn her over as if she was something dirty that had been dumped there and needed to be inspected. 'Is she hurt?'

'Not much. The *gwrach* went for me, Trev. Look. Am I bleeding?'

Trevor sniggered. 'Nothing your Nerys can't lick away. What did you have to hit her for?'

'She'd have killed me, man.'

Trevor snorted. 'Well, you can take her in if she's a mess.' The boots stopped their probing. 'It's clear up there now, is it?'

'Still full of her *cach*, I expect.'

'Good. We need some tinder to get it going, Joni boy.'

'You're not going to let her back in first?'

'She had her chance. Now you get her down to town while I see to business up here.' Trevor's boot gave the silent mound in front of them another small nudge. 'She got anyone, beside that la-di-dah son of hers?'

'Oh aye, she pupped all right, a litter of little wasters. A son and a couple of daughters in those sties by the river.'

'Well, let them see to her.' He raised his voice. 'The least they can do, eh, old woman?'

Joni knelt down and levered up her head. '*Cach*. I didn't hit her that hard.' He let the head fall again and then dragged at the arm.

Trevor laughed. 'Looks like you're going to be in the *llaca* when they see that, *fy ffrind*.'

Joni paused, held the old face with both hands and bellowed into it. 'If anyone asks, you fell. Understand, you old crone? You fell.'

*

They saw the fire from the lakeside: a glow on the hill that drew the eye. But it was the nose that had been drawn first: burning, a rich odour of something other than wood. People said it was the smell of a life burning; all its hopes, its memories and disappointments. The old woman would not be consoled. Her daughters and then her granddaughters took turns in bathing her wound and talking to her, but she would not speak back. For days she sat outside their house in the street, on the wall and then on a chair, watching where a spiral of smoke beyond the lake grew smaller. People said she couldn't see and yet still she watched. And when it was entirely gone her eyes closed. Days later, when she opened them again it was obvious to everyone that her mind had gone too.

One

It is as if the land is coming on them in the dark, as if they are not moving, as if the sea is bringing it close: great cliffs each side, and in the distance the grinning crescent of a beach. At last, after all these weeks.

Everyone is on deck, the strange half-light illuminating their pale, silent faces. It is difficult to see, difficult to tell who is who. A single figure divides into two and then three: a slight ginger-haired man and his wider wife, then a child at their feet: Silas and Megan James and their child Myfanwy.

'I can't stand still,' he says and squeezes her shoulder slightly, but she keeps looking at the land. 'It's been so long,' she says, 'if we stop watching maybe it will go.'

That's what things do if you don't watch them.

There is a mewling from the shawl wrapped around her and Silas pats the warm small globe of material. Mine, he thinks, and allows a warm current of satisfaction to rise through his body.

He looks again at the land and then at the people watching. The light is gaining strength, dispelling shadows. He smiles. Everyone is dressed to the nines. Sunday jackets, and Sunday frocks, clean clothes on the children. Who are they expecting to impress? The Indians? Indians. The thought makes him shiver. Heathen and vicious according to some, given to marauding new settlements and carrying off the women and children. Will they be lined up on the shore ready to greet them? He peers out into the gloom, but still there is neither sight nor sound of life.

He is startled by a tug at his trousers. 'Dadda?' He reaches down and allows the soft small plump hand to close around his own. She is hopping up and down, restless and impatient.

'Calm, child.' They'll pay for this excitement later with her tears and protests. With his other hand he smoothes her head and feels the small springs of her curls bounce against his fingers – a shade halfway between his thin strands of vibrant orange and her mother's brown.

'Dadda, what are you looking at? Can I see?' Her small

11

quacking voice. Her hand tugging at his own like the string on a kite in the wind, but he doesn't feel, doesn't hear. All he can think about is the land – how it will feel to have something solid beneath his feet, to hear the sound of wind through the branches of trees, and to taste fresh food again – fruit, a few leaves and meat without salt. There are other thoughts too – shadows and wisps of something dark that he pushes away before they gather substance in his mind. Not yet, he thinks. Later, when there's time. Then he will let it take hold, let it do its damnedest and hurt. But not yet.

For now there is just what lies in front of them. Land. He shuts his eyes, leans against the railing, and tries to remember how it will smell: the aromatic tang of crushed leaves, the barn-like fog of hay and cut grass, the damp mouldy smell of the forest floor... the rich stench of a prize sow's muddy boudoir. Trotters churning up the *cach*. He smiles. Yes, just now, he longs even for that.

He opens his eyes again and peers forward. It is still hard to see. There is a great bank of cloud covering the sun and everything is grey. The shore seems lighter than he'd expect and there's something strange about the flatness.

'Dadda?'

He looks down at her and she tugs again at his trousers. Her voice, when it comes this time, is complaining and threatening tears. 'Why won't you lift me up? I want to see.'

The weight of her always surprises him. She clenches her knees at his waist and hooks her arm around his neck and then squeals as the sun comes out. 'Look Dadda! Yellow!'

The sudden sight of it winds him like a blow to the stomach. Behind the white beach the land is almost as pale, and is bordered by cliffs that look as if they have been painted there by a madman's brush – jarring oranges and more yellow. Even though the sunlight is weak the land ahead is glowing. Something grips his lungs, squeezes them tight. No trees. No grass. Too yellow, too bright. He closes his eyes and opens them again but the brightness stays. It is unreal, untrue, a brash, feverish dream.

'Dadda!' Myfanwy wails, 'stop it. Let go. You're hurting me.'

Her voice brings him back. Something real. He is holding her too tight, crushing her to him. He releases her and then carefully draws her head towards him so he can feel her burning cheek with his own, then, still looking at the land, turns his head slightly to kiss her. Sorry. Oh Myfanwy, *cariad, cariad*. Still holding her to him he squints ahead, trying to see something of promise. Not a single tree. Not a single patch of grass. Some off-white patches which could be tents, and a brown hulk of a wreck protruding from the water ahead of them. Apart from that, just yellow cliffs pitted with holes, too shallow to be called caves, and a few scraps of vegetation: dead-looking bushes and something that looks like it could perhaps be a bramble.

'This can't be the place,' he says. 'Soon someone will realise. That drunk of a captain has made a mistake.'

Megan gives no sign that she's heard. She's glaring at the land as if she's waiting for it to change into something else. As the sun climbs everything is becoming clearer and more vivid. A flock of birds erupt from a cliff with a couple of loud calls, and then settle again almost immediately. 'Seagulls!' she says, and grips onto his arm.

Two

It is the 27th July 1865, midwinter. The sun rises timorously from the South Atlantic to no great height then slumps back down towards the desert of Patagonia. The day is cold and clear. Somewhere near the beach, which so far has no name but one day soon will be called Port Madryn, a cannon fires and causes some of the children to cry. At noon a keen-eyed child claims to spot a flag billowing on a pole – green on the bottom, white above with a faint indication of red in the middle; *the red dragon*, the child says, turning around to catch any approbation – and shortly afterwards a schooner appears in the bay from the north.

'That's his,' says the first mate, who seems to have the eyes of an eagle. 'Mr Lloyd's. I reckon I can see him on deck. He'll have brought some fresh supplies down here from Buenos Aires.'

The *Mimosa's* dinghy is launched, and Silas follows it across the bay. It merges with the sea and then re-emerges again, disappears and appears then seems to disappear for good. His eyes are weaker than the mate's. If he squeezes his eyelids together hard he can just pick out the schooner – a small brown smudge against the cliffs of the Península Valdés they passed yesterday.

Silas shakes his head slightly. They're wrong. A whalers' schooner, that's all it is. Silas has heard how they come after the whales, *Right Whales*, the ones that are easy to catch. Just the week before they thought they'd come across one of these ships, and for a while it had been comforting to think they had some fellow humans this far down in the South Atlantic. It had been days since they'd seen another ship. But when they came closer the 'steam' from funnels turned out to be the V-shaped fountains of whales exhaling as they reached the surface.

As Silas watches, the smudge across the bay seems to lengthen slightly and then divide into two. He blinks. A slightly smaller smudge and then something that moves steadily back towards them: the *Mimosa's* dinghy.

'Yes, it's him, I'm sure of it – Edwyn Lloyd! The man himself – coming over here to see us!' Silas turns to find his brother-in-law, Jacob, at his shoulder: a great fat moon of a face and a pair of stupidly adoring eyes. He grabs his sister's shoulders. 'At last you'll meet him, Meg!'

No. Silas shakes his head slightly. That isn't Edwyn Lloyd and this is not Patagonia.

But the dinghy is coming closer and Jacob's grin is broadening. Even Silas can see that there are three heads now, and the blackness of a beard and a hat on the one at the front. Silas has never met Edwyn Lloyd before but he's seen pictures in the papers, and this is how he is always dressed: tall black hat, striped waistcoat and chain. Stylish, slightly rakish. Explorer, adventurer, but also a man about town, proprietor of the press at Caernarvon, a friend of the Welsh gentry, of Gabriel Thomas and the rest of the emigration committee. He is thinner than his photographs, quite gaunt in fact, and fairly tall. Silas feels the muscles in his back clench, as though he is bracing himself.

'Edwyn!' Jacob calls out, as soon as the people in the dinghy are in earshot.

'*Brawd*! It is so good to see you.' Jacob leans over the side and half-pulls the man up the rope ladder, and, as soon as he has two feet on deck, engulfs him in a hug.

Silas watches Edwyn's two long, elegant hands on Jacob's back.

The fingernails are clean and neatly trimmed and there are small, thick black hairs in two clumps along each finger. Then they catch hold of Jacob's arms and push him firmly away. When the two men are a foot apart they look at each other; Jacob's broad slack smile is answered by a sudden flash of teeth.

'At last! All of you, here! It's been so long. I was beginning to think the day would never come!'

'With the help of our dear Lord.'

Edwyn's smile is extinguished. 'Indeed, *brawd*, indeed.' He touches Jacob's arms again, then turns and leaps up the few steps to the quarterdeck.

'*Fy ffrindiau…*'

My friends. Silas blinks – did he imagine that slight catch in the voice? Silas takes a couple of steps forward, but the man's face is hidden beneath the shadow of his hat.

Edwyn swallows briefly and then continues: '*Fy ffrindiau*, I am so glad to see you here at last.' Beneath the shadow of his hat Silas can just make out a pair of intense blue eyes moving slowly from face to face. 'Welcome to America, and welcome to the start of a grand adventure…'

'Dadda, I'm cold.' Myfanwy hugs his legs and he draws her to him. It won't be long now. In a minute Edwyn will have to break it to them that they have come too far south. They need to go back, he'll say, he's very sorry but that's how it is. They'll have to follow him back up the coast, where it is more like Wales and the vegetation is more lush and the air is warmer. Silas reaches out and grabs Megan's hand. She squeezes his in return. 'We're here!' she whispers loudly. 'Everything's going to be better now.' He opens his mouth to whisper back but Jacob hushes him.

Edwyn is leaning forward now as if he is sharing a secret with the women immediately in front of him. '*Ffrindiau, ffrindiau*. I know you have suffered. I know what you have endured: a hard voyage, and before that theft, ah, so much has been stolen from us – our land, our language, our culture! But soon we shall endure no more. Soon you will see our promised land. It is there waiting for us. The land we deserve, just a few miles south. Cattle! Trees. A splendid river. And grass – oh you should see it – mile upon mile of the most verdant pasture. The best grass you can imagine, *ffrindiau*. *Y Wladfa*. Like the old Wales but better.' He smiles – a quick flame of light that is soon extinguished again – then raises himself upright and looks at the rest of them. 'Pristine, it is. Unspoilt. No one to interfere…' he throws back his head. 'A land for the Welsh. Just think of that! A great nation with our own laws. No English landlords trying to cheat us with their taxes. No English clergy demanding that we pay their tithes. A prosperous place. A place where every Welshman helps his neighbour. No poverty. No cheating. No drunkenness or debauchery. A place where God's law shows us the way!'

'Halleluyah!'

'Halleluyah, indeed, *brodyr*!'

Suddenly he stops. His pale eyes – startling against the tanned darkness of his skin and the blackness of his beard – dart from one face to the next. Silas notes his hair: thick and dark and oiled, a contrast with the meagre covering of his own freckled scalp.

'Are you ready, brothers and sisters?'

There is a mumble of assent.

'I didn't hear you, *brodyr*. Are you ready?'

This time the rumble is louder.

'Praise the Lord!' someone says excitedly.

'And praise Edwyn Lloyd!' Jacob adds.

Edwyn shakes his head. 'No, my friends, we should praise Gabriel Thomas. Without his vision and perserverance, there would be no *Y Wladfa*!'

He waits for an echo of approval and nods at them all.

Silas shifts on his feet, and lifts Myfanwy to him. The child is shivering. She rests her head against his shoulder and he feels her teeth rattling against him. The wind is rising with the sun and becoming bitter. He undoes his jacket and gasps slightly as her body makes closer contact with his own. Too many words. It is too cold to stand here and listen.

'But there are others to thank too – my wife and Selwyn Williams. They've been waiting for weeks to meet you.'

'And we want to meet them too!'

He pauses. Acknowledges Jacob's shout with a nod, and then looks around at them. 'It has not been easy, friends. The Lord has tested us severely. You'll see.'

Silas tries to catch Megan's eye. It is time they got out of this wind. But Megan doesn't notice him. She is looking at Edwyn with the same expression as all the other women: something close to adulation. He tuts, and as Edwyn Lloyd begins to speak again, looks again towards the coast. No grass. No trees. Nothing. But it's as if only he can see it.

Three

The young men are eager to disembark. They go with Edwyn Lloyd in the small boat and row to the shore. Silas expects they kiss the land, imagines they dive from the boat and race each other to get there first. That is what he would do, if he were younger, or if he were unattached like Jacob, but as it is he has to wait until the next day. He has to help Megan and his two infant daughters to pack, and he has to listen to the wails of another mother who has lost her child in the night. The sound makes him gag on his morning biscuit and clutch Myfanwy so closely to him that she grumbles to be free.

'I want to play.'

He shakes his head fiercely and draws her closer. Stay.

'I want to go.'

'You can't.'

'Why not, Dadda?'

He mustn't cry. Not yet. Not now. Not any more.

The other women cry too but Megan is quiet. It is as if she can withdraw her mind. Nothing flickers in her face. He watches her as she packs carefully, folding each item of clothing into the smallest possible space. She pauses over nothing. She makes no sound, looks impassively around her, checking to see that nothing of their life here remains – as strong and silent as a stone.

The sea is gentle in this inlet, almost like a lake, and it takes just a few moments for Silas' oars to fall into rhythm, sliding into the water in time with the first mate's. If he shuts his eyes he could be back on the Conwy estuary again with its smell of salt and seaweed and the cry of birds. Just ahead would be the small house where there seems always to be a bright patchwork of washing spread to dry on the gorse of the surrounding headland. But here there are just cliffs, and behind him, the beach. He keeps twisting in his seat to look; a flat land coming closer, a haze of brown vegetation turning into small stunted trees and bushes. A strong wind blows from the land into his face, becoming colder and drier with every stroke of the oars. A persistent wind; it has not let up since they've anchored here. He shivers and checks that Myfanwy and Gwyneth are huddled into their mother. Megan is looking ahead, her eyes sometimes darting to his, and then back again at the coast, a grimace fixed onto her face by the wind.

'Nearly there now,' he says, not expecting a reply, 'nearly on land.'

Winter. Maybe that's all it is. Everything looks dead in the winter. In the spring there will be leaves, flowers, grass. He tries to hold onto the thought and believe it.

The oar slips into the sea, drags at the water and then emerges again. They are in time with the waves crashing and then dragging at the beach.

Browner. Colder. Beside him, Megan's head swivels. Everything is clear now. Every detail. Yellow patches of cliff become pockets of dead gorse and weeds like bramble, and in between them the ground is bare, sandy, infertile. This is more than winter. It is as if something has killed everything. As if there's been a plague. Nothing moves. Nothing makes a sound. Nothing lives.

Megan's eyes widen. 'Silas…?' She says. 'Silas?'

Nothing but banks of mud, pale cliffs. Sea.

He reaches for her hand.

'Silas…?' It's as if she's come alive. As if she suddenly sees.

He is holding his breath. As soon as he realises he lets it go – and a brief small mist appears and then disappears in front of his nose. It is so cold it almost hurts him to breathe. He concentrates on the sound of his breaths and the way these small sighs fit between the quiet splashes of his oar.

Then another sound. Something higher. Megan again. Her mouth open; clutching the babies so closely to her they are beginning to cry. 'We have to go back,' she says. 'We can't go there.' She tries to stand and a slug of the sea spills in, adding to what is already there on the bottom.

The first mate turns to look at her. 'Sit down, woman. You'll drown the lot of us.'

'We'll die if we go there.' Her voice is high and hoarse, and her eyes are staring unblinkingly at the shore. 'Those birds – it's a sign. There is something wrong. Something evil.'

Silas wants to go to her, but all he can do is reach out with his hand. 'Sit still, *cariad*. The children are frightened. We'll soon be there.'

He needs to hold her, whisper to her that everything will be all right, but she is pulling away from him and trying to stand again. 'No. I can't. We have to go back...' Her voice ends in a sob.

'Please, Megan, sit.' He presses her down and she collapses onto the seat, but she is still staring ahead. 'Can't you see? Blackness, death... we mustn't land...'

As the boat grinds against the sand she wails. 'Too late, oh sweet Lord, help us.'

'Megan!'

She looks back at the *Mimosa*. Soon it will be gone. Soon they will be left here, and there will be no way back. 'I can't leave him, don't you see? My poor baby. He'll be searching, calling. I can't leave him.'

Silas reaches over, grips both her arms and stares into her face. '*Cariad, cariad*. He's in the Lord's arms now.'

She shakes her head, tries to shake his arms from her. 'No!'

The hard thick skin breaking, the hurt coming out. If only he could draw her to him, but the boat rocks whenever he shifts. Already their feet are wet.

'Come now. We have to go on.'

She shakes her head. 'No, no, not without Richard... oh *cariad bach*, I can't leave you out there.'

Silas can feel Myfanwy's face on his, the whiteness of it, as it turns and looks at her mother. 'Hush, hush. You can do nothing for him now. He's at peace... in God's arms.'

'NO!' A pure sound. Loud. It seems to sear the air.

The men hauling trunks and boxes up the beach stop and look. Silas stands, then heaves himself over the side so he is thigh-deep in water. It is too cold to hurt. He pulls at the boat until it is in shallow water, then lifts Myfanwy onto the sand. 'Sit here,' he tells her, 'make a lap for your sister.' The little girl sits quickly, her serious eyes never leaving him. She crosses her legs in front of her and smoothes out her skirt. Then he removes the shawl containing Gwyneth from around Megan's neck and places the child in her sister's arms.

'Come,' he says to his wife, and with the first mate's help he pulls her from the boat. She is shaking now, sobbing loudly, but that is good he thinks – better to let the poison out, better to make the wound clean. He clutches her to him on the beach, smoothes back her hair then holds her face between his hands.

'He's gone, hasn't he?'

'Yes, *cariad*, he's gone.' The dark shadows of memories creep out from where they have been hiding. Richard.

Richard. He remembers the first time he saw him. Black hair caking his head like a well-fitting cap. Eyes the colour of indigo. Pink skin well filled with flesh. He wasn't sure what he had been expecting, but it hadn't been this. Most of the babies he'd seen were thin, weakly-looking with tired eyes. Richard's eyes stared at you right away, looked at you with something close to defiance. Who are you? What do you want? What am I doing here?

They'd still been in Rhoslyn then, tenant farmers on a small-holding. He was a tailor by training but gradually he'd swapped his needle for a spade – a couple of years of decent harvests had meant that he was better off digging than sewing. Gradually they had acquired a bad-tempered but productive sow, some good egg-laying chickens and a few cows which were generous with their milk. Each market day he came back feeling more wealthy and every night he went to sleep with plans in his head. In a few months he could ask permission to build another barn, try another crop, get a few more cows, he could even employ a servant – and he would send Richard to school. For the first time in his life he felt powerful. It was as if Richard had been the missing piece in the puzzle of his life. Once he was born it seemed that everything had fallen into place. 'I have never been happier,' he'd tell Megan as they tiptoed away from the sleeping child, and she would turn her head with that lazy smile of hers, then reach out to him and it would be like a door opening and he would feel enveloped in her warm comfortable world.

Megan's body had always been sumptuous. Even on this cold beach he is aware of his fingers sinking through the cloth of her sleeves and into her flesh. The warmth there makes the rest of him feel colder still. He hugs her close and feels his own body wake to her touch and smell. She is shivering, and the clattering of her teeth sets his jaw trembling too. The dip in the sea has chilled them both. He helps her up the beach and to the side of the fire someone has made in front of some unfinished huts.

He finds Myfanwy at the shoreline with Gwyneth, watching the waves creep towards them. She is so young, so serious – everything she does is done with such determination. He picks them both up together; glad at the way the weight of their small bodies tests the strength of his arms. He tucks Myfanwy's head beneath his chin but she complains and tries to squirm free.

'Be still, now. If you're not, I'll drop you.'

'But I want to walk!'

He carefully lets her fall and she walks at his side, her hand clutching a piece of the cloth of his trousers then letting go. Independent. Always a fighter – from her very beginning.

'Silas!' Sometimes the memories of voices seem so clear it is as if they are beside him still.

'Silas!' Ah yes, his mother-in-law, Elinor, her voice sharper than usual – trying to cover her panic. Then, of course, his own heart quickening in response.

'It's breech. You have to go get the doctor, now, *ar frys!*'

Ar frys – oh yes he'd been quick. Ten minutes on Bessy to fetch the doctor, and then the man not hurrying enough – more concerned in tutting and protesting. 'Breech? You should have called for me before now. You're a fool, man. Why didn't you call for me from the beginning?'

Then, once the doctor had been pulled into their cottage and the door had been closed, the sound of the birds chirping: a couple of sparrows and then a blackbird on a tree. As if nothing was wrong.

He closes his eyes. Remembers. His axe smashing through wood, and his words, bargaining with God: Don't let her die. Spare her and I'll never tell another lie. Let her live and I'll never curse the fat old sow nor that cockerel in the morning. I'll even listen to her old fool of a father.

Then a scream. The memory stops him breathing even now. The only time he'd ever heard Megan scream. And then a door slamming and the doctor shouting orders and he'd flung down his axe and covered his ears. Don't let her die.

He touches Myfanwy's head. Good girl. She looks up and

smiles at him and he reaches out suddenly and draws her to him so he can feel her warm sweet breath on his face.

It's always the same. Once the memories come they loiter in his head. There's Elinor's shadow passing over him; her face too calm, too serious. Then that thought, that hideous idea. He tries to drive it away but it won't go: Megan or the child? If he'd had to choose what would it be?

He'd taken a breath, asked the question. 'Is she all right?'

Megan or the child? Which would he have chosen? Megan, he'd have said.

He buries his face in Myfanwy's hair. Forgive me.

Megan, Megan, Megan.

'Hush,' Elinor hadn't answered but had held Richard out to him. 'Look after your son.'

But he hadn't taken him, not straightaway. 'Is she dead?'

Too loud. Blurted out. Elinor had shaken her head. 'Hush, think of the child.'

Then they'd both heard: a weak crying and Elinor had shoved Richard into his arms and hurried back, shutting the door behind her.

Then, for a long time, not a cry, not a shout, not even the murmur of conversation, until at last the door of the cottage had opened and the doctor had called him, his face long and unsmiling. 'A fine girl,' he'd said. 'You're a lucky man.'

'And my wife? I heard her...'

For a few seconds the old devil had played with him, shaken his head slightly but then looked up and at last he had smiled. 'Lucky for you I managed to turn her. They are both well. Your wife, Mr James, is a courageous young woman. A gem, in fact.' He smiled more broadly. 'A bit of a polish now and again and she'll sparkle for you, I expect. But now she needs to rest. Leave her be a while.'

Both well. As soon as the doctor had gone he'd rushed in.

'Mam, can you give that fire a prod? There's more wood by the stove.'

Myfanwy had been in her arms, her head twisting and her mouth rooting.

She'd pretended not to notice him. 'Not as pretty as her brother, poor thing – looks too much like her father.' Then she'd looked up at him and smiled. Ah, that smile – how he'd wanted to hug it to him then and make promises he had absolutely no hope of keeping! If only he could see it again now.

Megan is sitting where he left her, legs drawn up, her chin resting on her knees, staring into the fire.

'Megan?' She makes no sign. He calls her again and she turns towards him.

The light is strange. The sky is too open. The flames and smoke are being churned violently by the wind and make shadows that flicker on her skin. He looks at her sunken eyes, and the flesh drooping from the bones of her cheeks. How can she have changed so much without his noticing?

'Gwyneth needs you, *cariad*.'

She holds out her arms in silence. He watches as she tends to Gwyneth, guiding the child's mouth onto her nipple and then stares again into the fire. His gem. His precious stone. Something he should have cared for. He slumps down beside her and holds her hand in his. His fault. Every promise he made himself, he's broken. I'm sorry, he says. We shouldn't have come here.

He looks around. Desert. A cold desert of bitter winds. He squeezes her hand again. Then wraps his arm around her shoulder, holding them both to him. Sorry, he says again.

Four

Yeluc

This I know: the world belongs to Elal. Where his arrowheads touched the ocean floor so the ground rose up. Great rivers drained the water from the land and the memory of this is imprinted in the dry gorges and wide empty canyons. This was before man came. Before man became. Before Elal thought of us. He planted forest, swept out plains with his arms, drew up mountains with his fingertips, and then he thought of us: his Tehuelche. He made us large and strong like himself and he gave us legs so we could wander around his great creation. I suppose he wanted an audience, animals who would talk more loudly than the *mikkeoush* and armadillos. So he thought of us. His people. His guardians for all that he had made rise up from the ocean. He filled us with promises and hope. He told us that when we die he would see that we would take our places in the firmament and shine as stars. Elal. A god but also a man. A giant but also small enough for us to see. It is his land, he allows us to dwell here because of his great munificence. It is important to remember this. Important to know. Important to tell those around us and to remind the children that come after us. Elal. Great one. By looking after his land so we look after ourselves.

When I saw the big swan on the ocean I knew that Elal had not sent it. Even though I know Elal is used to swans and first learnt to shoot his arrows through her feathers I could see this was not his bird, not his carriage. Of course I have heard of such things before: large birds that bring men. But I had never seen one, not in front of me, not like this, even though I am old and have seen much of the world and am wise to its ways. I watched it grow big and bigger still and then voices came to me, calling, shouting, words I didn't understand, not even the words the Mapuche use or those whiter men from the north. I am used to their words from my father and even speak them a little, but these words were full of spit, clearings of throat and growls. Later they told me it was the tongue of heaven, but no one has ever heard the stars speak.

But even before I saw them I knew they were there. I could feel them coming. Strange creatures in the air. Their spirits and their helpers making the other world restless. Disturbing my sleep. Making the *rou* skittish.

By the time they came close enough to see, the sun was high: a weak sun, doing his best to warm up the air and the wind blowing his efforts away.

From the shore there was a boom, like a small thunder, and then they detached themselves from the swan. Like fleas. No, larger than fleas. Like rats. Rats disturbed from a nest. Falling into the water and crying out when the water grasped them, swimming like rats do, frantic and clumsy, their heads above the water and then one of them stepping on the land first, jumping up and yelling to the rest who were going back to the swan. Trouble, I thought and wondered if Elal knew. Trouble, I thought then and I was right and wrong. Nothing is all one thing or the other. So it was with these men and their women, especially their women.

Five

They unload their possessions onto the beach. There isn't much; most families have easily packed all they own into a single large trunk. They haul them up the beach to the shelter.

Silas unlocks his and peers inside – thirty-eight long years on this earth and so very little to show for it. He riffles through baby clothes, rolls of cloth, rugs, pots and pans until he finds what he is looking for – a couple of old blankets. He pulls them free and with them comes something else – a roll of old bills and orders. He briefly glances through them: small sums marking triumphs and then larger sums with accompanying demands, threats and denials. One paper is caught by the wind and carried towards the sea. He runs after it, catching it just before it reaches the water. It's nothing more than an old bill; the ink a little faded but still legible. He snorts – if he could only read it. Yet he knows every word. He walks back slowly, glancing round to check that no one seems to have noticed his sudden frantic movement. No need for anyone else to see – even though each man here will have similar secrets.

The doctor's boy had chased after him at the market. The shrill 'Mr James' had forced him to stop and look around, and the boy had thrust the bill into his hand with a short small bow of his head.

He had waited until he was alone before breaking the seal: the doctor's scrawl had meant little to him, but the long line of figures and the sum underlined twice at the end had meant rather more: more zeros than he could ever remember seeing on a piece of paper before. They'd wobbled in front of him while the rest of the world had retreated, like a column of hungry mouths exclaiming O, O, O.

Even Elinor's placid words failed to reassure him.

'We can help you out, *bach*.'

He'd shaken his head. He couldn't bear the thought of his father-in-law smirking as he reached into his cash box. He would do this himself. 'Don't tell *anyone*.'

'I won't, if you don't want me to, *cariad*, but...'

'Promise?'

She'd nodded slowly once. 'I promise.'

Ah, Elinor – how he sometimes misses her gentle words. He smoothes down the bill and adds it to the bundle of other papers. Why is he keeping all these? What good is it all now? The demand of £10 from a man in Chester for a church that was empty each Sunday; then one for £37 from the Melrose estate to be paid by Lady Day for his one-room cottage and land; and then the smaller bills: the £3 he owed the saddler and the shillings he owed the grocer. Then those more inconspicuous chits written in Megan's hand – each one recording a small heartbreak – the sow and then his eight cows and then his dogs: Polly, Benny, Sammy.

More faithful than humans, he always told Megan.

Soft you are, Silas. My father was right.

And more intelligent too. He sits on the top of the trunk to force it closed. Well except for that night when they had followed their urges rather than their brains. That night. For a few seconds he sits still on the wooden box. If it hadn't been for that night he would still be in Wales, still in Rhoslyn. Still have a wife and three small children. Three. The day seems to darken. That night it had been cold and autumnal. There had been bonfires somewhere; he remembers smelling them. Even though it was dusk Silas could make out white fluffy backsides in his cabbage field; no doubt their owners helping themselves to supper. The dogs were on them at once of course; through the gate and yelping and barking for kingdom come.

Silas smiles at the memory. Always too optimistic, especially that Benny. Those cabbage fields were riddled with burrows, and the dogs had never a chance of catching them, but still they persevered. He'd whistled, but they'd taken no notice. He'd laughed. Daft old creatures. So he'd waited until they'd come back with their tails slunk down between their legs, and he'd given each one a friendly wallop on their backsides.

But someone had been watching. He'd heard hooves on the road, as he was telling them off, and that night Trevor Pritchard, Melrose's gamekeeper, had called. As usual he'd just tapped once on the door before barging in with his two oafish sons. They'd stood at the doorway leering while their father had crossed the room in two paces and started poking around the place with his stick.

It had taken a couple of minutes for Silas to speak. 'What are you doing?' Then, annoyed at how ineffectual he was sounding, had quickly added, 'Get out, or I'll set my dogs on you.' Which, it turned out, was exactly what Pritchard had come for.

Silas shuts his eyes, remembering the old cottage. There had not been much to see – apart from the large pieces of furniture everything else is with them still, packed away in the trunk. To one side was the cupboard bed with the children's low bed beneath, a small cupboard set into the wall and the bible and a prayer book propped up by a jug on the deep windowsill. In front was the great dresser festooned with jugs and plates and cups. To the other side a table and chairs, and the settle pulled up toward the fire. Apart from that there was just the ironwork hanging above the grate and a ladder leading to the small loft stretching across half the room. The floor was made from slate flags – a recent addition replacing beaten earth – and Megan had just completed a long rag rug in bright jewel colours which ran down the middle of the floor.

'Call them, James. There'll only be more trouble if you don't.'

There was nothing he could do. The three men were large and they each had sticks. In the end it had been Richard who had called them. Richard, with his quivering little voice questioning Silas, and then accidentally calling out their names, whereupon they had appeared of course – from the only place they could be, under the bed.

Pritchard's sons had made smart work of them; cowing them with sticks before trussing them up with rope and shoving them into sacks. Then, leeringly licking his lips, Trevor Pritchard had written out a receipt with their names.

'What are you going to do with them?'

They were moaning like pups.

Pritchard grinned nastily. 'Not in front of the children. This won't be the end of this little matter either, don't you worry. Mr Melrose is most particular about his stock of game. He'll be here directly, to see how things stand.'

That weekend Melrose and a couple of his English friends had come trampling over Silas' crops and scaring the milk from his cows. The following week Silas had been summoned to the solicitor's in town.

'Mr Melrose is giving you notice to quit,' the round little lawyer had said.

'He can't do that!'

'I'm afraid, Mr James, that he can – and has. Apparently there was some issue with the game.'

Silas had tutted and shaken his head. 'Nothing happened. That sly snake of his, Trevor Pritchard, has been making things up.'

'Well, he's using that... not that he needs a reason.'

'I'm going to see him.'

'There's no point, Silas. He won't listen. You know that.'

He'd slumped back in his chair and looked at his hands, suddenly defeated. 'What can I do, Mr Roberts? I've put my soul into that place.'

'I'm sorry Silas.'

'Is there nothing that can be done?'

'We-e-ll...' Roberts had fiddled with the gold chain which always looped out of the watch pocket on his waistcoat. 'Maybe he would consider your renewal if you would agree to an increase in rent.'

Silas had gasped. 'I can't. I can barely afford to pay what he wants as it is.'

'Well, then...' Roberts had yanked at his watch chain until a large gold watch had landed in his small white palm. 'Stopped again, damn it. I'll have to take it into Thomas' again.' Then he had risen to his feet and clapped Silas on the shoulder. 'I'm so sorry, old man. There's not much else I can suggest.'

'But I've a young family, and that land is all I have, all I had...'

'I know, I know. You're not alone. It's small consolation, I know.'

'What can we do?'

'No one is allowed to become destitute in this day and age. The council will...'

'We're not going to the workhouse.'

'Well, you'll have to find something else then.'

'What?'

'Really my man, I have no idea.' He was looking at his watch again and frowning. 'I did hear there is a good living to be made on the coalfields.'

'Down the pit?'

'Yes, it's hard work, I know, but there's money to be had.'

'But there are accidents, explosions, people are killed...'

'Well, if you don't feel you can do that you'll have to find something else then.'

'What?'

But Roberts was clearly not listening. He'd given his watch a few careful winds and was now examining its face. 'My father brought me this, you know. All the way from London.'

But Silas had gone, slamming the office door shut behind him.

Six

Yeluc

They took their time to disgorge themselves from this craft. Now it was close, twisting and straining the sinews that held it where it was, I could see that this was just what it was, a craft, a distant relative of the ones I'd heard about, the ones the bowlegged ones use in the colder lands. Not like theirs though, no, not like theirs at all. This was large, several *toldos* sewn together floating on a raft of trees. And between the *toldos* and the wood were the people.

Signalling to Seannu and her sisters to keep down, I crept closer to see; my hair part of the thorn, my body close against the ground. There were people waiting. Two men and a woman, the swimmers and then some others I hadn't seen before, emerging from their own *toldos*, a few horses and a few other animals rounded up and chomping at the ground. Why had I not seen them? They ran along the beach to welcome them, their arms waving, shouting their language the same words again and again, running into the surf and out again, pulling at ropes that were thrown at them, then pulling at the small craft that had been born of the large one and followed the people that swam like rats into the water.

Step back. Close my eyes. Time is a god too, powerful but he can be tamed. Sometimes I can make him stop, go back and he will show me again what I know.

It is dark. How long have I been here? Seannu and her sisters have stolen away, following some quest of their own and left me here. No matter.

Their great swan is whispering to itself in the waves: creaks, sighs, promises of return. They have built a fire on the beach below me. Over the fire the women have assembled poles and pots and now things spatter, jump and boil within. Meat. It is something one of them killed.

Ah yes: a great roar from one of their sticks and then a small cry from something nearby.

Trouble, I said to Elal and he answered me in the wind. Yes, Yeluc, trouble. He prefers the silence of the *bolas*, the calmness of an arrow.

The spirit in my stomach grumbles at the smell and I begin to crawl backwards, my old legs snagging branches, making them crack but the sound does not matter. Eventually I stand but they do not notice. I am thin, dark against the sky. There are many of them clumped together in groups around the fire. They talk without meaning, words changing into songs and songs into chants. And something changes within me. The spirit that grumbles is suddenly quiet and still. I listen. Many voices entwining becoming one. Something loud, something strong. Something that clutches at the spirit inside me and makes him strong too. Elal. It must be Elal. They know him too.

Seven

There have been more speeches like sermons, more sermons like speeches – all three ministers having their turn – and they have buried the poor child who died in the night, on the land above the cliff. Silas thought it an almost unbearably bleak ceremony which caused Megan to weep new tears.

'He didn't suffer, did he, Silas?' Her voice is so quiet he has to huddle closer to hear.

'Richard?'

A nod.

'No, my love, he went peacefully.'

'You think he knew?'

'Only that he was going to heaven. I told him that soon he would see the Good Shepherd and He would gather him up in His arms with all the other little lambs that He has called that day to be with Him.'

'Did he believe that?'

'I'm sure he did. He smiled at me and murmured that he hoped their fur would be soft.'

'And do you, Silas?'

'Do what, *cariad*?'

'Believe.'

'Of course I do,' he says gently, and strokes her head.

There is nowhere to sleep. The only shelters are the half-built roofless sheds, and so the hold of the *Mimosa* is being stripped of all its timber. As the men carrying the planks come near, Silas thinks he can smell the stench of the hold still held within its grains, and for a moment he is back there, in the port of Liverpool, the *Mimosa* still captured in its dock on the Mersey. Someone is hacking away the mermaid figurehead which has been deemed too scantily dressed for respectable eyes, while below there is the sound of hammering and sawing as the bunks are put in place. Then, above that, there is the sound of the town – the yells, the calls and the laughter. In his mind he walks through the clamour, along the dirty streets with their ripely smelling piles of horse dung and discarded, rotting wares and into the quieter and more dignified reaches of a suburb. A Welsh suburb. He remembers the waiting; the days turning into weeks as the emigration committee tried to find a ship.

There had been so many rumours: a government paper declaring that the place was besieged by Indians; then a newspaper questioning that there were enough funds; and then, worst of all, there were the posters on the wall outside the chapel. Each week there would be a new bleak 'report': the Argentine government was reneging on its promises; there was not enough land; and finally the whole thing was a wild goose chase and the Welsh would be back within a year.

'English gossip and scaremongering,' Jacob had said, when he'd read it all to them. 'Take no notice. Edwyn Lloyd warned me about this. Keep the faith, he said. A new Wales for the Welsh. Think only of that.'

It was too much for some; and when a promised ship, the *Halton Castle,* failed to appear, several families packed up and went home. A few weeks went by before another ship was found. It was an old clipper – used to carry tea rather than people. Gabriel Thomas, the colonists' benefactor, had to spend yet more of his wife's money kitting it out with bunks and tables, but soon the *Mimosa* was ready for boarding.

May had been warm and the great grey Mersey had seemed to smell of the life they were discarding. Old pieces of clothing and furniture were floating on the surface; half-decayed carcasses of animals stank from where they were caught under jetties; swirls of browns and reds, greys and black. A dirty old soup of a river.

Silas shuts his eyes and hears it again. Wood scraping against wood, then all of them climbing the ladder, Megan slower than usual and protective of her bump, and Jacob so excited he'd actually hugged Richard and Myfanwy to him until they had howled their protests. It's starting, he'd said, our great adventure. But then they'd been interrupted.

'Hey, you!' English. They'd turned to the direction of the voice to see a large, very hairy young man, wearing the tattered jacket of a naval uniform. 'Welsh? Coom-raigh? Understand, eh?'

They'd left it to Jacob to reply.

The hatch with its two doors propped open was across a deck scrubbed so hard that its knots stood out like sores. They'd walked across it unsteadily trying to get used to the slight movement beneath them. Silas had stood back until last holding Myfanwy. Already the hold had its own stinking miasma seeping out onto the deck: fish, seaweed and the contents of a latrine.

'You can pass down the child now, Silas.' He'd had a sudden urge to run away but instead he'd forced himself forward and nudged Myfanwy toward the hole.

'No!' she'd said, as soon as she was close. 'No! I'm not going down there Dadda, it smells of *cach*.'

But a pair of hands had grabbed her, and swallowing hard he had followed Myfanwy's sobs into the gloom. There'd been a tangle of arms and legs, and then a mass of bodies. Like maggots, he'd thought, and then followed the movement of one of them into the edge of darkness. The bunks were crude – hastily made from unfinished planks. Then there was a screen made from rough pieces of wood. On each side were bodies, each one with a face looking up at him. Then, eventually, they found a vacant bunk – just enough room for the five of them.

Home for the duration, Jacob had said cheerfully, the smile in his voice apparent even in the darkness.

For two long months that bunk had been home. Towards the end of the voyage he knew every stain, every knot, every twist in the timber. It had been their table, their bed, a place for the children to play. Gwyneth had come whimpering into the world there and Richard... had left.

He looks away from where the men are piling the timbers ready for fixing and blinks.

That sand again – every now and again the wind suddenly sweeps up vindictive little handfuls of the stuff and blows it into everything: clothes, shoes, food, and, worst of all, Myfanwy's eyes.

'I expect you're wondering where this new Wales is, my friend, are you not?'

Silas starts and looks around him. Edwyn is beside him. He wonders how he managed to come so close so silently.

'Perhaps you're thinking the Lord has let you down...'

Silas says nothing.

'...or I have let you down.'

There is another pause and Edwyn smiles. 'Ah, I can see you might be thinking that and rightly so. But do not fear. This is but a temporary shelter, *brawd*.' He raises his voice so that the other men can hear. 'Our promised land awaits us, over there,' he says indicating a small valley to the south. 'Milk and honey, brothers. Tall trees and meadows. Cows lowing and the sheep bleating. It won't take long. Just a few more miles and we shall all be in *Y Wladfa*.'

Eight

Silas is watching Edwyn Lloyd. The man fascinates him just as much as he fascinates everyone else. On board the *Mimosa*, Jacob had talked of very little else so Silas has had plenty of time to imagine the man who had encouraged everyone to come here. It was a description so extravagant it was bound to lead to disappointment: 'The voice and heart of a lion, eyes as soulful and deep as an ocean, revered by everyone that encounters him.'

Jacob was clearly a man smitten. His eyes seemed to drift off into some sort of reverie whenever he mentioned his name. 'Ah, *brawd,* we are honoured to have him as our guide.'

Silas smiles. He had, he realises now, been expecting someone bigger – not taller, perhaps, but certainly broader, with dramatic, memorable features. Instead he finds a face that, apart from the full and undisciplined beard, appears to be neat rather than striking and a frame that is memorable only because it is so tall and lean.

However when Edwyn talks they all listen, and his voice does carry, although it is distinct rather than truly powerful. He moves constantly and rapidly with the muscular grace of an athlete: one moment helping with the dismantling of the ship, the next taking a turn at cladding the roof. And when he is not doing something with his hands, he is talking, talking, talking. In fact Silas is already tired of his voice: greeting the young Irish doctor in English, or barking out instructions in Spanish to one of the hapless servants, or greeting one of the ministers in his perfect Welsh. Now he walks up to where the women are making the evening meal, smiling at one face and then another, wheedling so subtly no one notices: 'Would you mind, Mrs Davies? Yes, that's right. If you would be so kind... yes, that would be perfect.' While the men are herded together to listen to his plans: 'And yes, Mr Humphreys, if you could ask your brother to join us. Yes, splendid. Just what I wanted.'

Everything about him is elegant: his voice, his walk, even the way he climbs onto a slightly higher piece of ground. Silas whispers to Myfanwy to go with her mother, and then goes to stand with the other men. He notices that one girl, Miriam, is loitering, hoping, no doubt, to remain unnoticed between her brothers. She is tall like them, and so thin and flat-chested that she could pass as a pretty young man; but Edwyn spots her and with a wink directs her to go and stand with the other women. At first she pouts and doesn't move, apparently immune to Edwyn's charm, but then after a nudge from her eldest brother, slouches off to join the women.

Edwyn, meanwhile, is gesturing for quiet with his arms. After a few seconds they are quiet. The wind has picked up and is whistling over the cliffs and it is a strain to hear. Silas shivers and hunches up his shoulders. Just the sound of it makes him cold. Like everyone else he is wearing as many clothes as he can find, but still the wind finds a way through. Edwyn, however, seems unaffected. Occasionally he has to bow his head to dodge some debris swept up by a sudden flurry, but his voice goes on unabated.

'Now, *brodyr*, we need to cross this stretch of land to the south of here, a distance of forty miles. It is a cold and barren place, a wilderness in fact.' He pauses and looks slowly around him. 'We are to be tested like the Israelites in the desert, and like Our Saviour Himself.' He smiles suddenly. 'But not, I hope, for forty days and forty nights!' There is a smattering of uncertain laughter which becomes more confident as Edwyn's grin widens. Silas sighs. He is in no mood for jokes. However long it takes will be too long as far as he is concerned. If it is south of here surely it will be colder still. He imagines trudging through a wilderness of snow and ice. He allows himself to slump against a rock. The voyage was so long and hard. Everyone is exhausted. Some of the colonists were already weak from months of poverty when they first boarded the *Mimosa*, and of course they are no better now. Some are suffering from fever. Five children have died – and there is one woman sitting so languidly that the Lord will surely welcome her into His arms soon. The thought of these people walking anywhere seems so utterly unlikely that Silas wonders why Edwyn Lloyd does not despair, but he does not. 'But, *brawd*, I know with all my heart that we will be victorious. A test is a good start for any nation and it can only make us stronger. We will come through it together. Arm in arm; each Welshman supporting his comrades through the wilderness. In fact Mr Selwyn Williams, who knows about these things, has suggested that this is how we should proceed.' Edwyn pauses, lowers his hands which had been indicating the land behind him and continues. 'The numbers he suggests are groups of twelve or more. Safety in numbers, isn't that so, Mr Williams?' He waits for the large sunburnt man who is standing close to Silas to nod grimly in agreement. Then, grinning at him, adds, 'Thank you. As you can tell, my friends, Mr Williams is a man of many words.'

His sarcasm brings another small ripple of laughter.

'But I have confidence that what he says is right.'

Silas' eyes travel to Selwyn Williams. Selwyn is a massively built American whose wild, wrinkly beard is so blond that at first glance it looks white. This, together with the weather-worn leatheriness of his face, gives an initial impression of age, although the easy way he moves and his little-used voice betray his youth – he is really only twenty-eight. He obviously doesn't share Edwyn's sartorial interests; his clothes are ill-fitting, his jacket too short and missing most of its buttons, and his trousers are torn at the hem. His hat consists of a pelt of pale brown fur, almost indistinguishable from his hair, and any shape that it once had has long disappeared. The contrast with the elegant Edwyn is striking: whereas Edwyn stands erect with his shoulders invariably thrown back and his chin up; Selwyn slouches into his clothes, almost as if he'd like to disappear into them. Selwyn seems reluctant to speak, but when he does his views are so unrelentingly gloomy that Silas feels an immediate empathy. Oddly, despite his dress and pessimistic outlook, he seems to be attractive to women too, and already Silas has overheard a couple of the younger single women discussing his attributes with some enthusiasm.

'A little boy in a man's great body.'

'Lovely eyes.'

'Needs looking after, though – look at those clothes.'

'I saw him first, Annie Warlock. Don't you get any ideas. He's mine.'

An innocent, a child – as Silas watches him pull his fingers through his colourless beard he can see what those women mean. There is an oddly childlike unselfconsciousness about the man and if he is aware that he is the object of Edwyn's ridcule, he doesn't show it.

Edwyn Lloyd begins to sort the men into groups. 'So... yes, how about you, Mr Rees? Could you be spared, do you think? Good man. And your brother? Yes, that's right...'

Edwyn Lloyd, Silas notices, has two smiles: a sudden grin for public consumption and one that is more like a spreading of his lips which is only for himself. This private smile is smug, small, almost hidden beneath his beard and betrayed only by slight changes in the flesh adjacent to his nose. He smiles this private smile now as his eyes sweep over the men before him. It remains on his face as he turns to where one man is actually trying to catch his attention with a small wave of his hand. His smile broadens as he pretends to miss him. 'Is no one else willing to be part of the advance? Are you sure? How disappointing.' The man waves more vigorously and makes small coughs, and Edwyn's private smile expands. Only on the third pass of his eyes does Edwyn pretend to look startled. 'And you Mr Griffiths?' His surprise is staged, obviously overdone, and around him some of the other men smile too.

'How very kind. Yes, thank you, Jacob. Now we can all be assured that the party will be in safe hands.' His voice now has a slight sneer about it but Jacob seems oblivious of both this and the snigger of the men around him. He seems to hear just what suits him. As soon as Edwyn used his Christian name, Jacob seemed to become larger. He looked around him and smiled triumphantly at Silas. Now he steps forward eagerly, grinning at Edwyn who nods and grins his public smile back.

'When are we going, Edwyn?'

'Ah, I had tomorrow in mind. Unfortunately, I shall be unable to come with you myself. My work is here for now, with my wife.' He looks around, balances on his toes so he can see over their heads, then he motions someone forward. A slightly built, pale-faced woman picks her way between them. She is in her mid twenties, brown hair scraped into a small hat, and with symmetrical, even, small features that seem to Silas to be almost completely inexpressive. If she were more lively she'd be a beauty, he thinks, but as it is she looks defeated. There is something in the way her body droops that betrays exhaustion. Her clothes look expensive but well worn: a heavy dark-green skirt and blouse of wool, and a shawl with a subdued paisely pattern wrapped tightly on top.

'It's been hard work, so far, hasn't it, *cariad*?'

Cecilia Lloyd nods seriously.

'We almost felt like giving up some of the time, didn't we?'

She nods again. For a few seconds her eyes seem to travel passively over the faces around her and then they slip smoothly back to the floor. Vacant, Silas thinks, nothing there, and he wonders if she is truly as stupid as she seems.

'Ah Captain!' Edwyn calls out in English, 'here, if you please.'

Silas looks up with interest. He can't imagine that the thug of the *Mimosa's* captain would respond happily to a command, but even Gidsby seems under Edwyn Lloyd's spell. He comes through the crowd of men meekly when summoned, listens carefully to what Edwyn says then responds quietly. Silas tries to match the voice he hears speaking to Edwyn with the one he remembers on board the *Mimosa*, but fails. The voice in his head, the one he heard so frequently on the voyage, was uncouth and aggressive with such a vocabulary of swear words that he made Jacob blanch. But to Edwyn Lloyd, Captain Gidsby's tone is mild and civil. He appears to be explaining the workings of the compass with some patience, although Edwyn has the condescending air of someone listening to an idiot. They confer quietly in English for a few moments before Edwyn passes on his instructions in Welsh. 'He says you have to just keep following the needle south,' he says, making it quite clear he is merely passing on the information. 'You line the north up like that with the mark on the rim, then go in the opposite direction. Due south. If you keep going that way, you can't go wrong.'

He thanks the captain and dismisses him, and the captain mutely dips his head, before returning to the beach. Then he walks along the sand, looking backwards from time to time, before continuing as if making sure that Edwyn Lloyd had finished with him.

'The *Meistr* has something on Mr Gidsby, I reckon,' Selwyn Williams says quietly as they watch him retreating down the beach. 'Seen him snooping round the ship yesterday. Guess he found something.' Selwyn smiles and looks at him. 'Any ideas?'

Silas thinks for a few seconds, then shakes his head. Gidsby was always very secretive.

Selwyn looks disappointed. He pauses while the captain scuttles out of sight, then says. 'Must be something the captain is very keen to keep quiet.'

Then suddenly Silas remembers the Mimosa tipping, and the captain struggling to fasten something down on deck. Something he wanted no one to see.

'There was something…' Silas says, '…at the beginning of the voyage, during a storm, a particularly bad one…'

He thinks back. The storm had only been going for a couple of hours, but already the ministers had begun to nag God in relays. Eventually Megan had clapped her hands over her ears in the shadows of their bunk: 'If I were God I'd drown the lot of us.'

Everyone was sick. Only Silas seemed to be immune to the constant tipping and swaying. While the storm raged they were kept in darkness; the hatch was fastened down with just the cracks each side of the door reminding him of sky and open air. He kept looking at the narrow slits of light. Eventually the smell of other people's vomit and excrement made him gag too. He needed to escape, he thought, just for a minute. So he had lurched his way past the bunks of groaning bodies and buckets, groped around for the ladder and then climbed slowly towards the light, making sure of each handhold. Then he'd hammered on the hatch until it had given way. There'd been a sharp waft of air and a glorious sliver of daylight. The ladder had swayed and heaved but still he'd pressed his face there. The sky was darkening. Beyond the deck was the sea, or at least the smell of it. And there was the sound of the waves breaking across the deck – an entirely different sound from the thunder against the hold. Then, above it all, another sound – a man's voice, hoarse, young and desperately trying to hide his panic: *Tell them to clear off, we don't need them. Tell them to go and mind their own damned business.*

'Contraband,' Silas says.

'Yes,' says Selwyn, fingering his beard thoughtfully. 'That'll be it. A good few bottles tucked away somewhere – and Edwyn knows about them.'

The younger men are eager to start. Too eager. As soon as Edwyn Lloyd has divided out the equipment one of them starts off alone. William Bowen is young, a surly curl to his lip and nothing but an insolent word for everyone.

'Mr Bowen?' Edwyn Lloyd calls after him.

'You catch me up,' he says without turning and continues on the track.

One of the women tuts and Edwyn's face colours slightly. 'Mr Bowen, you are not to go out there alone.'

But the man doesn't turn.

'William, come back at once!'

'Shall I go after him, Edwyn?' Jacob asks, but Edwyn shakes his head. He is still watching the boy go. 'Such stupidity,' he mutters, then looks at Jacob and smiles. 'Not yet, my friend. We mustn't allow the reckless actions of one man to threaten the survival of the rest. We must get you ready. Make sure you are all properly equipped.'

Now Lloyd's movements are slightly quicker and more agitated. He makes frequent glances into the desert and when he does so, his fists clench tightly. The *Meistr* is angry, Silas thinks, and trying to conceal it. Silas wonders if anyone else notices the two small lines deepening in the centre of his forehead, or the quiet tutting as he waits for each man to acquire a gun, a ration of food, a blanket, a shovel or spade. When one of the servants asks a question the *Meistr* gives an impatient answer back, and repeatedly punches a fist into his palm as he waits for the man to return with a horse and a barrel of water.

'Just to tide you over, until you reach the valley,' he says to Jacob, Gidsby has been very kind...'

Jacob looks up, his mouth open. 'The captain... kind?'

'Yes, yes. The captain...!' Edwyn retorts. 'He has kindly loaned us his lifeboat to deliver the rest of our supplies to the valley by sea. The sand bank won't trouble a small boat like that, not like it might ground the *Mimosa*. His men are loading it for us now.'

William Bowen has long disappeared.

'He should have listened to you,' Jacob says, as one of the women calls after him to come back.

Edwyn waves away his words with an impatient flick of a hand. 'You must try to catch up with him.' He looks around him. 'Now, let me see... Mr James?'

Silas turns.

'I hear you can hold a note.'

Silas nods hesitantly. The last song he sang sent Richard to sleep.

Edwyn inspects his face. 'What do you say? A song to send our friends and brothers on their way?'

Silas doesn't answer. He looks at the trail of William Bowen's footprints. The sand gradually gives way to a light soil, but the land is desert: cold and dry. He imagines the boy stopping, looking around and realising he is lost.

'Maybe if we make enough din, he'll hear us.'

Maybe William Bowen is already cold, shivering, walking frantically around in circles...

The children and women are clamouring excitedly around now, exchanging kisses and hugs with those about to depart. It is becoming noisy – the laughs are too loud, and the conversation is beginning to have a frantic and desperate edge.

'Silas, a song, if you please,' Edwyn interrupts loudly, and there is quiet.

Silas looks around. Every eye is on him.

'Just a note we need,' Jacob says, 'to get us going.'

'Dadda?' Myfanwy is at his side. 'Are you going to sing?'

Silas takes a breath. How can he refuse. His voice wavers and almost stops. It's been so long. He swallows away the hurt, and tries again. By the time he reaches the end of the fourth line he is caught up in it. He opens his mouth wider: *'Hallelujah, Hallelujah...'*

It always finds him: this joy springing up from somewhere, this sound that makes him feel powerful. They are all joining in now, each face transformed. This elation – they all feel it: eyes shut, mouths wide open – each man, each woman. Even Edwyn is swaying in time with the song, his voice strong and controlled. It is as though, just for that instant, they have become a single being with one voice.

At Edwyn's nod, Jacob begins to lead his horse away up the trail and the rest of his party follow, each man peeling away the women and children. Their voices fade and Silas looks around him – without so many able-bodied men the community on the beach looks diminished and vulnerable.

Nine

Silas sniffs himself. A distinct odour of kipper. It is too cold to wash, too cold even to undress. His shirt and trousers seem to have become part of him. Sometimes he thinks that shedding them would be like peeling away skin. He takes a few steps down the beach, rounding his shoulders against the cold. The hut has a roof now, but it is still not very comfortable, and there is a separate shelter on the beach for the kitchen. Someone is cooking bread in a pot. He stops, relishing the smell for a few seconds, then walks on. As he comes closer there are other smells too: bacon, porridge and the simple steamy smell of water being boiled for tea. He is hungry and he loiters close, hoping to be fed.

'If you want breakfast, you'll have to get me some water.' Megan rises from where she has been stooping over the fire and hands him a bucket.

The water has to be carried from ponds a little way inland. He takes the bucket and runs to catch up with Selwyn Williams, who is similarly encumbered and striding in the same direction.

At first he answers Silas' questions with nods. It is only when they arrive at the ponds that he seems to find something to say.

'Lucky,' Selwyn says, tipping his head in the direction of the water.

'What do you mean, lucky?'

'Lucky there was a storm. A week before you came – poured it down, it did. Lucky.'

They plunge their buckets into the deepest part and collect some water then begin to walk back.

'Before that, it was dry as bone,' Selwyn adds suddenly a few minutes later. It is so long since the rest of their conversation that Silas has to think back for a few seconds for his words to make sense. 'What about a well?' Silas asks. 'Isn't there water in the ground?'

The big man laughs a little and shakes his head. 'Come,' he says, 'I'll show you.'

Selwyn is the son of Wisconsin settlers. They loved their language and were keen to preserve it. However they soon became dispirited: their children learnt English at school, and having learnt it, used it almost exclusively to talk to those around them. Their Welsh culture, they realised, would be lost within two generations. So when they heard about the proposals for a new Welsh colony in Patagonia, they were enthusiastic: in an isolated colony surely their language would thrive. But Selwyn's father now had an arthritic leg and his mother could only truly see when the light was bright. They were too old for new adventures, they decided, and so they volunteered their son in their place. So Selwyn was shipped across to Liverpool and thence on to Patagonia with little say in the matter. He didn't much mind. Although his complaints seem to be many, they are, in truth, merely his pessimistic commentary on the world he finds around him. And since he finds conditions in Patagonia to be just as unsatisfactory as those in Wisconsin, he finds himself equally discontent – and at least in Patagonia no one laughs at his accent.

Silas and Selwyn walk a little way inland behind the tents housing the servants that have brought some of the animals overland from Buenos Aires.

'Those men'll be going back soon,' Selwyn says. 'The schooner's waiting. Daresay they'll be anxious to be gone.'

Selwyn slows at a patch of ground that has been cleared of bushes and has been trampled into a slight hollow. Silas goes to walk forward but Selwyn holds him back. 'Careful.' The ground is softer than it looks, each foot causes the sandy earth around it to break. It is disconcerting; even Silas leaves large wide footprints, and he has the impression he is treading on a crust which is covering a mighty hollow.

'Over there,' Selwyn gestures with a massive finger. 'Slowly now, be careful.'

In front of them is a great hole. They ease themselves forward until they are lying at the edge with their heads just over the side. Once it had obviously been deeper than it is now; the ground around it has toppled over the side widening the top, but there is still a wide, deep cleft through the sand and then the rock. At the bottom Silas thinks he can see black-coloured water.

'Our well,' Selwyn says and smiles ruefully. 'We were at it for days – an order issued by the *Meistr* before he and his wife set off on one of their many important missions to Buenos Aires.' He sighs, eases himself back and sits up.

'They all said it couldn't be done, but the *Meistr* insisted. He took each one aside, in private, and had a few words.'

'He speaks Spanish?'

'Enough. We both do. Don't know what he said, but each one came back with a scowl and got back to the digging sharpish. Didn't last long though, whatever he said.'

'What happened?'

'Well, we found the water, see. Brackish, of course, like I said it would be, and the men were so fed up they got themselves out and left me down there as punishment. *Meistr's* representative, see.' He grins sardonically to himself.

Silas stares at him. 'For how long?'

Selwyn shrugs. 'A day, a night, maybe two. I lost track.'

'Weren't you frightened?'

'Only at the end. First I thought, well, a prank, I guess. They'll get me out soon. But then, when it grew dark...' He pauses, smoothes his beard with the palm of his hand, gets up, waits for Silas to follow him and starts walking back towards the tents. 'Could hear them in the distance, see. They were... enjoying themselves, I suppose... they'd broken into our storehouse like children. And were eating and drinking everything.'

'How did you get out?'

'See that man?' He points to one of the servants in the distance – a big man with blue-black skin.

'I'd given up hope. I was so thirsty I was thinking I'd drink the water, even though it would probably kill me. There was a grey light, I remember that – either early morning or dusk, and then suddenly – a face peering over the edge! When I asked him why he'd helped me he just said "Lloyd" and crossed himself. I guess he'd figured that the *Meistr* would be back soon enough, and didn't relish the consequences if Mr Lloyd found things not quite how he'd left them.'

Selwyn is abruptly quiet. Silas inspects his face. He looks drawn. Beneath the outer leather his skin looks quite bloodless and pale. They walk back to the tents. The servants look just like ordinary men. They nod at Selwyn and Silas as they pass.

'And now you just carry on as if nothing has happened?'

'What else can we do? This is a hard, cruel place, *ffrind*, make no mistake. And anyway, they'll be gone soon with the schooner – maybe tomorrow or the next day.'

'But where we're going will be better, won't it?'

Williams shakes his head gloomily then glances around to see if Lloyd is anywhere near. 'I wouldn't bank on it. One or two of the men have been south of here and they say it gets no better, just colder. And then there's always the Indians.'

'What about the Indians?'

They have reached the fire on the beach now. Selwyn pauses and looks around him. There are several other men there, warming themselves near the flames. At the word 'Indians' several of the men have stiffened where they sit and their heads swivel with interest.

'Well, the Indians round here, they've got a grudge, see. The land is theirs, they reckon, and they were expecting payment. And you know how they go about settling these things.'

The men look nervously at each other. They have all heard the stories, and on board the ship they have practised loading and taking aim with the rifles again and again. It was something Jacob organised with great relish, marching his little army of volunteers up and down the few yards of deck as if they were tin soldiers.

'There was a colony just over there not so long ago.' Selwyn points to the peninsula ahead of them. 'They swooped down without warning one Sunday. Not one man escaped.' He slices the air with his hands along his forehead. 'Scalped, each one of them. And the women and children...' his voice fades and he shakes his head.

'What happened to the women and children?'

He lowers his voice so they all have to crane forward to hear. 'Slaves to the Indians... each one of them.'

Several of the men noisily draw in breath through their teeth while several others tut.

Selwyn takes a deep breath and then frowns as though it hurts him to continue. 'Worse than death, that's what everyone says. They mesmerise them, you know. Decent God-fearing folk are turned into savages... tribes with light-coloured women, and do you know what people say...?' Selwyn pauses dramatically. The men around him hold their breath. 'These women are put under a curse so they don't want to come home again. They say they're happier where they are. The Devil's work, it has to be. How can a God-fearing woman be happy living like that?'

A few of the colonists echo his tuts while the rest look around them as if they are being watched.

'How can we know if they're close?'

'You can't. They creep around in big soft-skinned boots, see, and no one can hear them. But you can smell them, all right. They light fires, and they smell strongly of smoke. It's like the Devil, isn't it? Brimstone and ashes. The smell of Hell.'

The group is silent now, each face looking around.

'Didn't Edwyn Lloyd know this?' Silas asks suddenly. 'Didn't he know about the desert, the cold, the Indians? I'm sorry Selwyn, but I don't think all you say can be true. Surely the *Meistr* wouldn't have brought out women and children – his own wife, *brawd*, if he knew it was like that.'

Selwyn raises his great bear-like head and glances towards the bay where Edwyn Lloyd is issuing orders to some of the sailors. 'Well, what is paradise for one man is hell for another. My advice, *fy ffrind*, is not to expect too much, then you won't be disappointed.'

Megan is getting better. A day ago he heard her laugh, and the sound had made him forget what he was doing and just look at her in gratitude. She'd been playing with Myfanwy on the sand, drawing pictures and then decorating them with stones and shells. Then the little girl must have said something because Megan had given a small joyful whoop and shoved her a little. It seemed like a sound from so long ago that Silas felt tears smarting in his eyes. He remembers Megan when he first knew her – walking arm and arm with her friends; the way she would glance over her shoulder to check that he was following and then that sound, that whoop of laughter, as she'd nudge her friend just as she nudges Myfanwy now. Inside the woman there is still the same girl.

The beach is bleak; when the wind blows it is cold and dry and both Myfanwy's and Gwyneth's mouths are chapped. Megan spreads a little grease on the corners of Myfanwy's mouth and she moans at the pain.

'I know, *cariad*. But it won't be long now. When we reach the valley this cruel old wind will be gone.' She glances at Silas for confirmation but Silas, as usual, is watching Edwyn Lloyd. Ever since Selwyn had told them about the Indians the men have been subdued and edgy. A few of them have been looking longingly at the *Mimosa* as if they are contemplating returning.

But now Edwyn Lloyd has clambered onto a trunk and has motioned for them to come forward to listen. His voice is steady and serious, his face still and straight. 'Last night I dreamt of the valley.' He pauses, and looks around at them, picking out one face at a time. 'Oh *brodyr*, we are blessed. Truly it was as the good book says, "A land that floweth with milk and honey".'

Silas looks around him. Everyone is listening, staring intently at Edwyn.

'Yes, *ffrindiau*, *Yr Wladfa* is the start of great things – God's kingdom on earth. I am sure that is what the dream was telling me. If only we persevere we will one day be a great nation – a people with power and influence.'

Silas folds his arms. Despite himself he is a little impressed at the drama of it all. Is it possible that the Lord has chosen them? That somehow they can make a great nation from a desert? He shakes the idea from his head. No, it's just words. That's all they are, words without meaning. They change nothing. He glances at Selwyn who nods back: do not expect too much.

The schooner has departed for Buenos Aires with the servants and the bay seems empty without her. The *Mimosa* is alone now, creaking impatiently at every turn of the tide. The women trudge back and forth with bottles, pans and buckets to the pool by the beach – the one they share with the animals. The water is cloudy at the edges where the mud is churned and some of the children cry when they go too close because it has a rankness that reminds Silas of a pig sty. They swing their pails far into the middle of the pond and pull them out, then carry them back to the beach to heat on the fire. The water is too precious to use for anything but cooking and it is too cold to risk washing in the sea. They get used to the smell of each other's dirt.

The *Mimosa's* lifeboat has still not returned from delivering supplies to the colonists at the valley to the south, and Gidsby is anxious to be off. Every morning Silas sees him pacing up and down the headland looking at the ocean, watching for the return of his lifeboat or a change in the weather. At last he demands to see Edwyn Lloyd. They walk off together down the beach from where snatches of only Gidsby's strident voice carry up to the people at the fireside.

'We have to go. We can't wait forever.'

'When, then?'

'Well, you're going to have to bloody do something.'

'I don't bloody care who you tell. Do what you bloody like.'

Selwyn looks quizically at Silas and then at the *Mimosa*. Whatever it was that Edwyn was using to hold the captain here is weakening.

Silas is needed to make up numbers. There are six of them altogether: Silas, two sailors, Edwyn, Selwyn and Miriam's father, John Jones. They pick their way along the coast at low tide, escaping to the higher ground when the sea flows back in. Edwyn leads the way, striding out so the rest have to hurry to catch up. Beyond the first promontory they come across barrels floating in the sea and then, in the next bay, find the *Mimosa's* lifeboat caught on a shallow platform of rocks. Waves are smashing over it, pushing it inland and the crew are passing the cargo from man to man onto the beach. The colonists and sailors join them and by the time the boat has sunk, later that evening, most of the supplies are safe.

It is too late to return so they make camp.

'They'll be waiting for us in the valley,' one of the crew of the lifeboat says, looking towards the south.

'Aye, if they've got there.'

'Their stomachs will be empty by now.'

'They will be well, gentlemen, the Lord will provide,' Edwyn says.

'Provide them with what?' mumbles Silas but Edwyn gives no sign that he hears.

Silas shifts nearer to the fire and hugs his knees. It is beginning to rain again and the wind is bitter. Edwyn is smiling and looking into the distance. Sometimes it seems to Silas that the man has lost his sense.

The bay is empty now. The *Mimosa* has sailed away without her main lifeboat, the captain dismissed with a curt nod of the *Meistr's* head. He had scuttled away onto his ship as if released from some spell, and could soon be heard, even from the shore, cursing his crew with renewed venom.

Silas looks around at the sand, bushes, cliffs, and their small huts and pitiful pile of supplies on the beach. Alone. Thousands of miles away from anything they've ever known.

Even though the bay is empty Silas has the uncomfortable feeling that he is being watched. He looks at Edwyn and then Selwyn – they too are looking around them: to the cliffs, and then inland, and then back to the cliffs again.

'Well, if you're not going to ask him, I shall.' Megan shoves Gwyneth into his arms, and walks up to Edwyn with her arms folded.

Edwyn glances at her and flashes his smile. 'Ah, Megan, isn't it? Silas' wife? How is your little one? Gwyneth, I believe?' Edwyn removes his hat and bows slightly. 'I've been meaning to offer my condolences. I should have spoken to you sooner. Cecilia has told me about your sad loss.'

Megan slumps a little. She'd be surprised that he knows, surprised and saddened at being reminded. 'Thank you,' she says quietly then straightens herself again with a shake. 'I would like to know what you're doing about my brother and his companions,' she says. 'They went with nothing. How do we know they're not starving to death down there?'

Now it is Edwyn's turn to look surprised. His face darkens slightly and he opens his mouth to respond but Megan interrupts him. 'Because if you're not going to do anything then I will.'

Empty words. It is obvious that there is nothing Megan can do, but a small group around them is listening now, and it is quite clear that Edwyn doesn't like it.

'I am doing something, *chwaer*.'

'What's that, then?'

'I am sending the sheep.'

'How are you going to do that?'

'Sit down, Megan, and listen, everything is in order.'

Silas grins to himself. The *Meistr* is irritated. He is obviously not used to women standing up to him. He has rarely heard Cecilia say a word.

'John Jones is making himself ready,' Edwyn continues. 'He says he can drive the sheep south...' Edwyn smiles suddenly, as if he has had an idea and looks at Silas '...if someone will volunteer to bring up the rear.'

The two look at each other. Edwyn's smile is smug and his eyes are narrowed.

'But I'm no shepherd!' Silas says at last.

'Nor is anyone else here. But I am sure you want to do all that you can to help your brother-in-law. Don't worry. Just do exactly what John Jones tells you to.'

Now all eyes are on Silas. How neatly the man has shifted their attention. Gwyneth whimpers in his arms and beside him Myfanwy pulls at his trousers. 'Dadda,' she says softly, 'what's happened? I'm frightened.'

He looks at Megan, wanting her to turn around and look at him, but she stays exactly where she is, glaring at Edwyn.

The sheep are not only needed by the men in the valley, Edwyn points out, but will be needed by the rest of the colonists when they get there, and the only way to get them there is overland – the flock is too large now to go by any small ship. Someone is going to have to go sooner or later – and they will be doing the colony a great service if they go now. Edwyn shifts a little away from Megan's gaze and then locks Silas' eyes with his own. 'What do you say, Mr James, are you ready?' He tips his head to one side and a grin twitches beneath Edwyn's beard. 'Or are you afraid?'

There are a few moments of silence before Silas gives the only possible answer.

Ten

Yeluc

For some time I waited. Songs turned to chants and chants into the mumbling of wind over weeds. As the men quenched their fires the women led the children away and their bodies became shadow and the shadows became night. My stomach reminded me it had not been fed, so I crept down to where their embers still had reddened sleepy eyes. There was meat there. I could smell it – small pieces they had dropped. It was overdone, spoilt, but I was hungry. My feet made no sound on the sand and I bade Elal entice the wind from its sleep to blow sand over my tracks.

I saw where they slept. There was one guarding the entrance to their chamber with one of his sticks but he slept too. They had drawn up the ground to make a shelter. They had assembled one stone upon another and on top of this tied down reeds and bits of twig. They were like the Cristianos then: they do not like to wander after the *rou*, instead they build houses and keep their animals with them. These animals are sad beasts. They are kept in pens with earth walls and their misery when they see the world and yet cannot go out into it, gives them the long white fur of an old man. I know this. I have heard them bleat. Sometimes the bleats are angry but mostly they are sad. It is a sound that travels across the desert and has greater power than the wind. Anyone who hears it becomes a little sad too and is moved easily to tears.

Ah Elal, are these your beasts too? Or are there some you do not own? I heard some of these animals lowing close by but I didn't go and see them then. Instead I crept to where these strangers slept. I stood still by their entrance and watched them sleep. They had one small lamp but it allowed me to see them all: men in one place, women and their young curled beside them in another. Their air was foul with their breath and the walls held it there – still, fetid, the sealed inside of a carcass left too long in the sun. Then, as I watched, one of them stirred. A girl-child. Even though she was as tall as a young warrior and her breast as lean as a boy's, I could see what she was. The line of her jaw was soft, her cheeks full and dark, her hair like the many twisted twigs of the *calafate*. She raised herself up and seemed to look at me but she didn't see me. I was as still as a reed on a windless day. For the count of five heartbeats I saw the lamp shine off her eyes and then they closed again and she fell back. She murmured to the body that lay next to her and moved closer, curving herself around the other, her arm reaching out. And I remembered how that felt, how it was to be wrapped in the body of another, and I remembered Seannu and longed to be with her again.

So I climbed the hillside above their camp and clicked behind my teeth for Roberto. Seannu and her sisters had left and gone inland. I knew from the signs they had left in the fire – a round stone and then a longer one pointed to where the sun rises – where to find them. But it was dark so I lay below my mantle and listened to Roberto tearing at the dead grass beneath the thorns. It is a comforting noise and it always makes me sleep, even when my stomach is growling at me and memories are trying to prod me awake.

I awoke with the sun and the strangers calling to each other on the beach below. Only one of them noticed my footprints: the girl who woke in the night, I saw her following them then looking up to the cliff where they stopped. She didn't see me. Elal has bestowed upon me a gift: I can become thorn even to a passing *mikkeoush*, and I am silent because Elal guides my steps.

I watched them as they went to where the cattle lowed, the hogs grunted and their white *rou*-like creatures were entrapped. Beside them was a pool, encrusted at the edges with salt, pink as flamingos, and the men trod through this with short, sharp shouts as if they had seen something great, when really they had seen nothing at all: just a pool that will pass, something that comes with the winter rains and then disappears as soon as the sun stays longer in the sky. But they took the water from this place and smacked their lips.

It takes them a long time to return for they are laden with water. I can hear each footstep as they snap twigs and break through the crust of sand. They have barrels which it takes two of them to carry, and buckets and some have bottles which I watch to see if one breaks for if it does I shall remember where it falls and scoop up the fragments: a piece of bottle is precious, Seannu would pounce upon it, the blackness of her eyes surrounded at all sides with white.

But nothing fell, everything was carried as carefully as a mother carries her young, and they were singing a low tune in time with their steps. For a time I listened, then my mouth moved with theirs, and then quietly, so quiet my voice was just a murmur, their words became mine, a sound like their animals staring at the fence, deep in my throat.

Careful Yeluc. Even though you are far away and they don't look back, they still might see you. Elal doesn't own them as he owns you. His power might slip. Your voice may grow loud and there are things you cannot help.

The sun rose in the sky and soon I could smell the camp: meat boiling in water, the fragrance of wood turning to ash, and another smell, sweet, intoxicating, making me want to go closer. But I did not.

That smell, and with it a word that they used that can be rolled on the tongue. *Bara*. Bread. The promise of sweetness in the mouth, the shell of the outside and then softness within. A nut and then the gentleness of young meat. It was that day that I smelt it first, with the strangers, and I knew then that I would know them, because of that smell, because of what they could do.

Eleven

The sheep have evil eyes, their pupils like slits, and the irises a poisonous yellow. When they bleat it is as if an old man is groaning, and Silas is sure they are complaining to each other as they trot. John Jones is a small tired-looking man with a large family; the grown-up children of his first late wife having been left behind in Wales. He whistles and his dog comes to heel – a fine obedient animal, and Silas feels a pang of jealousy. He remembers Polly, Benny and Sammy, the way they always seemed so anxious to please, and the way Polly in particular used to look at him with such unconditional adoration and trust. Then he remembers the last time he saw them – trussed up by Trevor Pritchard's sons – and quickly blinks away the memory.

John's dog pants, its tongue lolling from its mouth.

'Good boy.' John pats the animal on its head, and the dog's tail whips the air. 'Ready?' he asks Silas. Silas nods. They have enough supplies to last a couple of days, which Edwyn has insisted would be enough to take them to the valley.

'Besides, you are sure to find more water, there will be ponds, just as there are here,' he assures them.

'And the odd fountain appearing miraculously from a rock, I expect,' Silas mutters to himself miserably. But there is not much else they can do – there is a limit to how much water a man can carry, and if they carry too much they will travel even more slowly.

'Faith, Silas,' Edwyn says, clapping him on the shoulder.

'I've got faith,' Silas says, shaking him off.

'You'll see when you get there.'

They glare at each other for a few seconds more and then their eyes drop away.

John sets off, whistling at the dog to follow, and for a few minutes the dry valley to the south is filled again – this time with sheep instead of white, dirty water. Silas gives Myfanwy and then Megan and Gwyneth a long tight hug.

'You look after your mam now,' he tells Myfanwy and the child nods seriously. Silas laughs and runs his fingers lightly through her hair. 'Tell me if she's been naughty, understand? And make sure she eats all her dinner.' Then looking firmly forwards he begins to walk. When he is sure that they can't see the expression on his face he allows himself to look back. Stupid, he tells himself, blinking away tears, and slaps the rump of a straggler with the palm of his hand. It gives a surprised little trot and then scampers after the rest.

For a couple of hours they make good progress. John seems to know where to go without a compass. He heads off with a confidence Silas alternately admires and doubts. There is a driving wind that makes every move forward a struggle and the sheep are irritating – some straggle, while others stray from the rest. He runs after them as quickly as he can, encouraging them back on course but soon he is left behind, with just a few sheep near him. He slaps them all on the rear and encourages them onwards with a click from the side of his mouth – a sound that he usually reserves for horses. Then he looks around. John has disappeared from sight.

'John?' he calls but there is no answer. In the distance he thinks he can hear a dog bark. Suddenly anxious, he hurries towards it leaving the sheep behind. They will catch up if they have any sense.

'John?' he calls again, but there is no reply. Apart from half a dozen sheep, he is suddenly alone.

The wind has died down to a whisper but the pack on his back has thin leather straps which are eating into his shoulders. He stops for a short time to shift it into a more comfortable position and when he looks ahead again there is a fine mist drifting in from what he thinks must be the east. He hurries forward, calling out again for John and then the dog. The land becomes higher and the mist thicker. A mound he had thought was a sheep turns out to be a large pale-coloured rock. He stands on top of it trying to see, but the mist is rapidly thickening into fog. He listens for the sound of a bleat or a bark but there is nothing. In each direction the land, or at least the part of it he can see, is the same – undulating scrub, small thorns and tiny plants close to the ground like mould with sandy soil in between.

He hurries up a slope, his breath adding to the fog. His heart, drumming in his ears, is all he can hear. 'John, can you hear me?' he calls, but his voice is muffled.

Defeated, he sits and takes a swig from his bottle. In spite of the fog, which is making his clothes damp and heavy, he is thirsty. He squints anxiously at the sky searching for the sun, but the fog is too thick. How can the weather have changed so quickly? He searches again, thinks he sees a place where there is a glimmer of light, then pauses. Is it afternoon or morning? He guesses it must be afternoon by now – so over that hillock must be the west and that valley must lead south. He thinks of John and the way he strides out with such confidence. That way. It must be that way. He steps forward and immediately encounters his own footprints in the dust. Either he was going the wrong way before or he is now. He looks again at the sky. Maybe that patch of light isn't the sun after all.

There is a strong whiff of smoke. How can he smell smoke in the middle of nowhere?

'John?' he calls again.

This time there is a faint sound in return but it is not a sound he knows. He stops still, holding his breath. Indians. He remembers now. That is how they smell. Like smoke, that's what Selwyn Williams said. Like Hell. He sits as quietly as he can, and listens. The sound comes again. A distant drum. Very distant. Far, far away. He breathes again. A twig snaps close by. Snap. Another one. He tries not to move. Something is creeping closer, not taking care, not needing to take care because whatever it is is about to strike him or spear him with an arrow. He doesn't quite know what weapons they have, but he expects they have arrows. In spite of the cold a small trickle of sweat starts to roll down his side from his armpit. Then an evil eye peers at him through the fog and its eyelid blinks. It opens its mouth and lets out a plaintive bleat. A sheep. His shoulders sink and he breathes out. Just a ewe. He stands and the sheep runs away to where he can no longer see her. Silas sinks onto the ground, unpacks his blanket and prepares to wait. At the moment there is no point in trying to go anywhere. He covers himself with his blanket and shuts his eyes.

In the morning the fog has gone and so have all the sheep. He takes another gulp of water from his flask and shakes it. Almost empty. He thinks of John – he must be almost at the river by now, if he has continued.

At least Silas can see the sun now. He decides to head towards it. If he reaches the sea then at least then he will know where he is. He staggers forward. The land is barren in all directions, like a desert, like the one the Israelites had wandered around when they had been cast out of Egypt. Like the place God the Son fought against the temptations of the Devil. No doubt Jacob would call this a test. Silas snorts. He doesn't want to be tested, doesn't want to have to think. When he starts to think all that he finds are uncomfortable questions. It is better not to think at all. 'Be quiet!' he yells at the empty hillside, and it shudders back his voice.

Something moves in front of him: a small bush divides and an armoured animal with fur and a pointed face and tail emerges, looks at him and then scurries away making a trail in the sand behind it. He has never seen such a thing before – an animal with its own battle dress – and thinks of going after it. Perhaps if he hit it hard enough with a rock he could kill it and drink its blood. Rock into bread. The lessons from Sunday school are slowly coming back to him. He follows its track over the sand but the animal is too fast for him. He reaches the top of the hill and looks around him. He smiles. Satan must be losing his power: God the Son was tempted by visions of great cities, but all Silas sees is a sand dune, and below that, stretching out against a long beach, the sea. For a few seconds he just stands and looks at it – enjoying the soft crashing of the waves against the shore. There is something comforting about its sound. It is familiar, recognisable – the same sea that Megan is seeing now, part of the same one that his sister can see from her back door at Conwy. The Atlantic is nothing more than a very large pond connecting them all. He runs, shouting, across the sand.

He guesses that this way is south, but he doesn't care any more. He has used up all his water now and his throat is burning. When he swallows it hurts more. He tries not to think of drinking but when he does all he can remember is the spring he came across as a boy on his uncle's farm. It had been raining and one day he had spotted a trickle of water emerging quietly from the ground where all there had been before was lichen-covered rock and mud. He remembers the sound and the smell of dry rock that had suddenly become wet and the taste of the water, slightly chalky, but cold and sweet against his tongue and then the lush green of the ferns and grass where the trickle joined a stream a few feet away.

Silas looks around him. Grass – how he misses it. Not these yellow-green tufts but grass that is as lush as a child's head of hair, mile after mile over hills and fields, trimmed neatly with the constant nibbling of the sheep. He will never see it again, he realises, and treads onwards in the direction he hopes is south. The beach has given way to dunes, and he is walking along the top of these where the sand is harder and bound together with spiky vegetation. From time to time the dunes end abruptly in small cliffs. He stops at the end of one and looks around him. It is not that far down. He takes a few steps backwards and then runs forward and leaps into the air. The gap is greater than it looks. He lands awkwardly at the bottom of a gulley, his ankle twisted beneath him. A sharp burning sensation sears up his leg. He tries to stand but the pain causes him to cry out and collapse again. The wind sweeps down, channelled by the walls of the cliffs and he shivers. He manages to push himself near to upright on the leg that will bear his weight and finds a place where the wind has worn out a shallow cave in the sand.

He looks around him. This place has obviously been used by animals. He can smell the musty odour of old droppings. In the corner there is a heap of something that is partly black and partly white which he suspects is a carcass but has no intention of investigating more closely. If he were an animal, he thinks, he would crawl here to die. He curls up in a hollow, as far to the back as he can. At least here he is sheltered.

He sleeps. He dreams of the hilltop above Conwy and then, in a state halfway to sleep, allows himself to drift downwards through the castle gateway and the street where he first saw Megan. Such a beautiful girl – long, and not too lean, with long brown hair tied back in a blue bow of ribbon – and that way of glancing back she had, laughing at the stranger behind her, unafraid, slightly defiant.

Talk to me. If you'd like. If you'd dare. And for a long time he hadn't. For a long time he had been perfectly content just to look. If only he could see her now. Just one last look. As she was then.

He is smiling. In spite of everything he is smiling. He doesn't want to wake. If only he could continue with this half dream, half memory. But in his dream, he moves. He jostles for position. There's a fair in town and word is going round the fair that in one of the stalls there is the fattest woman in the world and she is sitting there, naked as the day God made her, smiling quite shamelessly at anyone who pays to take a look. Everyone is crowding close, keen to get in line. He is being nudged from both sides, tipping left, then right, laughing and crying out. Then behind him someone calls and he turns, knowing who it will be, anxious to see her, twisting around on one foot, all he wants is the merest glimpse of a smile, perhaps a word, or the touch of her hand, but all he feels and sees is pain – bursting through: white, searing, a scream burning everything else away. He opens his eyes. His ankle is twisted beneath him – and she is gone.

He closes his eyes again but there is nothing there. He shifts slightly but there is no point in moving. Eventually he will sleep and maybe he will return to his dream. It is all that matters. That dream and the girl with the ribbon. The one he loved. He will lie here and she will come back to him.

Outside it rains. At first all he notices is the cold, and then, incredulously, the comforting and familiar sound of the drops beating down. He thinks vaguely of puddles and reaches out with his hand so that it returns cold and wet. He licks his fingers then reaches out again. The taste of the water revives him a little. He crawls out and finds a small puddle and drinks it dry, scooping sand, mud and water into his mouth. He looks around. That small puddle was all there was and now the rain has stopped. He returns to his shelter and closes his eyes.

She doesn't come back immediately. It is as though he has to work through the rest to find her: the spring, the street, the fair. But at last she's there: a circle of light shining on her head as if there's a halo touching her hair. She's in front of him this time. It's his turn to reach out, tap her on the shoulder… but when she turns it is the fat woman who looks round, with long black hairs sprouting from her chin, smiling at him with a toothless mouth, and two small horns on her forehead.

Silas opens his eyes and hears the end of his own scream. Outside it is just becoming light. He is panting; sweat that has soaked into his clothes is making him shiver. He tries frantically to get rid of the images in his head. He crawls from the cave and down the gully until he can see and hear the sea. His heart begins to slow and he allows himself to furtively touch the memory: it wasn't Megan, not really, it was something else just pretending to be Megan.

He looks at his ankle. If he keeps his foot square to his leg it doesn't hurt as much. Perhaps he can bind it there so it doesn't move. He will go on, he decides, gritting his teeth as his ankle nudges the ground. It is important to keep fighting. Important not to forget.

He forces himself to his feet yelling out with the pain. There is no one to hear. It doesn't matter. He yells again, enjoys the sound, and sniggers. He can walk, just, if he is careful. All this shouting and crying has made his throat dryer still. He needs to drink. He needs more water – if only he could find a pond, a river, a sea. The sea! He can't believe he hasn't thought of this before. It's just a big pond of water.

He hobbles forward, a small man, more like a troll now than a man, his clothes hanging in ribbons where he has torn them on the thorn, his strands of hair grown long since they left the ship – a bright bedraggled ginger protruding from beneath the brim of a tatty, black felt hat. One deep footprint and then beside it a more shallow one – his good foot and then his bad one. The sea foams over the toe of his boot and he stops for a few minutes to sit down on the wet sand to remove it. Maybe the sea will cure him. He ties his boots around his neck and wades in to his waist. Cold. *Jiw, jiw,* it is cold. It doesn't matter if yelling dries his throat now. There is plenty to drink. He cups it in his hand and tries to swallow, but he can't. The salt makes him gag, but at least it is wet, and his legs are so cold he can't feel them. He wades out, relishing the numbness, then picking his way back up the beach to the high-tide line and its fringe of seaweed and detitrus.

The wind is blowing again, making him cold, and the seaweed is sharp on his feet. He walks on a little more. Despite the seawater, he is still thirsty – in fact even more thirsty than he was before. He licks his lips and tastes the salt again and he is thirstier still. He quickens his pace. The faster he goes the sooner he will reach the river, or at least a pond. Maybe it will rain. He mutters a tentative little prayer but all that happens is that the sun appears from behind a cloud and shines more brightly. Something glints in the seaweed in front of him. He staggers closer. A green bottle. The colour makes him catch his breath. Green fields, green trees, green grass. A sob escapes from him. *Hiraeth.* Such longing for home. It seems so cruel; he prays for a little rain and is rewarded with anguish. He stoops down to pick the bottle up, meaning to throw it as far away as he can, but stops. It is too heavy to be empty and the cork is still sealed in place. He finds his knife and hacks it out and sniffs: alcohol of course, and by its smell quite sweet, but at least it is something he can drink. Forbidden, but only by chapel; God Himself, he has heard, takes a more liberal stance. Didn't God the Son miraculously produce the stuff at a wedding? He smiles; he has never heard Jacob use that passage. He takes a small sip and swirls it around his mouth. He has never tasted wine before. He doesn't like it much, but he drinks again, more of a gulp this time, which tastes a little better.

He squints ahead. It won't be long now, he thinks. He must be nearly there. They'll be surprised to see him. And so will the *Meistr* when he eventually arrives there too. He imagines Edwyn Lloyd's smug little smile changing to an open O as he sees Silas waiting there for him with the rest. Did God tell you about this, then, Silas would ask, and for once the man would be speechless. Silas is laughing out loud now, weaving onto the beach and then onto the dunes. He is so happy he could sing, so happy he could dance. He gives a little leap, and then, ignoring the protest from his ankle, another one. He is making more progress like this. From now on he will not walk but jump.

He has finished the bottle now. It seemed easier to drink it all at once rather than to have to go to the effort of finding a way of carrying it without spilling any.

Above him a seagull cries and wheels.

'Thank you, *ffrind*,' he calls up to the sky and the seagull answers. The same birds. The same ones that followed them over here, swooping down on anything they threw out to sea, even Richard in his shroud, in his box. The shadow creeps over him with its fingers. He mustn't think of it.

Maybe the bird knows his sister. 'Do you know Muriel James?' he asks it, and the bird calls back that it does.

'Is her back any better?'

'No, just the same.'

'Come down here and talk to me properly.'

But the bird remains where it is, wheeling on a draught from the sea.

'Do you know Edwyn Lloyd? Can you see that valley he's been telling us about?'

'Yes, yes, it's very close.'

'Is it like he said it is?'

'How is that?'

'With meadows and tall trees.'

'No, nothing like that, you'll have to see for yourself.'

The bird wheels off, then dives suddenly into the surf, plucks up a fish and then flaps away down shore. 'Follow me,' it calls, and Silas staggers after it as quickly as he can.

The Welsh call it the river Camwy, the Tehuelche Indians call it the Chubut – the twisted one – because it is a river that writhes and squirms in its outsized valley. From its mouth sticks out a great tongue of sand, a sly thing, partly submerged and flicking back and forth, endeavouring to scoop up anything that passes by on the South Atlantic.

It takes Silas some time to realise that the spit of sand that he is hobbling along is skirted on one side by river and on the other by sea. He is moving erratically with his eyes on the seagull, crying out, gesticulating towards it, pleading for it to come closer. The bird in return does appear to be actually taunting him. It flies back and forth, never moving so far away that he completely loses sight of it, and crying out from time to time as if to attract his attention.

When Silas does eventually see the river he cries out, screeches insults at the seagull and limps quickly along its bank whooping. The river is broad and in full spate with high steep banks. He keeps hobbling to the edge and limping back, cursing and moaning, until he reaches a place where there is a slope – then he staggers headlong into the water. The river has the opacity of thin milk here, a pale yellow, and Silas comes up spluttering and choking before dipping in his head again and drinking. When he emerges he is white and shivering. The rock flour has converted him into a ghost. He shakes himself like a dog, flicking off water then resumes his hurried stagger a few paces along the riverbank. Then, without warning, he stops and vomits, again and again: first rock-choked river water, then something pink – the wine, then something paler and then a painful retching which produces nothing. His stomach is empty. He staggers on a few more paces and then collapses where he stands. Then, curling in upon himself, groans a few times and lies still and quiet.

The wind blows around him. For several minutes he lies there listening. There are the usual whistles and rustles though the branches of shrubs and then something else – a faint animal-like howl. He looks around him trying to see where it comes from. There is a path. It takes him a few moments to realise it, but when he does he jabbers to himself and continues along it quickly.

The light is fading when Silas appears. One of them yells at the sight of him, while a couple of men curse out loud. He looks ghostlike and surreal – a lurching, supernatural troll.

'What are you?'

But Silas doesn't speak. He creeps up to the fire and falls silently into a faint.

By the light of the fire Jacob Griffiths recognises his face. He shakes him cautiously. 'Silas? Is that you?'

Silas retches again and groans.

'Can anyone fetch him some water?'

'I was talking to a seagull,' Silas murmurs, his eyes still shut.

'Of course you were.'

'He told me that Edwyn Lloyd has been telling us lies.' His eyes open. 'He said the Camwy valley is just as barren and dry as anywhere else.'

'Well, you'll be able to see for yourself tomorrow.'

'Did you see Will Bowen?'

'Yes, we found him.'

'Was he all right?'

'Yes, in the Lord's arms now.'

For a few seconds there is silence. All that he knew about William Bowen was that he was young, headstrong and insolent – and wouldn't listen to anyone. He remembers Edwyn calling after him to come back and then imagines William waving his words away. It seems too severe a punishment for a little disobedience. He imagines the young man becoming lost, becoming frightened and then curling up, defeated and alone.

Silas closes his eyes again, the events of the past few days are coming back to him. 'I had some sheep.'

'What happened?'

'Where are they?'

The men are crowding round him now, saliva lubricating their words. It is days since they have had much to eat.

'They wandered off with John Jones.'

'All of them?' The voice sounds incredulous, desperate. 'Where did they go?'

'Back to the bay, I suppose. I don't know. I wandered around for days.' Silas' voice breaks. 'I was so thirsty. I'd no idea where I was. There was nothing to drink. Nothing to eat. I'm sorry. I'm so sorry.' He is sobbing now. 'There was nothing I could do.'

Twelve

Yeluc

The sun passed over the sky once, twice, and nothing changed. The strangers on the beach span around themselves like *mikkeoush* caught at all sides. Then a few of them walked on a trail to the south and didn't come back. More rocks were dragged from the ground to build their shelters and soon the sand was dark with tracks, one path leading the way to the pond and the animals. I noticed patterns; their lives were like the designs the women draw on skins and cave walls: a red line in the morning when they woke, made fires and ate. Then a zig-zag of yellow ochre as they fetched water, gathered more stones, and the women clattered metal vessels over fires. When the sun rose to its highest point another red line, marked on the day's mantle only they could see, and they ate again, and another when the sun set. Every day was the same: wake, eat, do, eat, do, eat, sleep.

My belly was tormented by their smells and caused me pain. Go hunt, it said, but in the daytime I pretended I did not hear. Sometimes I have to remind it who is master.

Eat, my stomach says again, and grips me so hard I stagger to where the cliff becomes shelf and the *rou* skip on their long legs, sniffing the air. At any sound they pause and their whiskers search the wind with small twitches. Even when a *rou* nibbles at a herb his eyes are searching around him. They are nervous, difficult to catch, and their meat is lean and unsatisfying but my stomach is desperate. I creep up close to where a young one is tearing at a *charcao* plant. He is more absorbed than the rest, chewing on the delicate fronds as if he is thinking. He dies with my single *bola*; an instant death, scattering his relatives into the scrub beyond. I salute his body and wish his spirit a peaceful journey, then, gripping him by his soft white underbelly, carry him close to the lagoon that the white men use. This *rou*, I decide, would be better boiled. I behead him, skin him quickly then divide his body into four. There is little meat, but my stomach gurgles in anticipation. I call Roberto for my armadillo shell which is tied to his saddle, and scoop some water from the lagoon. It is stale and coloured with mud.

A twig snaps. Close by. Like the *rou* I am sensitive to sounds, and even though my eyes both point the same way, like it I am always watchful. I have been hunted too. I quench the fire with my foot but I can do nothing about the smell of smoke. Holding my mantle close around me, I sink slowly to the ground and listen: footsteps moving towards the lagoon, human ones uncaring where they tread. Then a voice, a young girl's, calling. But nothing replies. It comes again. Two notes, the first one rising the second falling. She moves forward again. I peer out. It is the girl with the black *calafate* hair. She is carrying a large empty vessel to the lagoon, looking around its edge for a place to walk. Selecting a place she crouches then reaches out and dips it in, then looks up, around, at me.

Elal. Has she seen me? She stops, her mouth slightly open. She blinks once but does not stop looking. Then she speaks. Three words, rising at the end. She waits a few heartbeats then speaks again, a handful of words this time: two words, a space then the three again. Her vessel is sinking, the water is covering her arms and she turns to rescue it. By the time she looks back I have gone. She pulls the vessel from the water then looks back again to where I was, then at my bush where she would see my eye if she knew where it was, then to one side and then the other.

She calls again, and this time someone answers. She makes the sounds of a snake and flaps with her arms. Now there is quiet, and a time full of waiting. For a few long breaths nothing moves. Then she calls over her shoulder, a voice so full of disappointment I am tempted to stand and let her see me. She inspects her vessel and walks towards the answering call. I wait until I am sure and then I stand. My stomach reminds me it has not been fed and I walk back to the armadillo shell. Some other creature has carried away one of the *rou* legs but there is enough left to lull my stomach to silence. Then I resume my post at the top of the cliff and watch to see what will happen next.

Another day. Late, the sun already high, and a rain touching my skin as lightly as the brush of a fox's tail. The people on the beach below carry on with their pattern; the yellow ochre merging with the red. From time to time one of them looks out to sea, peers and then away again, and once a woman climbs near to where I shelter and looks out from the top of the cliff.

She is a tall woman with long black hair, like Seannu used to be but with more flesh on her rump and breast. Below us the smiling fish are making loops and circles above the waves and when she sees this she smiles too. Then she looks to the place where the sea bleeds into the sky. I know what she wants; for the swan to return but she does not have this magic. She holds open her arms and then lifts her hands to her head, then her knees fold as if they are too weak for her and she is on the ground, a moan as if her spirit is escaping, louder and louder until it breaks like a wave: 'Rich-ard', and a sob. I wait but she doesn't move. The air fills with water and still she doesn't move. Her thin mantle sticks to her body and I can see what lies beneath – more cloth with laces as if she needs something to hold her together. Elal begins to cry upon her; his tears large and cold, but still she does not move. She is quieter now, her head resting on the ground in front of her, so close that if I reach out I can touch her. My hand creeps out. I could smooth her hair – the way I smooth Seannu's – or touch the sodden cloth. If she lets me, I could ask my spirit guide to help me heal her. But there is a call from the beach below and her head starts upwards. She takes the thick cloths that cover her legs and sweeps them up to wipe her face. She is younger than Seannu, her face less worn and her hair not painted with grey. She stands carefully, her body shaking, then calls back.

Then there is another cry. 'Mam!': a word like a hum and she runs towards it. 'Mam?' She slithers and falls down the steps of the cliff, crying out and laughing, then runs to where a child waits and sweeps her up in her arms.

It grows dark. The sun hides behind a grey cloud so night comes early. The smell of cooked food drifts close to the ground. I creep towards it, hungry for its taste. I see them sitting about the fire in groups eating from bowls. The woman who climbed the cliff sits with a baby on her lap and a small girl with hair the colour of the fox's fur – the part of his tail before the tip – next to her. The *calafate* girl sits next to a pregnant mother and her son; the son asleep against her belly, twitching as if bewitched. Then the girl puts down her bowl and looks up and she sees me.

I call on Elal to make me disappear but she gives a small soft cry low in her throat. I smile and hold open my arms, but she makes no sign back so I step quickly backwards out of the firelight where only Elal can see me. I sink into the cliffs. I know each cave, each stairway of soft rock. Even though I am old and have lived through too many seasons, I climb as easily as a cat and just as silently. I rest at the top and watch again.

With the day they come to the cliff and look up. Have they seen me? Do they know I'm here? One of them starts to climb but the rest call him down. Then they huddle together on the beach.

Ah, Yeluc – is this long ago or now? Men huddling together, holding thoughts of you in their heads. Men talking in low voices making plans. As they disperse, you back away. Each movement is known, each pant of breath, each thud of the heart. As they form a line and move towards the cliff you rise to your knees. When they start to climb you are looking for your horse, clicking for him until he notices you. You call for him and when he comes you swing yourself on his back. You do not look back. You do not turn. Even Elal cannot protect you now. You press youself down against the horse's neck and whisper into his ear to go faster. Around a hill, following the twists of a valley so they cannot see you. But behind you are shouts. The fast ones have scaled the cliff. They have found that it is easy, there are steps, almost as if someone has made them. But you do not look. No, do not look Yeluc. Then, once, there is that sound that burns the air. Roberto lurches and you steady him with the reins. It is the only time you need to pull on them. Then you cry to him, 'Alo,' that word he knows. The word you invented with him when you were both foals. Go, most splendid one. And he goes. Faster than they are. Faster than what comes out from their sticks. South, to where you know they will not follow.

Thirteen

Yeluc

I have heard there is another god. My father, the *cacique*, used to speak of him. This god rules over everything, not just the land of the Tehuelches. He came with the white men and can divide himself into three. Once he was a man-god but now he stays in the sky with all the other gods and the ancestors, and watches over everything. But he cannot watch over your land as well as you, my lord Elal. I follow the paths you trod first for your people, marking them out with trees and patterns of hills and high ground so we might never be lost.

I guided Roberto with my words in his ear, past the small salt lake and the flamingos, through the small pass where the old *cacique* Namigo died, and saluted his memory, and on over the wide flat land edged with sea and low distant plateaux. There are spirits and demons everywhere. I can see them crouching in streams and in the shelter of rocks: there a face, there a body curled up like the whorls of a shell. Only I can see, only I know. I ride carefully past. If they are not sleeping, I frighten them away with powerful words.

I startled a small wild cat from the tangled branches of the *molle* thorn. As it ran through the undergrowth I thought I saw Elal's helper Gualichu in its fur, but I was wrong. It was a lesser spirit, chased away by my curse. I let my bag of charms slip back to its place beneath my cloak; it was not needed yet.

In front, growing larger and larger, the small tip of a finger in the sky, was something that would soon turn into a clump of trees. It marks the bank of the river and sweet water where Seannu would be. To the left of me was the ocean, hissing in its sleep, to the right side a spreading smoke spiral of a large camp fire, too far away to smell. They let me trespass. I harm no one and I eat little. And perhaps they are a little afraid.

Then I saw another trespasser I did not know. A stranger, one of those I'd seen, a small mantle on his head and below it the same fiery hair as the child. I dismounted and crawled closer.

When I was close, I saw he was lost. I have seen it frequently – when a warrior exchanges all that he has for a sip of the Cristianos' rum. They forget the land. They forget the ancestors and the spirits and they forget Elal. They move like this one was – crossing tracks without purpose and then crossing back again. This one though was quiet. The ones with too much of the white-man's poison roar and curse, laugh and fall over. This one was stumbling, checking something in his hand and then walking forward again. Once he reached the edge of a dune and jumped. He landed clumsily – like a child who is learning about his legs. His foot twisted under him and his face was red but not with ochre. Soon he fell and lay on the ground. I waited for him to rise but he did not. He yelped and crawled towards a cave and then curled up there like an animal waiting to die. I went closer still. He did not move. I could hear a rasping sound in his throat like the sound that the fox makes. Then, when I was almost on him, he threw something towards me. It was a bottle, it lay on the ground where it landed and nothing seeped out.

He was looking directly at me now but he couldn't see me. His eyes were pale like a summer sky overhead and for a few heartbeats I stared at them wondering what they meant. I tried to see if there was a spirit there but this shell was empty. His lips were bleeding and his body was making the shaking of the cold. I reached for the talisman that hangs around my neck and he barked at me as if he could see me. I hesitated. I asked Elal for help. Perhaps my Tehuelche spells wouldn't work on him, but I held onto my talisman anyway – it is the claw of the first animal I killed with a *bola*: the claw of a *mikkeoush* and it has not brought me great fortune but even so I keep it with me.

He shouted again and I began to run. Below the cave was a thicket of *calafate*, and even though its thorns tore at me I took refuge between its branches. I could still see the white man. Although he looked a little like a Cristiano he was not one of them. He was too pale, and his words were not their words. He sank back on the ground and lay still.

The sun fell onto the earth and still I waited. The wind breathed coldly on us and I buried myself deeper into my mantle, pulling it higher so it covered my mouth and ears. The moon came up, full and new, and I saluted it and asked it to bless me. It smiled on me and covered the ground with its radiance. The man with the bewitched eyes did not move. Asking Elal to wrap me in darkness I crept forward again. The man was asleep. I touched him first on his arm and then on his face. There was no warmth, and then, when I felt deeper at his neck I could detect just the faintest beating of life. I dropped a little of my water onto his lips and he groaned softly – a sound I could hardly hear like a breeze on grasses. Then, saying my most powerful spell to make life return, I rubbed a little juice of the *calafate* berry into his lip and waited again. No sound. No sign that he lived. I dropped water on his lip again and then shut my eyes.

Another place. Another time. Only I can travel. Only I can see. My spirit drifts from me and I look down at Yeluc sitting next to the white man in a cave. Down then, down and down. A dark place only I can see. The mist coming in and then, through the mist he comes. Tortuga. A turtle with a warm back. My helper. Then a place full of water and trees and the moon shining through. A small child with his pale shimmering hair full of fire. It is the white man. His spirit. Weak like a child. Sick. He cowers when he sees us, shouts at us and tells us to go. Then he shrinks into himself. As if he is leaving us. No! I reach out and grab his hand. Pull him onto Tortuga's back so he leans against me. Not your time, I tell him. Not yet. And he clings to me. Small fingers like pinchers. Like a brother. We are joined now, I tell him. Something stronger than blood.

It takes a long time to return. Every time Tortuga tries to hurry the child groans and tips from his back so I hold him there, keeping him safe.

Mind within body. Spirit within spirit. Yeluc's eyes open. Yeluc sees. The man's cave in darkness. The moon behind a cloud. The man smiling in his sleep and murmuring a word. 'Meg-an.'

I touched him and he was warmer. When I put water to his lips he drank. The child within him was quiet now and becoming stronger. I told him to sleep and waited for the moon to cross a hand's width across the sky. Then, since his breath came slow and deep, I left him and lay alone, watching the stars and wondered if that was where he would go too, if his god was like Elal, waiting to welcome his people to the heavens.

I was woken by a cry. The man. Shouting and screaming in the sea, standing with the water up to his shoulders and then I knew that some evil spirit was possessing him because he started to drink. The man full of the sea's poison. The wind blowing harder and the man shivering with pain. Then staggering along the beach to where the river makes its lazy entrance. Then drinking again.

Now a fight. The spirits from the sea and the spirits from the river. And the moon watching as the man groaned and retched. Vomiting like a snake, loud coughing retches that frightened Roberto so that he trotted towards me and then nuzzled my hand. I whispered into his ear and told him about how the man was fighting demons and that soon he would sleep. And he did. We lay close but he didn't know. In the night a puma came, his hungry eyes looking for meat, but we chased him away. The man slept on.

He is thin with hollows in his face. An old warrior and when he sleeps he speaks words with the voice of the wind: 'Dew, dew,' and then other words, and I follow them with my mouth· 'Meg-an, Rich-ard, Mee-ven-wee, Gwyn-eth'. And some of these words are sad as though the people that owned them have gone away and are now souls shining in the firmament. It is bad luck to talk of the stars, I wanted to tell him. Once Elal has shown his children to his kingdom they are no longer ours but his. But the man with the *zorro* fur spoke on and when he woke there were wet tracks on his face which he wiped away with his hand.

I will watch you, I told the man. I will be your guardian, your brother. I will let nothing harm you, and although he heard me he didn't see me. He turned and his eyes were haunted like the *rou's*. There was a kind spirit in them, like something young in an old shell, and I wanted to hold it to me and make sure it lived. I guided him along the river, shaking branches of the small willows so he knew where to go. He didn't see me. Not once. He walked as if he dreamed. And soon we came to where his own kind were and I could lead Roberto away, for then there was the smell of a fox cooking in a pot, and they greeted him with cries and a word that I now know must be his name: 'Si-las'.

Fourteen

Silas looks around him. By daylight he can see he is in some sort of brick-built shelter. The wind howls around the place, grabbing anything that is loose: door-hinges creak and the gaps between the bricks whistle back. He looks at the objects around him: chairs made from the skulls of large cattle covered in furs, tables made from boxes, shelves and beds built into the walls. He props himself up, tries to stand. No one is around. Through the open door he can see the remains of last night's fire being blown around – a swirl of ashes and small charred branches.

He is still weak. Beside his bed someone has left a cup of water and a small piece of biscuit. He sits back down on his fur-lined pallet and eats slowly, soaking the biscuit in the water to soften it before breaking off tiny pieces with his teeth. After he has finished he lies back again looking at the ceiling – it is a complicated structure of supporting beams. Who has built this place? Not Jacob and the men that came with him.

Holding onto walls and pieces of furniture for support he hobbles carefully to the doorway of the cottage and looks outside. Last night Jacob bound his ankle tightly in rags so that it couldn't move. There is a square with four large brick-built cottages each with doors and shutters for the windows, and in the centre a hearth for a fire and what looks to be a kiln. Around the cottages seems to be a high earth wall. It reminds him of a small fort, because at each corner is a small solid-looking cannon.

'What do you think, Silas?'

Jacob has returned with some scraps of tinder and is clumsily rebuilding the fire. 'There's a moat outside – apparently there's an old story that Indians won't attack over water, but maybe it was just that the fellow who built this place wanted to feel like some sort of lord.'

'Who was he?'

'We don't know, really. One of Edwyn's servants told me he remembered hearing about some Welshman called Evans wanting to start off a ranch in the Chubut valley but he gave up very soon, after just a few years. The man said there had been a rumour that the Indians had got wind of Evans' plans and made sure all the cattle scarpered to the hills before he'd even started.'

Silas sits beside him. Every part of him aches.

Jacob, he notices, is making a mess of building the fire. Even though he is easing each piece into place, he is getting it wrong, but Jacob is soon standing back and smiling contentedly at his handiwork. He looks at Silas. 'The Lord was clearly saving this place for us. Why don't you go outside and see?'

Silas stands slowly while Jacob looks at him and grins. Nothing seems to affect Silas' brother-in-law. Although almost as broad and tall as Selwyn Williams, Jacob's bulk is of the soft sort, consisting of blubber rather than anything as hard as muscle, and his hands, though large, are paw-like and too clumsy to be useful. As he blinks at Silas benignly, Silas wonders yet again how long it takes Jacob to shave carefully away at his cheeks, chin and upper lip to leave this ridiculous fringe of dark honey-coloured beard outlining his face.

Silas shivers. It is too cold to sit still for long. He stands and walks unsteadily towards the entrance of the fort and peers outside. The fort is on a small embankment surrounded by a shallow moat. The moat is dry now but obviously fills with water from the river when the tide is high or the river is in full spate. He takes a few steps outside the fort and looks around him for meadows but all he can see are patches of grass and thorn. It is certainly greener than the land he has so recently crossed, and he supposes that if you came across it from one of the barren slopes a couple of miles away you might have the impression of a meadow, but it is still more yellow than green, and beside his feet there are patches of bare ground where there is no vegetation at all.

'Well, what do you think?' Jacob has come to stand beside him. He is smiling and looking around the place as if he is happy.

'Where are the trees? I thought there were supposed to be trees.'

'Over there, look.'

Silas follows Jacob's finger. By the river a trio of willows droop over the river, but they are stunted and small.

Silas is too depressed to speak. The seagull was right. Away from the river, wherever the ground is higher, it is as barren as everywhere else: a few bushes and some scraps of thorn, and between them the sand or the earth, dry and dusty, scooped up by the wind into briefly-travelling vortices.

His legs suddenly give way and he sinks to his knees. It is a desert, just another desert. He thinks of the promises, the assurances, and Edwyn Lloyd and his carefully chosen words. Seven thousand miles for a desert. Did the *Meistr* think they wouldn't notice?

'Here, drink this. It's a sort of tea,' Jacob says, pouring some boiling water on to a couple of small twigs in a cup. 'It doesn't taste of much, but it's better than nothing.'

Silas sips. It has a faintly tarry taste and for a few seconds it fools his stomach into thinking it is being filled.

Jacob and the rest of the men there had given up waiting for the *Mimosa's* lifeboat several days ago, and Silas' confirmation that it will not arrive at all comes as no surprise. At first they had gone looking for game, trying to trap rather than shoot to preserve ammunition, but had been unsuccessful. Then one of the men managed to trap some sort of long-legged rabbit, and the next day they had come across an injured animal that seemed halfway between a deer and a goat. Neither of these had kept them going for long, of course. From time to time they have seen other strange creatures – a large bird with long legs that couldn't fly which was like nothing they have ever seen before; and sometimes something that seemed so familiar – a fox just as red and bushy-tailed as the foxes at home – that they were shocked into stillness. Once they saw a small tabby cat which looked quite tame but snarled and ran when they approached. Other times they have seen small dogs, mangy looking things that are also shy but seem much less wild. Then another week had come when they had not found anything at all and in desperation shot a few ducks – but they had been too rich for them and made some of them sick.

The fire is burning well now and the men are returning. Every morning they do their best to hunt, leaving Jacob to guard the place and tend to the fire. One by one they sit and warm their empty hands.

'Well, what do you think of the place, Silas?' one man says, waving at the buildings around them. 'It's quite a surprise, isn't it? Not much different from home. Sometimes when I wake I think I am back in my little place in Carmarthen and Mam is going to be in soon with a cup of tea, but instead in comes Jacob.' He laughs, then adds more seriously and quietly, 'but of course I wasn't starving to death in Carmarthen.'

'And it is a little less like a desert.'

'Yes, there is that, too.'

They return to stare at the fire, each one silent with his own thoughts for a few minutes until the last man returns with something heavy slung over his shoulder. He rests his gun carefully against the side of the house and then walks slowly up to the rest of them. They look at him with bright expectant faces.

'Bagged something, did you, Ivor?'

He lays the bird along the ground beside the fire and looks at Jacob.

'A bird of prey, *brodyr*. We cannot eat this. The good book forbids it.'

But little by little the bird is plucked, roasted and eaten. For another day their bellies are not empty. In the afternoons they go about their other work: some are clearing the ground, some are trying to make a track to the west, while others are digging out pits for the houses and gradually building up walls.

The next day they catch nothing, and the next day nothing again. Soon they will be too weak to even walk out of the fort.

'What's going to happen now?' Silas asks.

Jacob shakes his head. 'I don't know.' Even he has stopped smiling, and above his lip there are small hairs starting to grow.

Then, suddenly, there appears a dog. It comes from nowhere. A whippety sort of animal with long legs and a tail that stands up pointed and tall from its backside. It trots around as if it knows the place, sniffing and cocking its leg at every corner then sniffing again. It visits each man in turn, begging or nuzzling up, and then when it receives nothing but a pat on the head from anyone it runs out of the fort into the desert.

'Did I dream that?' asks Silas to no one in particular. 'Am I going mad? First a talking seagull and now a stray dog that comes from nowhere?'

But if the dog was a dream everyone else has dreamt it too. The men go to sleep in their houses while Silas and Jacob keep guard at the entrance.

The dog returns with a rabbit in its maw, and then something like a small deer. Each one has been killed with a single bite, expertly placed. Then he presents them with a fox and a couple more rabbits. He drops each cadaver at Silas' foot and then trots off again into the desert. The bodies are still warm. Silas gathers them together and Jacob helps him to skin them, then they assemble a spit over the fire and thread the six trussed carcasses upon it so they hang like fat beads on a string. When they start to cook the dog returns with a rabbit that he keeps for himself.

'What shall we call him?' asks Silas.

'*Antur*,' says Jacob, 'our hope, our future.'

The smell of cooking invades dreams. It is the odour of every feast, every Christmas, every Easter, and the men smile as they sleep. Then they wake shouting and laughing. Soon everyone is grabbing and eating – their faces glistening with trails of fat and their hair festooned with pieces of gristle. Silas has never felt so full; his stomach strains against the belt he has had to draw in to keep his trousers up. All may be well. All they have to do to survive in the place is to find enough game – and surely if a dog can do that then so can they.

The dog curls up on Silas' feet. He strokes its head. Just like Polly's head – the same size, the same shape. His favourite little dog – oh, how he'd loved that animal. Antur shivers suddenly, a single ripple spreading over his body like a pebble in a pond.

'Someone walking on your grave, eh, boy?'

In the night a brief shower turns the top layer of ground into mud. They call again for Antur but he has gone; the only trace of him is footprints leading out of the fort and quickly disappearing in the desert. They whistle again, but the empty desert whistles back.

'Is it possible for everyone to have the same dream, do you think?' Silas asks.

'No, it happened,' says Jacob, patting his stomach. 'Our manna from heaven. A sign from God. We are meant to be here, *brawd*. Even you must believe that now.'

Fifteen

Yeluc

Inside the river there are good and bad spirits. They are easy to see; even those without powers can hear their voices – young spirits laughing and playing tricks on each other in the mountains, and then, on the plains, the sighs of old men as they are swept out to sea. Sometimes they swell with anger, roar and fight each other for territory; bite at the land and swallow great mouthfuls, only to spit it back when they are spent. And they are sly, changing where they lie at a whim, flooding without warning, then settling themselves in to a new place with slurps and belches.

When I look at the river now I see it has changed again; it has claimed some new land for itself, and it twists in a great arc before it reaches the sea; smooth and languid, a great tongue of water mixing with the ocean, grey-brown then blue.

I offered the river a homage: a little of the *mara's* heart I had kept in a pouch, and it swallowed it without thanks. I told it about the strangers that have come and it said nothing back; but then the river spirits rarely talk to Elal's people, they talk only to themselves. So I rode Roberto silently along the Chubut's banks, trying to overhear words in the river's chatter, until I reached the high land. Upon this high land, which is all pebbles and small rocks thrown up by the river, is a piece of land that is higher still. It has been made by white men, so I have heard, and this happened not so long ago, when I was a child and still lived in the chief's *toldo*. This higher land they call a fort and it has four corners and an entrance near to the river and is surrounded by a shallow narrow lagoon of its own. It is usually quiet here. Powerful spirits haunt it and block the ear of anyone who goes near with the thickest skins so no sounds can be heard. Even when the sun shines it is cold and it is somewhere to ride past quickly to avoid being cursed. But it is here that Sil-as and his white brothers have chosen to rest and make camp.

Sixteen

Selwyn Williams comes over the desert alone with the pigs. It has taken him just four days. He is filthy, but completely unruffled, as if he has just completed a not very arduous stroll in the park.

'But there's a trail,' he says, when someone admires his time, and points back from where he has just come. 'Indian – hasn't anyone else seen it?'

The men shake their heads and wonder what he means.

Several groups of men have arrived from over the desert now – with horses, supplies and other animals – but no one has ever reported seeing a trail before.

'Tracks, marks...' he pauses, seems to think, 'things out of place... rocks, broken branches... difficult to explain.' Then he looks around him. 'Ah, Silas.' He strides forward, and hugs him. Silas staggers back grinning, struggling to breathe again after being in such close proximity to Selwyn's sweat-soaked clothing.

'It's so good to see you! When you didn't return with John... well, you can imagine how Megan is, poor woman.'

Silas nods then swallows. It is something that rarely leaves his mind. The thought of Megan hugging Myfanwy to her alone on that beach is his last thought before he sleeps.

'Where's everyone else?'

The men exchange glances. Jacob claps him on the shoulder. 'There's only us, Selwyn,' he says gently, 'we're all that's here.'

'But the women and children?'

'You left them behind in the bay, don't you remember?'

Selwyn shakes him off. 'No – they should be here.' He looks around him, as if he expects them to leap out from somewhere. 'Where are they?'

'There's no one here but us, Selwyn.'

'No schooner? One arrived from Buenos Aires, a large one, and the *Meistr* persuaded her captain...' Selwyn stops abruptly and closes his lips.

'You've got to tell us, man. Who was on board?'

'Women, children, the *Meistr*, the *Meistr's* wife.'

They stand still, letting the sense of it sink into their brains.

'All of the women and children?' Silas asks quietly.

'Nearly all.'

'When did it leave?'

'A few days before me. It should have...' He stops, looks round at the stricken faces. 'I'm sorry, I don't know...' He pauses again then adds lamely, 'I'm sure everything's all right.'

'Yes, of course,' says Jacob quickly, but his shoulders have sunk. He swallows then seems to straighten himself. 'We've built quite a little village here now, who do you want to show you around?'

The pigs squeal with merriment as they encounter the mud of the riverbank in the pens that have been made for them. The colonists have accomplished a lot in the four weeks they have been here: ground has been cleared, there is the start of a track by the river, a few mud-houses have been assembled from turfs and reeds, and the livestock is secure within earth-wall pens and fields. Everything is ready. There are plenty of men and animals, but no women and children.

The men work. They go to the coast and look out. They continue to work and then they go to look out at the sea again. Nothing changes. No one comes.

That evening Silas walks along the river too, following in the footsteps of the men who have gone there before him. After a few paces he encounters Jacob returning. The minister's step is slow and although his body is still broad it has lost a little of its bulk and his face is sunken below his eyes. Even so, he has obviously made some attempt to shave his face, but his skin is gashed, as though his knife was too blunt.

They stop on the path, facing each other. 'Any sign?' asks Silas, but he knows the answer. He waits for Jacob to shake his head, then turns to look over the river. It is the same both sides, quiet, nothing moving, nothing much living. He sighs. 'The new Wales – is this what we came so far for, eh, Jacob? Is it really any better than what we had?'

Jacob smiles. 'It will be better, *brawd*, you'll see. When Edwyn Lloyd comes...'

Silas' fingers curl into his palms. 'Edwyn Lloyd!' He spits on the ground beside him. 'It's his fault we're in this place. The man is a liar. Milk and honey, that's what he said. Look at it!'

'Have faith, *brawd*.' Jacob's grin diminishes, but only slightly. 'It will come to pass. We must have patience and all will be well.'

'I've run out of patience, Jacob,' Silas says slowly. His fists tighten.

Still Jacob smiles. It is a rictus.

Silas steps forward and prods him in the chest: 'We've lost everything, don't you understand?'

Jacob's grin is replaced by a slackly opened mouth as each prod nudges him backwards. 'Don't you care?' Silas steps closer, Jacob's breath in his face. 'They're all gone, Jacob, all of them. Your sister. Your two little nieces. Your nephew.' His voice breaks.

Jacob glances anxiously behind him. Below his heels there are pieces of wood and small branches being carried along in the river. It is fast flowing, deep, and very, very close.

Silas drops his voice so it is intense and quiet. 'They won't come back now, don't you realise that? Just because of that madman and his lies. We should never have come here, never have listened. How can you still believe in him now?'

Jacob smiles again and touches Silas on the shoulder. His hand opens and the broad fat fingers completely envelop the top of Silas' jacket. 'Whatever happens, they are in the Lord's hands now. It is hard, but we must take comfort from that.'

'I don't want them in His hands, I want them in mine,' he says, shaking his arms to throw Jacob off. 'I don't understand you, Jacob. You seem to have no sense. You've lost all that you love and yet you just smile as if everything is well.'

Jacob goes to touch him again, but Silas shoves him away, 'No, leave me alone!'

Jacob's mouth opens as his foot slips from underneath him, his eyes widening as the river looms beneath him. For a few frantic seconds he struggles to regain his balance, then he rights himself and steps away from the water's edge. He scowls briefly at Silas but then he seems to collect himself. He looks upwards and breathes out slowly then takes a couple of steps down the path and turns back to face Silas. 'You are upset and worried,' he says, 'and you don't understand the Lord's way. I forgive you, *brawd*.' Then he walks swiftly away, back to the settlement.

The days pass slowly. Five days and then six.

'Dead, the lot of them,' says one man.

'You can't know that.'

'Shipwrecked.'

'If you can't think of anything else to say, be quiet.'

The fire crackles and they watch the wood shift. Silas thinks of Megan hugging Myfanwy and Gwyneth to her and then calling out for him. He should have been with them. He feels a tear collect in the corner of his eye. When he blinks it travels slowly down the side of his cheek.

Seven days, then eight days pass. 'How can we have a colony without women and children?' Silas asks suddenly. Beside him Selwyn gives a quiet sniff and Silas looks up. The big American's face is wet with tears.

'What's wrong?' Silas asks.

Selwyn buries his face in his hands.

'A girl?'

Selwyn nods and swallows a sob. 'Annie Warlock.'

Silas remembers the large rough-looking blonde from Swansea, a servant with one of the wealthier families.

'She said she loved me, but I said nothing back.'

Silas pats him on the shoulder. He opens his mouth then closes it again.

'She'll never know, now, will she?'

Silas can think of nothing to say. Jacob is moving around the camp fussily putting things in order. He is folding blankets, picking up dirty cups, tutting over bones that have been discarded around the fire. How can the man carry on as if nothing has happened? When he feels Silas' eyes on him he holds out what he has collected and tuts again, inviting Silas to share his disapproval, but Silas looks away and squeezes Selwyn on the shoulder. The great bear of a man is shaking.

'We'll help each other, *ffrind.*'

Nine days and a flock of thirty ewes arrives from the north, and with them John Jones and another man – both of them tired but happy. John and Silas hug each other. 'Where did you go?' they ask each other in unison.

'Back to the port when I couldn't find you.' He stoops to smooth the back of his dog. 'You let me down, that time, didn't you, boy?' The dog pants and wags its tail. John pats him on the head. 'Never mind, not your fault, boy. These sheep are better behaved, *on'd yw hi?*'

'How's Megan?'

'Not good...' he trails off. 'But why are you asking me?' He looks around him still smiling. 'Where's the wife? Fine welcome from the woman, this is.'

When they are told they are not here both men grow pale and silent. They walk slowly into the fort with their heads hanging down. When they are sitting by the fire Silas asks where the sheep have come from and John tells him that Edwyn Lloyd managed to persuade the Argentines to send some more.

'That man can persuade the sun not to shine,' says Selwyn.

'Did you ever find the first flock?' asks Jacob.

John shakes his head. 'Gone for good, they are.'

Jacob looks from John to Silas and gives a smug little smile. 'Perhaps you had a better helper this time, John.'

Silas stands with his fists clenched.

John shakes his head again. He stares into the fire for a few moments. 'Couldn't be helped,' he says quietly. 'There was a fog, see. As thick as that *cawl* my Mary makes, it was.' At the mention of his wife John's voice fades to a murmur.

Silas turns away. No one wants to understand, no one wants to know. He walks away without thinking of where he is going – out of the fort and then along the path to the coast. How he wishes he could just walk backwards through time, back and back, across the desert, across the sea, taking Megan, Myfanwy and Gwyneth – and Richard with him. The thought of Richard's face squeezes his heart so tightly that he cannot bear to breathe. It thuds against the hollow spaces inside him, each beat making him gasp. Richard, Richard, Richard. He tries to make it go away, but it won't. It is as if there is a hand around his heart and with each pulse the fingers tighten. He walks forward and there are more sounds, more beats – thuds coming up through the ground into his feet – in and then out of time. Waves. The ocean's heart, reminding him of his own.

He comes to the end of the path and looks down. The moon is full, a long beam of cold light that reaches from the horizon to his feet. He has often seen great brown sea lions come ashore here and in the light of the moon he sees that there are some resting there tonight. They are on the platform below him – great huddled masses of flesh, all looking grey in this light, like mounds of something soft gone solid, snuggling together as if they are cold. They make no sound. He sits and watches them but they don't move. The heartbeat of the sea goes on and the fingers keep in time, squeezing and squeezing. He doesn't want to remember but he does. A heartbeat faltering. A quiet thud not keeping time. Slower and slower. Out there in the ocean. Another time. The shadows creep out and this time he can't send them back. He's there. In the hold of the *Mimosa* and it's happening again.

The doctor patting his arm and telling them he's sorry. The man walking away as if there's nothing to be done. The boy has a fever, he wants to tell him, that is all. It will pass. These things do. The fever will pass and the hatch will open and the storm will finish. And they will all go up the ladder out of this place with its sickening smells of death and Richard will wake and walk into the light – just as he did yesterday. He was walking then and he will walk again. How can he not walk now?

And Megan reaching for the lamp, smoothing back the boy's hair, his forehead, his cheeks, his chin. He will open his eyes soon. But he doesn't. She leans forward and kisses him lightly on the cheek. But even though they both watch he doesn't wake.

No one moves. No one speaks. The ship tips and creaks. The hatch to the hold closes, opens, closes again.

And suddenly there is Jacob: pushing through, dropping down, gathering the boy in his arms.

And it is as if they are both just there – warm statues no one can do anything about. Everything just happens and they can do nothing.

The world moves slowly.

The space where he was, the small dent that his body made. His body. His body. Not there. He looks again and again. Knows and doesn't know. Believes and doesn't believe. It hurts too much. He reaches out, touches the pillow, and draws away. Cold.

Then colder still. Wind in his face. Spray in his eyes and a small box slipping into the water, the lid slipping, the shroud unfurling, and for a few seconds it doesn't sink, he knows he should look away but he doesn't, something is holding his eyes, keeping them still, making him watch as the waves pull at the shroud a little more and a small hand appears, reaching out like one of those flowers on the beach which he knows are really fish, and he watches it sink, blue-green wave after blue-green wave, and then something inside him screams: a sound like a flame, burning, searing, cutting. Sorry, sorry, sorry. He grabs at Megan and draws her to him. His fault they came. Sorry. He believes it now. He knows it now. Her heartbeat and his, the only sound she makes, the only movement. Thud, thud, thud, like the sea.

The same sea beats now. Its waves creep up the shore towards the sea lions as the light fades and the moon rises. One of the sea lions has slithered laboriously into the water. A beam of moonlight picks out his head as he bobs in the sea, and as Silas follows it over the waves he thinks of how it must be to have a head full of nothing except the feel of cold water on a blubbery body, the slipperiness of fish as it slides down into the gullet and no worries of God or death or people gone and never coming back. Never coming back.

A cloud passes briefly over the moon and the world darkens and then becomes brighter again. Beyond the waves is something else – too big for a bird and too white for a whale. He squints ahead, wishing his eyes were stronger. It must be a sail – the sail of a ship – close and coming closer. He stares at it a little longer – even from here he can see that it is bedraggled and lopsided. A schooner! His yelp disturbs the sea lions and they look up into the darkness.

Seventeen

The men come quickly in the dark, gathering anything they can find that will burn to show the ship the way. They yell and shout even though it is impossible for anyone aboard to hear. Then, when they are too tired to do any more, they sit and wait. If they keep watching it will keep on coming. If they look away it will maybe go.

There are only a couple of men on deck of the *Maria Theresa*, and they work as if they are dreaming, not making a sound. Everything happens slowly. A rowing boat is lowered and the women and children line up to climb inside. Even from the shore Silas can see that they can barely walk. When they are near he can see their eyes are dull and blinking slowly.

Edwyn Lloyd is first to disembark. He sits erectly in the boat, a stick supporting him, apparently inspecting the way the crewmen row him ashore. He helps Cecilia from the boat and then walks stiffly up the beach alongside her, his arm supporting hers. The two do not look at each other; their faces are as still and as vacant as everyone else's. Silas barely registers them; instead he searches through the other faces on the *Maria Theresa* until, at last, he finds them, lit by a sailor's lamp. Megan helps Myfanwy climb on board the boat then pulls her under her shawl to protect her from the cold. Silas peers through the darkness. He can't see Gwyneth. Is her mother holding her, or is her shawl empty? He stands stiffly, waiting for them to approach. Then, as they climb ashore, Megan steadies what she is carrying beneath her shawl, and the shawl gives a whimper. She rocks the shawl a little, staring ahead of her. Then she stops. She sees him. For a few moments she stares with an open mouth and then tries to run towards him. She manages only a few steps before Silas reaches her. They cling to each other tightly without speaking.

'You're alive!' she says, 'thank God. I thought when John Jones came back...' She buries her head in his chest.

Then, when Myfanwy whimpers, he turns and lifts her far too easily into his arms. For a few minutes they stand where they are on the beach clinging to each other, waiting until one of them can find the power to speak.

'We thought we'd lost you, lost all of you.'

'There was a storm,' Megan says slowly, as if she is testing her voice, 'everything crashed around and the water barrels went overboard. Oh Silas, it was horrible, horrible. We were so thirsty and it was so cold. I thought... we'd come all this way, and... I thought...' She sees Jacob and reaches out for him.

'Oh Megan, Megan,' Jacob says, coming a little closer. He raises his hands, and then, unsure what to do with them, lowers them again. 'You should have more faith, I told you Edwyn Lloyd would make sure we were all right.'

She draws back as if stung, stares at her brother for a second and then buries her head again in Silas' shoulder. Silas hugs her closer and begins to walk a couple of steps along the path, but Megan stops. She struggles to free herself from Silas a little and then looks back at Jacob: 'How can you say that to me? You don't know what it was like, what we had to endure.' Her voice is trembling, but she fights to continue. 'We almost died and Edwyn Lloyd could do nothing, nothing. He's just a man, Jacob, human like all the rest of us!' She slumps back towards Silas, still looking wild-eyed at Jacob, panting and holding Gwyneth tightly to her.

'It is because of that man we are here, in the Lord's land.'

'Exactly,' Megan snarls, her voice stronger. 'Because of that man and his stupid schemes I have lost my son, almost lost my daughters, my husband, my brother, almost lost all of you.'

'Nonsense,' Jacob says, 'all of this – is the Lord – testing us. Edwyn Lloyd is our protector – doing all that he can to make the Lord's plan for *Yr Wladfa* come to pass.'

Megan narrows her eyes, leans forward and her voice hisses in the dark. 'He is mad, obsessed; he carries on despite everything.'

'Calm yourself, *chwaer*, this is doing no good.'

'He has no heart, no feeling, no sense.'

'*Ust*, watch your tongue,' Jacob says, frowning. 'The man has suffered as much as anyone, look at him.'

But she shakes her head. 'I will not look at him. I never want to see him again.'

'Megan! You mustn't talk like that.'

Silas steps back, straightens Myfanwy in his arms, and glances at Jacob. 'She can talk any way she pleases. If you don't like it, leave us alone.'

'Maybe it will be better if I do.' He turns to the group surrounding Edwyn, picks up a small box that has just been thrown ashore and walks stiffly up the beach alone.

Megan and Silas rest in the shelter of a low cliff before continuing.

'Was it worse than on the Mimosa?' he asks.

She nods. 'Colder... but the storm was the same, wind and rain and big waves, just like then....' She grows silent. He remembers too.

Above them the hatches had rattled, lifted from their housing by the wind even though they had been fastened down, and then the rope holding the luggage in the centre of the hold broke and some of the trunks had begun to slither from one side of the deck to the other. Then the hatch doors had opened a little more and banged shut again, and with each tilt water had flooded in, soaking anyone near with a short cold torrent.

Then, from somewhere close, came the sound of cracking and splintering, and the ship had tilted even more wildly. Silas wedged his family onto the bunk, holding them to him in the corner, bracing himself against the sides, while even more water had fallen through.

And then the wind had grown stronger still, until it was shaking the hatches like something strong and angry, roaring and moaning, then hissing and whistling. Waves crashed above them, louder and louder until each one was so like a small explosion that Myfanwy had screamed and covered her ears. Then, all at once, it had stopped and there had been a quietness quenching everything else.

Silas shivers at the memory. It had been the start of fear, the start of suffering. The boy had been in his arms, already ill and smelling of vomit.

'A big wave,' Richard had whispered, his hot body shivering, 'it's gone right over us.' And he'd clung to Silas – so tightly that afterwards, even after the child had died, there had been a bruise on his arm. 'I'm scared, Dadda,' he'd said, 'are you?' But Silas had shaken his head against him, and lied. 'No, *cariad*.'

On the beach Silas holds Myfanwy more tightly to him and shuts his eyes. It's as if he's there. He doesn't want to go back, but he can't stop himself: the hatches are shut tight and nothing comes through; the air is sealed in, motionless, the timbers creaking, one against the next, every movement a little creep inwards.

He opens his eyes again but the feeling is still there: the water pressing, squeezing, and holding them tight – a mile below and then another mile, and in all directions, more and more – an endless terrifying volume.

He'd thought of God, of reaching out, looking for a hand, praying that it would appear and he'd feel it holding his, but it wasn't there. Instead of a hand just the thread of a thought. He'd grabbed hold. Attached to the thread, some string, attached to the string, a piece of rope and then a larger rope, and maybe, at the end of that, God's hand, holding on. Don't break, don't break, he'd prayed. And it hadn't.

How long had it been? A minute? Maybe two. It seemed like time had stretched, as if it would go on and on. But eventually the crashing on the deck had returned, and everyone around him had laughed and there had been Richard again on his lap; his breath on his face – hot, real, and soaking in sweat.

'It's going to be all right now,' he'd said and the child had believed him.

But it wasn't, of course. Instead everything had become worse. Finally Silas manages to shake away the memory. That was then; this is now. They can start again. Thankful to feel Myfanwy in his arms again, he shifts her to lean against his shoulder, and helps Megan along the beach to the path.

Eighteen

Yeluc

There was a new moon shining over the desert. As I saluted her I thought about the sea and the moon's daughter who lives there, how she makes the waves shift and creep closer to the land in her anxiety to rise up and greet her mother's arrival. Then I thought of Seannu, how she emerges from the *toldo* smiling to greet me too, and how much I miss her, so I rode Roberto quickly away from the sea to the high place where the river forces its way through rocks to enter the valley, and the air is colder and drier.

Seannu and her sisters, they are there – in the elbow of the river, their *toldo* emerging from the ground like a large boulder, the entrance gaping open like a mouth in the direction of the far away sea. For a time I watch them. They are almost as blind and as deaf as the strangers: Tezza crouching by the fire; Mareea pegging out skins.

I let Roberto graze and creep closer on my belly. For a while, I watch the smoke drift up and billow into shapes in front of me. My mind wanders, time falls away, layer upon layer, until there is Seannu at the entrance to her father's *toldo*, as she was the first time I saw her: black-haired, pink-faced, tall, holding her mantle tightly around her, flashes of silver and bone at her neck, frowning at something at my feet. It is the body of a *zorrino* I found.

'Why do you have that, you stupid boy?' she asks, kicking the carcass with her foot. 'Take it away from here. It is a nasty smelly thing that no one wants.'

I look at her foot and then at her leg outstretched. It seems to reach up and up, lean, long and straight as a stem. Then she sees me looking and grins. It is like the sun coming out from behind a cloud. 'Are you Yeluc?'

I nod. It is all I can do.

She comes closer. I feel each muscle in my back stiffen; one then the next like a branch caught in a flame. Her two long cords of hair lift with her face. 'I've heard you're strange. I've heard you see things. A shaman in the making, that's what they say... is that why you have the *zorrino*?' She squats down to examine it. 'But it's dead. Why did you kill it? If it was a spirit...' Her questions stop and she pauses to look at me. Her frown makes two deep lines on her brow and I see how she will look when we are older. 'Do you not talk?'

And for now it seems that I do not. The smell of her breath is like every summer I have known, and every summer I want to know. Her mantle has fallen open and I can see the short garment she wears beneath – something that has been bought from the Cristianos – a piece of woven cloth, thick and red. Beneath it her legs are pressed together, and I examine the crevice between them, and the way it becomes wider and then narrower again to her knees. She is lean; but as she stands again there is something in the way that she holds herself – legs apart, chin jutting forward – that is powerful and reassuring. She looks at me, waiting.

'It was fighting with another...' I do not want to tell her about the battle, about the kicking and biting. 'I wanted to see what makes it smell. What gives it power.'

'Oh, it will give you power, Yeluc, you can be sure of that. If you smell like the *zorrino* people will not come close but run away from you.' She smiles again. Her teeth are even, small, still ridged at the edges like those of a child. 'My brother was right – you are strange. But I do not think you are going to be a shaman.' She catches hold of her mantle and draws it close. Then takes a few steps towards her father's *toldo*.

'Why?'

Her face is in shadow now, but her smile still shines whitely. 'Because a shaman cannot take a wife.'

So because of Seannu I tried for a time to deny what I saw and heard, tried to ignore the signs of Elal and the voices of the spirits calling me to journey. But a man cannot choose not to be a shaman just as he cannot pretend to be one. It is something that he is, something bestowed upon him by Elal, like five fingers on each hand and a head upon his neck. O Elal, how I betrayed you and the way you had blessed me. But Seannu haunted me with her own sweet spirit and I could not resist her. For just a few weeks our tribes would be camped around the same spot on the river and every day I made some excuse to go and see her until she would emerge at the sound of my horse's hooves, and then, at last waiting for me as she skinned meat or pinned out skins.

I was possessed by her, bewitched, my head felt hot and light as if I were short of water. One day my mother caught my face between her hands and looked at me, pursing her lips and frowning: what is it Yeluc, she asked, it is as if there is something inside you – can you not chase it out? But all I wanted to hear, all I wanted to see was Seannu. So I told my cousin Aonik to present her father with all that I owned: two fine mares, some brooches and bracelets for his wife, some pots and a pup my mother's dog had whelped. But Aonik reported that the chief had regarded them uneasily. He knew of me, knew what I was. The shaman should not marry. But Seannu had weakened him, as she weakens everyone. She tugged at his mantle, looked at him with her mouth turned down and then up, pleading and then placating him with promises of grandchildren until he relented.

Yes, Yeluc, it happened. Long ago now when you were young and so was she. I shut my eyes and remember: her blue-black hair oiled and decorated with threads of red, every piece of finery that she owns taken out and displayed on her throat and arms, and the women chanting, and then Seannu running between them, hugging, clutching, tongues leaping up, *la-la-la-la*, arms reaching out, tears, calls, sighs. And I sweep her up and she is there, *la-la-la-la*, pressed against my back, soft, warm, still they sing, *la-la-la-la*. She clutches tighter. Touches my neck with her lips. The shaman has a wife.

The smoke clears and time shifts again. I peer inside and there she is. Red face polished like stone. Grey hairs woven in with the black, but still the same amulets glinting beneath the gown. Her dog sits on her lap and she plays with its ears through her fingers. She looks up and smiles. 'Ah, Yeluc. There you are. I've been waiting.'

Nineteen

In spite of everything Megan is happy to have a home. It is not much: a house made from root-filled mud covered with thatch made from grass. There are small holes in the wall where the mud has already fallen away and the wind blows through; but at least it is shelter, and a place to stay, and Silas watches her as she arranges the things they have brought from home – her china and her small cupboard, their clock, her pans, some of the better rugs, the quilts and blankets. He stands at the doorway and watches her move. Her dress, the colour of chocolate, is loose on her now and is held in at her waist by a belt. He looks for the familiar curve of her rump or the swell of her breast, but there seems to be little under the cloth any more but more cloth. She makes a table of their trunk. They have to sit on the earth floor, which is not very flat even though it has been trampled over several times by the stallion, but once this is covered by rugs and the walls covered with blankets to keep out the draft, and the lamps are lit, it seems homely enough. Silas looks at her face in the lamplight, it is thinner and more drawn than it was, but when she sees him looking at her she smiles, and he smiles too.

'Here,' she says, passing him a tiny shoe. 'It's Myfanwy's, I was saving it for Gwyneth but it'll be better if you take it now instead.'

He looks at it dumbly.

'You bury it, Silas,' she says exasperatedly, 'don't you remember? You put it under the hearthstone for luck.'

Something inside his chest seems to clench and stop him breathing, like a fist of happiness. They are together again and it is all that matters. He lifts up the hearthstone and digs out a small hole and places the shoe inside.

'Good,' she says. '*Y tylwyth teg* will be pleased with that. We'll be lucky now.'

'*Y tylwyth teg!*' he says, grabbing hold of her suddenly around the waist, and laughing. 'Surely the little people can't follow us here!'

'They go everywhere,' she says, pouting. Fairies, demons, bad spirits – he can never tell how much she believes – but she has always looked out for them assiduously.

Together they make supper – a bowl of mutton stew – then they put the children to sleep in a nest of blankets in the corner. For a few minutes they allow the precious tallow to burn while they change out of their clothes. Myfanwy gives a quiet snore as she turns over.

'Here,' he says. She watches from her seat on a box as he opens a bag she has never seen before and reveals two soft sheepskins. Her eyes widen.

'A leaving present,' he says, 'From Muriel. She told me to keep them for you as a surprise when we got here.'

He spreads the skins out in front of the embers of the fire then reaches over to her and pulls her towards him. Her flesh used to spill from his hands but now his fingers fit easily around her. He breathes in the odour of her hair. Everything about her has become more intense: a musk instead of a fragrance; flesh that resists him rather than moulds to his hand – hot, savoury, tasting not just of salt but of something sweet. There are parts of her he no longer knows. He catches his breath. He longs for her so much it hurts. He pulls her down, presses himself to her, her convex back hard against his concave chest. Then he edges back slightly and raises his head so he can just see her face: it is motionless, watching the fire. He watches it too, the small glowing houses tumbling and crackling onto the earth.

She murmurs some words he can't hear and he glides his hands around her again. Ah, he had forgotten how this feels: Megan's skin, Megan's hair, the contours of her valleys. She twists her head and kisses him and he remembers another time, another Megan, a Megan that did all the enticing and all the kissing. A Megan that came to her window at the sound of his voice and pulled him closer; the Megan before this one. He shuts his eyes and again finds her mouth with his.

In front of them the houses of the fire village gradually darken. Roof timbers collapse and walls fall, sending small cascades of sparks into the room. He glances towards Myfanwy and Gwyneth – two dark unmoving mounds – then reaches up beside him for one of the blankets from home. The yellows and blacks are shades of brown in the dying light of the fire. He snuffs out the tallow and its greasy smell drifts around them as they cover themselves with the thick cloth. There is little light left now but he can see the reflection of the fire's glow in her eyes – and in the tears that are collecting on her cheeks. Beside them the tiny charred houses fall softly like snow from a steep roof.

Twenty

Everyone is crammed into the small warehouse they have built on the side of one of the earth walls of the Old Fort. Jacob stands on a small box so that everyone can see him while sacks of rice and flour have been arranged like pews and the women and children sit on these, the sacking itchy on the legs even through trousers and skirts. They are wearing their best clothes, but even these are starting to look bedraggled.

'There are other wildernesses, *ffrindiau*,' Jacob says, his voice strained with sincerity, 'hot places where nothing grows at all, and the Lord has called his people even there, and helped them to build His kingdom...'

Silas' mind starts to wander. From where he stands at the back he can just see the cliffs that skirt each side of the valley floor through the open door. On the southern side something rises: a bird, or maybe a wisp of smoke. It lasts just a minute. When he looks again it is gone. He glances around to see if anyone else has noticed but everyone else seems to be trying to pay attention to Jacob's sermon.

'Fountains burst forth from cliff, yea *brodyr*, water where there was just rock before. Corn grew where there was nothing but sand. Manna from heaven... then glittering cities where there was nothing but caves and shelters. A new land where His people can dwell in His glory! And that is what the Good Lord has promised us. Are we going to betray Him, *brodyr*?' Jacob pauses, his arms stretched out, but nothing happens.

'I said, are we going to betray Our Lord?'

'No, *brawd*,' says a single voice.

'No, *brodyr*, we will serve Him and labour for Him. We will toil without rest, labour without looking for reward...'

A few people around Silas fidget on their sacks and exchange glances with each other. 'Don't think that lazy dog Tomas Price will think much of that,' whispers one not quietly enough. His neighbour laughs and Jacob raises his voice '...knowing that the true paradise is in Heaven above. And what a place that is, *ffrindiau* – angels playing harps, glorious singing by the almighty chorus...'

There is more rustling and creaking as people shift on the

sacks of grain, their eyes wandering. Hands play with hymn sheets and buttons on clothes. One young man shyly reaches out to hold hands with a young woman who sits next to him while another woman straightens her dress, smoothes it down and then straightens it again. When a child cries several people immediately rise to take her out.

The *Meistr* is sitting with Cecilia at the front. They sit upright, still as two statues, their faces calm and without expression. From time to time Edwyn bows his head to draw a finger across his eye, and sometimes Cecilia nudges the hat on her head. There is a smugness in the way they hold their heads, and in the way they politely join in with the amens and halleluyahs. But even Silas has to acknowledge the contrast in reception: whenever Edwyn Lloyd speaks the people sit with rapt attention. No one fidgets. When children cry they are told to hush. There is something in the way he makes his voice rise and fall, swell and fade, and then there is the vibrato that Silas hates but which catches his ear just as much as it seems to catch everyone else's.

'Let us pray,' says Jacob, and Silas watches as the *Meistr* and his wife shuffle to their knees. His lips move without a sound. Her eyelashes flicker.

The service ends. Jacob appeals for another chorus of agreement but none is forthcoming. So Jacob orders Silas to give them a note for their hymn. Silas finds a 'Soh' from the middle of his range and leads them through the first verse. He has a large collection of hymns and songs in his head. It is something he has always found easy to learn. If the entire bible were to be put to music he is sure he could learn it in a month if not a week. Sometimes, when he is alone, he makes up new tunes for the words of old songs, and sometimes he makes up new words as well. One day he would like to find someone to write them down for anyone that is interested. It will be his legacy, something for Myfanwy and her children and her children's children. These are your grandfather's hymns, she could say, even though he couldn't read a note and did not know many letters, he knew his songs and he knew more words than the entire congregation of Rhoslyn. It is something he first thought of a few years ago for Richard. His voice fades slightly. Richard. His singing dies away altogether. A few people next to him notice and give him sideways glances. The child had a promising voice and could sing several complicated old tunes nearly note-perfect. 'I can hear them in my head, Dadda. It is as if there is someone in there singing them already – is there someone in your head singing too?'

Silas had enjoyed imagining the two of them sometime in the future, singing side by side in the choir, perhaps being picked out for duets – father and son together. Silas looks down, blinks. He can't read the words but he waits for the letters to become clear again on the paper.

A small hand squeezes his. Myfanwy. 'Sing, Dadda.'

He opens his mouth obediently. This is supposed to be a joyous day. Edwyn Lloyd has ordered it so. A holiday, he'd said. They had done enough building, digging and carrying for now, and were celebrating the start of the colony. There is a pig roasting on a spit and bread cooking in the oven.

After the blessing they burst noisily into the courtyard smacking their lips and inspecting the fire.

It is a fine day. One of the best they've had. The air has a clear quality quite different from the air in Wales – perhaps because it is drier. He looks around. He can see for miles. Something attracts the corner of his eye – something moving. It is another wisp of smoke, rising this time from the opposite direction, towards the northwest. It forms a thin neat column several feet into the air then stops. A second later another column of smoke rises. The air seems to be quite still because the smoke doesn't spread, just widens slightly as it rises until there are three fat heads of smoke slowly rising in a column over the desert.

Silas turns back to the fire, but as he does so, another head turns with his. Selwyn Williams has seen them too. Their eyes meet. Selwyn nods, his expression hidden by his hat. Indians.

There is a wreck in the river that is revealed at low tide. After the meal the men go to the riverbank and examine it for timber. Apart from a few willows, and the planks carried down from Port Madryn by the *Maria Theresa,* it is their only source of timber. Jacob says that he believes he could easily remove the cabin intact from the deck and that this would make an excellent schoolroom.

'You think so, do you?' says the *Meistr*. 'You don't think this ferocious current and turbulent water would cause you any sort of hindrance whatsoever?'

The people around him laugh at Edwyn's sarcasm, but Jacob seems quite oblivious to the ridicule.

'Indeed not, Edwyn, I should think that if we could hitch up a few ropes from the bank...'

Silas drifts away. Even though he dislikes Jacob, he can't bear to see him ridiculed. Megan's brother has always been hopelessly impractical. Just because a man can read Latin it doesn't mean he has more sense than anyone else. Silas himself can barely read, but he knows that trying to dismantle that wreck in such fast-flowing water would be suicidal. He looks back. He can no longer hear what is being said, but Jacob is still obviously causing much merriment.

Silas walks back towards the fort and is immediately convinced they are being watched. He turns around quickly but there is nothing there.

The warehouse is their committee meeting place as well as their chapel and there is such a shortage of candidates that Silas finds himself elected as representative alongside Selwyn, Jacob, John and seven other men.

The *Meistr*, of course, is leader. His position was taken as read.

'We will start with the potatoes and the maize,' he says, 'the land is cleared; all it needs is to be ploughed.'

'Too cold, here, for maize,' says Selwyn.

'We'll try using the oxen,' the *Meistr* continues pointedly, as if no one has spoken.

'Too late in the year for planting anything now.'

Edwyn sighs and looks at the doubting American. 'Mr Williams, why are you always so full of such cheerful optimism?'

There is the usual trickle of laughter and Silas' eyes meet Selwyn's. He tuts almost silently and Selwyn nods back, his face grim and still. *Brawd*.

'If the plough doesn't work with the oxen we'll try the horse. We must have faith, Mr Williams, otherwise we will accomplish nothing – surely you know that by now.'

As Edwyn commands so the work is done. Within a week the ground around them has been ploughed and planted, and soon, thanks to a recent light shower of rain, is covered in a patina of green.

The next Sunday Jacob revisits his sermon on transforming the wilderness, nodding at Edwyn each time he mentions a miracle.

Afterwards he catches Silas at the doorway. 'Have you seen, *brawd?*' he asks, pointing to the strips of green visible in the distance. His grin is triumphant. 'The Lord triumphs through Edwyn Lloyd!' he says, 'despite the naysayers,' he adds, looking at Selwyn who is trying to get past. 'Despite those with little faith.'

Now he looks back at Silas. 'This is just the start! Imagine the valley filled with fields, acres and acres – wheat, potatoes, and maize! Milk and honey, milk and honey, just as Edwyn always said. Do you still doubt him?'

And with that he sweeps away, his long coat billowing.

Twenty-one

There is something thumping at the ground. Selwyn and Silas stop and listen.

'Horses,' says Selwyn. 'Lots of them.'

'Indians?'

'Sh.' Selwyn drops to the ground and holds his ear to where the mud is covered with a little grass. 'They're moving fast. Coming this way.'

Silas hears himself swallow.

'Dadda?' Myfanwy has appeared beside him and is sliding her hand into his.

Around them people pause: a spoon hovers over a pot, a spade stands sunk halfway into soil, a mother leaves her child half-dressed.

Selwyn shakes his head. 'No, not Indians.'

The beat is too regular, deliberate and confident.

The spoon is dropped. The child is swept up into a blanket. The man with the spade pulls it from the ground and hurries back to the fort.

Soon they can see them: a narrow band, tightly packed, unfurling into a ribbon of bright colours and gold. Metal glints. The shod hooves of horses clatter on the stones. There is no stealth, no tentative scout. They have not been invited but they are coming anyway. Stand aside.

The horses are trotting sedately, their heads erect, great elegant beasts and on them soldiers, civilians and servants. Their faces fall slightly when they stop at the fort and the surrounding buildings; as if they had been expecting something more that what they see: poor people in their village of earth, smelling of river weed, dirty, clothes turned to rags. A few sheep bleat at their arrival, while the cattle and the pigs snort in the mud.

Spaniards. Silas decides that he doesn't like them. Not that they'd call themselves Spaniards of course, Argentines, they'd say they were, if anyone could have understood them, as free of their mother country as the Welsh were free of theirs.

There are several tall dark-bearded soldiers in uniform, with long black boots and silver stirrups, jodhpurs and long navy-blue tunics embellished with gold braid on the sleeves and shoulders and red on their collars. If they mean to inculcate respect they have succeeded. Even the youngest children are silent as they dismount. Their faces are half hidden beneath the shade of their peaked caps, and the one of them who looks like he might be in charge is brandishing a sheaf of papers.

The officer barks out a question and looks around. Edwyn Lloyd steps forward and, after a gesture that could be a salute, he says a few words in Spanish.

Of course the man speaks Spanish. Silas plays with a small stone near his foot. Around him he hears appreciative voices admiring Edwyn's linguistic skills. His eye catches Selwyn's. They exchange smirks.

'This is Colonel Julian Murga,' Edwyn says, turning around to the colonists to translate from Spanish to Welsh, much as he translated Captain Gidsby's words from English. More than a hint of smugness, Silas thinks, and wonders how much he truly understands. He expects it is less than the *Meistr* makes out because each of his words is accompanied by much gesticulating, and sometimes he notices that the Argentines look puzzled and look at each other to grin or shrug.

'A good man,' he continues. 'He is here to validate our treaty with the government. Shall we show them a little Welsh hospitality, brothers and sisters?'

He leads them into the warehouse where the women have been busy preparing food for the guests – mainly meat and bread, but Mary Jones, John's wife, has managed to find some dried fruit and made some small flat cakes upon her griddle. It is a cheerless party; the colonists and soldiers are hushed and stand around in small groups talking amongst themselves. Edwyn, however, is noisy. It is as if he is trying to fill the space with noise; his laugh is too loud, his gestures are too expansive, and his voice has a slightly strained edge. The officials seem to be taking it in turn to talk to him.

Silas nudges Megan towards Selwyn. He is standing close to Annie, who is helping Mary serve. Then, leaving the two women together to examine Gwyneth, who has been grizzling for the last couple of hours, he steers Selwyn forward to listen. Selwyn knows a little Spanish too; before they came down to Patagonia he had been obliged to spend some time in the capital, and although he claims to have tried very hard to remain completely ignorant he could not help but pick up a few words.

'What's he saying?' Silas asks.

'Stupid things,' he tips his head to one side as if that helps his understanding, '…about their journey here… and now he's asking about that government minister – Rawson.'

The topic of Dr Rawson seems to be causing much amusement because the soldiers suddenly burst into laughter. The *Meistr* looks less amused and asks Colonel Murga a question. Although he tries to disguise it with a smile he obviously does not like the reply. He asks another question and appears to like the answer to that even less.

'What's happening?' Silas whispers, but Selwyn tells him to hush. He listens again, and for a few minutes after Murga has finished he is quiet.

'What's he said, Selwyn?'

He shakes his head. 'That we're Argentines now, just as much as they are.'

The officer talks a little more. There is a flippant tone to his voice. Arrogant, Silas thinks. They're well matched. He watches his face and then looks back to Edwyn who is attempting to smile again: a flash of white through the growth of his beard.

Selwyn turns to Silas. His face is pale, set, angry: 'I don't believe it. The *Meistr* is just agreeing with everything they say. We're being used, and the fool doesn't seem to realise or care. If we are Argentines then this colony is Argentinean and they can claim Patagonia. That's all they care about – getting a foothold here before the Chileans do.'

Edwyn Lloyd speaks again and Selwyn stops to listen. This time after they finish Selwyn says nothing, just presses his lips into a straight line.

'What did he say?' Silas asks, but Selwyn shakes his head.

The soldiers are laughing – one and then the next as if some particularly amusing joke is being passed along the line.

'Tell me!'

'Can you hear them laughing? He just asked them where the fertile land is. A big joke. It's all desert, apparently, and hadn't anyone ever told him that?'

'But I thought he'd been here, that's what he said – cattle, tall trees, meadows...'

'That's what he told me too, but it's all rubbish, apparently. Desert all the way to the Andes.' Selwyn listens again. 'Oh, oh no.' He looks more downcast.

'What? What are they saying?'

'There was someone here before.'

'We know that, the Welshman – the one who built this fort.'

'No, not him, some of their own... *Impossible* – did you hear that? Like the English word. The crops grow, just a little, then the sun comes and everything fries. Too cold and then too hot.'

'But they let us come, even so.'

'Rawson, I heard him... he made promises. Told the *Meistr* he would look after us. But now they're saying...' He listens, frowns, and shakes his head. 'No, it's no good, I can't tell what he's saying.' He stops. Beside them one of the officers has been left behind. He is smaller and younger than the rest and is nibbling at one of the cakes with a serious thoughtful expression as if he is not quite sure whether he likes it. 'Just a minute,' Selwyn says and steps forward and talks to him. He is less fluent than Edwyn, and the officer has to repeat things several times but eventually he returns to Silas. When he speaks Selwyn does so through clenched teeth, his words spat out through barely moving lips. 'It's what I thought. Everything the *Meistr* has promised us is lies. We are allowed some land, but that's all. No more livestock, no more grain, no other help at all – and we're under their thumb. That's why they're here – to make sure we know who's in charge.' He shakes his head. 'We've been tricked, Silas. Everyone's been tricked.' His great, ungroomed beard sways from one side to the other, as if he is looking for something to kick. Instead he settles for a sack of grain and punches it too hard to make a seat. 'Ah *brawd*, if I could, I'd go back to Wisconsin tomorrow.' He sits on the sack and watches. Annie drifts up to him but when Selwyn barely responds to her words she drifts away again.

Silas looks around him. The rest of the colonists and soldiers are looking more happy and relaxed. It is pointless to say anything now. It is better to wait. Everyone will find out soon enough.

Megan comes over to him with Gwyneth held over her shoulder. 'I'm worried about her, Silas; she's not feeding properly. And I think she's got a fever.'

The baby is listless, her eyes half shut. He feels her face. She does feel hot but then his hands are cold. 'Maybe it's nothing,' he says, but he examines the child's face again. She seems tired. Her eyelids droop. For a few seconds she looks beyond him through half-shut eyes as if she is already dreaming and then she falls asleep.

Myfanwy comes to hold his hand. 'Why are you looking at Gwyneth?' she asks.

'Just to make sure she's asleep, *cariad fach*.'

In the yard the Argentines are making speeches.

'What are they saying Dadda?'

'I don't know, *cariad*. Go and ask Mr Williams.'

She sidles up to Selwyn but he shakes his head and waves her away.

She runs back to her father and tugs at his sleeve. 'Mr Williams won't speak to me.'

He pats her on the head. 'Never mind. Perhaps he's trying to listen.'

She looks back at Selwyn for a few minutes still holding on to her father's sleeve, and then tugs it again. 'Dadda?'

'Yes?'

'Mr Williams is crying.'

'No he's not.'

'Well, he looks like he is.'

'Men don't cry, Myfanwy. He must just have sand in his eyes.'

'But he looks sad.'

'No, he's happy. We all are. Look, they're putting up a flag.'

The flag is fastened on a pole outside the warehouse. It is pale blue and white and a yellow sun with a face is shining from the middle. Not the red dragon standing on a green field clawing at the white air, spoiling for a fight. For a few seconds there is silence, then Edwyn Lloyd yells out a hurrah with Jacob following immediately, then a bedraggled applause from some of the younger women. Cecilia, Silas notices, is mute and pale, looking first at her husband then at the flag and then at her husband again. He glances again at Gwyneth on Megan's shoulder and brushes his finger against her face. She seems less hot than before.

Now there are more speeches, in Welsh this time and it is the Argentines' turn to be bored. Jacob first, then finally Edwyn Lloyd.

'And in honour of that man,' Edwyn Lloyd says, 'we have decided to call our first settlement Rawson, because without Dr Rawson, minister of the interior, none of this would have been possible.'

Jacob leads the hurrahs this time, and this time the soldiers join in – at first just with their voices, and then, at Murga's nod, with their guns, quickly lifted from their shoulders and fired into the air. Myfanwy buries her head into her mother's skirts and begins to cry. The guns fire again and there is some more muted applause and cheering. Most of the children are crying now, and a couple of the very young ones are screaming. Silas' eyes meet Selwyn's and then look away again. The American is standing on his own looking out of the settlement to the river.

The guns fire again and Silas catches his breath. Gwyneth has not cried, not moved, not even flinched. She hangs over Megan's shoulder like a rag.

Twenty-two

Yeluc

Elal's land had been defiled. From the bay to the fort was a weal; the wet ground scarred by the marching hooves of a small army. When I approached the fort I could see them there: men wearing tight mantles in the bright colours of flowers, gold and silver sparkling from their shoulders, and beside them their strong large horses. The Cristianos. They stood in line and clapped and made the low loud sound of the elephant seals, and then numbed Elal's world with thunder from their firesticks. Then, in the middle of it all, appeared a patch of blue and white – the colour of the sky on a summer day – and in the middle of these stripes, a picture of the sun: the father of Elal's bride. And this small scrap of colour fluttered high over the roof of one of the huts and there were more shouts and one of the Cristianos started to talk in a loud voice to the rest. Then, when he finished talking one of Si-las' brothers began, and then another of the Cristianos. They had so much to say. I grew weary of listening to them, I led Roberto away for him to find new food.

By the time I returned the Cristianos had gone, marching northwards on the track they'd made. It had begun to rain and they marched quietly, the noise of their harnesses and hooves muffled by the low cloud.

That was then. This is now.

Si-las sits outside his grass *toldo*. On his lap there is a small child with hair like his own. The setting sun catches it and turns it into fire. Neither moves. Then, in front of him, a small mouse emerges from a hole in the bank and sniffs at the air. Si-las glances up and as he does so the child's head on his lap drops against his chest. The mouse disappears and Si-las looks down. For a single heartbeat the baby's head lolls outside his arms, then Si-las catches hold of the tiny object in his great wide hand. He brings it quickly towards his face as though he is going to kiss it then allows it to fall away again. Then he leans back against the doorway and roars – a scream turning into a single word, again and again: 'No, no, no.' A magic so strong even the river spirits listen. He clutches the head again and turns it towards him, looking at the face and screaming the same word and each time it is as the first time, 'No, no, no,' and even though his own kind come, even though they try to prise it from him he will not let it go. 'No,' he says, and it hurts my ears. And I turn because I cannot bear to watch, but when I shut my eyes I can still see it, a pale spirit drifting above us all, wondering where she is to go next.

They buried the child at the edge of the village. I watched carefully so I could tell Seannu: how they stood and chanted. How they all sang. How they wept. And the skin around Seannu's eyes softened, and I knew she was thinking of the small patches of ground beside the river where the soil never seems to heal.

Twenty-three

The doctor is young, Irish, and has picked up very little Welsh. He had joined the *Mimosa* fresh from medical college. He had few ties and was looking for adventure, but a life in Patagonia has not lived up to his expectations. He has an easy-going nature and has found life with these Welsh colonists a little too intense. 'Intense,' that is the English word he uses to Silas when they talk. Silas has to ask Selwyn for a translation.

'Too holy,' Selwyn explains, and grins.

Silas has noticed that the doctor himself grins little these days and has less to say. When he first came aboard he had made some effort to learn the language, but just recently he seems to have given up. Instead he has taken to resorting to signs and odd words.

'Why did you not go back with the *Mimosa*?' Silas had asked him once through Selwyn. It is what I'd have done, he'd thought. After all the doctor had the means – no doubt the *Mimosa* needed a ship's doctor on the way back just as much as she'd needed one on the way out. The doctor had shrugged in reply. 'I had to stay,' he'd said once, 'the colony needed me.' Another time he'd said Edwyn Lloyd had persuaded him. But eventually he'd admitted that he couldn't face another voyage on the same ship as Captain Gidsby.

'The man was… ill,' he said, pointing to his temple, 'up here.'

Then, when Silas had asked him why he'd said that, he'd pulled at his hair and grimaced: 'Nits. Remember?'

Silas had returned the grimace – 'nits' is a word the doctor came to know well on board the *Mimosa*. It was the first time any of them had encountered the Jones family; the daughter, Miriam, had been engaged in a tug of war with the captain. It had been a struggle that neither was likely to win since they were well matched in height and weight. John Jones' daughter was striking. Tall and thin with a black fuzz of hair topped with a small white cap, long pale face, sharp nose and small brown eyes like raisins.

'Mam, Mam!' Her voice had been shrill as the two had crossed the deck together in a slow strange dance – his hands entangled in her hair and her feet aiming kicks at his legs and at any other place she could reach.

'Mam!' By this time the other Joneses had appeared: Mary,

John, and two of their other four children. John was small and stringy and Mary was shaped like a cannon ball – her girth roughly matching her height – but their sons were both tall like Miriam, with arms like truncheons. They advanced on the pair together and then suddenly stopped. There was a glint of grey metal and polished wood: a gun. The Jones family paused for about three seconds and then Mary, six months pregnant and consequently more spherical than ever, reached forward and grabbed the gun. There was a single shot that caused everyone to drop down and when they all looked up again the captain and Mary were looking at each other with the gun between them on the floor.

It didn't take long for Jacob to find out the reason for the rumpus: the captain had been told by one of the sailors that some of the girls had nits so he had ordered the first mate to 'fleece the lot of them'. Unfortunately he, and the first mate, had chosen the first ewe unwisely.

The doctor, as an Irishman, and outsider, had been called in as judge.

'The Welsh are a clean race,' Jacob had said grandly and, thought Silas, somewhat sweepingly.

In the end the doctor, with a wry smile, claimed to find nits only on one person – the completely bald head of Caradoc Llewellyn, the Baptist minister.

There have been few smiles from the doctor since then. By the time they landed in Patagonia his face seemed already to set into a frown, with pair of perpendicular and parallel lines on his forehead that have deepened week by week. All he seems to be able to do is oversee the passage of children into the world – only to see them out of it again a few months later. Silas looks at his face with pity. How miserable it must be to feel so powerless one day after the next. Gwyneth is the third child to die in less than a month. He turns all these thoughts over in his head. It's not hurting yet. It's as if some large part of him has just been scalded and he is waiting for the pain to start.

'But why did she die?' he asks, but the doctor shrugs and shakes his head.

'It must have been something.'

'Fever,' he says, which they both know is no answer at all.

Megan is pale and mute. When Silas makes her some tea she sips it as if she is a child.

Myfanwy tugs at her dress. 'Mam?'

But Megan has retreated again. After she has finished the tea she stands, tucks in the blankets of Gwyneth's cot as if the child is still there, and then walks to the fire to rearrange the kindling.

'Mam?' Myfanwy's voice is uncertain. 'Mam?' This time it ends in a breathy sob. Silas picks his remaining daughter up in his arms. 'Leave your mother in peace for a while, *cariad fach*.'

'Why, Dadda? What's wrong with her? Where's Gwyneth?'

'Your Mam's sad. Jesus has called your sister to heaven to be with him too.'

'Will Jesus want me next?'

'No.'

'Why not?'

'Because...' His voice breaks. He can't carry on. Why? The pain has suddenly arrived in an overwhelming wave and taken away his voice. Instead he presses her to him and for once she doesn't struggle but rests there peacefully.

'Dadda?'

'No more questions now.'

'When will Jesus want me too?'

He rocks her gently against him. 'I said no more questions.'

She wrestles herself from his grip and looks at him. 'Dadda?

He can't bear to answer, can hardly dare to speak. He desperately thinks of something else to interest her. 'Did you see the soldiers go?' he says at last.

She nods her head.

'Did you see the track they made?'

She nods again. 'Where did they go?'

'Back to their home.'

'When are we going home, Dadda?'

The question jolts him a little from his misery. He is surprised she still remembers. Five months must seem like a lifetime ago to a five-year-old child.

'This is our home now, *cariad*.'

'But what about...?' Then she catches his eye and stops. She places the tip of her thumb in her mouth and frowns as if she is thinking. 'We're going to stay here for Jesus to find us too, aren't we Dadda?' She waits for him to reply and when nothing comes carries on. 'Otherwise he won't know where we are, and he'll look and look and look for us and never ever find us – and then we won't see Gwyneth and Richard in heaven.'

She waits a few moment for him to answer and when he does not tells herself, 'That's right, Myfanwy.' And leans heavily against him. 'Good girl,' she says dreamily.

In the morning Megan doesn't rise but lies quite still facing the wall. Silas leans over to look at her. Her eyes are open but it is as if she is staring at something far away. Myfanwy is still asleep. He picks her up gently and puts her to lie beside her mother. She murmurs and presses herself against Megan's warm back.

'Cuddle up close now, *cariad*,' he says and creeps out with a bucket for water.

'I'm so sorry,' Mary Jones says, when she sees him in front of the fort, 'John told me last night. If there's anything I can do to help...' Her voice fades for a few seconds, 'but I don't suppose there is, really.' She looks down at her baby cooing in her arms and the two toddlers standing passively each side of her, and Silas thanks her and says that they will cope. She looks at him solemnly. She manages her family with a serious unsmiling efficiency – now a brood of six children. With her stubby frame, and equally stubby face and nose, she is as unlike her lanky daughter as it is possible to be. Whereas John and Mary are small and quiet, their children are large and loud. The three older ones stride around the place like over-sized puppies, yapping at each other in conversation that includes no one else, although Miriam sometimes manages a smile at the people she sometimes notices around her. Although too pale to look truly healthy, they never seem to sicken and as he regards her three youngest children he feels a slight pang of envy. For the Jones family life seems to continue unremarkably, without incident. Even the birth of their latest offspring at Port Madryn was not dramatic. In the shade of a hill which now bears the child's name. According to the doctor it was an easy delivery.

Silas walks on to the river but someone is already there. Cecilia Lloyd wringing out clothes then piling them into her basket. She seems so young and vulnerable. She's aged about twenty-five he'd guess. Everything about her is unremarkable; from her ordinary-looking brown hair that is piled on top of her head, to her pale, unexpressive face underneath. It is so blank that it is as if her mind has been stubbed out inside. He sits out of sight behind a bush and watches her. Her face is perfect – each feature in proportion – but somehow not at all beautiful. Her eyes are a dull hazel, her lips neither broad nor thin, her nose neither retroussé nor long. As she passes him he can smell the soap she has used to wash the clothes and can see her hands red and raw with the coldness of the water and the wind. She's thinner than he'd realised, or maybe, like the majority of the colonists, she has lost weight. She walks slowly up to the fort, her head tipped down. After waiting a few minutes he fills his bucket and follows her back.

Edwyn's cottage has a prime spot, high up, using part of the fort wall for support. She spends several minutes laying the clothes out in the sun to dry and then enters the house. Although she draws the door to, it doesn't quite reach the doorframe. Silas sneaks closer, pretending that something on the wall has caught his eye and he is examining it.

'That Baptist minister – Llewellyn – is he alone?' Edwyn's voice, speaking softly yet clearly audible through the turf wall.

'Caradoc? No, he has a wife, Martha.'

'Anything I should know about her?'

'Martha – ah, a mousy little thing, prefers her own company – but she is secretly very fond of piano music which her husband thinks is akin to worshipping the Devil. She's had several miscarriages, I think – not one came to term – and she lost her mother shortly before the ship sailed. She's very quiet – much in thrall to that husband of hers.'

'Ah. And Caradoc himself is almost fifty – about ten years her senior. Is that right?'

'Yes. A second marriage, just like John Jones – do you remember? The first wife died twelve years ago.' Her voice, like her face, is almost without expression.

'Are they for us or against us?'

'A little against at the moment, though not as much as some.'

'And your recommendation?'

'The piano is important to Martha; I think she is envious of the little organ the Williams family managed to smuggle over. Maybe if you happen to mention your admiration for... Bach.'

'Bach? Are you sure?'

'Oh yes, Martha Llewellyn would be very interested. Mention

the Toccata and Fugue in D minor...'

Suddenly someone calls from the entrance to the fort. 'Silas! I'm so sorry! I just heard.' Selwyn. He comes hurrying towards him and the voices inside the cottage are suddenly silent. Cecilia's face appears at the door, her eyes slightly wide. She glances at Silas and her mouth opens. 'Have you...?' She stops and closes her mouth and Edwyn appears beside her. He steps towards Silas with his arms outstretched.

'Ah Silas, I heard about your loss. I'm so sorry. Gwyneth, wasn't it? Such a dear little one. All during that dreadful voyage south there was not a peep out of her. I used to say to my dear Cecilia it was probably because she was born at sea. That's right, isn't it?'

And suddenly it hurts. It hurts so much he can't speak. A scald. Searing his body like a flame. He drops the bucket and starts to run.

When he returns to his cottage Megan is dressing Myfanwy in her best clothes. They both turn to look as he stops at the threshold and sinks where he stands.

'I'm sorry,' he gasps and Megan comes close and holds his head against her skirt.

'I know,' she says, over and over again. 'I know, I know, I know.'

Twenty-four

It is Megan who is strong this time. She smiles and talks for Myfanwy, sweeps the house, cooks, even helps with the clearing of the ground and the digging, while Silas weeps, digs a little in the field and weeps again. 'I'm sorry,' he tells her, 'I'll get better.' And she smoothes his hair, kisses him and tells him that it's all right.

'How can you go on?' he asks her once, and she says she is holding it in like a breath – then letting that breath out a gasp at a time, and that way it hurts, but not as much.

Today she is in the warehouse with Jacob and Myfanwy. Jacob has taken it upon himself to make an inventory of the stock but he doesn't seem to have made much progress. Silas stops at the threshold, listening.

'How many was that?'

'Six, no, that was last time, eight... er...'

'Are you sure this time?'

'Well...'

A loud sigh and then: 'Shall we start again, Jacob?'

'I suppose we should.'

'And concentrate this time.'

'I always concentrate. It's your fault – you're not making a note when I say.'

'Well, you keep distracting me with all this talk about Indians.'

Silas steps over the threshold so they can see him. 'What talk about Indians?' he asks.

Jacob turns around, his mouth slightly open. A notepad trembles in his hand. 'Ah, Silas.' A pause. Myfanwy runs to her father and pulls at his trousers. 'I want a drink, but Mam says I've go to wait.'

Silas pats her on the head absentmindedly. 'What's this about Indians?' he asks again.

Jacob is grateful for the question. 'Just a request for trade,' he says, trying to appear nonchalant, 'a letter from one of the chiefs. Murga gave it to Edwyn – and we had a meeting to discuss it, but of course you... well, we didn't want to trouble you.' He pauses, examines Silas' face and then continues. 'Seems harmless enough to me, but Megan seems to think that we should be preparing for an attack.' He sits heavily on the nearest sack, his knees outspread, and the chain of his pocket watch glittering across his waistcoat. Now that things are more settled he has clearly managed to locate his shaving knife. He is sprucely turned out, but there is a small stain on the collar of his jacket, and his outspread fingers are covering a tear on his trousers. Not for the first time it occurs to Silas that Jacob is in desperate need of a good woman.

Myfanwy gives up with her father and stands by the door. 'Mam, I'm thirsty!'

Megan takes her daughter by the hand. 'I just think we should be wary, that's all.'

'But Edwyn says it's quite normal. Nothing at all to worry about.'

'Mam!' Myfanwy pulls her mother through the door and their footsteps fade into the distance.

Jacob and Silas look at each other. 'But we should take no notice of Edwyn Lloyd. The man is an idiot,' Silas says, 'and no one in their right mind should trust him. Look at the result of his lies. First Richard – and now Gwyneth.'

'That is the Lord's doing, Silas,' Jacob says gently, reaching over to him and patting him on the shoulder. 'It's not Edwyn's fault. The Good Lord called them to Him. It was their time.'

Silas shakes him off then steps back to glare at him. 'Why do you insist on defending him?'

For a few moments there is silence. Silas is aware of something giving inside. It is as if something is boiling within him. Something like milk in a pan.

'It's what happens. Children die. It happens at home and it happens here. You can't blame Edwyn Lloyd. If the good Lord wants them he will take them.'

Silas clenches his teeth and shakes his head.

Jacob sighs. 'I know he's got some things wrong, Silas, he's only human after all. But he's doing his best... and the way he handled the government officials – surely you have to admire that?'

The bubbles inside him rise – hot and uncontrollable. 'No! No, I do not.' He is shouting now but he doesn't care. 'The man has deceived us – haven't you realised that yet?'

Jacob tries to hush him but Silas takes no notice. 'Do you know why we're really here? Do you?'

Jacob is silent now, open-mouthed.

'We're just Argentine pawns, Selwyn told me. If we're here, the Chileans can't claim the land. They're not interested in the Welsh. All they want are more Spanish-speaking Argentines. What will be worse? The English or the Argentines?'

'I'm sure you're wrong about that, *brawd*. Edwyn Lloyd would have told us, I'm sure.'

'Would he? Are you sure? Come with me, look.'

Jacob follows him outside and Silas points to the flag. 'What is that? What does it mean? Is that part of a New Wales? Or something worse than the old one?'

Megan is mending one of his shirts when Silas returns to the cottage. The place has been swept, the dishes and clothes put away. She has a frantic air about her, as if she is finding it difficult to keep still. She smiles too brightly when he enters and agrees too vehemently when he suggests he makes tea. Everything is too slow and too difficult. The twigs he has collected for the fire burn too slowly; the rough table he has made is too rickety and uneven for the pot; and when he tries to pick up the kettle it slips from his grasp and steam scalds his hand. He slams it down and turns to her.

'Why did we come?' His voice is quiet and intense. 'Tell me Megan. Remind me.'

She doesn't answer, just continues with her sewing, stabbing the needle into the cloth again and again with swift vicious movements. At her feet Myfanwy plays silently with her doll, pretending to sew too. He knows the answer: Jacob. Her sanctimonious brother with his smug confidence in God and even greater faith in Gabriel Thomas – the principal of an insignificant college for ministers in Bala. Jacob had made a career of confirming that man's prejudices and conceptions of the world and, in reward for this unquestioning support, had been granted a position teaching at the college. It was there that Jacob had heard about Gabriel's scheme to populate Patagonia, and there that he had encountered Edwyn Lloyd. Oh, how unlucky it had been that the *Meistr* had happened to come along to the college with his big ideas just a few weeks after the incident with Trevor Pritchard and his dogs. Silas had always suspected his brother-in-law of a certain missionary zeal, but never expected to be amongst his potential converts.

Silas remembers opening the door to Jacob that day: his inane smile on his broad big face, made to look even more inane somehow by that carefully cultivated fringe of beard. The cottage was almost empty, all their good furniture already sold to pay off their debts. Jacob had taken it all in as he'd stood on the doorstep, his pale-green eyes blinking underneath the shadow of a wide-brimmed hat.

Jacob had been told the story immediately – crisp short sentences from Megan – while he'd stood in front of the fire, his jacket open, warming his hands. Then, when she had finished, he had turned to them with his shoulders squeezed up to his ears, one hand clutched in the other in front of him, grinning – like a child anticipating a treat.

'Oh, this is the Good Shepherd's work! He has sent me here for you now!' Then he had shut his eyes and clutched his hands together in front of his face. 'Thank you Lord, your servant is listening.' Then he had looked around at them and grinned. 'Wait until you hear. Oh such wonderful news – at last my Lord has told me how I am to bear witness for Him.'

Then he had told them about Patagonia, and the Emigration Society in Liverpool that was set on establishing a colony there. It was then that Silas had first heard the name of Edwyn Lloyd: '…a great man, you have to meet him. He has been over there with one of his gentlemen friends from Port Madoc. They scouted around the place and he says it's a wonderful place, a new Eden, a paradise.' He'd looked around to make sure everyone was listening. 'And the best news – I am to be the minister. Such a great honour. That is why I am here. I have to persuade more people to come with me.' He'd paused to draw breath. 'Will you come? You have nothing to keep you here, have you? Nothing at all. In Patagonia you will be able to do what you want when you want with no interference from anyone.'

Silas had looked at Megan and to his surprise she had immediately smiled back. 'Why not?' she'd said. 'Jacob is right. What have we got to keep us here? Mam is gone. Da is gone.' Then she'd swept her arms out to indicate the bare walls of the cottage. 'And soon all this will be gone too.'

'But where is it? How far? There could be wild animals, or people! No!' He'd folded his arms and shaken his head. 'We can't just leave home just like that!'

'The children would grow up free citizens,' Jacob had said, watching Myfanwy totter towards him on her newly discovered legs.

But Silas had sat down on a box and shaken his head. They were both mad. Patagonia! He didn't even know where it was.

Megan had walked up to him and put her arm around his shoulder. 'Please say yes, Silas. There's nothing left for us here, you've said it yourself.'

He looked up at them both: the two broad faces both smiling appealingly at him. It was as though something heavy and powerful was pushing him along, something he couldn't resist, but still he had to try.

'No,' he'd said, 'I can't. What about Muriel? I can't leave her.'

'Muriel doesn't need you, Silas – she's got Sam. Please, Silas! Just think of it – isn't it extraordinary that Jacob should come here today, of all days, with this news?'

'It will cost twelve pounds for each adult and six pounds for each child, but you only need to pay a fraction of this now...' Jacob had paused and continued more quietly '...and I have it on good authority that any Welshman who wishes to go, will go, regardless of payment, the Emigration Society will see to that.'

'You see, Silas – we won't have to pay a penny! Everything's worked out for us. It must be fate telling us to go!'

'No, Megan – the Lord.'

'Then we must!'

Silas wanted everything to stop. Surely it was not too much to ask for time to take a breath, to stand back and consider – but he was not going to be given the chance.

Megan had smoothed his head as though he was her favourite cat. 'What do you say, Si?' she'd said softly.

'I'll think about it.'

Then Megan had smiled – they both knew he had lost already.

If Megan remembers all this she says nothing. She just continues to sew and smile. He paces up to the fire in the hearth and pokes at it with a stick. Not my fault, he thinks. He can't bear the quiet so he sits next to her on the crude bench and starts to talk. He tells her about the Argentines and Edwyn Lloyd, about Selwyn and her brother, and all the while Megan continues to silently smile and sew, the needle not pausing in its movement, one tiny glint of metal swiftly following the last. At last he stops and holds her to him. Not her fault, either.

Twenty-five

Outside, rain is coming down in a heavy burst.

'Just like Welsh rain,' Silas tells Megan, and laughs grimly. She groans and throws another shawl over the one she has wrapped around her already.

'Good for the crops,' he says, and imagines the tiny potatoes and the shoots of maize he has planted drinking it up and growing stronger.

But this Patagonian rain doesn't stop. It goes on: a downpour and then a drizzle, a shower and then another torrent, rain driven into sheets by the wind then falling quietly and continually, on and on until the river creeps upwards over its levees and banks, seeps onto the lower ground by the side, forms pools which grow larger which interconnect to form swamps, then lakes, until the valley is just one big lake – the sky reflected in it like a hazed mirror. Meanwhile the walls of the houses start to weep: tears wash down their outer skins, exposing the capillaries and veins of roots. The land is reclaiming its own, Silas thinks, mud going home to mud, as if the house is melting like tallow before the flame, everything becoming slurry.

Silas wakes. There's that emptiness again. That feeling that something's missing. Then his eyes open wide. The walls are coming away from the roof and water is running across the floor from the back wall to the front. Part of another wall collapses softly into the pool outside with a subdued splash. He walks over to the hearthstone and lifts it. The tiny shoe is still there. For a few minutes he looks at it, then carefully replaces the stone into position. He rouses Megan, quickly scoops up Myfanwy and a few of their more fragile possessions, and they all run to the fort.

The warehouse is crowded. There is little room to lie down and rest. Bodies lie jammed next to each other breathing in the stench of the churned-up river, and the pervasive smell of mud. Outside the sludge sticks to clothes, to shoes, to skin. It comes over the rims of boots and oozes inside. Every movement is difficult and slow, and the children demand to be picked up because the mud sucks them down so fiercely and deeply they are afraid of drowning. In front of the fire it dries and falls off in flakes. The flakes disintegrate into a dust that is spread with every movement. It is in everything they eat and drink and in every gulp of air. Outside something bleats and bleats again, but no one takes any notice. It is too wet to go anywhere.

One day of rain follows another: sheets of water that are blown around in eddies; heavy bursts that batter walls and faces; interminable drizzle that penetrates through to the skin; and then an onslaught of drops that seem as hard as small pebbles.

Silas lies on a mattress of grain next to Megan and Myfanwy and listens with his eyes shut. The relentless drumming makes his mind wander. He imagines himself falling in time with its beat, deeper and deeper.

And then it stops. In the sudden strange silence everyone looks out. Before the rain started, and it is a time difficult to remember now, there were the sounds of animals all around them: pigs grunting, cows lowing, but most of all sheep bleating – eight hundred of them, enough to cover a sizeable hill. Now it is quiet.

'The sheep,' Megan says, and looks at Silas, 'I can't hear them!'

Silas and John Jones rush out to the pens but they are not there. The earth walls have been washed away and next to them the ground is churned up by many running hooves. A few of the men follow the tracks a couple of miles to the north but they peter out at the edge of the valley. The sun is shining now, and the air has become humid and hot. They shade their eyes and look, but the sheep have gone as far as their feeble little legs will carry them. Silas notices one guanaco that tears off in the distance but not a single white behind. John says he thinks he hears a distant bleat and for a few seconds the rest of them hear it too. But it is far, far away, as if it is taunting them, and although they go on a little way to see if they can see it, there's nothing there and that is the last they hear or see of them. They walk slowly back to the fort to tell the rest.

'All of them?' says Edwyn incredulously. 'All eight hundred?'

The voices in the warehouse stop to listen.

Silas and John nod.

The *Meistr* looks at them both for a few seconds then abruptly turns away. Jacob chases after him and taps him on the shoulder. 'Perhaps we should call a meeting. Perhaps I should discuss my inventory, Edwyn, so we know exactly what we have left and how long it will last.'

Edwyn nods curtly, then takes a breath so deep his shoulders rise a couple of inches and then sink again. Then, without turning, he walks quickly away to the outside of the village.

When they see him again he is smiling. But it is the smile Megan smiles these days – not a smile at all but a determined stretching of the mouth. 'All will be well,' he says with a forced brightness. 'You'll see.' He sits, and then gestures to Jacob to continue.

Silas sits silently, but is not listening. All gone. It's as if something inside him has collapsed and left a void. Everything – sheep, crops, houses, shelters. All that work. All those days scraping at the mud.

Jacob takes the floor. He describes the items from his inventory that are probably safe and then pauses for approval. When no one speaks he frantically fills the silence with more words. Eventually he finishes and looks around the room as if he is waiting for someone to stand up and speak, but no one moves. In fact everyone is so intensely still and silent Silas looks around him. People are either looking at each other with frightened faces or glaring at the figure who sits at the front of the room next to Jacob: Edwyn Lloyd. The *Meistr* sits quietly. From time to time his eyes flick around the room as if he is looking for something, but whatever it is he doesn't find it.

Faces turn. Now Mary Jones is standing up and quoting from the report they all know so well: 'Meadows and tall trees, wild cattle and other game... that's what it says, does it not?'

Edwyn says nothing – instead he seems to be waiting for someone else to speak with a weary silence. He does not have to wait long.

'And where exactly did you see these wild cattle, when you first came over here, Mr Lloyd?' Annie Warlock asks, 'Because they're not here now, are they?'

'They were here.' Edwyn's voice sounds strained. 'It must be the Indians, maybe they chased them away, like they did before.'

Mary opens her mouth to speak again but Caradoc Llewellyn interrupts her. 'The important thing, *chwaer*, what we should be concerning ourselves with, is our current predicament, and what we should do about it, not prodding bruises we can do nothing about.'

She opens her mouth, looks to her husband for support but he shakes his head so she sits down.

Caradoc stands, and leaning on his walking stick, looks at Edwyn: 'The important question is how long will the supplies that we have left keep us?'

Edwyn Lloyd looks around at them all and then looks down again at his hands. The glares are becoming more intense. A few people around Silas are tutting loudly. The *Meistr* looks more than weary, Silas decides, he looks broken. 'Without the ewes, without crops – I would say five months, at the most.'

A few of the women gasp. Each face is directed towards him, listening intently.

'There is nothing else? You've made no other plans?' Caradoc says sharply.

The *Meistr* looks down, shakes his head slowly, 'No'.

Mary Jones tuts loudly.

'Nothing at all?'

Again his head shakes.

'What about the wildlife?' Jacob says. 'Couldn't we live off that like the Indians do?'

'We'd have to trap them,' says Selwyn. 'Do you think we could do that, find enough to feed the entire village?'

'What about the guns?'

'We have to preserve the ammunition,' Caradoc says firmly, 'in case we have to defend ourselves against the Indians.'

'But there're none here.'

'They'll be here soon,' Selwyn says. 'You can count on it.'

Everyone seems to be holding their breath. Edwyn Lloyd seems to be becoming smaller.

'So we are going to starve, then, unless something is done,' Annie says shrilly from the back, but no one looks around. Everyone is still looking at Edwyn Lloyd, watching him crumple. Mary speaks again, 'Well, we're going to have to ask for help. Sometimes, Mr Lloyd, even God needs a helping hand.' She rocks her baby in her arms so resolutely it seems afraid to cry. 'Someone,' she says, 'is going to have to go to Buenos Aires to ask for more supplies.'

Edwyn looks up, a faint glimmer of hope in his eyes.

'But I don't think it should be you, Mr Lloyd,' Mary says, 'I think you have let us down. I think it should be someone who has gone through all that we have gone through, and still shown their mettle.'

'Selwyn Williams would do very well,' says Jacob, and Edwyn's head jerks suddenly towards him as if he's been stung. His mouth opens and then closes again. Jacob blushes and then bows his head. There is a general murmur of agreement.

Selwyn looks embarrassed and pleased at the same time. 'But I don't speak much Spanish.'

'It's good enough, I think,' says Mary, 'and you speak English?'

Selwyn nods.

'Then I think you'll do.'

Everyone is standing now, crowding around Selwyn to congratulate him.

'Shouldn't we put it to the council?' says Jacob, plaintively, 'vote for him, properly?'

'We have voted,' says Caradoc loudly and there is a general agreement. No one except Silas has noticed that Edwyn Lloyd has crept away, down the side of the hut where it is dark.

Twenty-six

There is something in the way the *Meistr* moves that causes Silas to follow him, carefully, slowly, out onto the broad flat plains where they are clearly visible from the surrounding escarpments and Silas shivers, imagining who might be watching them.

Silas looks around him as if seeing it all for the first time: after the rains it has suddenly become high summer and already the plants are changing colour from green to something more yellow. They look as if they are ripening, swelling with something as if they might burst and he stoops down to inspect a bush – something like a thorn that grew outside his mother's house but with tiny green leaves and red buds. He looks closer – there are orange things like beads dotting the branches. Each one is pitted with a hole that looks too perfectly bored to be the work of an insect. He picks one off – it is just like a bead – then puts it in his pocket to show Myfanwy. Another plant smells vaguely of pine when he steps on it. But it's not pine, he reminds himself, of course it's not pine. He feels a sudden intense desire – a *need* – to walk under trees, to feel the crowded loneliness of the woodland, with the branches crackling beside him with the weight of animals and birds. But instead there is this, and only this – mile upon mile of scrub and grass interrupted by occasional lifeless slopes – a wasteland leading onto a desert. He looks again for Edwyn Lloyd – the man is still striding away to where the land rises in white cliffs. They look unnatural, too white, as if they are made from salt.

Edwyn doesn't look back. Silas watches from the shelter of one of the larger beaded bushes. The *Meistr* reaches the base of one of the cliffs and begins to climb. There is no easy way up. He reaches just a few feet up and then comes slithering back, then tries again somewhere else with the same result. Silas smiles. He takes a step forward out of the shelter of the bush and Edwyn Lloyd chooses that moment to turn round. For a few seconds Edwyn stops. He sees him. Silas stands his ground. Edwyn moves back towards him, his gaze never moving from Silas. Silas stares back, ignoring his urge to run back into the fort and hide with the rest.

As Edwyn comes closer Silas is aware of his eyes. Blue. Out here, in the achingly bright sun of a Patagonian summer, they seem to have acquired an extra intensity. As the *Meistr* comes closer Silas notices them briefly leap around in their housing as if they are following a bird or a butterfly in flight.

'Why did you follow me?' The eyes become still, and the effect is even more unsettling. His intense unwavering stare gives Silas the uncomfortable impression that he can see inside Silas' skull. He can't think of an answer so instead he lies. 'I was after one of our hens.'

Edwyn Lloyd snorts derisively but then seems to decide to continue the polite charade: 'Well, no sign of her out here.' For a few seconds he seems to inspect Silas' mind a little more then says, 'I would have liked to have known you a little more, Silas.' Then when Silas says nothing in return, 'you have suffered more than most, I know that, but I think we could have been useful to each other.' He reaches out to touch him but Silas steps back and for an instant Edwyn's arm is held in front of him, the cloth of his sleeve emptily drooping down. Silas' eyes flick over him. The *Meistr* too has lost weight. His face is drawn; there are small hollows where there should be flesh.

'Ah well,' Edwyn's arm drops again. 'So be it. I have tried with you, Silas. The Lord knows.' He sighs and turns slightly away. 'I had such plans... I imagined you my comrade.' He laughs dryly. 'Too late now, though. I am taking Cecilia back to Buenos Aires.'

Silas' mouth opens. 'Why? There is no need for you to go too. Selwyn Williams is our representative now.'

Edwyn's eyes drop. His eyelids are long, elegant, fringed with luxuriant eyelashes. A spasm seems to pass over the rest of his face and when he looks up again his face seems to be held tightly in position. 'My wife is not well, and besides, my place is not here. That has been made perfectly clear to me by all of you.' He walks stiffly back towards the settlement.

The *Maria Theresa* has been patched with pieces of timber from the wreck in the river. She looks old and ill, as if her voyage with the women and children exhausted her; even her sails are bedraggled and yellowing. Edwyn and Cecilia's journey to her is stealthy. When Jacob sees them carrying their bags and boxes from the entrance of the fort he just stands there with his mouth gaping open for a few seconds. Then, as Silas watches him, he runs, his arms like broken windmill sails, his feet making an uneven pattern of thuds, until he is standing next to them, grabbing hold of their arms and then gesticulating for them to go back. Edwyn glances back at the fort and shakes his head. When they go to move on again towards the ship Jacob runs on a little further, holding his arms out wide, blocking their passage, remonstrating with them once again. But Edwyn forces a way past him and Cecilia follows, their bodies straight, their faces looking ahead of them. Jacob goes to follow them again, runs a few paces and stops. He continues to stare after them and then his shoulders sink. They are going and there is nothing he can do. He slumps back, face downwards, looking at no one.

All of the colonists watch the *Maria Theresa* depart. As they lose sight of her Silas turns and reads the faces around him. They are depleted and vulnerable. Besides Selwyn Williams and Edwyn and Cecilia Lloyd, there are others on board who could take no more and have given up – the doctor, one of the three ministers, and several others. They have the means to go elsewhere, and it is not just Silas who envies them. There are just over a hundred souls left now, and as they turn to troop back to the fort Silas realises their isolation: to the north, four hundred miles away over a dry wasteland is the nearest settlement – the outpost of Patagones on the Río Negro, a lawless place; to the west are unexplored mountains reportedly riddled with savagely ruthless Indians; and to the south there is just more wasteland becoming colder and colder until the land ends at Tierra del Fuego; and to the east an empty ocean. They can call on no one. Their one link with the outside world is disappearing beyond the headland. They have to survive alone on the little they have left, and unless Selwyn can persuade the Argentine government to help them and send more supplies they will starve to death. Patagonia is not somewhere anyone passes except to round the straits, and not many people look landwards as they do. No doubt they are forgotten already – completely out of sight and utterly out of mind. The adults walk silently back to the fort, even the children are subdued.

Jacob is standing at the front of the warehouse wearing his best clothes – a darker version of the clothes he always wears: a black woollen three-piece suit, with small white collar showing. He is thinner than he was of course, they all are, but this loss of weight suits him.

He smiles uneasily and clears his throat, but no one looks up. The council members are slumped around the room as lifeless as the sacks of flour they are sitting on.

'*Ffrindiau*, we must not give up,' he says, 'there is still time to sow seeds if we work hard.'

No one replies. A few of the men sink back against the wall, their faces dour and immobile.

Jacob tries again. He claps his hands half-heartedly and forces a smile. '*Brodyr*! Listen to me! All is not lost. The good Lord means for us to be here.'

One man snorts, 'I think you're wrong there, Mr Griffiths, I don't know where the Lord meant us to go, but if it was this place then He has a strange way of showing it.'

His neighbour nods in agreement.

Slowly Jacob's smile fades. He searches the face of one man then the next, but they all look down or pretend to be engaged in conversation with the man next to them.

'Well, there are still things that need to be done. I need a volunteer to help me with the track into the fort…'

Silas sighs. It's hopeless, everyone knows it. He eases himself forward off the sack. There is no point in staying here – no one is deciding anything. He starts off towards the door but someone else is moving too, someone at the back: Caradoc Llewellyn.

Caradoc simply stands where he is and looks slowly around the room with a deliberate eye. He's a stout small man, but with both hands on his walking stick, holds himself high. 'Mr Griffiths is right. We have to continue, *brodyr*. There is still hope, still something we can plant. Let us show the Lord what we can do.'

'It's too late now,' Silas says flatly. 'Summer, it is, not spring. No one tries to sow seeds in the summer.'

'But no one can know what will happen in this place! It is untouched, untried. It is up to us. With the Lord's help we could still make the desert bloom.'

John sniffs quietly. 'I suppose it would do no harm to try.'

Caradoc looks over at him and nods. 'Yes! We must try. The ground is prepared. It is soft now, ready for planting.'

Two of the men near John sit up slightly and look at each other. 'It should be easier this time.'

'And the weather is fine.'

Caradoc looks at them too. 'Exactly. What is there to lose?'

There is a murmuring as if they are rousing from sleep.

Caradoc marches over to where Jacob still stands, his stick against his shoulder, talking quickly. 'We can still succeed, my friends, I am sure of that. The Lord is with us. He has left us with enough grain to try. It is a message. Hope. Remember the dog he sent us? Antur. Our future. Our promise. There is still something we can do.' Now, standing next to Jacob he breathes in and then out noisily, and then taps with his stick against one of the sacks. 'Come, gentlemen! Look lively!'

Silas looks around him. Something has fallen from all their faces. They are talking, planning, and some of them are beginning to stand up. Yes, they should try, they might yet succeed, certainly if they do nothing they will not.

Caradoc looks around at them, nodding his approval. 'Yes, yes, that's right.' His voice is becoming louder and more clipped. 'We should start today. This minute. No time to lose…'

'You, indeed!' says Jacob, his face brightening too. 'We should…'

But Caradoc is already leading them out into the sun like the Pied Piper.

Silas follows. The rest of the colonists are walking briskly now; some of the younger men are actually trotting. They call to each other and soon everyone is there, chatting and laughing – even Megan – almost as if Caradoc has announced a celebration. They go in groups to their plots, concentrating on ground they worked before – between the meanders where there used to be grass. Silas rakes over the soil. It does not take long – the soil is light and already prepared. At the end of it he looks at his work and shrugs. It will do.

Twenty-seven

Yeluc

Elal has many people. To the north of the Chubut are the men of the pampas, the Günün-a-küna, shorter, more irascible, picking fights with any they come across, but they are all 'Brave-people', all Tehuelche. They speak our language, although some of the words they have are strange and the way they say those words stranger still. To the south of us are the Selk'nam and Haush and to the west of them the people that spend their lives cross-legged in canoes: the Yamana and Kaweskar. Then to the west, where the hills start to become mountains, are the Mapuche: aggressive and hostile. They live in houses in one place like the Cristianos and like them grow food in gardens and make pots and weave clothes. They would smother us if they could as they have smothered our brothers the Puelche. They would take Elal's people and tell us their tales so loudly it is all we would hear and we would forget the great god Kooch who made the world, who was so lonely surrounded by cloud that he cried for a long unimaginable time and made the sea. And this same god, who is not theirs, sighed and made the wind which drove away the clouds and gave us light, and made an island where the great Elal was born – the offspring of a cloud and a giant.

And now there are other people. People Elal doesn't know. Si-las my brother, Me-gan, his woman, and Mir-ee-am, the girl with the *calafate* hair. I let their names rest on my tongue then roll them around. Si-las, Meg-an. Like a song. Like a dream. Seannu says that I say them in my sleep.

Seannu and her sisters are well fed and happy now. They crouch about the fire and sew or play cards or cradle their dogs. They shoo me from the *toldo* and then the hearth. The *bolas* are ready and the horses harnessed. The knives are sharpened, the traces mended. Go Yeluc, they say. Hssst. There is nothing for you to do here. Go and hunt. So I rise early, my old limbs creaking and stiff from the sleeping, and summon Roberto from where he is foraging for grass.

My people are close. I can smell their fires. Sometimes I think I can hear their prattle. Sometimes I imagine I can see them as Elal would see them, aloft on his swan, peering at his world from behind her black, outstretched neck; their *toldos* clustered together like thirsty *rou* around a spring, their fires lighting the dark like a sprinkling of eyes. They know I am here. If they want me they come for me.

Then, near the river, there is Si-las and his people. Meg-an. Jay-cob. Sel-wyn, Mir-ee-am. I hear them calling. I see them working. Not like we do. Not the lighting fires and then the moving on, careful not to make a mark. No, Elal. These people scrape at your land. They scar it and make it raw. Ah, it makes me angry and sad. All this is no good. I need to watch them, Elal. For you and for themselves. If they continue like this it will be the end of everything.

Twenty-eight

Caradoc sits squarely and massively on the sack at the front, even though he is fifty there is little grey in his beard; but his head is as bare and as shiny as a horse chestnut. Until Edwyn left, Silas had scarcely been aware of him; as head of the Baptists he had seemed remote. But now he is frequently to be seen strutting around the place with his small troop of Baptist brethren in tow. He is a stern figure with a brisk way of both walking and speaking. His wife, when she is seen, which is seldom, is softer and meeker.

'Has anyone else seen this smoke?' Caradoc asks, examining each face around him in turn. Almost everyone nods. 'And this noise that Jacob heard?'

They all nod again. 'A drumming.'

'And horses, maybe.'

'I heard someone calling, as if they were lost,' says a small voice at the front.

Caradoc looks at her, and then, very unexpectedly, smiles. 'Did you, my little one?'

The child hides her face in her mother's skirts and the people around her laugh.

Caradoc's smile abruptly disappears again. 'We need a reconnaissance,' he says. 'Three brave souls with guns to see if there's really anyone out there.'

'Yes!' Jacob says quickly, 'I'll do it. Anyone willing to join me?' He looks around eagerly but although some of the women smile encouragingly back, the men look away. For a few seconds there is silence, and Silas feels Megan's eyes on him.

'I'll go,' he says. Jacob isn't the only hero. The men around him relax a little, and he is rewarded with a squeeze on the arm by Megan.

Caradoc tips his head in a nod. 'Anyone else?'

'He'll go,' Mary says, indicating her husband who looks faintly startled. He shakes himself a little. 'Oh yes, I'll go.'

'Good man.'

Mary smiles complacently. She is dressed entirely in black as usual, the collar of her dress pressed down by the jowls of her face. The woman appears to have no neck at all. Silas looks away quickly before she catches him staring.

'Three. Good. You'll need the two stallions.'

'And the largest of the mares, perhaps?' asks Jacob.

'Yes, yes, I was just coming to that. And guns, and plenty of ammunition, of course. If you prepare for trouble you'll most likely not have any.'

The rifle feels heavy strapped to his chest. He doesn't like the touch of the metal, the way it becomes so quickly cold when exposed to the air and chills him. Jacob is leading. Of course Jacob is leading. Ever since it was first mooted at yesterday's meeting Jacob and Caradoc have referred to this as Jacob's mission, as though he is about to convert a horde of Indians to the Christian cause. John comes next and Silas takes up the rear on his diffident mare. They are riding close together. It is as if it is something they have agreed although nothing has been said. Jacob seems to be careful not to go on too far ahead of the rest and keeps glancing back, slowing or stopping and waiting then going on again.

He waits now, his head swivelling from side to side, scanning the valley floor and then the slopes so that Silas looks too. There is nothing there, but still Jacob looks. When he catches Silas' eyes he smiles, but as soon as he looks away again his face becomes still and tense, with two small lines extending the outline of his nose upwards into his brow. 'Nothing yet, *brawd*,' he says, his voice careful and even.

He swings the horse away again, and continues along the flat piece of ground by the river. John follows behind him without comment; his body rigid in the saddle. Silas follows closely. They are being watched. The further they get from Rawson the more strongly he feels it. There are eyes in the undergrowth, shapes in between bushes, shadows where there shouldn't be shadows. But when he turns they are gone.

There is a sound. A twig snapping. Silas pulls on his horse to stop and looks around him. Nothing. Everything is quiet. There are no birds, no insects, just the sound of the river and his heart thudding in his ears. He looks again, his eyes resting on each bush around him in turn. Too quiet. Not a single warble, squeak or rustle. As if someone has frightened everything away. He waits. Still nothing. He breathes out slowly.

Ahead of him Jacob and John have stopped and are looking back. Everything waits. Silas searches around him for footprints, old campfires, skeletons of dismembered animals... nothing. A cricket starts to hum. A bird gives a short sweet call, and then Jacob calls out. 'Silas? What's wrong?'

Nothing. He shakes his head and then the reins of his horse and she trots quickly to join them.

A narrow passage between rocks opens out to a small meadow and Jacob smiles back at them, opening his arms to indicate the expanse. Silas looks around him again. It is too open here. He feels suddenly exposed. Anyone watching them could pick them out with an arrow one by one. He eyes a distant patch of vegetation and digs his heels into the horse's flanks. Faster. She grumbles a little but trots more quickly. Faster. He catches up with John and Jacob, points to the vegetation, and then waves at them to hurry. Jacob nods once, his eyes flicking around him.

Once they are under the cover of the bush they listen.

'What is it?' Jacob's eyes are wide. 'Have you seen anything?'

'No.'

'A pity,' he says, but his face relaxes.

They pass quickly from one island of cover to the next. Even Jacob is silent now. His face is like John's: tense, his jaw clenched.

Now it is John's turn to stop. He has smelt something. His head twitches sharply like a deer that has sensed a dog, or a guanaco that has smelt a puma. Silas comes close.

'Can you smell it?'

Silas nods. Something burning – strong, aromatic, close. A scorched piece of twig tumbles over the ground in front of them.

'What is it?'

'Shst!' Jacob's voice is too loud.

They listen again. A piece of loose vegetation is picked up by the wind and for a time they all follow it with their eyes.

'Indians.'

'Where?'

Silas shrugs. 'I don't know. Can't you smell them?'

There is a sudden sharp crack of twig nearby. They all turn towards the sound. The branches of a bush part and a small cat steps through, hisses and then bounds from them.

Silas gives a small laugh. He has been holding his breath. It is a relief to let it go.

Jacob snorts. They can still smell smoke. He looks around. 'Maybe they're hiding from us.'

'No,' says John. 'Look, over there.' John points towards the cliffs to the north.

'Where?'

'Can't you see it? A fire.'

He narrows his eyes. He can just make out a line of smoke, but it is faint and distant.

They ride on carefully. No one talks. No one even tries to whisper. Even the horses seem to know they must be quiet and tread where the mud is wet and soft by the river. Jacob prays in silence, his eyes open, and his lips barely moving.

The sun climbs higher. They follow the riverbed, sinking behind an embankment and then out again. A wind has started to blow from the west and they can no longer smell the smoke even though they must be riding towards it. Jacob slows as he climbs, then stops and waits for John and Silas to draw level. He is looking at where the fire was and laughing silently to himself. 'It's just the cliffs. Not smoke at all. A crack in the rock. Look.'

Now the sun has moved it is easy to see.

They carry on alongside the river. It is low in its bed now; even Silas' timorous mare can be persuaded to cross. Jacob crosses it again and again; to cool the horse's feet, he says. But he doesn't mention what they all know – that this will also disguise their tracks if anyone is following. They look behind them, checking to see if they are being followed, and then ahead again and to the side.

The sun sinks and they mount the bank again, each man starting as something noisily disappears into the water beside them. Silas strokes the mane of his mare to soothe both of them. There is someone watching. The horse knows. No matter how much he smoothes down the mare's ears they prick up again. She seems to be listening. A shiver travels along her flank and she neighs softly. Silas looks around him; ahead of them is a small canyon and Jacob is foolishly leading them through. The man doesn't think. Sometimes he seems wilfully stupid. But it is too late to stop him now. To make a fuss now would only draw attention to them. He smoothes his horse's head again and urges her forward.

The wind picks up. It gusts down the gulley so ferociously that they have to tuck down their heads and fight to make headway. Then all at once there is a howl. It is human, loud and close. They stop, their eyes wide, searching the steep slopes around them. Silas pats down the hairs on his horse's neck and then his own.

'Just the wind,' says John. But he doesn't sound certain. Then the sun disappears behind a scrap of cloud.

Silas shivers. The shadows are becoming darker and deeper. He hears one rock grind against another. Whoever is watching has come closer. The walls of this gorge are steep but pitted with small caves and strange-looking boulders that stand proud of the rest: what had been a brilliant orange in the sun is now grey and brown and black.

'Move,' hisses Silas, 'we can't stay here. We should never have come. We're asking for trouble.' Each crevice could contain an Indian. He imagines the Indians watching them pass, waiting for them to get into range of an arrow or spear.

Jacob attempts to laugh. 'Don't be afraid, *brawd*. The Lord will protect us.'

Silas looks at the man cowering in his saddle. 'The Lord?' he says, 'where is He?'

Jacob's face is partly hidden beneath his hat, but Silas can just make out that he holds his finger to his lips.

'If He is with us, why does He never say anything? And why are you afraid?'

'Hush, man.'

Silas takes a breath. He has had enough. If they are going to kill them let them hurry out of where they are hiding and finish the business now. He is tired of waiting. 'Why doesn't He talk to us, eh, Jacob?' He takes another breath and starts to shout. Above the wind his voice echoes faintly off the walls of rock. 'Perhaps He has abandoned us too. Have you thought of that? Perhaps He was never there at all!'

Jacob and John are rigid in their saddles, staring at him with open mouths.

Silas laughs then gallops forward. He stops and shouts again. 'Is anyone there?'

Above him a few pebbles scatter down the hillside. He turns towards the sound. 'Is that you? Whoever you are. Whatever you are. Why don't you come out and show yourself?'

Some more pebbles come tumbling from the slope as if someone is walking there, or trying to scramble away.

'Coward! Come out. Show yourself.' Silas peers upward but it is difficult to see. The sun is setting and it is becoming darker. A few more pebbles fall in a small sharp torrent, and Silas' mare suddenly takes fright. She neighs loudly once and then gallops wildly with Silas clinging onto her mane until the valley floor opens out into a plain, then stops just as suddenly, snorting and stamping her feet.

Behind him Jacob and John follow almost as noisily, then they trot a few more yards to where a small willow grows between two boulders. Jacob dismounts and immediately disappears behind the nearest boulder to relieve himself. When he returns, he falls to his knees and jabbers out a few words to thank the Lord for their deliverance.

They light a small fire and take turns to sleep alongside it on their saddle blankets and furs. They hear growls and the sound of something heavy moving close by but nothing comes close. When dawn comes Silas can at last see clearly where they are – in a lush-looking valley too broad for its river. But the patina of yellow-green is a deception; only part of it is vegetation – most of it is a strange yellow rock; this place is nearly as much of a desert as anywhere else.

But when he wakes, Jacob's eyes open wide. 'A valley,' he says, standing and looking around him. 'A wondrous fertile valley. Do you see God's hands? Oh *brodyr*, this is a message. Even though we doubted Him, He shows us this!'

Everything is faded and parched. It is becoming hot, the sun burns at the ground and on their backs, but still they go on – Jacob with his head held high, the brim of his hat low on the back of his neck, turning around again and again to smile and ask if all is well.

'A paradise,' he says when they stop. 'Praise the Lord.' But he is fingering his gun, a strange distant look on his face.

It is too hot to think. The sun seems to be becoming more intense with every day. Even though they rest during the hottest part of the day the heat seems to cling to the ground late into the afternoon, making every movement slow. No one speaks. The only sound is the clatter of hooves on rock and gravel. It is as if everything has burrowed underground or moved to the mountains in the west to get out of the sun. Once a fox barked close by and a skunk ambled nonchalantly across their path, but there have been no guanaco and no ostriches and just a few of the long-legged rabbits making their strange circuitous routes to their holes as soon as they approach.

They are aching: sore, chafed where they rub against the saddle or where sweat drips. Silas is tired of turning his head, tired of checking. He slumps with every footfall of the mare, until he feels himself in danger of falling, and forces himself back into his saddle. At the back of his head an ache is spreading over his skull. It is the strain of knowing they are being watched. He knows the eyes are still there. He can feel them on the back of his head. But he is tired of waiting for something to happen. He droops again.

They have been climbing for the last two days, but now, still keeping close to the river, they start to climb more steeply. The wind is stronger with more frequent gusts and the air is cooler. Plants cling more tightly to the ground, and in each depression there are the remains of winter ponds, crusted with salt, the footprints of birds like perfectly preserved fossils at the edges.

The summit of this hill leads on to a higher one and then beyond that to a hill that is even higher. Both horse and rider pant. The air must be thin. Silas looks around him. The land is bare – just rocks and sand. He sits up, feels oddly jubilant. They are almost at the highest point now. Something lifts from him as he realises. No longer the watched but the watchers. High and invincible. A view that stretches for miles. Nothing can touch them.

'Closer to God!' Jacob cries out. He turns to Silas and John. 'He has delivered us, *brodyr*! You see? Our faith has been rewarded.'

The valley spreads out before them to the east. From here it looks misleadingly lush, much greener than the higher land that surrounds it.

'Our promised land,' Jacob says happily.

They have reached the end. Above them the river forces a way through a sheer-sided granite block and there appears to be no way through. Even so they attempt to scramble up and succeed in peering through a narrow gap. The land continues to rise in barren slopes towards distant mountains.

Jacob climbs higher up the rock face, reaches the end of a spur and pauses. Silas can see his jacket riding up and then down again as he breathes. He is only halfway to the top, with a great mass of rock still above him, but he plants his feet out wide as if he has conquered something significant and grins down on them. 'You see, the Lord has thought of everything. He has given us a haven. No one can get through here. We are quite alone in our paradise! Praise be to His name!'

Twenty-nine

It takes some time for the rest of the people to assemble. The crops that seemed to be thriving by the river a short time ago are withering, but no one understands why; some of the colonists have been trying to save them by adding a little manure from the pig pen to enrich the soil, but it has proved hopeless. They are hot, tired and dirty but at the sight of Jacob they brighten – the fact that he and his companions have returned so quickly must be good news.

Caradoc dismisses Silas and John with a small wave of his stick, and Jacob is invited to the front to speak for all of them. Silas glowers, attempts to correct the inaccuracies in Jacob's account, which are many, but each time his words are swept away by Caradoc's hand. 'It will be less confusing if only one speaks,' he says, and motions for Jacob to finish.

'The end of the valley is impenetrable,' Jacob says. 'It rises in a great mass that no man can cross.'

Silas looks around. Everyone seems to be smiling – even Megan. He tries to catch her eye but she is watching her brother with a studied determination.

'So we are quite safe. There will be no attack from the west. The Lord has seen to that,' Jacob concludes and sits down with his arms folded.

'But they can come from the north or the south,' Silas protests, ignoring Caradoc's glare. 'There are breaks... in the escarpments... between the cliffs. Places easily breached. We saw them again and again. Why don't you tell them about that, Jacob? Have you caught the *Meistr's* disease of never speaking the truth?'

Caradoc frowns at Silas and tuts. 'There is no need for that, Mr James.'

Silas looks around him; the majority are listening to him, so he continues, 'There are places where a whole army of savages could break through, as quickly as they like, and the first we'd know about it would be an arrow in the back, or a knife at our throat when we woke.'

A woman at the back gives a small wail.

'You are upsetting people, *bachgen*. There's no need for that.'

'But Jacob is giving a false impression. The Indians could be at our doorstep any day they choose.'

Jacob's face reddens. At his waist the finger of one hand points half-heartedly in Silas' direction. His voice, when it comes, is high and strained. 'Which is why I am about to tell you my plan, if you would just pause for a while to hear what I have to say. We should spread out, take the land allotted to us and spread out along the valley. The Lord has given us this land, so it is up to us to guard it and ensure it is safe.'

'But surely you're not proposing we risk the women and children...'

'But Silas,' Caradoc says, 'your journey has told us the valley is empty for now.'

'But we didn't search everywhere.'

Caradoc raises his voice and talks over him. 'Whichever way the Indians come, we'll keep a watch for them... warn each other, have a series of fires as they did in earlier times...'

'But what if we don't see them?' A few people around him mumble their agreement.

'We can't miss a whole tribe of people,' Caradoc says firmly, and for a few minutes everyone is quiet, looking from Silas to Caradoc.

'Well, I think it's hopeless,' Mary says at last, 'but I'll make sure that husband of mine builds a pyre, now he's back. It'll stop him getting in my way...'

Up until now the only structures that have been built outside Rawson have been shelters – one-roomed affairs, crudely built on the higher land out of reach of the river – just a place for a man to shelter from the wind, rain and sun when he goes out to his land to tend it. But now they are beginning to extend them in stone and brick, a bedroom and then a scullery with two or three cottages clustered together to form a hamlet where one colonist's land meets another.

Joseph Jones comes running and yelling along the path from the beach, followed by his oldest brother and sister, all three of them running, 'A ship, a ship! Mam says to come at once!'

All is not well. This stretch of water with its treacherous sandbank has already claimed one ship. The Jones family are already there yelling warnings, the eldest three charging along the beach waving anything they can find, but if the captain can see, there seems to be little he can do.

A gust of wind drives her suddenly closer and there is a loud splintering and then a crash and the three youngest Jones children cover their ears.

'Can't we do anything?' Jacob asks. He shifts from one foot to the other. 'They might go under. They might all die.'

But all they seem to be able to do is watch while the ship comes closer and the splintering louder.

'Go back!' yells Jacob, gesturing with his arms. 'Back!'

But the ship comes closer still.

'What's that captain doing?' Caradoc asks, 'can't he bring her about?' Then he starts to wave and shout too, his stick describing directions in the air.

Silas watches with his arms folded. It will do no good. He remembers Gidsby saying that a ship in tight waters like these is as unpredictable and as uncontrollable as a woman. Steer one way and she'll go the other.

But this ship seems to pause and a small boat is dropped over the side.

'Selwyn!' Jacob cries and they all run down to the side of the river to help him ashore.

'Where's everyone else? Where's Edwyn?'

'Buenos Aires,' he says. His mouth opens to say more but Annie forces her way through to hug him. 'Selwyn!' she says, 'have you missed me?'

'But where's Edwyn?' Jacob asks plaintively.

Annie swings round to face him. 'Leave him be now. Plenty of time for him to answer questions later.' Then turning to brush some dust from Selwyn's jacket, she picks up one of his bags. 'I baked some bread this morning. Are you hungry?' Then, without waiting for a reply, grabs him by the arm, marches him back to the village.

The ship is laden with supplies he tells them later, as soon as Annie allows him to speak. 'They've agreed to a grant,' he says, '£140 a month – so I bought us some more transport. Nice little ship, at least she was – called her the *Denby*. The *Maria Theresa* barely made it into port.'

Caradoc taps Selwyn lightly on his arm with his stick. 'You've done well, *bachgen*. A good ambassador.'

But later Selwyn admits that it was the *Meistr* who was mainly responsible for this coup – stubbornly demanding day after day to see Dr Rawson and then the British Consul until something was arranged.

'Where is he? Why didn't he come back?'

'I don't know... something to do with Cecilia. He talked about sending her back.'

That night the colonists celebrate with singing and a feast of new food. It is January at last and 1866 has started well. Soon they will start sowing wheat again, earlier this time, that way the shoots might have a chance to establish themselves before it becomes too cold. They toast Selwyn and then Dr Rawson.

'And Edwyn Lloyd!'

'Yes, indeed – our absent friend!'

The merest mention of his name and the colonists are clapping and cheering. It is as if that meeting a few months ago never happened.

Megan shifts beside him and leans her head against him with Myfanwy asleep on her lap. He draws her to him and feels a comfort in their warmth in his arms.

'All's well,' he tells her, trying to mean it.

She smiles and nods but it is just her mouth that changes, nothing else. It is as if he can see the thoughts flicker over her face. He holds her closer, but there is nothing he can do to make them go away.

Thirty

Yeluc

Seannu and her sisters grumble. It is not time for us to move, Tezza says. We are getting too old. Then, when I tell them where I want them to go, they protest more loudly still. That is not our place, Yeluc. It is not where we go. It is not time. The spirits will be angry. But Mareea begins to pack away her skin, and presently Tezza joins her, muttering under her breath and shaking her head. You're trouble Yeluc. That's what they say, and they're right.

But then Seannu comes smiling from the *toldo*, big gaps in her mouth where her teeth have gone, her little dog in her arms. Maybe we can trade, Tezza, she says. Maybe they will take some of our skins and those feathers Mareea found. We could buy tea, cloth, sugar.

Then Tezza nods at the thought and begins to loosen the poles of the *toldo*. Yes, trade, she says. And I can see she is thinking about what she will buy.

Then they dismantle the *toldo*, put out the fire, lash everything we own onto the horses and slap them into a trot.

Where now? asks Tezza when everything is ready.

Just down the trail and to where the sun rises, I tell them. Where the Chubut curls before it meets the sea.

Where Si-las is, Seannu says, is that it? And she looks at me with her eyes narrow.

Yes, I say, I need to see what they do. I need to let our tribesmen know I am with them. I need to know they are safe.

Thirty-one

It is May and every day the wind blows a little colder. As soon as the sun drops behind the mountains far to the west the coldness starts to penetrate and lasts well into the next day. A week ago they finished clearing the land of the shoots that withered away over the summer, and have sown more seeds directly on top. Since then there has been a fine rain.

Silas, Megan and Myfanwy walk along the riverbank. As they pass the patches of cultivated land, Megan inspects the ground on either side. 'Something's growing again, look.'

Here and there are small spikes of green. They look fragile as if the smallest wind will sweep them away.

At last Selwyn has married Annie. Since he's returned from Buenos Aires she has rarely been from his side, escaping from her domestic chores at every opportunity, enticing him with her voluptuous charms, until they now seem one being instead of two, his hands constantly guided along some part of her ample anatomy until he goes an inch too far and is slapped back into place.

As Selwyn had promised the service has been short and songs are about to follow. No drink of course, but he has promised there will be enough meat to fill everyone's stomach. Instead of waiting with everyone else, Megan had suggested they take a walk to try and take their minds off their stomachs. But now, as they approach, Silas thinks he can smell bread baking and the fragrance of something sweet and his stomach rumbles. He thinks of cake, the sort his mother used to bake at Christmas when she had the money – dark and full of fruit.

Megan has stopped to inspect one of the small plants. She lets go of Myfanwy's hand and the child runs ahead of them. As the child heads for the river she threatens her gently: 'I'll let you go, but you stay away from the river, understand? If you fall in there, it'll carry you away and no one will be able to save you.'

The little girl nods seriously, regards the river for a few seconds then runs along the path keeping pointedly away from the side.

Silas looks around them. Sometimes the desolation beyond the river overwhelms him. Beyond the fringes of the riverbank where they have planted the seed there is nothing but bare ground and scrubby vegetation. How could Edwyn not have seen? How could he bring them here and then go? The man has escaped to where everything is much more pleasant and civilised and abandoned them here in this: a wilderness with poisonous soil. Maybe he is not even in Buenos Aires any more but has accompanied Cecilia back to Wales. Wales. Sometimes he wants to go back so much it feels like an ache somewhere deep inside, close to his stomach. If Edwyn Lloyd's wife has returned then so – somehow – can Megan and Myfanwy.

Myfanwy has stopped ahead of them and is sitting on the ground waiting for them to catch up. Beside her is the *Denby*. It is still beached on the riverbank because no one has the energy and inclination to mend her. Silas stares at it, considering. Maybe he could persuade John and Selwyn to help him. Together they could make her seaworthy. Surely they could get her up to Patagones just up the coast, just a few hundred miles, and from there they could find a passage too, if not to Wales then to somewhere else.

'Silas! Why don't you answer me?' Megan stands in front of him. 'You're not listening. Why do you never listen?' She grabs Myfanwy's hand and strides on ahead.

They have almost reached the fort now; the earth walls seem smaller than they were, but the cannons are still in position – small pompous things, incapable of anything much except a loud noise. Over the last few months more cottages have been built outside the fort, on the higher ground, further from the river. It is quiet. At the entrance the mud is churned up as though there has been a horse stampede. Silas looks at it, and then glances at Megan who returns his puzzled expression; they don't have that many horses. They walk more slowly. Megan calls Myfanwy to come back to them and then grabs her – with her other hand she reaching for Silas. 'Look,' she whispers.

But he has seen already.

Four tall Indians, one old man and his women, are walking, silently and haughtily, leading horses and clutching to themselves long cloaks of supple-looking skins decorated in faint daubs of red and yellow. It is too late to run; the Indians have half turned to look and are watching Silas and his small family approach. All they can do is keep on walking.

The colonists seem transfixed: Caradoc, Jacob and the

bridegroom at the front in a line. All of them are still in their Sunday best. The new Mrs Williams has put flowers in her hair since the service to match her pale-coloured dress. It is a maiden's dress of fine cotton, and looks incongruous below her worn face and matronly body. Her chest swells from her waist rather like the chest of a strutting army officer or cockerel. She stands only just behind Selwyn beside Mary Jones and looks by far the fiercest of anyone there. Her face is scarlet and even from here Silas can hear her breathing noisily in and out. Perhaps she is annoyed that they have interrupted her wedding day. It is too late to bring out their guns. No one dare move. Instead, for a few minutes, they stay where they are, staring at each other. It is just as he said, although he is too frightened to feel triumphant; the Indians have crept up without warning. How long will it be before they summon the rest of their tribe and finish the business? Everyone knows what they do – kill the men and take the women and children as slaves. But when the Indians come to a halt in front of the three men they do nothing – just wait expectantly and silently.

Silas inspects them carefully. Their cloaks are held in place with their folded arms. The dun-coloured leather is decorated in splodges of chalky-looking pigment and joined together in a complicated pattern of shapes. Around the neck is a collar of fur that obviously continues inside the hide. The hair is held back with cloth bands, dirty looking, and the women's hair is arranged in two braids, like a child's. The older woman's hair is almost white and divided at the centre while the two younger women have darker hair cut off in the front to form an uneven fringe. All four of them are frowning as if the sun is in their eyes. They do not look friendly.

'We have nothing,' Annie says, 'you might as well go on your way. You'll get nothing from us.'

Caradoc looks at her sharply. The woman is unpredictable, rough, inclined to say what she thinks without much prompting. Silas has heard that she is used to fighting; a servant in some place that was close to being a brothel, before she was adopted by the family who brought her here.

'Go on, off with you!'

Again there is just the sound of the river gently murmuring. Then one of Mary's babies gives a short wail and this seems to nudge the old Indian into speaking. His words come out slowly, creaking from him like twisted pieces of metal. He holds his hand to his mouth.

'Heathen words,' Mary whispers loud enough for everyone to hear, 'they make no sense.'

But Jacob tips his head to one side slightly then smiles in triumphant recognition. 'I think they want some bread, I heard a word, something like *pan*,' he says. 'It's a bit like Latin, I think they must be talking in Spanish.'

The Indian speaks again, and this time Selwyn looks at Jacob and nods. 'Part Spanish, part something else.'

A new waft of sweetness reaches them. The Indians must know what it is, and what it means. No doubt they have tasted bread when they have traded with the settlers in Patagones. Mary sends Miriam into the warehouse where the cakes and bread are cooling and she returns with a small loaf in a cloth – a plait of dough with a brown and glossy top. The smell and sight of it makes each stomach grumble. Caradoc holds out his hands to receive it but she ignores him. Silas smiles. The girl is confident to the point of being brazen. She walks quickly up to the Indian and holds out the loaf. She is as tall and leggy as the tallest of his wives. He steps forward and takes it carefully in his hands as though it is a baby. Then he examines it, turning it over and over, holding it up to his nose and then holding it at arm's length and examining it again. Then he nods, breaks off a piece and passes it to one of his women, the woman that seems his equal in age with grey in her braids and a face as crumpled as last year's windfall. She chews and smiles and murmurs something to him then he breaks off another larger piece and feeds himself and then the other two younger women. He nods to Miriam and she goes back to stand next to her mother. Then he offers a piece to Caradoc.

If Caradoc were a bird he would be preening himself now, smoothing out his feathers and looking around him. Some of the fibres in his green suit are iridescent in the sun. He holds up his head, seems to swagger without moving much from where he stands. Obviously he thinks this token of bread is an acknowledgement that he is in charge. He looks around at Selwyn and then Jacob and Silas to see if they've noticed, which of course they have. They watch him break off a piece and put it in his mouth. He smiles. 'Good,' he says, 'well done, Mary. Good bread.'

The Indian, still chewing slowly, walks away from the fort

followed by his women. Then, a few paces behind, come Caradoc, Jacob, Mary and Miriam. Selwyn waits for Annie, reaches up to put his arm around her shoulders, and then they walk forward together, with the rest of the colonists. The Indian walks a few paces onto the ground beside the fort. The earth is hard, but here and there are small aromatic bushes. He turns to squat before one that is still bright with old yellow flowers. Then he motions to the two younger women who gather up small bundles of dried-up twigs from around the other bushes. They bring them to the old man who is tapping out sparks from two stones he has removed from his saddlebag. Eventually the tinder catches light and the flames of yellow blossom are replaced with the bigger blooms of a small fire. After several minutes it burns down and the air is thick with scented smoke. There is no wind and so it ascends in a diffuse column. The Indian folds his arms. He seems to be looking for something – first in the hills to the north and then the west. Silas looks too, but there seems to be nothing there, just the lifeless slopes with their salt-like screed of fine rubble. But the Indian seems to be happy. He nods slowly and walks back into the fort.

The settlers follow in silence. Silas grabs hold of Megan's arm with one hand and Myfanwy's with the other. He will not let them go. Never. Not even if the Indians come. Even if they come at him with spears and arrows. With his last breath he will hold on. He looks again to the hills to see if he can see anything move, but it is perfectly still. He can hear his heart pounding in his ears. If the Indians were coming, if they were riding towards them whooping, surely they would see them. He wishes he had his gun. Silas can see Selwyn looking, wondering too – what if they were to jump on him now and wrestle him to the ground? What would happen then? Would the rest of the Indians see? Would they come streaming from the hills? The old man and his women stop beside their horses at the entrance to the fort. They seem to be waiting for something. They look at the settlers and the settlers look back. For a few seconds nothing happens. Then Jacob swoops forward and grabs the Indian's hand, shakes it vigorously and lets it go. 'Pleased to meet you,' he says.

The Indian inspects his hand for a few seconds and then looks at Jacob. Then he reaches forward and grabs Jacob's hand back, shakes it hard and lets it go again.

Jacob grins and holds out his arms suddenly so the Indian flinches back. 'Come,' Jacob says, beckoning them forward with both arms, 'follow me.' He turns, walks into the fort for a few feet and then turns and beckons again with his hand. The old Indian looks at his oldest woman who nods briefly with her head, and then he follows behind Jacob, into the warehouse.

Inside the barn someone has managed to find tablecloths to lay over the boxes and cases to make them look like tables, and on them are several loaves of bread thinly sliced for the wedding, some jars of jam, some honey oozing from its small comb on a plate, and some sugar. There are also some big teapots and an assortment of mugs and cups. Some of the adults gasp while the children just stand silently and point – it's been a long time since there was so much to eat and drink. Jacob smiles and urges the Indians forward. 'Come, eat,' he says, but the Indians do not move. 'Eat!' he says, miming with his hands and mouth, but still they stand. The two younger women with the dark, partly shorn hair talk quietly to each other.

So Jacob tries again, walks up and down past the table, naming the bread, the jam, the honey, then when they still do not move, their faces motionless and impossible to read, he takes a few small slices on a plate with a spoonful of honey and hands it around, repeating the words slowly as if they are young children: *'Bara a mêl, bara a mêl.'*

The Indians' tent is pitched close by the river. Silas watches them assemble it using poles and skins. It seems to be the job of the two younger women, hammering one line of poles and then another, one row higher than the next until the highest row forms the opening. Then they take vast skins and throw them over the poles, anchoring the edges down with small rocks. It is a curious thing, like a cup half buried in the ground, one side open towards the sea and away from the wind from the west. As soon as the awning is assembled the two women begin to gather tinder for a fire, while the older woman unloads pots and more skins from the horses. At first the old man does little but sit on the ground near where the fire is being built and smokes a long pipe, but then he removes a bag full of tools and sorts them: there are knives and a couple of guns, and several things that Silas cannot identify.

Silas lowers himself onto his belly and moves closer. There is a slight rise in the ground and it enables him to see quite well. The old man seems to have many animals: all sorts of horses and mares and foals, in many different colours and sizes, and, it seems, temperament. There are also many dogs yapping around the place, one or two of which seem rather small and useless. One in particular seems to have as little to do as the old man and spends most of its time either lying on a skin or curled up in the old woman's lap.

Several of the horses have elaborate saddles and some of them glint with silver. Silas wonders how a man like this can have so much wealth and imagines raids on the colonies of white men and their horses driven away in the dark. Although obviously quite old, the man looks strong and active and his face is scarred with old wounds across his cheeks, and Silas wonders how many men he's killed. Silas rests his head on the ground. The Indian could easily be a killer and thief – there is a sly look about him, and there is something about the way he holds the blades as he sharpens them that makes Silas think of Selwyn's gesture as he mimed an Indian removing a scalp.

The two younger women, who are middle aged rather than young, seem to be constantly busy – as soon as they have finished assembling the fire they fetch water from the river and begin to cook on the fire. Meanwhile the old man and woman have begun a game of cards together. They play silently, both of them smoking, and both with a dog lying on their laps.

The water on the campfire seems to be boiling; Silas can see the steam billowing away from the pot in clouds. One of the women exclaims, reaches forward and pours some of the liquid into cups. They are making tea. Silas can smell it – that green tea everyone seems to drink around here. Just like us, he thinks, and sidles backwards. The old woman looks up as he does so, and as her eyes meet his he realises that she is not surprised. She looks at him calmly, her face turning slowly from him in such a dignified way that his alarm turns swiftly into a slight feeling of shame. Then, as he shuffles backwards he sees he is not the only spectator. Further along the mound, behind some bushes, he spots the backsides of Joseph, Miriam and Ieuan Jones.

'I suppose they'll want to trade with us like they do with the folk at Patagones,' Selwyn says. He untangles himself from Annie's arm so he can stand more upright. 'In fact they might prefer it. Patagones is a long way for them to go, I reckon.'

'They seem wealthy and are well armed,' Silas says, 'with guns, knives, and lots of horses – I've seen them.'

'Too true,' says Mary Jones. 'They could be waiting for dark to strike us in our beds. Maybe we should act now.'

But Jacob shakes his head. 'We are all God's children,' he says, 'and these Indians are innocent, even more like children than the rest of us. They are uncorrupted, pure...'

'Straight out of Eden, I suppose,' snorts Mary.

'We should treat them as the Lord has instructed us to treat all of his children. We could teach them the Lord's way.'

'Of course we can't trust them,' Annie says, and a few people nod and murmur agreement. 'Like children they may be, but even children can be wily and cruel.'

'We could minister to them too,' Jacob says loudly, as if he hasn't heard, then he raises his voice a little more. 'Maybe one day they would take the Lord into their hearts and know Him too.'

Mary snorts again. 'As long as our bones aren't being picked over by the vultures by then.'

Silas nods and Mary notices him. 'See, there are some who agree,' she says. 'I say we should see to them before they see to us.'

'What do you propose – that we sneak over there and kill them as they sleep?' Jacob's voice is high and soft, as if he is astonished.

Mary folds her arms. 'Perhaps. That would be an end to the matter.'

'No madam, it would not.' Caradoc spreads his knees apart and leans over his stomach towards her. 'They have friends, Mary,' he says menacingly. 'Did you not notice the fire? Do you believe they roam the desert alone? Once their blood is spilt we will be stained forever. Their friends and relatives will come for us.'

'Excuses. Some of you are too afraid. We should act now before it is too late.'

'Are there many that agree?' Caradoc asks, looking around at everyone, while everyone else looks around too, seeing who sides with whom. Most faces are blank, but there are a few who are nodding and murmuring yes.

'Then you are overruled. This is the new Wales, God's kingdom. It is ruled by God and we obey God's rules.' Caradoc looks at Mary, John and Annie then slowly shifts his gaze to Silas. He looks back and for a few seconds the two men stare at each other. 'And those who think they would prefer to live by other regulations should perhaps think of living elsewhere.'

Thirty-two

'I don't trust them,' Silas tells Megan, 'And Caradoc and Jacob are too stupid with them.'

But she looks away. 'You don't mean that.'

'I do. They're being naive, weak. Those Indians are no more like innocent children than any of the rest of us. They're sly, vicious, just biding their time.'

'Why do you say that?'

He shakes his head.

'Tell me, Silas!'

'I don't trust them, that's all I'm saying.' He stands and walks to the door then looks back at her. She is pale, her mouth drawn, and her eyes slightly wide. Frightened – or angry. 'Why don't you just tell me? It's ridiculous to tell me just hints and half truths – worse than telling me nothing at all. I'm not stupid, and I'm not a child.'

He sighs. Everything he does is wrong. 'It's just something Selwyn has been telling me...' he says, and pauses, trying to think how to tell her.

'Tell me!'

'About a place north of here, a place called Bahía Blanca.' He stops. Despite her insistence she looks alarmed. He is not making it any better. 'But that's five hundred miles away...' he adds quickly. 'Oh *cariad*... please, I don't want...' He steps back to her and tries to throw his arms around her, but she pushes him away. 'The rest, Silas, I want to know the rest.'

'It's nothing, nothing...' His voice trails off, continuing only when she glares at him. He takes a deep breath in. 'He says they came on the Sabbath, stealthy like cats. No one was spared, not even babes in their mothers' arms. By the time they had finished, all that was left was a line of scalps.

She stares at him, her mouth open. Slowly, she shakes her

head. 'No,' she says quietly, 'I don't believe it. They wouldn't...'

Silas forces out a laugh. 'Yes, it's probably just a story. Just something someone's made up to keep their children in order. Anyway, the Indians down here are a different tribe – Tehuelche – more peaceful.' He smiles. 'Well known for it.' He laughs uneasily, kisses her smartly on her disapproving mouth and opens the door. It is cold, the end of June, the beginning of winter. He draws his jacket around him and allows his teeth to rattle loudly. 'I'll try to get some more flour,' he says.

The supplies from Buenos Aires are being rationed. There are a few voices around the village complaining that this should have happened earlier and that things are worse now than they were when the *Meistr* was in charge. People are tired and irritable and a little hungry again – even Caradoc's waistcoat is beginning to sag emptily over his stomach.

Every day the old Tehuelche visits the fort with his wife, and every day he picks up a word from the Welsh, and they pick a word from him, and in that way a new language is fast developing – a pidgin Welsh, or a pidgin Tehuelche. Selwyn was right – the Tehuelche has come to trade – his guanaco hides and feathers for whatever the Welsh can give them in return, which turns out to be not very much at all and is getting less with every passing day.

When Silas reaches the village, the old man is already there in the warehouse. Silas can smell the huge, garishly coloured skin he has with him, as soon as he enters. It is not smoke that he can smell at this distance, but the rank odour of improperly cured leather. The man is throwing the pelt out in front of him over the floor so the colonists can inspect. It is made from the skins of several animals sewn together and Silas can see it has small scraps of dried-up flesh adhering to the outside. The smell is strong as it unfurls. The old Tehuelche shows how they wear it, the fur inside, drawn to his body with folded arms. Then he unwraps it from himself and offers it to them.

'*Bara*,' he says.

Caradoc shakes his head. Silas wonders how he can bring himself to touch it, the thing is probably alive with lice or something worse. 'This is worth more than bread.'

The old Tehuelche shakes the mantle again. '*Bara*'.

Caradoc looks at Jacob and Selwyn. 'How can I accept this? How can we tell him?'

For a few minutes the men look at each other, then the old man hurries outside to where his horse is waiting. In one of his saddlebags is a note. He hands it to Caradoc.

'Spanish, I think a letter,' Caradoc says, examining it and turning it over. 'Can you make any sense of it?' He hands the note on to Selwyn.

'It's a list, things they'd like in exchange for the guanaco mantles or feathers – yerba for maté, sugar, flour, bread, biscuits, tobacco, ponchos, handkerchiefs, blankets,' he grins, '...and alcohol. That seems to be the most important of all.' Selwyn reads on a little further. 'Ah, I think it says he's glad we're here. The people in Patagones are... thieves, I think... and horses, yes, horse-thieves. I wonder who wrote this... it ends telling us not to be afraid, calls us friends, says there's plenty of food here for everyone... plenty guanaco, plenty ostrich.' He stops suddenly and looks at the old Indian who is listening intently. 'Thank you,' he says and claps the Tehuelche on his bare shoulder – underneath the mantle the Indian wears just a pair of skin trousers and boots. Then he turns to Caradoc. 'I think this means they are willing to share their land with us. It's very...' he looks at the old man again '...kind.'

'Fetch him some bread,' Caradoc says to Jacob, 'Mrs Rhys was baking this morning, tell her I'll make sure she gets some flour in return.'

Silas tuts. He has been standing listening for several minutes. They seem so willing to be taken in, a few words on a piece of paper and they are ready to believe anything. The old Tehuelche has shifty eyes; they rest on nothing for very long. It gives him a haunted air and it makes Silas feel uneasy.

'We're almost starving and yet you are giving away our food?' Silas says. 'These people can find food of their own, they don't need ours.'

'We can spare a little.'

'We can't spare anything. We're all hungry, Caradoc!'

The Indian points to Silas. '*Háchish!* You... *aoukem.*'

The men look at each other.

'*Aoukem!*' The old man rotates one hand around his head then mimics stabbing at something on the ground.

Silas has understood but still he shrugs and asks, 'What does he want?'

'I think he wants you to go with him to hunt.'

Silas laughs. 'Me?' he asks incredulously, then laughs nervously, 'I'm not doing that.'

The old Tehuelche's name is Yeluc. His skin is the colour and texture of an old leather chair Silas once saw in a minister's house. Around his forehead is a band of cream cloth holding back hair that is long and streaked with grey. Held around him at all times with a hand that looks as if it is set into the shape of a hook, is the huge enveloping cloak.

He greets Silas with a curt nod, and then presents him with a horse – a pied thing, obviously selected for its bad temper. Then he sits back on his own horse with the suggestion of a grin on his face, and watches as Silas attempts to mount, and then cajole his horse into action. This horse is nothing like any horse Silas has ridden before. It is more like a mule than a stallion. For about ten minutes it refuses to move at all, then, after he has given it a couple of hard nudges with his heels, it bucks and tries to throw him, arching its back and then its neck, dipping and throwing up its back legs, until Silas is thrown several feet away onto the soft mud of the riverbank. He lies there for a few seconds trying to decide where he hurts the most, and then sits up and stares angrily at Yeluc.

'That horse is not broken.'

The Indian smiles and shrugs, then without leaving his own horse leans out of his saddle, picks up the reins of the piebald and offers them to Silas again. '*Hogel... ketz.*'

'No!'

The Tehuelche shakes them at him, the small pieces of metal jangling together, but still Silas doesn't move. He hurts everywhere, he has decided, but mainly down his left arm and leg which are burning as if alight. He groans and lies back again. He is too old for this. The Indian should be teaching the younger members of the colony – they mend more easily.

Someone coughs. Someone quite close. He looks around but sees nothing except Yeluc and his horse. But someone is watching. The Tehuelche smiles and shakes the reins again and reluctantly Silas gets up. He is not a coward. He will not give up. He swings painfully back on his horse and looks around just in time to see Jacob striding back to the fort.

Yeluc shows him how to keep his place by holding on with his knees, and how to soothe the animal with a whispering voice. Then, when the horse is calm, Yeluc taps Silas with his stick until he is sitting upright in the saddle, his back straight. Yeluc nods without smiling. He is sitting with his arms folded. Good, he seems to be saying, that will do.

The next day he is waiting outside Silas' house when he wakes. As Silas opens his back door he hears the snort of a horse – and stepping out he sees Yeluc there sitting erectly, smiling.

'Today – bolas… *chume*,' the old man says, and draws something long and heavy from his saddlebag.

Silas peers at what the old man has in his hands: two fist-sized round pebbles, each with a long leather thong tied around a carved shallow channel. He counts them, offering one and then the other towards Silas. '*Chuche, houke…*'

Silas nods. 'What are they?'

Yeluc stares at him uncomprehendingly.

Silas pretends to throw them away and then shrugs at the Indian.

'Ah…' Yeluc smiles suddenly, then flaps his elbows at his sides. '*Mikkeoush*,' he says, then allows his head to flop to one side with his tongue out and eyes closed. Then he opens his eyes and sits upright again. '*Chuche, houke…*' he says, taking the thongs from Silas and letting the two stones dangle, '…*mikkeoush*.' Then taking out another stone on a lead counts again, '*Chuche, houke, aäs…*'

'Three stones?'

Yeluc nods and imitates something trotting along with his fingers.

'For guanaco! Ah I see, two stones for ostrich and three for guanaco! That's right, isn't it?'

But the old man has gone. There is, apparently, no time for breakfast. Yeluc points to where the piebald is snorting impatiently, and Silas calls out goodbye to Megan and swings himself into the saddle.

Yeluc makes him throw the bolas again and again at a target until his arms ache – the pitch of the old man's grunt only changing slightly when Silas misses and when he hits. After an hour of this he motions for him to follow him and they return to his camp. The women are busy as usual; one of the younger women pegging out a skin while the other one is sewing two smaller skins together with sinew. The older woman stirs something in a pot that is dangling over the fire. There is a smell of herbs and meat that makes Silas realise he has missed breakfast. They are chattering quietly together, the two younger women laughing at whatever the older woman is saying. When they see Yeluc they stop what they are doing and gather around the fire.

Yeluc directs Silas to sit on a small pile of skins.

'Seannu,' he says, pointing at the old woman, who nods and smiles.

Silas nods.

'Tezza,' he says, pointing to the thinner of the two women with a fringe, then 'Mareea.' He points at Seannu again. 'Seannu.'

'Ah,' Silas nods and smiles. The women are something to do with Seannu, then. He mouths the words, trying to remember them and they look at him expectantly. Seannu's skin is dark and polished like her husband's but Tezza's and Mareea's are slightly paler and their eyes wider and more oval. Mareea, he notices, seems more inclined to smile than the others and it is she who offers him some meat wrapped in a small piece of skin. Still they watch him as if they are waiting for him to say something. He takes a bite of the meat. It is tender, covered in a flavoured fat. 'Good,' he says.

'Where are your people?' Silas asks. 'Where is your tribe? Your village?'

They look puzzled so he draws on the mud. Four stick people indicating that they represent Yeluc and his women, and then many more at which he points and gestures at the empty valley around them.

But Yeluc grins and doesn't answer. Silas watches him and says little else. You understood, he thinks, you understood very well. Where are your people, the other Tehuelche? You don't want to tell me. He looks around him. Hiding, waiting. He takes another bite of his meat. This show of friendliness means nothing. He will not be fooled. He will keep on his guard.

Silas is not the only one Yeluc has selected to train. He has picked out various young men in the village including Joseph and Ieuan

Jones, Miriam's brothers, but he refuses to take Miriam herself even though she dresses in her brother's trousers and makes a fairly convincing boy.

After several days Yeluc seems to be convinced that his apprentices are competent enough to be taken out on the hunt, and smiling he allows Miriam to join them too – acting as beater with his three women.

The hunting ground to the north of the valley is flat, and almost empty of vegetation. From time to time a small swirl of dust builds up into something larger – a ghost-like cloud hovering above the ground. Up until now it has seemed to Silas that that is all there is: distant layers of higher rock and closer small lakes crusted with pink salt and matching flamingos and various ducks, then small bushes and bare ground in between. But as the old man approaches things change. It is as if he breathes magic into the air. A swing of his arm and what seems to be just a bush changes into a smaller bush with deer; a series of scattered rocks suddenly moves and becomes a flock of the small Patagonian rhea. The guanaco flee gracefully while the rhea make a strange strutting zig-zag. When they open their wings they cease to look like birds but sweep along the countryside like small sailing boats, tacking to catch the wind.

Yeluc has learnt a few words now and gives them quiet clipped instructions. They have left the women to come on slowly behind them, making as much noise as they like, scaring anything with legs from their lairs, while the boys and men move out in a semi-circle, gathering the game in front of them like a human net.

Yeluc picks out a bush with a grunt and a finger.

Silas squints to look. He wishes his eyes were stronger. All he sees is the desert, yellow-green and yellow-brown.

'Sil-as!' Yeluc's voice is a harsh whisper.

Silas follows his finger and one of the brown mounds moves. A guanaco. It is alone, separated from the rest by the galloping hooves of Joseph's horse and the fence of noise that the women have made with their horses and chatter. Silas takes out his bolas and slowly unravels the sinews that hold the stones together. Yeluc nods, checks to see that Silas is holding it correctly, and then nods again. Silas is practised now. He grips the end of the leather rope tightly and then twists it around above his head until it is making the air throb, then lets go as it reaches its highest arc. The three stones seem to stagger in the air, one dropping below the other two before it hits the animal on the nose. The guanaco falls silently and at once.

'*Kow!*' Yeluc gives a wide grin of approval then bows his head and invites Silas to inspect his kill. It is only then that Silas dismounts, grins, and for the first time dares to turn his back.

They return to the village singing: Yeluc attempting to join in the chorus but his old voice wavering and out of tune. The Jones siblings and the rest of the young men return to their families, while Silas returns to the barn where Megan has arranged to meet him with Caradoc and Jacob. It is his first hunt and they are anxious to hear what he's done, what he's learnt. Jacob, as usual, is interested in the Indians – how they live, how they speak, their gods, their habits, but Silas can tell him little except for how they hunt. The man, or at least Yeluc, seems to spend his life hunting, and when he is not hunting sitting at his fire smoking or playing cards or mending his tools and weapons; while the women pin out skins, cook, sew, gather wood and water and are constantly busy, and like Welsh women they like to keep their houses clean. Twice now he has been cleared out of the way so that Yeluc's wife can finish her sweeping.

'Just like us, then,' Megan says.

'But innocent, like children,' says Jacob.

Silas shakes his head. There is so much he doesn't know, so much Yeluc won't tell him and keeps to himself. 'They are not children. They have more guile than a child, more animal cunning.'

Caradoc takes the carcass and turns it over. It is a fine animal, not too large but with a lot of flesh. 'If this carries on we are going to eat like lords,' he says, 'there must be enough meat on that thing to feed at least two families. You have done well, *bachgen*.'

Despite himself, Silas stands a little taller.

Thirty-three

It is July – their second winter in Patagonia – and the weather is cold. The first anniversary of their arrival at Port Madryn passes without comment. The supplies from Buenos Aires are slowly petering out and there is an uncomfortable and widely-held suspicion that without the Indians – without Yeluc and his patient teaching – there would be no Welsh colony at all.

In his discussions with the council Caradoc bluffly tries to take credit for their good fortune in encountering Yeluc, and then, when that is dismissed, reminding them of what he considers to be his tactful treatment of the old man. 'He respected my age and experience,' he tells them, 'he trusted me.'

Jacob prevents an embarrassed silence. 'I am sure he did, *brawd*. But he is clearly a kind man, don't you think? I think he could see...'

'That we were on the verge of starving to death,' says Annie.

'Yes, food for the birds we'd be now, if it weren't for Yeluc.'

Mary and Annie have become Yeluc's enthusiastic champions. They are teaching his women how to make bread and they, in turn, are showing them where to find herbs for cooking and healing. Annie is pregnant and Mareea has shown her where to gather weeds that might help her morning sickness.

Yeluc rarely comes near Silas' house, preferring instead the warmth and activity of Mary's table. Whenever Silas visits the Jones household, Yeluc seems to be there sitting at the table with one of the younger Jones children on his knee, while Mareea or Tezza stands next to Mary watching all that she does. The woman is an excellent cook, proficient with both baking pot and griddle, and she seems to enjoy the old man's attention and appreciation. She feeds him titbits as if he is one of his wife's little dogs and his vocabulary is improving daily. However, when Silas asks Mary if she has changed her mind about the Indians she shakes her head. 'Just Yeluc, and his women,' she says. 'As for the rest of them...' she shrugs, 'who knows?'

Gradually Mary and her daughter are becoming experts on the Tehuelche way of life. They love to show off what they know, and as a result Jacob too has become a frequent if not quite as welcome a visitor, quizzing the two women, and, Silas suspects, hoping to befriend Yeluc as well. With the slightest prompt Miriam will explain how the Tehuelche are dependent on the guanaco, how the old hides are used for the awnings, while the younger ones are used for blankets and the youngest ones, especially the skins of those killed while still unborn, are prized for making the softest cloaks or mantles. She will tell how the Indians waste nothing, and this is somehow part of what they believe, their religion. The necks and legs are used to make boots and the remainder used to make harnesses and leads. How the animals are revered almost as gods, rhea is useful for fat, feathers, and their sinews good for thread, but the meat is dry and sometimes fed to the dogs. She will tell how they follow the herds, how they have done so for centuries – inland to the breeding grounds in the summer, out to the coast during the winter. Then she will take a breath and tell how it seems to her that their voices change when they talk about their world around them, how they seem to feel part of it, as if it is something living, and how they seem to value and cherish everything they find and everything they kill. Then she will tell how much she doesn't know, how much she has to learn: about rituals she has seen only fleetingly – strange gestures over the kill and muttered words at places that look just like everywhere else, but nonetheless seem revered.

Jacob sits entranced – either at the sound of her voice or at what she has to say, while Mary clears up around him. 'If you're so interested in our friends why don't you ask them yourself?' she asks him, and he smiles and says that one day he hopes that the Lord will give him an opportunity.

Throughout the early winter there is rain, and by August the crops are still green but growing slowly. The patches of green are small – they have planted just where there was growth before – but Caradoc assures them that this will just be the start. Few of them are farmers, he reminds them, but he is sure that the Lord will guide them if they persevere.

So they nod and smile and stamp their feet to drive away the cold. At least their bellies are not empty, at least they are still here, and at least the Good Shepherd seems to be keeping a watchful eye over them – clearly, in Patagonia, says Megan, he sends Indians rather than angels.

Thirty-four

Jacob has come to bless Silas' house. For the last few weeks Silas has been making it ready and now there is enough space to accept visitors. There are just three rooms – a living room, a bedroom and a kitchen with a scullery in an outhouse – and it is bigger than anything he has lived in before. They have nine guests – the Jones family, Jacob, Selwyn and Annie. It is not very comfortable, there is not much space, and the children – the three youngest Jones children and Myfanwy – are sitting on skins on the floor, but even so they are all in here together. It is going to be just a short ceremony because they have collected their rations together and Megan and Mary have prepared a feast of bread, meat and cheese in the kitchen next door. Miriam has also picked some berries that Seannu has assured her are safe to eat, and made them into a jam with a little sugar. It is the sweet smell of this jam, newly made on the stove that Silas has constructed in the kitchen, which is making Jacob's voice so moist with saliva that he hurries through his words, obviously anxious to be finished.

It was Jacob who insisted that the house be blessed, and he has spent the morning inspecting the place and passing comment. Of course everything that Silas has constructed is wrong: the hearth to the chimney is not wide enough, the outhouse is inconveniently located and its door pointing the wrong way, and the bedroom is too small and lacks proper ventilation.

It has taken several months for the work to be complete. Silas, John, Joseph and Ieuan have constructed the place from stone and the Jones family seems to be taking as much pride in the result as Silas. When anyone admires their handicraft they smile at each other and then at Silas. All this from nothing. A miracle. The walls are straight, the thatch neatly finished, and the dried guts of rheas used to 'glaze' the windows. In return Silas has helped them build their own larger house close by. A short path, lined in some places with gravel, connects the two.

'Safety in numbers,' Mary Jones had said, and for once John had added his voice: 'You build yours right next to mine, Silas, so we can watch out for each other. We can't be too careful... and despite what that old fool Caradoc says, you can't trust those Indians. I've heard tales that would make you afraid to shut your eyes in your bed.'

Miriam is a frequent visitor. She spends quite a lot of her time walking the path between the two cottages in order to take a message from her mother who seems to be always busy at home, or to collect Myfanwy so she can play with the younger children.

Even though they are all still very young, Miriam is endeavouring, with some success, to teach the children to read. In Wales she was a bit of a scholar, her mother tells Silas in one of their many conversations at her table.

'She wanted to be a teacher.'

'Maybe she could still be one.'

'Here?'

'Yes, with Jacob.'

'Jacob?' Miriam looks up, wrinkling her nose as if she has smelt something unpleasant. Mary and Silas grin at each other, and when she sees them Miriam snorts. 'I would be very grateful if some people would stop talking about me as if I am not here.' And she sweeps by, her skirt almost up to her knees.

Miriam is in front of him now, singing along to the hymns that Jacob insists they sing. Her mother seems to have found enough material to make her a new dress since she has grown so conspicuously out of her old one. It is a dark check, the colours so muted they are almost indiscernible in this light. He finds himself watching the cloth – the way it stretches and relaxes when she sings. It is trimmed with a high lace collar. This is obviously an uncomfortable feature; from time to time she pulls it away from her throat quite roughly and sighs then glances irritably at her mother who takes no notice. Silas smiles and nudges Megan, but she is busy with Myfanwy. He guesses that the wearing of the collar is the result of a battle that Miriam lost. He imagines it will be ripped off at the earliest opportunity.

Even though everyone is hungry, Jacob continues to talk. Silas isn't listening, but everyone around him seems to be listening or pretending to listen, with rapt attention. Everyone, that is, except Miriam. She has her head bowed and is obviously trying to smother a smile. Her head turns slightly and her eyes slide towards his under her fuzz of hair, which seems to have been worked into a neat arrangement involving a slide, and he knows she has been aware of his scrutiny. His face warms and he looks away.

Jacob is still talking. He is so self-absorbed, so self-righteous, so convinced that everything he has to say is worth everyone's attention, but the children are becoming restless. The baby is whimpering and Mary is now looking at him with such a face of irritation it seems incredible that he hasn't taken the hint. He threatens and then soothes and cajoles. Our Lord can be wrathful, he says, kind but always good. He has learnt a lot from Edwyn Lloyd's rhetoric and is improving with practice. His eyes roll and his voice rises to a thunder. Then, without pausing, his voice softens so everyone has to strain to hear: whispering threats, muttering promises, sharing secrets of eternal life. But then there is another noise too. Silas turns to where it is coming from – a scratching at the brittle rhea gut of the window, and behind it the shadow of a head, and then another one. Silas is not the only one who has noticed. Selwyn goes quietly to the door, opens it a little then closes it again. 'Indians,' he mouths to the rest of them, while Jacob continues his sermon. There are lots of them, about twenty, he says quietly to Silas, and more around the house. Megan creeps into the kitchen and comes back nodding. 'More Indians,' she whispers. 'Strangers.'

'Sing,' Jacob orders, and indicates to Silas that he is to give them their notes. He chooses a loud defiant *re*, and then the line of the first verse praising and yet also appealing for help: 'Oh God, Our Help In Ages Past'. They sing out loud, some of their voices shaking when they delve downwards in pitch.

'Another!' calls out Silas when that is finished. So they keep on singing: all the loud defiant hymns that they know, one after the other, and the door opens and the Indians fall in, staggering and then walking upright, peering into the colonists' faces, breath rancid as old fat, cloaks ragged and smelling of animal, bands of old dirty cloth wrapped tightly round their heads, faces pitted with old wounds and sores, skin dark and polished like hide, and hair hanging down in knots. Megan closes her eyes. Myfanwy's voice trembles a little, and Silas' hands closes around hers and squeezes it once. They sing while the Indians inspect each face in turn, peering into eyes as though they are trying to see something inside, picking at clothes and rubbing the cloth between their fingers. They touch the blond hair of one of the younger Jones children and the child squeals and buries his face in his mother's skirts. But still the Welsh sing. They are becoming a little hoarse now but still they sing. Then the young Indian boys with them pick their way around the room touching, lifting things up, tapping and dropping them and then grunting. The colonists sing until their breath runs out and Silas nods at Jacob.

'Now let us pray,' commands Jacob and falls to his knees.

Stupid. Silas is aware of his exposed neck at just the right height for a sharp blow downwards, but the Indians just watch for a few seconds and then a couple of them do likewise. The rest of them continue to stand. There is little room to move now. Every patch of space is covered with legs or hands. These Indians are tall, even Miriam and her brothers are dwarfed by them; they have to bend just to peer into the Welsh faces. But Jacob takes no notice and starts to recite the Lord's Prayer loudly as an invitation for everyone else to join in.

'Amen,' says Jacob at the end.

'Amen,' the congregation echoes.

'Amen,' says another voice at Silas' elbow. He opens an eye. The child next to him is kneeling too. 'Amen,' says the child again, and gives a quiet short giggle.

'Glory be to the Father and to the Son and to the Holy Ghost,' says Jacob.

'As it was in the beginning, is now and ever shall be, world without end. Amen,' they answer.

'Amen,' says the boy, happily. Now a couple more of them are kneeling, looking at the colonists' clasped hands and then holding theirs together too.

'Glory, honour, praise and power be unto the Lamb forever. Jesus Christ is our redeemer. Halleluyah, Halleluyah.'

'Halleluyah,' repeat a few voices all around them.

Miriam makes a strange little choking noise. Silas opens both his eyes to look at her. Her face is red with suppressed giggles but now they seem to be escaping from her in an eruption of quiet snuffles. Now she laughs out loud, her mouth wide with bellows and snorts. He looks around him. The Indians have gone. The door of his house is open and bangs shut in the wind.

'The grace of our Lord Jesus Christ and the love of God and the fellowship of the Holy Ghost be with us ever more,' Jacob says with relief.

'Amen,' they reply. They stand up, looking at each other incredulously. They are still alive. John feels himself all over as if he is trying to check. They didn't kill them. They hug each other and congratulate each other in loud high voices, while Selwyn checks the kitchen. The Indians have gone and so, unfortunately, has the bread from the table – but not the meat and not the horses in the yard. So Jacob instructs Joseph to take his horse and gallop back to the village warning everyone he meets along the way that there are more Indians heading down the valley. Then, after they have packed away what remains of the food, they all follow in the cart or on horseback.

When they see Rawson they stop. Camped outside the village is another village, just as large, of many tents, horses, dogs and people.

'There must be a hundred of them at least,' Jacob says in a hushed voice. Silas nods and Megan holds Myfanwy tightly on her lap. Even Miriam and Joseph are silent and pale.

'Who are all those people, Dadda?' Myfanwy asks.

'More friends,' Silas says, trying to sound certain.

Thirty-five

The colonists are surrounded. The women and children have retreated back to the fort and for a few days they huddle together inside. Just until they see what happens. Just until then.

Silas is lying next to Megan in Jacob's cottage. Myfanwy is the only one who is sleeping. They have arranged layers of skins on the floor to keep out the chill of the earth, and even though they are quite comfortable they are still wide awake. When they are not talking they are listening. The sounds of the Indians are all around them: dogs barking, horses stamping the ground, children crying, adults laughing and calling out. And they can smell them too: fires burning, and meat and fat cooking on aromatic wood. Every time they try to sleep there is another waft of smell and another animal sound to remind them that they are not alone. After a year of solitude in this place they are finding it hard to bear.

The next morning the Indians are still there. Silas creeps from Jacob's house to the low ground outside the fort wall. He looks around. The collection of about twenty tents is like a strange miniature city; the shadows in the early morning making each tent appear longer and more important than it really is. Each opening points east, the curving skins providing a shelter from the wind that usually sweeps in from the Andes. It is very quiet and he assumes everyone is asleep; he can just see their bodies lying beside the glowing embers on the floor. Then he notices that there is one man sitting and watching, his eyes following Silas, a rifle over his lap and a dog lying on his feet. The dog pricks up his ears and then his head, and then a few other dogs notice him too and come running up; an assorted selection, some as thin as whippets, and some as docile as old sheepdogs. Perhaps these are the relatives of Antur. He holds out his hand and one of them kisses it with his nose. The dogs follow him as he walks away from the tents and the village to where the wilderness begins. He empties his bladder. The small rivulets in the sandy soil disappear instantly, leaving just the impression of their passage. The dogs come over and sniff. 'Shoo,' he tells them, buttoning up his trousers but they just come up closer to him and sniff again. He smiles to himself – like Benny and Polly they seem particularly interested in his crotch. 'Go away,' he says, waving at them with his hands but they take no notice. A few more are coming and he begins to feel uneasy; suddenly he seems to be surrounded by a pack and some of them are large and don't look tame. When he starts to walk away quickly one of them starts to growl.

'*Wati!*' The man keeping guard calls out and the growling stops. '*Wati, wati, pespesh.*' The dogs stop and slink away. Silas holds up his hand to the man in greeting, but the man doesn't seem to see him.

They are Yeluc's people, the northern Tehuelche – of the same stock but loyal to a different chief. Tribes change; Yeluc has told them, drawing pictures in the sand to add to his words. They form and reform as they migrate across the desert – sometimes just a small family group, sometimes a few families coming together for the big hunt in the early summer. The winter brings the guanaco to the coast where the weather is milder; in the spring and summer they go back to the breeding ground hundreds of miles inland and wherever the guanaco go, the Tehuelche follow. It has been like this for centuries, even before the Cristianos brought the horse. Each tribe has its own territory and each member of the tribe carries a clear map of the boundaries in his head. There are trails and signs, the old man has told him, and soon he will show the Welsh exactly where they are. It will be better for everyone if they know.

'What about you?' asks Silas. 'Where is your tribe?'

The old man shrugs.

'But you must have a tribe,' Silas persists. He feels comfortable with the old man now, they have spent many evenings like this – smoking and talking.

'Many men,' the old man says, stirring the mud at his feet with a stick, 'and one.'

Silas frowns at him: 'Stop talking in riddles.'

The old man smiles and gradually explains with words, pictures and expressions with his hands and face. He was cast out. He draws a line between a figure representing him and the rest of the tribe.

'Why?'

'Old one sick. They call – Yeluc, Yeluc – and Yeluc come…' He makes a strange gesture with his hands, as if plucking something from his forehead, then holding out his hands palm downwards in front of him.

'What?' Silas frowns and then realises. He thinks Yeluc is making the sign for a spell or curse.

Megan used to pretend she was joking when she talked about such things: old women she knew who could turn milk sour, and make children ill. She would deny believing in such things but would nevertheless avoid them if she encountered them in the street.

'But she die.' The old man allows his hands to fall back into his lap.

Silas nods. 'And they thought it was because of you?'

The old man nods his head. 'Yes, *brawd.*'

'What happened then?'

'I go. They afraid of Yeluc. I go with *toldo* and horses and dogs. I have Seannu. I happy.'

'What about Tezza and Mareea?'

'They have men. Men die. They cut hair.' He motions with his hand across his forehead. 'They see Seannu. They come with us.'

Silas dabbles at the ground with a stick. 'Don't you mind?' he asks. 'Don't you miss other men?'

Yeluc shakes his head. 'We meet. We talk. We trade. With Tehuelche. With white men. With bad men at Patagones.' He smiles. 'With the good men at Chubut. Is good. Yeluc happy.'

Silas returns to Caradoc's house. The old man is dozing but Jacob and Megan are awake and talking over the fire as they cook breakfast.

'Are they still there?'

Silas nods, but from the way Jacob turns away it is obvious that he already knows the answer. Yeluc comes to talk to Caradoc and Selwyn, reassuring them that all is well. Using a mixture of Spanish, Welsh and Tehuelche they manage to work out that this tribe is well known to him; Chiquichan, their chief, is an old friend. Yeluc tells them that Chiquichan will want to trade, and so all day they wait for a visit from their chief. It comes at sunset when the temperature of the air is dropping fast. Chiquichan is huge – tall like Yeluc but massively covered in flesh as well. Yeluc shows them how the chief's mantle has had to be made larger than most with an extra couple of skins just to ensure that it overlaps at the front. He is heavy not just with flesh but silver too. He has silver clasps and pins on his cloak and trousers, silver spurs on his boots, and more silver inlaid on his saddles and bags.

'He play cards,' Yeluc says quietly, out of earshot of everyone but Silas, 'for silver. At Patagones. He say Chiquichan win, but no. Chiquichan no win,' the old man shakes his head. 'They cheat. They thieves. No one win at Patagones.' He spits on the ground.

When Chiquichan reaches the entrance to the fort he opens his arms in greeting, exposing a rounded smooth belly that seems as stuffed full as the faggots Silas' mother made as a treat for Christmas. He throws his head back and smiles so widely his eyes are drawn shut into slits. He reminds Silas of Polly, the way she used to roll over for him to scratch her belly. Yes, just like a dog, Silas thinks, and wonders if he is as trusting – but he suspects not. Caradoc and Selwyn step forward to greet him while Silas and Yeluc look on.

Chiquichan grabs hold of his cloak and draws it together again with his folded arms. There is a short explosion of Spanish, and Caradoc looks at Selwyn for an interpretation.

'I think he wants drink,' Selwyn says, looking at Yeluc. 'Is that what he said?'

Yeluc nods. His folded arms hold his mantle closely to his body.

Caradoc nods to Selwyn and Selwyn walks quickly into the warehouse. He returns with three bottles.

'It's all we have,' Caradoc says, holding them out to him. 'We don't drink strong liquor. We have this for when we're sick.'

Chiquichan looks puzzled, but takes the bottles, prizes open one of the corks, sniffs and grins, then he slaps Caradoc on the back and laughs. His cloak falls open and through it Silas glimpses the large elaborate buckle of a belt holding up his trousers. Around his neck, half-hidden by his mantle, is a large red neckerchief. The man's face is florid. He fires a few words at Yeluc and Yeluc replies in the same tongue.

'He happy,' Yeluc says. 'He friend. If Chiquichan friend, then all the Chiquichan tribe is friend.'

The chief has a grin as wide as his face. He climbs upon his horse and the animal sinks perceptibly beneath his weight so that Silas feels a pang of pity for it. Then the great *cacique* Chiquichan digs in his silver heels and gallops back to camp.

The night brings more noise. There are the sounds of many hooves, snorting, dogs yapping and barking, and hushed voices calling and whistling.

The next morning they wake to find the city of tents to the north of the river has a satellite to the south.

'Gallatts,' says Yeluc.

The two tribes look across the water at each other.

'Big meeting... *aix*. Many *tchonik*... people. Smoke, talk, trade – horses, skins, feathers, wives, anything,' Yeluc explains enthusiastically to Caradoc and Selwyn in his usual mixture of Spanish, Welsh and Tehuelche. 'Find women,' he says, and smiles. 'New blood – strong women, then strong *coquetra*... children.' His voice drops.

'Do you have any children?' Silas asks Yeluc later.

'Yes, many.' He holds up all his fingers.

'So where are they now?'

'Gone.' The old man's voice is quiet. Silas has to move closer to hear. 'Up.' He points to the sky. 'With gods, heroes. *Áàskren*... stars?'

Silas nods.

'Yes, with stars. With sun, with *showan*.' Yeluc throws open his arms to include all the sky. His old eyes brim with tears. 'To Elal and... sleep.' He gestures with his hands, closing his eyes. 'With old ones? Yes?'

Silas nods. 'In heaven.'

'With stars?'

'Yes.'

'Good. Where dead ones go?'

Silas nods.

'Some man say up there hunting grounds. Much guanaco, much ostrich.'

'Maybe there is, Yeluc.'

'And in Welsh hea-ven? What there?'

'My father, my...' his voice breaks. He forces it to continue. 'My Richard, my Gwyneth.'

The old man reaches out to him and draws him close, holding his head firmly against his padded chest. 'Is good, Si-las. Good place. Fine place. If they there.'

In the morning the chief Chiquichan leads a white mare over to the entrance of the fort and leaves it there. The horse is flawlessly white, and it stamps the ground with a fine but strong hoof.

'For drink,' explains Yeluc, 'he happy. He get drink. Gallatts did not. He very happy. He thank you.'

Thirty-six

After a year of seeing just the same hundred or so faces, they now have to get used to seeing more. It is too much change. They have become used to having space, spreading out, laying claim to all that they see, but now they are surrounded, and feel hindered and watched.

The Indians allow or send their children first, peeping in at windows and around doors, and then approaching more boldly when they smell bread.

'Do you want some?' Silas asks holding out a piece of crust. The child comes closer. A little too pretty to be a boy, but long dirty hair and a band like they all have, and her own small gown of guanaco fur held around her body. She wears a thong of leather around her neck with what looks like the carcass of a very small animal hung in the middle. Silas guesses that it might be some sort of charm or talisman. No shoes of course, but then neither has Myfanwy. The child looks at the bread for a few seconds then darts forward and grabs it from him.

'Like a wild animal,' Megan tuts. 'I know dogs with better manners.'

The child chews carefully, her eyes never leaving them all: Silas, Myfanwy, Megan, then back to Myfanwy again. Myfanwy herself is enthralled. The two stare at each other unguardedly, and for a moment Silas wishes he were a child again, able to take in the world just for what it is, without preconceptions.

'More?' he asks, holding out another crust.

Megan tuts again. 'Stop that. You're only encouraging her. We haven't got enough food to give away.'

This time the child comes forward more quickly.

Silas smiles and whisks it away. '*Bara*,' he says, 'you say it.'

The child steps back and looks at him.

'*Bara*,' repeats Myfanwy, 'go on, you say it and he'll give it to you.'

The child looks from Silas to Myfanwy. The two look as if they could be the same age, although the Tehuelche is taller and more strongly built.

'*Bara*,' Myfanwy says again, more slowly. 'Go on, your turn.'

'*Bara*,' says the child, slowly, and Myfanwy claps her hands.

The child steps backwards at the sudden sound then smiles as Silas gives her the bread. '*Bara*,' she says again, and Myfanwy claps. 'Good, good, see Dadda, I'm teaching her.'

Either the child is a quick learner or Myfanwy is a good teacher, but by the end of the day the two seem to be understanding each other enough to have built a small *toldo* of their own in the yard just outside the house. It consists of just a few large rocks and a blanket but the two children stay there most of the next day and the day after that.

'Tomorrow Leesa is going to bring us some real skins,' she says, 'and we're going to look for sticks.'

'Well don't go far.'

Within a week there is a small tribe of six making their own village outside Silas' back door. When he goes past them he listens to them. They seem to be developing their own language. There are a few words of Welsh that he recognises but the rest is strange, probably Indian or something else they've made up. They play intensely and seriously, hardly noticing his passing.

In the village the visitors are older and more intrusive. 'They never leave us alone,' Annie says, during one of her visits for tea.

'Every hour I have one at the door, begging for something or offering me an ostrich feather or one of their smelly blankets. What do I want with that?'

Silas murmurs that being surrounded by so many must make things feel a little awkward.

'Worse than surrounded,' Annie says, 'invaded.'

She presses down her dress, proud of the tiny bulge that lies beneath there. Even a friendly invasion is tiresome, she says. 'I don't feel I can leave the house otherwise they'll be in there, helping themselves to whatever they can find.'

When no one replies she continues. 'It's the young boys who are the worst. You know, if they come in the house, I have to turn them upside down and shake them before I let them leave? And usually something comes falling out, doesn't it, Sel?'

Selwyn nods. Silas smiles – with a wife like Annie, Selwyn rarely finds the need to speak.

'A spoon, or a knife, or something like a thimble. Anything shiny, and anything useful.'

Silas and Selwyn laugh.

'It's not funny.'

She turns her back to them. 'I'm sorry to have to say this, Megan, but I blame Jacob. He's too keen to please, too keen to let them do just as they want without anyone saying anything. Children, he says. Well I don't think they are innocent at all. I think they know exactly what they're doing. And anyone with any sense could see that.'

Megan slams down a cup of tea in front of her with such force that some of it slops over the side onto the table.

She is frowning, but Annie doesn't seem to notice. 'Thank you,' she says, smiling happily. 'You'll have to come to our place after chapel next week.'

'I'm not going anywhere near her,' Megan says after they have gone, 'and I wish she wouldn't come here.' She narrows her eyes. 'Do you invite them, Silas? Is that why she comes?'

'I thought you could do with the company. I thought you liked her.'

'Why on earth did you think that? All those stupid things she says. Indians, my brother, thieves. Of course it takes one to know one.' She sits at the table. 'You know where she comes from, don't you?' She doesn't wait for him to reply. 'The docks at Swansea, with all the prostitutes and pimps.'

'Megan!'

'It's true, Silas, you know it is.' She picks up Annie's cup and drops it into a bowl of water so that the suds splash against her clothes. She brushes herself down with quick angry movements. 'When she's not talking about that, it's her stupid morning sickness, babies, birth, whether she wants a boy... or a girl.' Her voice breaks, and he reaches out to her but she shoves him away. 'The woman has no sensitivity, no regard for how other people feel.' She buries her face in her hands. 'I don't want to hear, Silas, I don't want to know. I just want to be left alone.'

But Mary says that Annie talks because she is afraid. Silas has come looking for Myfanwy, knowing where she'll be. The little group of friends have moved camp to the Jones' house because Mary is more generous with treats and gentler with her tongue than Megan. They are all sitting inside their dilapidated-looking skins contentedly munching on crusts of bread. Inside the house sits Seannu with Mareea and another woman Silas doesn't recognise.

'We're having a chat,' she tells him. 'Miriam's making notes.'

The girl looks up and grins at him. She had been so quiet in the corner he hadn't noticed her. 'There's so much they know – a herb for everything. Miriam's writing it down and trying to guess what they mean.'

It was Annie who gave her the idea, Mary says. Annie with her cure for sickness and her anxiety for something to help her when her time comes. 'Her mother died in childbirth, and left her penniless. Now she's frightened. I know it's difficult to believe, but she is. She told me that she heard her mother scream, as if she were being ripped in two. But I've told her, she's big-boned, it'll be to her advantage. It's midgets like me who have to worry.' She smiles. 'Not that I've ever had much trouble.'

Spring is coming and Annie swells a little with each month. The colonists wait for the rain clouds to come and for the Indians to move on but the Indians remain where they are and the sky stays clear. There is talk among the colonists of a conspiracy. It seems too much of a coincidence that both tribes have arrived at the same place at the same time and are staying so long. Even Jacob and Caradoc agree.

'They're trying to intimidate us,' Caradoc says, 'but if that's their plan they can think again.'

There is a murmur of agreement, but then Jacob clears his throat and fixes his pale unblinking eyes on one face after the other. 'We must remember that they're children,' he says. 'Remember they belong to the Lord just as much as we do.'

The men around him fidget and Annie Williams looks down at her hands.

'We must treat them with kindness.'

'Yes, give them no reason to attack,' agrees Caradoc.

'But what if they do? What if they're in their tents now, sharpening their spears?'

'Then there is nothing we can do.'

And for a time everyone is silent remembering stories: the attack at Bahía Blanca and at the Península Valdés. But they were Puelche, Caradoc reminds them, the smaller, more vicious race to the north, well known for their raids and aggressive behaviour. Like the Chiquichan, the Gallatts are Tehuelche in the main, the Puelche element subdued by the relative calmness of their leaders.

If only he had known what he knows now, Silas thinks, he would still be safe in Wales with a family of children. Sometimes he dreams he has gone home again and Richard is there. He wakes with the taste of their conversation still in his mouth and for a few seconds he remains in a more pleasant land, unwilling to wake.

He tries to fill his mind with his life as it is now: Myfanwy, Megan, his cottage, this farm. He walks around the house from sun to shade then sun again. This time last year their houses were dissolving around them in the rain. Now the sky is cloudless, the sun bleaching it with an intense white heat. No wonder the crops are wilting. It was never like this in Wales – there the heavens could be relied upon to open at tediously regular intervals. They inspect the soil – underneath the surface, which is dry and cracked, the ground is still wet from the winter's ample drenching. But they throw on water, bucket after bucket, careful not to scorch the leaves, but anxious to keep the ground wet. It does no good. It must be that the earth is poor, and perhaps by watering it they are making it poorer – all the goodness is leaching out, flowing back into the river. The crops go from green to yellow to brown.

They look at Caradoc, but he can find little to say. In his thick suit he is feeling hot and tired. 'Keep trying, *brodyr*,' he says, quietly – and rather hopelessly.

The heat is affecting the Indians too. Their youth are becoming boisterous – one night they gather up their horses and tear around the village and settlements, whooping and snapping their whips into the air. The cattle moan and the villagers hide in their homes, fearing for their animals and what is left of their crops. In the morning they inspect the churned-up mud and count their livestock. The next evening it happens again while the Welsh watch: the young men gathering like a pack in each camp then gathering their animals, their voices and laughs becoming louder and more excited. This time the ride finishes with a mock battle between the young of the Gallatts and the Chiquichan. They shout, charge and laugh into the night and the air smells strongly of burning and fat.

Yeluc sits placidly in front of his fire and smokes his pipe, smiling as Silas winces at each whoop and nearby gallop.

'Can't you stop them, Yeluc? They're driving everyone mad.'

The old Tehuelche shakes his head. 'Even Yeluc young, long time ago. Even Si-las. No?'

'I was never young like that.'

'No?' The old man regards him, calmly. 'Silas good? Quiet? Sleep all the time?' He smiles, and Silas smiles back.

'Maybe I made just a little bit of noise,' he says. Maybe he did, but that was in another life. Far away, long ago, but all he has to do is close his eyes and he is back there again.

The streets full of people and the market square crammed with stalls. A puppet show, a fortune-teller, and a man who promises to cure toothache by extracting all the teeth. Stalls with potions, ointments and liniments and ridiculous claims, but best of all the seven wonders: a gigantic man and a midget, a man with six fingers on each hand and seven toes on each foot, a woman who can fold herself up so she can fit into a bucket, a man with so much hair he looks like a monkey, the fattest woman in the world and a woman with no ears.

Then that girl. Long brown hair shining as it fell down her back. A smile that made everything else disappear. A glimpse. Just a glimpse but he longs for more.

'Do you remember the fair?' he asks Megan, and she nods sadly and squeezes his hand. Another world. One far away now.

A dance in the night. Great braziers along the front. A band playing the tune of a fast dance. A complicated running in and out, swooping forward, breaking off and looping hands, pairing and breaking free, shouting, laughing, kissing. Lips that purse, lips that stay open, lips that reach for his and lips that peck. But not her lips. Fat hands giving way to thin hands: hands that are rough with hard work swap with hands that are slightly smoother. But not her hands. Grabbing, holding, grabbing again and letting go. One girl and then the next, but not her, not the one. Circles, rings, pairs. Girls that hold themselves stiff and girls that don't, girls that shirk away and girls that grab back. Girls that hold you and then hold you closer, girls that wait for you to kiss and then make you kiss deeper. Girls that smell of the field and taste of fresh butter. Then at last the one that smells of bread and tastes even better. Brown hair knotted and gnarled but her smile still intact. Megan. The one. He'd reached out and held on. Kissed her and not let her go. Knew then that he'd never let her go. Not ever.

Ah, it seems like another life now. Another Megan. That girl and then this woman. That night and now this one. Noise and now quiet. A joyous expectation and now nothing.

Thirty-seven

In the field by the river each shoot is limp and brown; some lie flat against the ground. There is something in the ground, Megan says it is some malicious spirit drowning or poisoning everything that they do. Everything dies here, he thinks, everything withers – crops and children. The shadow returns suddenly, swamping everything, weakening him. Shuddering, he kneels beside one of his shrivelled shoots and supports it with his fingers. No one can survive here. It's hopeless. He pulls the shoot from the ground and with a shout throws it towards the river. It flutters weakly and lands close to his feet. He picks it up again and with a roar runs and throws it again. This time it reaches the water. It floats and is rapidly carried to a rock pool and is caught out of reach.

John Jones has a new horse.

'Three loaves and a bag of sugar,' he says, happily, patting the animal's rump. 'I've been promised another one for tomorrow.'

'But that's not enough,' says Jacob, 'you're cheating them, surely.'

John shrugs. It is Sunday and Jacob has just finished the morning service. Mary has stayed at home with her children as usual. She has been little seen for two months claiming that her children cannot be seen in public because they have nothing decent to wear, so today John has come for all of them – and to show off his horse. Silas admires it with everyone else. It will do to pull the cart he says, and John nods his head vigorously – he has talked enough for one day. He whispers into the horse's ear and the horse shivers slightly. Then, with the aid of a clack from John's mouth and a twitch on the reins, the horse and rider trot off to their house to the west.

'Well, the Indians have horses to spare, I suppose,' says Silas.

'And I'm sure John would not have haggled.'

Caradoc and Silas catch each other's eyes and Caradoc gives one of his rare smiles. The thought of John Jones saying more than a couple of words to the Indians – or indeed anyone at all – is comically unlikely.

'Maybe I ought to do a bit of trading of my own,' Silas says, ignoring Jacob's tut.

'Remember their innocence,' Jacob says.

'Yes, I shall.'

But before Silas can do much to protect that innocence the Indians are gone. One group and then the other. Silas sees them passing his land early in the morning, following the guanaco, going west towards the Andes and the summer-breeding grounds, over a hundred of them, like ants from a disturbed nest, each one on horseback, the women carrying babies in cradles on their backs, and the horses laden down with poles and skins.

The number of them disturbs him – they seem more powerful

like this, one after the other, each one astride a horse with a few more horses trotting between. Silas sits where he is, caught in a hollow in his dry field, out of sight, pressed against the ground, not moving, not even breathing, trying to see their cottage and wishing Megan and Myfanwy had stayed in the village with the rest. But the Indians stream past peaceably, the young men making sorties to the land each side to pick up rocks, and once to peer inside Silas' brick store at the edge of his field and Silas stiffens as they look towards his cottage as if they are considering going there, but do not, until the last Indian stops beside him and looks, looks right at him, just looks and looks.

For a short time after the rest of his people have gone Yeluc lingers. He seems reluctant to go. He tells Silas he feels old, too old to keep moving and Silas looks at him surprised. But that's what you do, isn't it? That's what you've always done? The Tehuelche can't stop, can they?

'Sometimes we stop, Sil-as. Sometimes Elal call us. Sometimes he call our children. He take them on big bird in sky. Then we stop. Then we bless land, the big bird go in sky with children in feathers. Ah, Elal – he stop me many times.'

Whenever a white swan comes close Yeluc inspects it to see if it belongs to Elal. 'That how Elal go, Si-las. On back. In feathers. Some day we go too. We fly up to stars.'

'Is that the only time you've stopped, Yeluc?'

The old man shakes his head and sighs. 'No, *ffrind*, one time I stop with white man, with Cristianos.' He spits. 'I live with Cristianos. They give me name. Antonio.' He sings it again, bitterly, one syllable after the other, 'An - ton - i - o.' He stops. 'Is white man name. Is not name my mother give.'

'Your father is Cristianos?'

Yeluc laughs. 'No, no, she love the white man game. She play like this.' He mimes the dealing of cards with his hands. 'She not win. She give Yeluc away as prize. So I white man's child. I learn write, read. Many things. Then one day white man die too. Only wife left. Go live with pigs, she say. You dirty like them. So I run. I find my own kind and then I run again. They not like Antonio. Antonio sees spirits, ghosts. Bad things. Make bad things happen. So I Yeluc now.' He looks up at Silas. 'We run, yes? All of us. Cristianos, Gallatts, Tehuelche.

Run, run, run. All the time. Why, Si - las? Why we always run?'

The afternoon before he departs Yeluc visits Mary's kitchen with Seannu, Tezza and Mareea. Mary has put on a little party for them all and feeds them with freshly-made bread, cakes full of local berries and black tea. She has taken her best white tablecloth and covered their table. Yeluc's eyes open wide and seem unable to move from the table even when Silas speaks to him. His wife and her two sisters grab the freshly cut bread and ram it quickly into their mouths before they have even reached the table. Mary is trying not to smile. Silas can see her lips whiten with the effort to keep them still. Yeluc sips cautiously at his tea, declares it even better than whisky, then sits back in his chair.

'We go, my friend.'

'I know, we'll miss you.'

'We come back. Soon.'

For a few minutes they all drink and eat in silence.

'We pass our children,' Yeluc says suddenly.

Silas frowns and looks at Megan, who is sitting quietly and still in the corner. 'Where they're buried?' he asks.

'Yes, *ffrind*. We not talk. We listen. We know, here.' He slaps his chest then looks at Silas. 'They play, my friend, together – a happy place – in the stars.'

Silas swallows and looks at Megan. She sips at her tea and looks ahead at the wall. 'We believe our children go to Christ, Yeluc,' she says suddenly.

'Christ? You believe in Christ like *Cristianos*? Like thieves at Patagones?'

'Of course.'

'But you not *Cristianos*. *Cristianos* cheat, lie, thieve. You not *Cristianos*...' He bangs the table with his fist so all the women around the table start. 'No! Not *Cristianos*. You different tribe – *Galenses, Hermanos*. Not *Cristianos*.' He stands up, sweeps Mary, John, Miriam, Silas and Megan up to him one by one and then steps back again. 'My friends. *Galenses*. Not *Cristianos*. No.'

He hugs them all again and then stands by the door while his women too are hugged.

'We back soon. We not forget.'

August turns into September and then October. It is spring, a time of showers and wind, a time when crops should be bursting forth, sprouting upwards. A spring, in the wrong months, perhaps, but still a spring – but not this – not three months with hardly any rain at all. If the crops were not already dead they would perish now. In November the weather turns hot. Caradoc calls a meeting of everyone and they cram into the warehouse – men, women and children. Everyone waits, muscles tense. Caradoc's voice is strained and high. He tries to retrieve his joviality from a few months ago but fails. They have been in Patagonia sixteen months, he tells them, two winters, two springs and are on the verge of another summer. They have survived so far but can they hope to survive any longer? He goes from one man to the next, asking for reports. Silas feels Megan slump beside him and sigh. He points to each man in turn, waiting for his response.

'No yield,' Jacob says and hangs his head. Even the way he sits is subdued.

'No yield,' repeats his neighbour after him, his voice dull and exhausted.

'Nor me.'

'Enough for a mouse, no more.'

'Nothing, nothing at all.'

'Silas?'

'None from me, either. It's pointless. No one can live here.'

'John Jones?'

'Nothing – like everyone else.' Mary answers for her husband. 'Things grow at first but then something happens. It's the same everywhere.'

'Selwyn?'

'Nothing.'

Everyone is quiet, waiting.

'We should leave,' says Annie, 'we should run down what is left of the livestock and leave,' and this time several people murmur their agreement. Silas looks around. Everyone is nodding.

'Somebody is going to have to tell the government in Buenos Aires. No matter what they say we can't stay here.'

Thirty-eight

The *Denby*, the ship that Selwyn bought to bring back their supplies from Buenos Aires and wrecked on the sand bar, is their only way out. For two months they work together patching it up using parts from the ancient wreck that lies further downstream. Silas is happy. He feels lighter, as if something has flown from him. They will go somewhere else. All of them. They will start again. Together. There are enough of them to ensure their Welsh and their culture will survive. They will be free of the English, the cold, the dryness and they will be free of Edwyn Lloyd. The man still haunts the place. He is there in the houses, the distribution of the plots of land, the track in between them – even in the pattern that the plough makes as it turns over the toxic soil.

It is decided that Selwyn, Caradoc, Jacob and Silas will make the voyage to Buenos Aires. Caradoc assures everyone the ship is now seaworthy, but it seems uneasily balanced on the water, and when Silas is about to leave Megan grips his arm. 'It's not safe. Don't go.' Her voice is strained as if she is trying to keep herself from crying.

'All will be well,' he says and tries to hold her to him but she shakes him off.

'I don't want any of you to go.' She goes on to her brother, clings onto him, tries to pull him away from the gangplank. 'Megan!' he says, 'what's wrong with you? It's just a short journey up the coast, nothing to be afraid of.'

'It doesn't matter how short it is,' she says, then her voice gives way to a wail, 'don't leave me.'

Annie tries to comfort her, but she bats her aside. She watches, breathing hard, while the gangplank falls away and a small stretch of water separates them.

'There was a halo around the moon last night,' she cries out, 'didn't you see? It's a bad omen. There's going to be a storm, like there was on the *Maria Theresa*. You'll drown, all of you, and I'll have no one left.'

Silas tells them he'll stay behind, but Annie reassures him. 'Don't worry, Silas, Mary and I will take care of her. She's tired, that's all it is.'

A new moon. She hadn't mentioned it to him – but recently

she'd become more secretive and querulous. Another child hadn't come, and she'd been looking for reasons: single birds, lights in the dark, even something breaking unexpectedly when she cooked, were all signs of some malign presence. She had always tended to ponder over such things looking for a meaning: omens, spirits, the *Tylwyth Teg* – all these rested uneasily alongside ideas of God and the Holy Spirit. Megan believed firmly in everything.

They watch her from the deck as the ship moves away. Annie helps her slowly up the beach. When they are no bigger than matchsticks one of them waves from the headland. Maybe that was Megan, Silas hopes, but he knows he is wrong.

It takes them a couple of weeks to travel up the coast. It is February, midsummer, when they approach the vast estuary of the Río de la Plata and the clear water of the Atlantic becomes turbid.

'*Dulce de Leche*,' says Selwyn, standing next to Silas on the deck, 'that's what they say it's like, sweet milk boiled until it's burnt.'

Silas nods. As they round the next promontory the water begins to smell of the land, and in some ways seems to be a mixture of the two. The whole estuary is a caramelised cream, a great expanse separating Argentina from Uruguay, Buenos Aires from Montevideo. There is so much silt it hardly looks like water at all.

'We have to be careful now, stick to the channel.'

The ship edges forward in the shallow water. In the distance he can see the beaches and behind them something green – maybe a forest or at least lush vegetation. Trees.

He longs so much to reach out and touch them. Inside him something flickers into life. A memory. Walking under the trees with his mother's hand in his. The shadows of the trees touching them with their cold fingers, something snapping under his foot and the smell of fungus in his hands. His mother is singing and he is joining in; already he can sing in parts, his soprano melody and her alto accompaniment. She smiles at his voice and squeezes his hand as the song picks up speed. Soon they have reached a slope and they are running, not through necessity but because of the song, as if it is driving them forward. They lose some of their mushrooms from their basket but they don't mind. At the bottom they throw themselves down and look up at the roof of moving rafters above them and listen to the wind swishing through the branches. They grow silent listening and watching – endlessly moving patterns and shapes, a world in their leaves.

'Look, Buenos Aires!'

A hut and then another hut, then small flat-roofed houses, then larger ones. The greenness fades to brown, and the houses become higher. Then there are sounds, single voices calling out and then more, then bangs and a roar. The *Denby* approaches the land more closely, noses its way through the brown water until it is surrounded by other ships.

Silas looks around him from the deck. So much noise – a great clang of voices and colours. Selwyn tries to talk to him, but he shakes his head. No point. So many people, he had forgotten there could be so many people. They walk unsteadily along the gang plank into the dockland of one of South America's most prosperous cities. Silas is conscious of his worn boots, his frayed shirt and misshapen jacket. He pulls it down, and tries to polish his boots by spitting on them and wiping off the spittle with a rag. He thinks he can smell himself and he hasn't shaved; an untrimmed beard now accompanies his moustache.

The people around them are a mixture: some blond-haired, blue-eyed, some of them dark-haired and olive-skinned, some of them obviously Indian, and some of them have the intense black-blue glossy skin of negroes, but all of them move quickly and talk loudly. He is not used to being shoved, not used to being ignored. He tries out some of the Spanish he has learned from Yeluc and Selwyn but no one seems to be willing to stand still long enough to listen. Sweat is trickling from his armpits. He would like to remove his jacket but is afraid to expose the griminess of his shirt.

They go through slums which have masked their poverty with gaily coloured paint, peopled by women and bare-footed children who have clothes as shabby as his own, then an area of cheap hotels and boarding houses with foul-smelling gauchos playing cards outside – looking lost and ill without their horses. The place stinks. Once Silas had visited his sister in a place called Newtown: a miners' village. The houses had been built rapidly in rows and at the end of the street had been the privies: a row of seats draining into the brook behind. There were tales of old people falling in and never coming out. It seems as if these people in Buenos Aires are drowning in their own effluent too. They move quickly on, silently, so they can hold their breath. Then they turn another corner and it is as if they have entered a different world: huge stores flank impressive avenues lined with trees, affluent-looking shops look onto small tiled plazas, offices with great mortared balustrades and elaborately grilled windows loom over carefully arranged parks. Everyone is fashionably and immaculately dressed. Women sit under sunshades and sip coffee from tiny cups; men loll back and read newspapers. They walk on and the street disappears under market awnings. Farmers with polished burnt skin sell trinkets and fruit, Indians thrust out skins, feathers and blankets. Birds in cages squawk, while a monkey in a small jerkin chatters on a fat man's arm. They walk quickly through, their hands guarding their pockets.

'We're too far east,' says Selwyn.

'I thought you knew the place.'

'It's changed since I was here last.'

Caradoc tuts then turns around to face them all with his hands raised. They have reached a shaded quiet street with brightly painted walls in yellows and pinks, and at one door there is a small inoffensive-looking dog lying outside. All at once there is a burst of music and a man and a woman appear at a door shouting and in some sort of embrace. She is young, dark, her hair falling down her back in waves, her mouth picked out in red in a way none of them have ever seen before. She throws back her head and laughs and the man grabs her by the waist and pulls her back inside.

Caradoc tuts loudly, then marches on briskly, his stick tapping occasionally at the ground beside him.

'Was that a loose woman, do you think?' asks Jacob.

Selwyn grins at Silas.

Silas looks back at the door, hoping it will open again. Inside it looked cool and light, the floor tiled and through another door he thought he saw a garden, with a fountain of gently falling water. He wonders if Edwyn Lloyd is living in such a house. It seems cool, comfortable – a paradise.

They huddle closer together trying to retrace their steps. Selwyn is right; they must have come too far. The offices of the Minister of the Interior would be in a more salubrious area of the city, somewhere closer to the plazas and the women sipping their coffee. Selwyn stops a tall thin man in sombre dress and he points and indicates a direction with a nod of his head. They walk past grand churches with their doors open, releasing the smell of incense, dust and coolness to the street. Silas drops back to peer inside and marvels at the statues and small wooden confessionals.

'Come on,' says Caradoc, 'it's getting late.' The rest are moving quickly away. They hurry to catch them.

They turn off a busy main road into a street that is quieter than the rest. The buildings are plain, grey and massive. There are guards everywhere in bright uniforms and stern expressions, blocking their way and insisting that they do not enter. Eventually they find a small new building with a mortared frontage and a balcony on the first floor. It has a grand entrance, with two large doors opening into a cool tiled entrance hall. The civilian porter directs them to a room lined in dark polished wood where they wait until a young man ushers them into an office.

The sign on the door says Dr Guillermo Rawson and behind the desk is a tall balding man with an unsmiling face and melancholy eyes. He stands to meet them and holds out his hand, then says a few quick words in Spanish. The room is large. Books line two walls, and on a third is a large map. Besides a large desk there are also a couple of winged leather chairs arranged by a table near the window. There is someone there. Someone reading a book: a silhouette in the light of the window. They are just turning to Selwyn for his translation of Dr Rawson's words when the man sitting in the chair stands too. For a few minutes it is difficult to see his face, but then he steps out of the light and into the centre of the room.

'Edwyn!' Jacob says, and leaps forward with his arms outstretched.

When the *Meistr* hears their plans he is quiet. His beard has grown longer and more grey since they saw him last, and the skin beneath his eyes is creased and dark as though he is tired. He combs his long fingers through his beard then says quietly and incredulously, 'You want to move from the land the Lord has kept for us?'

Caradoc blusters and reddens a little, while the other men look down, embarrassed. Silas glares at them. In the presence of Edwyn Lloyd they seem to lose their resolve. They seem shy of him, as though their backbone dissolves away.

'*I* didn't,' says Jacob plaintively and for a few seconds there is an awkward silence.

'Nothing grows,' Caradoc says defensively, 'the shoots come up but then they just wither away.'

'But the Lord gave it to us. He wouldn't give us land that was infertile!'

Turning his back on Jacob, Caradoc turns to face Edwyn. 'Everything dies, everything. That's how it is, Edwyn. We can't carry on. We've tried our best.'

'I see.' The *Meistr* glances around the room, and looks at each man in turn. The darkness of the skin around his eyes makes them look deeply set, and as they settle on Silas he has a curious feeling of falling into them – as if Edwyn Lloyd's eyes contain their own small world.

Guillermo Rawson coughs quietly and they turn to look at him. Selwyn apologises to him in Spanish – in the excitement of seeing Edwyn Lloyd again they had almost forgotten he was there. Selwyn takes a piece of paper from his jacket. On board the *Denby* they had spent most evenings discussing what they would say to the minister of the interior and how they were going to say it. In the end Silas had suggested that someone should take notes and this is what Selwyn looks at now. He examines it for a moment as if refreshing his memory or formulating what he is to say then starts speaking slowly to the minister. It is clear immediately that if he used to be fluent in Spanish he is not any longer and after a few minutes of speech during which he has stumbled over words and Rawson's face has become fixed with a frown of puzzlement, Edwyn asks quickly if Selwyn would prefer it if he took over.

Rawson's eyes follow the conversation. 'I speak English, yes?' he says in English. 'Is better?'

Edwyn shakes his head and speaks a few words in Spanish. Rawson smiles, nods, and gestures for them all to find themselves seats.

After looking at the rest of the party Selwyn slowly hands over the sheet of paper.

Edwyn Lloyd talks quickly to Dr Rawson, and then turns back to them. 'He says that last year there were droughts everywhere and that is probably why the crops have failed. It has been exceptionally dry. People have had problems all over Argentina.'

The colonists look at each other then talk quietly together while Edwyn turns again to Rawson, talks and then turns to them again. 'He says he thinks it is too soon to give up. He thinks you should give it another try.' Then he lowers his voice. 'He seems to think he could persuade the government to come to some sort of arrangement over supplies.'

'Would they give us a ship?' Caradoc asks.

Edwyn Lloyd turns to Rawson again. 'He says he thinks that might be possible. He says to go away and think about it.'

'But how do we know what Rawson said?' Silas asks everyone later. 'How do we know Edwyn's telling us the truth? How do we know what he's telling Rawson?'

'I trust him,' says Jacob, 'I don't think he'd set out to lie.'

'Well, I think he would. In fact I think he's rather good at it. Do you remember seeing trees in our little paradise? Or lush meadows?'

Jacob is silent.

'Perhaps he exaggerated a little...' Caradoc says.

'A little? A little?' Silas is shouting now.

'Hush boy, everyone will hear you.'

They are in one of the plazas in the centre of the city. They are sitting together on a shaded piece of dried grass to keep out of the sun. Silas is thirsty, hot and angry.

He waves Caradoc's words away with an impatient flick of his hand, and continues even more stridently, 'He's obsessed, mad. Doesn't care how much he twists things... he'll do anything to make us stay in his precious valley, anything at all. He doesn't care if we starve to death or we drown in the river or Indians come and murder us all in our beds. He doesn't care how many of us die, how many children...' His voice breaks abruptly. The sob that he is trying to fight back makes his throat hurt. Richard. It hits him again. The smell of that fetid hold and the boy's hand in his, the grip weakening. Gwyneth's pale cold head resting on her mother's heaving chest. The emptiness is expanding, thoughts falling into it like the banks of a river in spate. It is all there is, nothing else. 'We can't stay,' he manages to say. 'We can't. We've tried long enough.'

Jacob reaches over to him and draws him close.

Caradoc coughs. 'We'll sort it out, *bachgen*,' he says stiffly, 'don't you worry. We'll find someone in the embassy to help us. It's too much for Edwyn Lloyd to do on his own anyway.'

Buenos Aires' river, the Río de la Plata, is the result of a confluence of two only slightly smaller monsters: the Río Paraná and the Río Uruguay. They flow through the land north of Buenos Aires. It is a wild place, tamed only at strategic intervals with forts, monasteries and small domed churches, and in this stretch of land, sandwiched between the two great rivers, is the area known as Pájaro Blanco. It is popular with settlers, one of the government officials tells them, they might want to take a look, so Silas together with Jacob and Selwyn travel along the Paraná river to investigate.

After the cool dryness of Patagonia the delta of the Paraná river is steamy and tropically hot. The river is immense, more like a slowly flowing lake, and the land each side seems well watered and fertile. Silas sits on the deck and stretches out. The sun is hot but there is a pleasant breeze from the water. There are cattle and horses in every direction and Silas wonders if it is true what he has heard – that they are the result of a few escaped horses and cattle which bred so successfully on the nourishing land that there are now thousands running wild, belonging to no one.

Living off these rich pickings are the gauchos, solitary men on horses, their dress so similar it has now become an unofficial uniform: small hard hats, brightly coloured neckerchiefs and wide-legged leather trousers with belts and sashes. They have a reputation for hard living and wildness, but as Silas passes them they look peaceful enough and contented, one or two of them waving and shouting a greeting when they are close. He imagines living here, owning his own *estancia* and clearing the land for more cattle. He would build one of these vast whitewashed buildings with their low red-tiled roofs. Then he imagines Megan and Myfanwy standing outside, scrubbed, clean, smartly dressed and well fed. They could even have servants and then Megan could be like those women he saw in Buenos Aires sipping indolently from a delicate cup. Yes, he decides, he could live here. The air is warm, the area lush and fertile. The work might be hard at first but it would not be the unrelenting grind that there was in Chubut. They could afford to relax a little, smile again, and talk.

They stop at the larger settlements. First, the city of Rosario, with its sandy beach, flat-roofed villas, bustling with boats, proud of being the place where General Belgrano first raised the Argentinean flag forty-five years ago. It is fast expanding now with European immigrants and anxious to attract more. Then they reach Santa Fe itself. Silas wanders through the streets with his mouth open; he had thought it would be a frontier town, dirty, unkempt – like the poor part of Buenos Aires. But instead he finds shady plazas, cathedrals with domes instead of spires, beaches by the river and lakes and houses that are whitewashed and bright in the sunshine. Inside, the buildings are just as bright and immaculate. There are tiled floors, white walls, elaborately carved wooden ceilings and through each window the sunlight splashes; a reminder of God, Jacob says, and for once Silas understands exactly what he means. Santa Fe. Even the sound of the place is beginning to feel good in his ears: 'Silas James of Santa Fe'. He could import his own piece of Wales up the Paraná river – dressers, settles, chairs, tables, blankets – he could even help to furnish a chapel and have his name on the family pew. It would have to be simple of course, like this Jesuit Iglesia, but without the domes on top, a fusion of Welsh and Spanish. They would go every Sunday dressed up in these smart severe costumes the locals wear: black and tailored, a little whiteness at the neck. Yes, that would suit the Welsh colonists very well, they would fit in, and like these colonists they are not afraid of a little hard work. All they need is a chance, and land that will respond to their labours.

'What do you think, Silas?'

He smiles his approval.

Edwyn Lloyd is less enthusiastic. He meets them again in the lounge of their hotel when they return to Buenos Aires. 'If we go there, we will lose our Welsh.' His voice is quiet, strained.

'If we stay at Chubut we will lose our lives.'

Edwyn Lloyd looks at Selwyn and fastens him with his eyes. 'You haven't given it a fair chance.'

'We nearly starved, Edwyn,' Selwyn says, 'you weren't there to see us.'

'Nevertheless we should go back, try again.'

'No, Edwyn. We've decided,' Caradoc says, 'we are going back to the colony to tell them our choices, while you sort out the details. We'll leave it to them to decide, of course, but I'm sure I know what they'll say.'

Edwyn Lloyd sits abruptly, his face set. Silas looks at him, trying to decide what he sees there – maybe anger, defeat, or resolve – it is difficult to say. His eyes are staring into the distance, the shadows beneath them emphasising their blueness, and as Silas examines his long straight nose, his glossy lush hair and full beard, he remembers what Megan told him once – that Edwyn Lloyd's face was beautiful, perhaps the most beautiful face she had ever seen. He becomes aware of Silas staring and his eyes change, flick suddenly from looking at some distant thing to something closer. He smiles tightly, 'Ah, Silas, *ffrind*, what do you say?'

'What I have always said, of course – we should leave the Chubut and find somewhere better.'

'Ah, of course, you too.' The black beard shakes.

Thirty-nine

Like the Indians the colonists pack horses and ride. It doesn't take them so long to reach Port Madryn this time. They follow the scar that the Argentine soldiers made almost two years ago. There is no getting lost, no running out of water. They know exactly where they will go and exactly what they will do. First they slaughter most of the animals that remain: there is not a single pig left, and not a single sheep. Then they pack all they can carry, and then that little bit extra that they love. Then, just before they kick the rump of the nearest cow to send it on its way in front of them, they take firebrands and touch each hearth with its flames. They smell it burn. They can hear it crackling behind them and they don't look back. What they have started the Indians will finish. Then they follow the track until they reach Port Madryn again. And then they stop and look around them. The cold beach. The caves. The sea. It is as though the last two years have never happened.

The decision had been simple and made soon after Silas, Caradoc, Selwyn and Jacob had returned.

'We can't stay here.'

'The Río Negro is no better.'

'Santa Fe might be worth a try.'

'So we go there.'

'Agreed.'

'Any dissenters?'

Of course there are always some.

'Overruled.'

Caradoc had folded his arms, nodded and told them he would return with Silas and Jacob to Buenos Aires on the new clipper that brought them here to report their decision. Dr Rawson, Caradoc reassured everyone, would be quite happy.

Selwyn would stay with his wife to help look after his child, a large, healthy boy, who had entered the world very noisily but safely.

That night Megan had clung to Silas and begged him to stay with her too. 'Tell me about Santa Fe again,' she'd said, and her eyes had smiled as he had talked.

'We want another child.'

And they had looked at Myfanwy asleep beside them.

'She needs a brother or sister.'

And for the rest of that night she had been his Megan again; drawing him to her, soft and smiling, murmuring when at last she slept.

In the morning she'd clung to him again. 'Don't go.'

But he had shaken his head. 'I have to.'

At Patagones their ship drops anchor. They have made good time from the Chubut, but now the captain needs to take on more supplies. Patagones is not a place they particularly relish, though it is pretty enough, with steeply inclined streets of adobe houses, a church and fort. Silas leans over the rail of the modern little ship that has brought them here and waits for the instruction to disembark. There is something run down about Patagones, he thinks, the houses are not quite white, the adobe crumbles away from the walls and the scrubby vegetation has been allowed to grow unchecked over walls. Yeluc hates the people here, he reminds himself, and looks at the small taverns, each one faded, and the plaster chipped. Stray dogs wander around the place and there are a couple of lame-looking horses eating whatever weed is growing from the track. They do not appear to belong to anyone; perhaps they have strayed in from the

Pampas. Silas is glad they are not staying long.

'What's that?' Jacob grabs his arm tightly. 'Look Silas, is that what I think it is?'

The *Denby*. They'd recognise it anywhere. They know each plank of wood, each kink in the ropes, each patch in the sails. She had been declared unseaworthy by the port authorities in Buenos Aires and they had been forbidden to return in her, yet someone has managed to sneak her out, someone who must be good at persuading people and getting his own way.

'Edwyn Lloyd!'

Silas hangs onto the rails, a sudden feeling of dread making him weak. Jacob sounds so joyful, so excited to see the man. It is as if the sight of him causes him to lose all sense. If Edwyn Lloyd is here it can only mean that he has something to tell them, something that couldn't wait.

'I bring great news,' he says as soon as they see him. Silas realises that his voice has regained its strength – in Buenos Aires he was intense but quiet, his voice hardly raised above an exclamation – on board the *Denby* it booms over the deck. 'We have another agreement with the government. I have managed to persuade them to support us a little longer in the Chubut. We can stay, *ffrindiau!*' he says – as if it is what they had always wanted.

He stands with his arms raised slightly from his side as if he is going to embrace them. His eyes are wide, light, elated. 'Isn't it wonderful? They have agreed to most of the conditions that I've asked for. We will be well-supplied, comfortable for at least another year.'

Jacob is smiling as if he has seen something he loves.

Caradoc, with a puzzled frown, looks at Edwyn and then at Jacob. 'What are you talking about, man?' he says crossly. 'We told you – we've had enough. We left them all packing up to go. They'll be waiting for us at Port Madryn by now.'

Edwyn's face loses its shine. 'You've told them to leave?'

'Yes. It was what we decided. We can't just tell them to turn round and go back.'

'But they have to. The Argentines have decided. It's the Chubut or nothing. They won't help us go anywhere else. They won't countenance it.'

'But... but... I thought...' Caradoc's splutterings end in silence.

He presses his lips together and glares at Edwyn.

Edwyn turns to Silas. The *Meistr's* smile is wide, loose, quite unlike the tight smiles he used to smile before. It doesn't stay in one place but seems to slop around his face. A lie. Silas is certain of it. There is no new agreement, no promise of supplies – just some notion that has appeared in Edwyn's head. He's lied before, why shouldn't he be lying now?

They take a bunk in the *Denby*; as Edwyn says, it gives them more of a chance to discuss what they will do next. Silas lies in the cabin alone, thinking of the Chubut and then the Paraná: one river unpredictable, treacherous, opaque and sluggish, the other like a small languid sea, warm, the surface catching small sparks of sunlight, clean and transparent. Santa Fe was like a dream of a glittering paradise; somewhere Megan would be happy and like the girl that he married. He punches his hammock. He is determined to go. There is no reason to trust anything Edwyn Lloyd says. Even if it is true that the government will no longer help them move elsewhere there have to be other ways. There will be others who will want to come too, the Jones family perhaps or the Williams. Edwyn Lloyd has cheated them once; they will not want to be cheated again.

Yet Edwyn Lloyd seems to have lost none of his ability to persuade. Jacob, of course, had been like a faithful hound whose beloved master had returned; he had keeled over immediately, wagging his tail and exposing his pink belly. Caradoc, however, is proving more difficult to convert.

Silas sees Edwyn Lloyd eye him up, consider his strategies and decides on offering a bone. The first one proves insufficiently enticing.

'The Argentines have been most generous,' he says, 'they say they are going to extend our grant indefinitely.'

'We had a grant before, Edwyn; we can't go on like that forever. We need to be independent.'

'It was an extremely dry year. Everyone is talking about it.'

'But that could happen again, couldn't it? What would we do then?'

The four men row ashore, walk around the streets, buy a little meat and bread from one of the traders there – a rough-looking man with a large elaborate crucifix shining from the grime of clothes – and sit on the shore to eat and drink. Behind them there are shouts and raucous laughter from one of the taverns, and presently an Indian staggers out, his face pale. He manages just a few paces before he tips over and is sick onto the track.

'This is an evil place,' Jacob says. 'Full of the Devil's work.'

'And we should get as far away as we can,' Silas says.

Caradoc nods. 'As soon as possible.'

By evening Edwyn is trying again. When he thinks there is no one else around he corners Caradoc on the deck of the ship. Silas presses himself against the cabin and watches unseen.

The *Meistr* smiles broadly and holds out his arms as if welcoming Caradoc into an embrace. 'Caradoc! I've been meaning to speak to you.'

Caradoc plants his stick in front of him. 'You have? What for?' His eyes travel warily over the *Meistr's* face, and the tip of his tongue licks the inner edge of his top lip.

'Jacob believes that without you no one would have survived.'

Although he shakes his head and tuts, Caradoc is clearly pleased. He stands a little taller and a small smile settles on his lips. 'Does he, indeed.'

'Yes, he says that the way you dealt with the Indians was masterful.'

'Well, I just used my common sense, and of course as a minister...'

There is a pause, and Silas shifts slightly to ease the numbness in his foot. He manages to glance at their faces – both are cautiously smiling.

Over dinner the talks begin again.

'How many have said they wish to go to Santa Fe?' asks Edwyn, 'It was unanimous, I think you said?'

'No, not unanimous.' Jacob tells him. 'There are some who wished to stay.'

'How many?'

'I'm not sure.'

Edwyn turns to Caradoc. 'What do you say? More than twenty?'

'Yes.'

'A fair proportion then?'

Caradoc shifts warily in his seat. 'I wouldn't say that.'

Edwyn smiles again. 'I know, I know, it must be difficult to tell. But the rest – do they all want to go to Santa Fe?'

'No, some of them have said they'd prefer Buenos Aires, or even this place – God help them.'

'So the colony would be divided. Is that so?'

'Well yes...'

'And so there would be no Welsh spoken within a generation.'

'Well...'

'Reverend Gabriel Thomas has seen this, Caradoc. Unless a colony is large, self-sufficient and isolated from more dominant tongues, the language and culture are lost.'

Caradoc is silent for a few seconds and examines the watch chain threaded into his waistcoat.

'How can you say that?' asks Silas. 'Surely every case is different.'

Edwyn shakes his head.

'Maybe it would be better if we were try to stay together,' Caradoc says quietly. He looks up at Edwyn and nods curtly. 'Maybe it would be better to do as Edwyn says – stay in the Chubut and give it another try.'

Silas knows that the *Meistr* is looking at him but he refuses to look up.

'Silas?' Edwyn says gently. It is halfway to a question.

Silas keeps his head bowed and says nothing. He is alone and defeated.

'Silas, I need to have the assent of you all.'

It is as if something is opening inside. A gulf of nothingness, and if he moves or says anything he will fall into it.

'Silas?' Edwyn touches him lightly on the arm. 'Will you come with me and take some air on the deck?'

There is not much to see: land, river, land, ocean, land, river, land ocean. For two circuits neither of them speaks.

At the start of the third Edwyn stops. He smiles. 'What's troubling you, *fy ffrind*?'

The same smile that he smiled at Caradoc. The same gesture. Silas speaks through clenched teeth. 'Are we friends?'

Edwyn's hands drop. 'I would certainly hope so,' he says

quietly, and for a few seconds holds Silas' eyes with his own.

'Why are you being so obstinate, Silas?' he says at last. 'The Chubut is our only hope now. Why do you refuse to see that?'

'Because if we go back there we will all die. Nothing will grow.'

'But last year was dry – an exception. Dr Rawson told you that.'

'What has he told us? We have learnt everything we know through you – or Selwyn.'

'Don't you trust me, Silas?'

Silas is looking at the ocean. It is morning and the sun is reflected there, as if it is lighting a shimmering passageway east. Home to Wales. He feels an ache in his chest. It catches his breath. He glances briefly at Edwyn. 'No,' he says, defiantly looking at him. 'You've lied to us more than once, deceived us and then abandoned us. Why should I believe anything you tell me now?'

Edwyn Lloyd lowers his eyes slightly and then turns away. 'I was doing my best, Silas,' he says softly. 'I know I made mistakes, but I was just trying to do what I could.' He pauses, takes a breath. 'I know we shall succeed in the Chubut if we give it time.'

'We gave it time! You haven't been there, you left us.'

'I was exiled.'

'You exiled yourself – to a warm civilised city.'

'It's not what you think. It wasn't easy. I had to work hard on the colony's behalf. I had to do things I didn't like. I had to…' He pauses, breathes in deeply and continues. 'I had to make friends, influential ones that could help us. I had to do certain things, things I didn't like… my wife, Cecilia…'

'Is in Wales.' Silas finishes for him meaningfully.

'She found it difficult…'

'But at least she didn't starve. At least her children didn't die.'

Edwyn doesn't reply. Silas waits. He cannot see his face any more; it is turned from him. His narrow shoulders are slightly hunched. Silas notices that his jacket is hanging from them as if a much larger man used to be inside. It quakes slightly.

'Perhaps we can continue this discussion later,' Edwyn says, and without turning around he walks quickly to the cabin and shuts the door.

The next time Silas encounters the *Meistr* he looks drawn – in just a few hours he seems to have lost his colour and the skin under his eyes has darkened and sagged. The eyes themselves look at Silas sorrowfully and appealingly. Silas is careful not to feel pity. The man is a liar, he tells himself. A cheat. Nevertheless when Edwyn opens his mouth he listens.

'Silas,' he says, 'please think again. I need your support.'

'Why? It seems to me you have everything worked out.'

They are alone at the captain's table. Edwyn's voice is quieter than Silas has ever heard it before, weak in fact, as if he is ill or very old. For a few seconds there is silence. The clock on the wall ticks.

'Silas, I need a strong man on my side. A partner. Someone who is not easily swayed and knows his own mind.' Edwyn pauses a few seconds, tilts his head as he waits for him to respond but Silas says nothing. 'The whole venture depends on you now, *brawd*. I need you to agree. Only if the decision is unanimous can we hope to start again in Chubut.'

The clock ticks again. Silas thinks of the cold Chubut river and then he thinks of the warmer gold-flecked Paraná.

Eventually Edwyn sighs and then clears his throat. 'Silas, I have a proposal. Would you be willing to give the Chubut another nine months before coming to a decision?'

'I've made my decision.'

'But it's the wrong one, man!' His voice cracks. He looks down, rubs his forehead in his hands. 'Just give it a little more time.'

'We've given it enough.'

'Please, Silas.'

'No.'

'At the end of it, if there is no improvement, I shall recommend that the colony is removed to Santa Fe. I shall put everything I have behind that instead. You will have my backing and you will have Dr Rawson's and the Emigration Committee's in Liverpool. I shall see to it. But please give the Chubut another chance, *ffrind*. Please.'

Nine months. So much can happen in nine months. Silas stands and looks out of the cabin window at the shore. There is a woman sitting at the door of her cottage, knitting.

'Silas?'

He stands, walks the short length of the room and back again. A child comes running up to the knitting woman and she passes her a little wool to play with. The same scene could be repeated anywhere, even in the Chubut. In spite of everything, there have been moments of contentment, if not happiness. Another nine months. Perhaps they could survive. If they moved to Santa Fe they would have to start all over again. Find a space, build a house, and clear the ground. Tiredness moves up quickly from his legs. They couldn't do it alone. But even if he got a few people to come with them, without any aid from the government it would all end in disaster. He looks at Edwyn and nods once.

It is as if the sun has suddenly come out. Edwyn stands, smiles, and gives Silas a light punch to his chest. 'Good,' he says, 'I'll send Guillermo a message and let him know. He wanted us all in agreement. He sent me after you. The government had come to a decision to back us just after you'd all sailed: but if we couldn't all agree there'd be nothing for any of us.' Then, just as he goes through the door the smile changes to something more familiar and hidden.

That private smile. Silas feels cheated but he doesn't quite know why. He kicks at the table leg. It collapses at its hinge and the table thuds against the wall. Stupid. He throws himself down on a chair. The shimmering dream of happiness darkens and disappears into the widening void. Stupid, stupid, stupid. He thumps his head hard against the wooden wall. Nine months. How could he throw away his dream so easily? He thumps it again. Nine months in a wilderness, in the cold, in the wind.

On the shore the woman continues to knit. Nine months before he sees paradise. Somehow part of the fault is hers. It is as if Edwyn has told her to knit, told her to mesmerise him with her hands. Told her to trick him. If he could, he would reach out, snatch the needles from her hands, take her work and unravel it, row by row, stitch by stitch.

Forty

The colonists are waiting for them, as promised, on the beach at Port Madryn. Silas sees their smoke as soon as they sail into the circular bay past the Península Valdés. There are several fires, a collection of irregular dark shapes on the pale sand, and when they get closer, he hears them shouting and calling. The old *Denby* drops anchor where the *Mimosa* creaked two years ago. Everything looks the same. They row ashore and the colonists stream out to greet them, exclaiming at the sight of Edwyn.

Myfanwy's face is a miniature of her mother's. She holds up her arms to be picked up, first by Silas, then by Jacob.

Megan quickly kisses him. 'I've missed you,' she says, curtly, 'don't you dare go again.'

They are using the caves in the cliffs for shelter, and even though it is cold and wet, at least it is out of most of the wind and the rain. Some of the women and children have slept there while others have sheltered as best they can in crude huts, assembled from what remains from two years before.

Soon they are once more sitting by the fire on the beach roasting pieces of meat. It is already dusk. Annie Williams' baby grumbles in her arms and as she rocks him back to sleep she looks at the *Denby*. 'When are the other ships coming?' she asks, 'because we won't all fit on that.'

The mumbling of voices stops. Everyone looks expectantly at Edwyn.

'There will be no other ships,' Caradoc says, 'we're going to stay in Chubut. It is decided.'

Silas hangs his head. There is a short shocked silence.

'You have spoken for all of us?' Mary asks incredulously, 'what gives you the right to do that?'

'All the representatives were in agreement,' Caradoc says coldly.

'All of them?'

When he nods, she turns open-mouthed to Silas and says quietly, 'And you too, Silas? I thought we could depend on you.'

Silas shakes his head. He can't speak. He can't explain. He looks at Edwyn with narrowed eyes and the man merely nods back.

'Of course you can go somewhere else if you choose,' Edwyn tells Mary, 'anywhere you like.'

Mary looks at him and snorts.

'But I'm afraid you will not get any help from the Argentine government if you do,' he adds.

For a few minutes the colonists are silent.

'But we've slaughtered our animals!' John says suddenly.

The man rarely speaks in public and it is startling to hear his voice. It is as if it wakes the people around him, and several of them start shouting out complaints.

'And set light to our houses!'

'And traipsed miles over the desert with the children.'

'And how are we going to get back there again, anyway?' Joseph Jones blurts out.

Edwyn blinks. Silas notices that the man's fingertips are trembling. He turns to Selwyn. 'Is all this true?'

Selwyn nods and Annie slips her arm around his shoulder. 'It wasn't his idea,' she says, 'everyone decided together.'

Edwyn sighs and shuts his eyes. He brings his fingertips together and rests his chin on his forefingers, and his head sways slightly. 'There is a solution,' he murmurs. 'All is not lost.'

They wait a few moments but the *Meistr* says nothing else.

'I'm sure the Chiquichan will lend us a few horses, if we ask them,' says Caradoc quickly.

'Yes, I'm sure they will, if we can find a way of sending word.'

But Edwyn doesn't seem to be listening. His eyes are shut and he is sitting motionlessly by the fire. The people around him start to murmur, but Jacob holds up his hands to quieten them.

'But we can't go back to Chubut now,' Mary says, taking no notice. 'I can't understand how this has happened. We were all agreed to go and start again in Santa Fe.'

'We've been tricked,' Silas says, looking at Edwyn. He speaks as though someone has him by the throat.

Everyone is silent, looking slowly from Silas to Edwyn and back again.

'We could have gone to Santa Fe, we could have gone anywhere we like, but somehow this man has stopped it.'

Everyone waits, but Edwyn doesn't stir. His eyes are still shut; his body still immobile, but underneath his beard his mouth is beginning to move. There are small flashes of white as his teeth shine through. Then, suddenly, he opens his eyes and rises to his feet. He goes to stand where the fire lights his face and smiles at them all.

'My most beloved brothers and sisters, how very grateful I am to you. How you have greeted me so warmly! I have to confess I was a little apprehensive after all that had happened, but when I saw you all… when I saw that your spirit wasn't broken, despite everything… how very glad it made me feel – that I knew you all. That you were my people. How very proud! *My* people, I would tell Dr Rawson, again and again. I know them. They will not give up. They work hard. They have faith. They are stubborn and are not afraid of a little adversity.

'Ah, my valiant friends, I can do nothing more than admire you all. The way you have learnt from the Indians! The way you have co-operated. It is unheard of. Unique.'

Everyone is quiet now. Several are smiling almost as broadly. Silas sinks back onto his heels and groans. The man has so many tricks.

'It has been hard everywhere, a strange unusual time of drought and everyone has been suffering – but Dr Rawson says that none have coped as well as the Welsh. He was talking of sending someone down to Patagonia to learn from you. You can't give up now. Today is the twenty-eighth of July 1867, *brodyr a chwiorydd*. Two years to the day since we landed here. As Dr Rawson remarked, it takes a special people to make a desert bloom. And the Welsh are those people!'

'Amen, *brodyr*!'

Several people cheer.

'Are we going to do it? Are we going to work together and show the Argentines what we can do?'

'Yes!' Several of the men are standing now, clapping and cheering. Silas looks at Megan, and even she is smiling. Silas shifts on his haunches, and goes to stand, but a hand clamps down on his shoulder. Mary. She shakes her head at him. 'Not now,' she mouths.

Silas looks around him. The only eyes that meet his own are Selwyn's, Mary's and Megan's. His wife's smile slides from her mouth then she reaches out, tries to touch him on the arm, but he walks away up the beach. All lies. He wraps his jacket around him and shivers in the wind. The wind – it is needling his eyes with dust and sucking away moisture from his throat. He swallows but the hurt in his throat will not go. That man has destroyed everything. He reaches one of the dilapidated sheds and beats at the walls with both fists. He cannot stay here. He will take Megan and Myfanwy and whoever else who wants to come with him and walk across the desert up to Patagones if he has to, and if no one will leave with him he will go on his own.

'Dadda?' A small hand reaches into his own. She has run after him. He reaches down and picks her up and sobs into the soft cushion of her hair.

Forty-one

The houses are remarkably intact; the roofs destroyed of course, but the walls and even some of the furniture still untouched. The colonists immediately start to work on them; the wind sweeping through, helping them get rid of the smell of ashes. When the Indians had realised that the fort was empty they tried to continue what the colonists had started – re-lighting roofs that had become extinguished, and throwing on more fuel where they could in an attempt to make the houses uninhabitable. The *Galenses* had turned out to be welcome neighbours; the *Cristianos*, however, were not. But then the rain had come and put out everything.

Silas' own house had required just some repair and then some cleaning. They had swept it out, and made more crude furniture from driftwood on the beach. Then he had repaired the stove and mended the doors and windows using timber from the old wreck in the river. Within a few weeks it was better than it had been.

Even though it is November and the middle of spring, Silas and the two older Jones boys have decided to go out looking for game. They are still waiting for the promised supplies from Buenos Aires and the stocks of food are low. Everyone is a little hungry and foraging for anything they can find. The guanaco and rhea have migrated inland to the breeding grounds of the west and the Indians, of course, have followed them. There is little left near the coast but a few of the smaller mammals and birds. It is hard work catching anything but every day he, Joseph and Ieuan manage to catch some small animal to eat. The rest of the colonists are busy clearing and turning over their ground, but Silas doesn't bother. He hunts to feed his family now but he is doing nothing to prepare for the future. Just five months left now and they will go to Santa Fe.

The sun becomes hotter as the summer approaches – a burning smouldering light with no clouds to filter it. He remembers last year, how he'd worked so hard with the hand plough, how he'd laboured with Megan pulling up weeds from the fertile-looking stretch of land near the river, how he'd sown seed and the land had been green with seedlings, and how at first they'd grown and everyone had been happy – and then they had all withered and died. No, he decides, there is no point labouring again if they will be gone from here in a few months. The thought of leaving lightens his step. He watches the rest of the colonists at work by the river, bending, pulling, and then bending again. Every back aches. Each pair of hands is rubbed raw. For nothing, he thinks, nothing at all.

Silas walks to the edge of his plot and looks at it; like all the other plots it consists of a dry dead-looking part and a more fertile-looking portion beside the river. If seed comes back from Buenos Aires he will plant it, but he will waste no time preparing the ground near the river. Instead he will plant the seed in the ground that is clear already because nothing grows there – the earth is pale and cracked with long deep fissures. This, at least, will be easy to dig. He tests the earth with his spade – it is soft and easily worked. He looks at the patch and considers it – yes, this will do. It will not be much effort but at least no one will be able to say he hasn't tried at all.

Forty-two

Megan sniffs him cautiously, and then steps aside. Sometimes he smells too strongly of the pigs or the sheep or the dung of cattle.

'I'm sorry,' she says, 'I've not been feeling well – that is, I've been feeling sick.' She looks at him meaningfully and pats her stomach.

He dives towards her but she backs away, laughing. 'Later,' she mouths.

Beside them Myfanwy is practising her letters using chalk on the table. She looks up at him and smiles and Silas pats her on the head.

'She would improve with some paper,' Megan says.

He nods. At last their long-awaited supplies have come, and together with the food, seed and agricultural equipment he has heard there are a few less essential things like paper and ink and books for the children.

'Jacob's talking about starting a proper school.'

Silas had snorted. 'It's too early for that.'

'No Silas, it's important. Just because...' She stops and finds something to pick up from the floor. Just because you can't read, that's what she meant to say, but she won't. She straightens up and smoothes out an ache in her back and looks at him. 'The children need to learn to read. Books, paper, pens, and pencils – they make things feel less desperate. Anyway, Jacob says everything's waiting for you.'

Silas had been putting off going to the warehouse for days.

'Get it over with, man,' Mary had told him. 'You've got to do it sometime. Take the cart.'

'Two sacks each, that's how it works out,' Edwyn says.

.   Silas takes his without comment.

'We will have a harvest this time, Silas, this seed is superior, by all accounts.'

He nods and lifts a sack onto his shoulder. He will bide his time. Only five months before they leave – less than one hundred and fifty days.

'If we all work together, we will succeed, don't you agree?'

Edwyn holds Silas' second sack against his body and waits for him to reply.

Silas sighs. 'No, I am not agreed. We both know what will happen. The seed will be sown and then it will die and then we will leave. All of us. This stupidity will stop and we will start again – somewhere green, with grass and trees and cows that I have seen with my own eyes.'

'It will grow, Silas. It is important that you believe that. Only if you believe in success will you succeed.' Edwyn tries to fix him with his eyes but Silas looks determinedly away.

'Are you going to give me that grain, or aren't you?'

'Why will you not give the man a chance?' asks Jacob plaintively, striding beside him as Silas determinedly leads his horse and cart out of the village. 'He has done so much for us all. We should all be grateful, all of us.'

'I can never be grateful to that cheat, that liar – you, of all people should be able to understand that. Richard and Gwyneth would still be with us, if it wasn't for him – and his lies.'

'You can't know that, Silas.'

Silas stops. The man is always so earnest and righteous.

'We should try to love one another. Turn the other cheek.'

Silas grips the horse's reins so tightly the horse is beginning to strain away. 'I can't.'

'You can, Silas, pray, ask for forgiveness.'

He turns so that Jacob can see his face. The minister makes a couple of backward steps, his eyes blinking.

'Me – ask for forgiveness?' Silas' voice cracks. 'What about him?'

'Edwyn doesn't need to.'

Silas lets go of the reins. 'Go away from me, Jacob,' he says carefully, keeping his voice steady. His hands curl into fists, and rise slightly in front of him.

Jacob blinks more rapidly and takes another step away. 'I'm just saying you should examine your conscience, Silas. It is not good for your soul to hate a man as much as you do.'

'GO AWAY FROM ME!' He makes a single lunge forwards, his fist an extension of his words and Jacob's teeth clink together like small pieces of china.

Silas stops and looks at his hands. It's as if they don't belong to him. As he watches they fall back down to his sides.

Jacob feels his mouth. 'You hit me!' he says incredulously, looking at the blood on his hand. Then his round astonished eyes travel up to Silas' face and for a few seconds stay there while a small, satisfied smile tugs at his lips and a dribble of blood appears. 'You hit me!' he says again, wondering, and then scurries away towards the fort.

Silas washes his hand in the river and tells no one. After a day of deliberately forcing the scene from his mind, he finds he can convince himself it has never happened at all. There was no blood.

Jacob's teeth didn't rattle. On Sunday he makes his usual excuse that, like many of the colonists, he feels his clothing is too scruffy and unsuitable for chapel. It is weeks since he has been.

'I shouldn't think the Lord minds how you are dressed, as long as you praise him,' Megan says, as she lowers herself into the cart with Myfanwy. She is heavier now and the cart sinks beneath her. 'They miss your voice.'

'But not the rest of me, then.'

'Silas!' But he notices that she doesn't deny it.

He is out in the field sowing the seed when she returns. At first he doesn't see her. He has made a brush from a few branches of thorn and has attached this to the horse. Now he is coaxing the horse up and down the field to brush the loose earth over the seed. It is easy this way because the soil is dry and friable. Too dry, too friable – it is just like last year – if there is any growth it will be short-lived.

He stops at the head of the field nearest the cottage. Megan is on her own, Myfanwy off with Miriam and the three younger Jones children, and for a few seconds he catches her just standing, gazing over the fields at nothing, short strands of hair playing in the wind. Her face is still, but he can tell she is angry: her fingers straddle her hips, and her chin thrusts upwards. Then she sees him, and turns to face him.

It is hot, late spring, and she is wearing a thin blouse, her best Sunday one, newly made from some pale material that came with the last supplies. She waits before he is almost beside her before she speaks.

'Is it true?' she asks.

'Is what true?'

'That you punched my brother?'

'It was hardly that.'

For a while she glares at him. 'Are you going to tell me what happened? Or am I just going to have to rely on what they say?'

After he has told her, she looks distractedly around her. Her hands clench and unclench. Say something, he thinks. Anything. She walks a few feet away from him and kneels down to inspect the soil while he stands exactly where she's left him: stiffening, waiting.

'Why are you planting the grain *here*?' she says at last. She keeps her head down so he can't see her face. Her voice is strained, tight, as if she is struggling to keep it under control.

He wants to run to her, shake her, make her tell him he's right and they're wrong. But all he does is swallow. 'Because it's easier,' he says. 'It is all going to die anyway; there's no point looking for work.'

'But the soil by the river looks more fertile.' One careful word and then the next. Ignoring all that he'd said before, as if it means nothing.

'I don't care!' His voice comes out too loud, too close to a wail.

She makes a couple of steps towards him and grabs his hand. Her eyes are glistening; too wet. 'Oh Silas, please try and make it up with them. We've got to live here. You've got to get on with them. I want to be included.'

Silas snorts.

'I can't bear it, Silas!'

He turns away from her and strides across the field that the horse has just brushed, making large deep footprints in the soil.

'Silas, stop!' She is coming after him. Her smaller boot prints are beside his, two for each of his one. She catches his hand. He looks sideways at her. The slight bulge beneath her skirt is lifting her hem a few inches above the ground. The thought of this new life calms him and makes him triumphant. His child. There is nothing more precious. Maybe he should feel pity, perhaps try to forgive – just a little – but he can't; every time he tries he discovers new lies, new deceits. Richard. He closes his eyes. If he forgave Edwyn he would betray his son, his daughter. Thoughts creep in on their own. It's as if they're falling into a void: the boy's head arched back on his pillow gasping for breath, one wheeze and then another; an old man's lungs in a young boy's chest. He opens his eyes and looks at Megan. Her eyes are searching for his now: anxious, slightly beseeching. 'Please try,' she says.

He reaches out and draws her close before she can struggle free. 'If we stand together,' he says, 'nothing can defeat us. We don't need anyone else.'

He releases her and she frowns and smoothes down her dress as if she is brushing away the impression of him. 'No, Silas, I need more than that. Two are not enough. A couple can't survive here on their own.' She stands upright and regards him. 'Will you try to fit in? Would you just agree to do that?'

He nods resignedly.

'Thank you.' She steps smartly up to him and kisses him hard on the lips. She pats her stomach fondly, then looks around her. 'Look at the river!' she says abruptly.

It is twenty yards in front of them, part of a shimmering silver meander. 'It is high, this year,' she says, 'have you noticed? Much higher than last, I think.'

'Perhaps.'

'I know so. Last year it stopped down there.' She points. 'Don't you remember?' She points to an area now covered in water. She looks around her. They have had to climb steadily to get onto the levee made by the floods. 'Look, it's higher than our land this year... Silas! Look, will you?' She stamps her foot and he stirs – he had been gazing at her in a reverie, not listening.

'The river, look at the river.' She points with her arm stretched out. 'It's higher here than where you've planted the seed.' He follows her finger and nods thoughtfully. The river is higher. Along its length there are several levees of gravel and sand, left there by floods of high water, and behind this the land where he has just sown the seed is lower and drier.

'You know, if you dug a channel through there, and it would only have to be a narrow gully, the water would spill through. You could water the land as much as you liked and then block it off again.'

'Not sure it's worth it.'

'It would only be a small channel – I could help.'

'No you can't!'

'Well, I shall do it unless you say you'll do it.'

He looks at her. She has her hands on her hips again, her feet are planted firmly apart and her lips pressed tightly together, her bottom lip protruding. Her determined look – it's a long time since he's seen it. He knows it is pointless to try to resist but he offers her a token anyway: 'Maybe in a few weeks if these seeds show no sign of sprouting.'

'No, now, Silas.'

'But it's Sunday!'

'All right, tomorrow then.'

It is decided. Megan grins at her victory.

The digging is not quite as easy as Megan thinks it is. The ground is either weed-choked or so friable it is difficult to stand and gain purchase. At last he manages to enlarge a small natural opening and work backwards. The water pours in behind him as if it is grateful to be let out of the river. It swirls forcefully at the sides of the gully until they collapse and the channel widens quickly behind him. He feels the water lapping at his feet and he digs more quickly, wondering if he has done the right thing and then worrying that he will be able to close it again. He digs a little deeper and the water seems to gurgle appreciatively, nudging at the soil, urging him onwards. He reaches the edge of his field and looks back. The water is forming small lakes and then tributaries of its own as more and more of it flows onto the land. But it is calmer now; the initial flood has slowed. He breathes out loudly. His feet are wet and most of his legs too, but he is happy. There is a hot breeze and it is quite pleasant to feel the coolness of the water. He clears away the final stretch of gravel and the water gently escapes into the lower ground. It seeps forward without disturbing anything and the soil, which is a rich-looking black and smells strongly of loam, is soon covered in a few inches of water. He finds he can block off the river easily with a few shovels of the dug out soil, and then makes another small channel connecting this higher field to one that is lower to the east. Soon there is a shallow lake of water over all his land. He calls Megan and Myfanwy to see. A stray flamingo comes to look too, makes a swift haughty inspection, and departs. Then Myfanwy calls the younger Jones children, and they come to gawp too, but by then the water has almost gone, sucked away by the thirsty ground. Silas inspects his barrier to the river and ensures it is tight – a little controlled inundation is welcome but he doesn't want to wake up tomorrow morning to find his cottage surrounded by a lake.

In another week there will be just four months to go. But today he has to go to the village, and the shortest route is along the river. This errand is something he has put off for as long as possible again, reluctant to face Jacob or Edwyn – but now there are things that he needs, and he is hoping that he will be lucky and Selwyn or Caradoc or one of the other men will be in charge. It is such a beautiful day he has decided to walk alongside his horse and cart to give the animal a rest. There is a cool breeze providing some relief against the heat of the early sun and even the Chubut is looking desolately beautiful. He looks around him indolently. He will take his time – he has little else to do. The sky is reflecting in the river and it is bluer than he has ever seen it before. Beyond it the ground is so dried out it is a bright yellow. He admires the intense colours. He will tell Megan about it when he returns. He clears a slight mound. He sniffs at the dry sweet air. The breeze is unusually slight. In front of the blue river the soil will be a rich brown. Brown, blue, yellow: the colours of the Patagonian desert.

He stops. Not brown but green. Bright green, as if the blue river and the yellow ground beyond have been mixed together on a palette. As he comes closer he notices something stranger still: this green is changing with the wind – darker then lighter. Yellow-green and then moss-green. A haze: sap-green, leaf-green, new-growth-green.

Silas had divided his plots into rectangles and has brushed in the seed in turn – one direction for one patch and then another for the next. It is like a patchwork of fragments of the same cloth with different naps – the weft of one against the warp of another.

He starts to run then stops. Stands, and then looks again. The ground is covered in small green shoots, rough row after rough row.

He looks again. He calls, once: his voice high with excitement: 'Megan, come and see this!'

Then Megan is turning with her basket of clothes; trying to run and then giving up; trotting – in his old boots because her own are too tight; then slowing to a quick walk with her arm around her bump. Her mouth is wide, anxious. No, not anxious, amazed and happy. 'Silas! Oh, Silas.'

They grip hands and half turn; dance.

'Oh. Oh. Look.'

They squeeze themselves together. In between them is the small bump and a feeble kick. Silas grins: a warble in the stomach.

He kneels in the mud to inspect the shoots. They are healthier than last year, stronger-looking, greener and not so straggly. Last year they seemed to grow too quickly, as if they were searching for something they couldn't find.

He reaches out and puts his arm around her again. She is trembling. 'I thought something dreadful had happened,' she says, 'I thought that maybe the seedlings had all been washed away.'

He draws her close. 'No, my love, they're strong, very strong –

quite different from last time. Maybe that was all that was wrong – it wasn't too much sun, but not enough water.'

She clutches him to her. 'Everything is going to be all right, Silas, I know it. The new Wales! This is the start. Edwyn Lloyd was right all along.'

Just now he is too happy to argue.

Forty-three

Word travels fast. Within two weeks the whole of Rawson has come out to Silas' farm to look at his fields. The crop is continuing to grow strongly, whereas elsewhere the wheat is wilting like last year.

'It needs more water,' Silas says. It is obvious now – why didn't they see it before? In a couple of weeks he has become Rawson's expert, and is revelling in his new authority. He visits the other farms passing judgement and giving advice on where to dig channels – as if he has spent years in the field refining his expertise.

Megan is inside the house resting. Her feet and hands are swollen and Mary Jones has instructed her to sit with her legs up whenever she can. She has also released Miriam from her duties in the Jones household so that she can be, according to Miriam, 'an unpaid skivvy' to Megan instead. She does not come graciously. Sometimes Silas eavesdrops on the conversation.

'Miriam, are you busy?' calls Megan.

'Yes, I am.'

'Well, if you aren't would you mind gathering more gorse for the stove?'

'In a minute, Myfanwy and I are drawing a dog.'

'Well, I suppose that's much more important then.'

Silas grins and then walks noisily in through the door. Miriam's chair immediately scrapes back.

'I'll just go and get some, then,' she says, making a face at Myfanwy, and rushes through the door.

'I'm going too,' says Myfanwy and hurries after her. Silas has heard Miriam explaining to Myfanwy that her own sister is just a baby and not much good as a conversationalist, so she has adopted Myfanwy as her favourite sister instead. So far she has taught the child to skip, knit a long tube of wool though a cotton reel with four nails hammered into it, write several names from the bible and draw the various animals they see in their excursions to the village. She also tells her long stories about the angels she has seen in the clouds and on the sides of mountains, and sometimes in the light above peoples' heads.

'It's their soul escaping, see. The angels take care of it – they either put it back or they take it up to heaven.'

Like Megan she also believes in the *Tylwyth Teg*, but whereas Megan's fairies are malign, and held responsible for every pail of milk that turns sour and every plate or cup that is cracked or chipped, Miriam's fairies are helpful, leading her to find buttons she has lost and warning her of potential disasters that lie ahead.

Although self-confident, she is young for her seventeen years and handsome rather than pretty or beautiful. She seems like a drawn-out version of her snub-nosed mother; but whereas Mary is dextrous, Miriam has an awkwardness that is not improving with her years. She is intelligent, however, and a proficient reader and writer and Jacob has already proposed that she should join him at the school he has started. Silas suspects that the man is sweet on her, as until recently he made a point of stopping at the Jones house to speak to her whenever he came out to visit Megan. Silas was amused to see that she was either not interested or unaware of his attentions. Often she would choose the moment of his arrival to ride away on the horse she had persuaded her father to buy for her, or would hide herself away reading one of the books Jacob had left for her the week before.

These visits had become much less frequent recently of course; since their latest altercation over Edwyn, Silas has only seen Jacob from a distance, and he has taken to visiting Rawson on a Thursday when Selwyn was in charge of the store and Jacob was nowhere in sight.

But Jacob's tentative courtship, if indeed that is what it is, has recently been curtailed altogether. One Thursday in December Silas had arrived in Rawson to learn that another ship had arrived with supplies and almost immediately had departed again for Buenos Aires carrying Jacob as an additional passenger.

'There was a berth spare, I've heard. Next we knew he'd gone,' Selwyn says. He looks awkward, as though he's given something away by accident. 'Suppose Caradoc or Edwyn should have told you, not me.'

Silas waits for him to continue. No one had even thought to tell Megan. She will be hurt and upset. Everything seems to upset her at the moment.

'According to the *Meistr*, Dr Rawson liked Jacob.' He sniffs. 'Didn't notice that myself.'

Neither had Silas – as far as he could remember the two hadn't exchanged a single word.

'Said the settlement needed a representative there, his right-hand man.' Selwyn smirks at his words and then looks around to check that no one is in earshot. 'I reckon he just wanted him out of the way. Since you and him had that tiff the *Meistr's* found things a little awkward, I reckon. Been saying things about social harmony, and maybe he thinks this is the best way to get it.'

Megan is lying on the day bed Silas has made for her so she can see Myfanwy and Miriam work and play together. Her feet are so swollen now that it hurts every time she walks. Her fingers are swollen too – so much that she cannot knit or even shell eggs. 'I am like one of those whales,' she moans. 'A useless whale landed on the beach.'

She still has a couple of months to go and Silas can't see how she could get much larger. Across her stomach is a network of red and blue weals where her flesh has torn beneath.

She fans herself with a paper Myfanwy has folded for her and decorated with flowers and birds, and for a few minutes after he has told her about Jacob she is silent.

'He slipped away,' he tells her, 'like a thief in the night.'

'Silas!' she says, 'he's my brother! A man of the cloth too. You shouldn't say that.'

'I only said "like a thief",' he says.

'Well, he'll be back soon I expect. He'll want to see his new niece or nephew.'

But he isn't.

The January sun shines. 'It is relentless,' Megan says miserably, 'I can't get cool.' But outside the wheat is growing strongly. When it shows signs of wilting he reopens the channel and allows the fields to flood again, and the plants swiftly recover.

'It's an inspiration!' Edwyn says. 'Silas' field shows us what we all can do!'

Silas looks down. He will not change his mind. It is still the *Meistr* underneath, he reminds himself, still the same snake.

'How wide do you think the channels should be? Better ask Silas!' The *Meistr* slaps him on the back. 'Here's your expert!'

The *Meistr* grins as if he wants a grin back. When he doesn't get one, he laughs. 'Too modest! That's what he is, *brawd*! Too modest to say.'

Forty-four

Yeluc

In the summer the *rou* go inland close to the mountains and we follow. It is a beautiful place with trees, lush grass and many streams and ponds. There are bright birds flashing through trees and fish glinting in pools. The *rou* have their young there and it is a busy time for us. The soft pelt of an unborn *rou* is a prized thing but rarely taken.

But as the mountains are fertile they are also cold and soon the *rou* sniff the air and smell the winter coming. Then they begin to drift back towards the sea.

These days Seannu and her sisters grumble. 'Why can we not just stay here?' they ask. So I tell them about the cold. About the spirits that live there, how they are malicious things that drink the blood of women and crack the bones of men and soon they are rolling up the skins of the *toldo* and stamping on the fires more determinedly than I am.

Are we going to see Si-las? they ask, but I shake my head. Patagones, I tell them, and wait for their howls of disappointment.

Forty-five

Silas goes out to the field early each morning looking for signs that the crop might be ripening. That, at least, is looking promising. Each stalk is straight and each ear full.

New families have arrived from the United States and Selwyn is busy introducing them to the ways of the colony. They are wealthy, young and vigorous and have inspired everyone with their scientific modern methods. They are used to farming on a large scale, and have a certain amount of swagger to them, but they are friendly and happy to share what they know and own.

They have told him it is most important to harvest just before the wheat bursts into flower.

The weather turns, the air becomes colder and Silas lies in bed beside the sleeping Megan and thinks about the baby ripening alongside the wheat. Sometimes he imagines the grains are like miniature babies growing plumper inside their casing. Then he imagines the baby ripening too, growing fingers and toes, hair and fingernails, and its belly becoming round and its legs kicking. He thinks of it like the frogspawn he once saw and the way the tadpoles became frogs, one set of limbs and then another and then the tail shortening. A gust blows at the window making the rhea gut rattle and beside him Megan squirms and moans. 'What is it?' he asks, grabbing her arm. 'Is it time?'

She doesn't reply.

'Answer me, *gwraig*!'

He struggles out of bed then fumbles with a tinderbox. When he can eventually see her face it is grimacing with pain.

'Do you want someone?'

She nods, and then gasps again. She swings her legs over the side of the bed and tries to stand then cries out as her feet touch the floor.

'I'm getting Mary.'

Her nightclothes have risen up above her knees and trickling down her legs is something that is not quite red enough to be blood.

'Quickly, Silas, quickly.'

Myfanwy is at the door looking in. He takes her by the hand and leads her into the kitchen. 'Stay here, understand?'

The child nods.

'Just for five minutes while I fetch Mary.'

The birth is almost silent: there is just a single cry and then a subdued mewl.

Mary opens the bedroom door just for a few seconds to tell Silas that the baby is very weak, and Megan is weeping that the child is going to die. An hour later she sends out Miriam to him to tell him to fetch the minister so they can at least baptise the child. The girl looks pale and frightened, her hands trembling by her sides.

'Well, at least tell me what it is before I go.'

'Another girl,' says Miriam, and Myfanwy looks up and smiles.

'A sister!' she says and claps her hands. 'Can I see?'

Miriam tells her to hush. 'Not yet,' she says, and glances at Silas, 'Mam said I had to tell you both she's resting and doesn't want to see anyone.'

The dawn is coming. There is a pinkness to the sky in the east, and despite the wind it is a pleasant morning. It must be the wind that is making tears in his eyes – no man can mourn a child he has never met. And anyway Mary might be wrong. How can anyone tell for sure if a baby is to die? Miracles happen, and even the sickliest-looking children sometimes survive.

Caradoc pulls on a jacket over his nightshirt and steps quickly into his trousers.

'Not always right, these women,' he tells Silas kindly and Silas nods.

But when they see the child they know that Mary is right. The baby is a strange pink-blue, her skin translucent with her blood vessels and ribs showing clearly beneath. She makes little sound except a faint wheeze and her chest seems to be fluttering rather than breathing. They have little time to see, because as soon as they enter the room Megan snatches the baby from the bed where she is lying beside her, and wraps her so vigorously in a blanket that Silas is afraid that life has been quenched from the child already. Mary glances at them and frowns, then motions them from the room.

'I think her mind has been affected,' she says when they are in the kitchen. 'She wouldn't speak to me, even when... even when the baby was coming. Even then. She hardly made a sound, not even at the end. It was as if she was determined not to speak. And she's not looked at her, you know. Just keeps moaning that the baby will die and that she will die too. I don't know what to do, how to make her comfortable. She has let me bathe the child, but cries and snatches her back if I try to put her in her cradle.'

'Perhaps if she rests...' Silas says.

Mary turns to the minister. 'I'm sorry, Caradoc, but I think you've had a wasted journey. I don't want to force her to give up the child.'

They return to the room. Megan's face is flushed but it is too early for childbed fever, and her eyes are brighter than they have been for months. Myfanwy rushes in and throws her arms around her asking excitedly to see the baby, but Megan pushes her away as if she doesn't know her.

'Mam?' Myfanwy steps back then turns to her father, her eyes like two small, overfilled ponds in the dim light. 'Dadda?'

Silas picks his daughter up and looks at the woman on the bed. 'Mam is not well, *cariad fach*. Don't worry, she'll be better soon.'

Mary tells Miriam to take Myfanwy home with her. 'I will stay here a while, if you like.'

'*Diolch yn fawr*,' he says, thanking her for her quiet competence.

Forty-six

Yeluc

Many times the gods have summoned me to their place in the firmament so that I can see their power. The first time I journeyed there I burnt with a light as intense as theirs and everything I touched was seared: my outline on the shell of my faithful Tortuga, my footsteps like blackened holes on the membrane of their kingdom, and my breath burning the air in front of me so it smelt of soot. Other times they have permitted me to enter their lower world and in there is a black sea with a grey beach of cinder skirting its edge. It is a place of small fires: points of lights rising in the distance, each one an island, sometimes spurting out columns of red liquid rock. In both these places is Tortuga, and sometimes his friend Piche, both of them armoured animals: one with the shell of a turtle, the other the mantle of the armadillo. Tortuga is silent, but Piche talks like a mountain-brook. Sometimes I can choose where I wish to go, but most often it is decided for me. I shut my eyes and enter with the beat of a drum, or the taste of the black herb, or sometimes I need nothing at all, just my body becoming so numb with hunger and fatigue that my soul escapes.

It is all this that makes me a shaman, chosen by Elal to see his world. I can bring good spirits and bad, and because of this I am to be feared and left alone with Seannu and her sisters. Yet sometimes they come to me: the Gallatts and the Chiquichan. There are some things only a shaman can know and do. There are some things only I can do. I know the ways of both Cristianos and Galenses, and sometimes they need me to help them.

This time Chiquichan comes with a message for the government. He wants payment for the land he thinks is his, and he trusts me to get it. No one can own the land, Chiquichan, I tell him, but he shakes his head. You live too much in the old times, Yeluc, he says. The old spirits are getting weaker, and the Cristianos have different rules. And he tells me to go to Buenos Aires with one of the Galenses called Ed-wyn. He is their chief and a good man, he says. And when I am there he knows I will make sure that Chiquichan has a voice.

So I leave on one of their swans. Not one with white mantles, but one which breathes hotly and noisily in its sleep. It rocks me so hard that it wakens strange dreams and demons. My body burns. My breath comes bursting from me. Oh, such sickness in the stomach. I cannot heal it. I shut my eyes and ask Elal to help me make a journey but I go nowhere. I call out for Tortuga, but he doesn't come. The white men shift before my eyes like ghosts. The one called Ed-wyn smiles and says he is my friend, but I don't know him. I call out for Elal but he covers his ears and I don't know why.

Forty-seven

There is no talk of leaving now. Nine months have gone past but Santa Fe is just a vague memory. It is autumn and although all the colonists now have fields of wheat only Silas' field is ripe. It is the colour of ochre, as lush and as perfect as any you would find in any of the provinces to the north. Silas fingers the ears; each one is full, firm, close to perfection. They rattle and whistle slightly in the wind, crack and snap when he comes too close. His sickle is ready. A few people from the village have come to see – Edwyn, Selwyn and Annie and the Jones family with Myfanwy. It is the colony's first crop. He looks towards his cottage but of course no one appears. It is then that he notices the light: in front of him, to the south, the sky is black-blue, darkening like a bruise, but from behind him the sun shines. It lights the field with a surreal brilliance. For a few seconds he enjoys the colours. But the sky means that rain is approaching – perhaps a storm that will flatten all this and make it worthless. They need to work hard to bring it all in and under cover before it comes.

'Now?' asks Silas.

'Now,' nods Selwyn.

Silas grips his sickle and makes the first cut. The people beside him cheer and a few rush in to help.

That night he creeps in to Megan. He is exhausted but satisfied, every muscle in his back aching – a sweet sharp reminder of his success. It is done. Myfanwy is asleep in her bed clutching onto the doll Miriam has made her. Megan sleeps with the baby. The infant grizzles in her sleep every night as if she is unhappy to be alive. Silas has tried not to get too fond of her but the child has such an endearing face – rather long for a baby, with a largish nose. Megan keeps the baby constantly with her during the day, fastened to her breast in a shawl. She is anxious, constantly checking the child's breath as she sleeps, waking her if she sleeps too long. Only once has she relented her grip on the child, for Caradoc to bless her and name her: Arianwen.

Silas is wary of touching the child and strokes her long fine hair with trepidation. It is dark brown and thick. Every night he kisses her small, sleeping face.

Live, he thinks, and something warm catches light within him. Live, and I shall take care of you. Fight, my little one, fight for yourself – and your brother and sister.

Edwyn has called a special meeting of the council to discuss the crop. Everyone is smiling.

'It's a model for the entire valley,' Edwyn says. 'So far all of the farms that have irrigated have seen a similar miracle.'

They are all clapping him on the back now. When Edwyn proposes a cheer, a child starts to cry at the noise.

'I am keeping a note of yield, size of the field, the frequency of irrigation and the type of soil.' Edwyn grins at Silas, as if they are allies, but fails to catch his eye, then says, 'I shall tell Dr Rawson we have struck gold – a special sort of gold.'

Trickery, Silas thinks, that's all it is. The man has a slippery tongue and he will take no notice.

'Silas? What do you think?'

He looks up. They are all waiting for him to speak. 'I think we should look into blocking the river upstream,' Silas says, and a couple of people around him nod their heads, 'and investigate the building of canals.'

There is a general murmur of agreement. Silas bows his head again, but this time he allows himself to grin.

'We should make sure that everyone has access to a water supply,' one of the Americans says. 'We could set up co-operatives and work together.'

'Amen to that!'

'And we should survey the land properly...'

'Agreed.'

'If we used that old river bed we would save ourselves some work.'

Their voices become loud and enthusiastic. One of the new American families, the Parrys, have shown Silas how to thresh his wheat using a horse tethered to a point on the ground and a plate dragged behind the horse near to the surface.

'But first we need more supplies, more equipment, more money from the government. If I can take all this...' Edwyn waves his notes at everyone, '...then I'm sure we will have a strong case.'

'Are you going on board the *Denby*?' someone asks.

What else is there? Edwyn nods. 'I'm sorry, yes, I'm afraid I shall have to.'

The *Denby* is anchored in the river. Her last journey south from Buenos Aires has left her even more dilapidated, and every day someone is there, hammering or mending. It is the colonists' intention to make her seaworthy again using the old wreck that lies just down-river, because without her they feel isolated.

'I'll take her just as far as Patagones,' he reassures them. 'I can take the steamer from there. Then Ivor can bring her straight back to you.'

'But is she safe?' Mary says.

'The captain assures me that she is – but that is another reason not to take her back to Buenos Aires. The port authorities might declare her not seaworthy and I don't want them to commandeer her again. Much better if she comes back and I go on by steamer. Now who will come with me?'

There is a chorus of volunteers.

Megan is listening. He knows she is listening even though she makes no sign that she's heard. She is concentrating on Arianwen. She fusses over the small rash on her chest, and then inspects her anxiously while she feeds. Every other chore has been left. Her knitting remains half finished by the stove, and her sewing is gathering dust by her bed.

'Edwyn is going to Buenos Aires tomorrow,' he tells her, 'with samples of my wheat.'

But she says nothing, merely divides Arianwen's hair and peers at her scalp. Miriam, however, is listening with interest. He likes the way she gives him her full attention, apparently absorbed in what he is saying or wanting to finish tales of her own.

'He's going to tell them about the irrigation,' Silas continues, mainly for Miriam now, 'the way it has changed everything. He wanted me to come too, he said I could be expert witness since it was my idea...' he glances at Megan, 'well, since I was the one that made it work... but I told him that it was more important for me to stay here so I would be on hand to help everyone else.'

He is enjoying his new status as teacher. The threshing has worked well and now there are sacks of Silas' grain in the warehouse that he is swapping with the rest of the colonists for favours and labour. The bread that is made from this grain is particularly fine, he is told, though whether this is just sycophantic comment or truth he has yet to discover. Yesterday he gave Miriam two bags of flour, freshly milled by one of the women in the village – one as a present to her family and one for her to convert into bread for himself – and he is looking forward to finding out how it tastes.

He glances at Megan again. The baby has obviously finished

feeding because it is motionless in her arms. He walks over to her and then reels back.

'Let me have her, Megan. She's stinking of pee.'

Megan shakes her head, holds the baby close and starts to sing softly into her arms. The smell is so strong that it is making his eyes water.

'Megan, either you have to change her or I shall.' He reaches down but Megan rocks back and forth singing more loudly.

'Megan!'

He prises her arms away and uncovers the baby from the shawl like a bud from its leaves. Then he plunges in his hands and stops. Cold. Too cold. Megan's eyes are fixed on his own. Her head shakes slowly. 'No. No. No.'

'Miriam,' he says, trying to keep his voice from breaking, 'would you please take Myfanwy home and ask your mother to come and help me?'

Megan has propped herself up on her elbow and is watching him. Strange how he knows that her eyes are open and staring at him – even before he looks up. She looks at him in silence for a few minutes and then lies down again. The faint shininess, where her eyes were in the darkness, disappears. Soon she will speak again, he knows that. He just has to be patient. Grief has made her mute before, but she has always eventually found her tongue. It takes time, but soon she will come round and talk to him again. He squats in front of her and takes her hands. 'Please, Megan, you have to try. Smile, talk, say something, do something. We all need you. We can't go on without you.'

But she says nothing.

'Just squeeze my hands if you can hear me.'

He waits. Her left hand twitches and closes slightly around his. Its coldness raises the hairs on the back of his shoulders.

He leans forward and kisses her gently on the lips and tastes the salt of tears. 'What is it?'

She gives a sudden sob and lurches forward into his arms. 'I'm frightened to love anything – if I do God will take it away from me.'

He hugs her to him, grateful for her warmth and her voice.

'But we have to love, *cariad*. Without love, we are nothing.'

'I miss them so much. Every minute. The pain doesn't stop. As if someone has caught hold of something inside me and is wringing me out.'

She sobs again and then takes a breath. 'It is better not to feel anything, better not to love at all.'

He holds her from him: 'No, Megan, you're wrong.'

She shakes her head. 'It's too late.'

'Won't you try?'

He thinks she nods her head.

A new ship arrives in the river. She has jaunty sails, a naked mermaid as a figurehead, and negotiates the sand bar nimbly. The colonists crowd onto the shore to greet her, stamping their feet to banish the cold, the children laughing and pointing delightedly at the nudity.

Edwyn comes ashore with a large white-bearded captain who speaks no Welsh or English but sniggers at anything anyone says.

'Where's the *Denby*?' Edwyn asks, 'she left Patagones before we did.'

'Held up somewhere, I expect,' someone replies. 'You know what Ivor's like.'

The ship is loaded with cattle, seeds and agricultural equipment – with the compliments of the Argentine government. A present from minister Rawson to celebrate the promise of harvest. The colonists forget the *Denby* as they gleefully unload ploughs, rakes, sowing and tamping machines – the best, most up-to-date equipment anyone can buy. The men are delighted, their voices high and excited as children's at Christmas. Most of the machines will be communal. Some of them are even new to the Americans and they take it in turns to experiment with them, laughing as the ploughs go askew, and the harvester leaves the wheat intact.

'We can't fail now,' says one, and a row of heads around him nods. 'With all that we've learnt, and this. We could be rich, gentlemen.'

'With the Lord's blessing,' says Caradoc.

'Amen.'

Miriam runs out to meet him.

'She's not back,' she says. 'I don't know where she's gone.'

'Who's with her?'

'She's on her own. The children are in bed asleep.'

Last night he'd caught Megan weeping over milk that had turned sour.

'The *Tylwyth Teg,*' she'd said, 'they're playing tricks. I have to find out where they're coming from.' He'd had to stop her going out there and then, eventually persuading her to mutter a prayer instead – one that had sounded more like a spell than a message to God.

He walks to the Jones' house and looks around him. The land is slightly higher there and he can see for a long way in each direction. The landscape is as empty as it usually is – almost flat without interruption to the hills and to the river. It is not quite night and everything is a shade of grey, blue or black. When he thinks he can see a slight movement in the vegetation towards the river he walks towards it.

She won't have gone far. She has no shoes, just some slippers Silas has sewn together for her from hide. Closer to the river he spots her footsteps, almost circular like the Tehuelches'. They lead along the bank, keeping close to the water's edge.

He comes upon her suddenly, sitting on a rock, looking out over the river.

She is staring at something ahead of her that seems to be absorbing her completely. Even when he climbs up beside her and touches her arm she doesn't turn.

'St David's lights,' she murmurs, but when he peers into the darkness he can see nothing.

'Megan?' he says gently, but she doesn't turn.

'Candles, burning on the water, leading the way.'

There are tears in her eyes. She blinks and they begin a slow track down her face.

'Arianwen, Gwyneth, Richard, Mam...'

'Come, *cariad fach,* St David's lights are for warning of what lies ahead – not for what has already passed.'

'I saw a bird, I should have told you. Outside the house. Sitting there. On its own.'

Silas sighs. Everything is a warning. Every sign presages death. When did this start? He can't remember. When did the girl that laughed all the time change into this superstitious woman?

'Come, Megan, time to go home. You need to rest. You're tired.'

But it is as if she is dreaming. She hardly seems to hear or know he is there.

'It's a sign,' she murmurs. 'From Dadda. Even though I didn't warn him, he's telling me. I shall be joining him soon.'

He takes her by both arms and shakes her slightly. 'Megan! There are no lights. It's dark. Look at me.'

He waits, but she doesn't move. So he takes her by the arm and gently pulls her, down off the rock and back onto the track for home.

'Why's Mam not speaking any more?' Myfanwy asks

Ever since the night by the river she has not said a word.

Sometimes he sees her eyes following something around the room, and sometimes he hears her muttering the spells she used to use to guard against the fairies. Often he finds her sitting up in bed with tears trickling down her face, silent and quite motionless.

'Can't you just talk to Myfanwy?' he asks her once. But it seems that she cannot.

'Edwyn is talking about going back to Wales,' Selwyn tells him. 'He says he needs to go back to get more people.'

Silas snorts. 'The man can't stay still. He skips around the place as if he has an angry little rat in his trousers.'

'He says now would be a good time to go – while there is good news to report.'

'That man would promise a vision to a blind man if he thought it would persuade them over here to Patagonia.'

Selwyn smirks. 'Only if they were Welsh.'

'Yes, and only if they were willing to lose everything they love and still show never-ending devotion to the cause.' But he is smiling too now.

'But he was right in the end, wasn't he?'

'How?'

'This...' Selwyn spreads his arms at the sacks of seed, the grain and the equipment.

'I think we have to wait and see, *ffrind*, it is only one crop, only one year.'

'He says Dr Rawson was dancing around his table.'

Silas is doubtful. The Dr Rawson he met was serious; he really can't imagine him doing such a thing.

'Well, maybe not exactly a dance,' Selwyn says, noticing Silas' face. 'But he did say he talked so fast his glasses clouded over, and he had to take them off and wipe them.'

Silas grins. That he can imagine.

But there is sad news as well. Selwyn takes his time to tell him, waiting until evening until they are alone together in Selwyn's house. At Patagones Edwyn had encountered Yeluc, Selwyn tells him. The old Indian was camping outside the settlement with his women. When he heard that they were going to Buenos Aires he demanded to come too.

Selwyn pauses, sighs, walks up and down the small length of his living room holding his latest colicky offspring in his arms. 'The *Meistr* told him not to go, but he insisted. Then the *Meistr* said a strange thing: Buenos Aires kills Indians – but of course Yeluc took no notice.' He pauses to peel the baby carefully away from him, hoping that the child is asleep, but a whimper causes him to press the child against his shoulder and walk again.

'The old man wasn't well, apparently,' he continues. 'Dreadfully seasick. Then, when they got there he was worse. *Ych-a-fi*! Buenos Aires is a filthy place, Silas. Edwyn says that there are cess pits and wells sharing the same small plaza.' He tuts. '*Moch*! They drink their own *cach*.'

He sits beside Silas, patting the back of the child draped against his chest. 'He got worse. Edwyn took him to the hospital but it was no good.'

For a few minutes he is silent.

Silas blinks away tears, but still the room blurs. Someone has snatched something from him. He can't trust himself to say anything.

'He had to tell Seannu. She said nothing. Just sat. He wasn't sure she'd understood.' He checks his child again and then walks with him to the cot.

'Edwyn went to see him before the end. Said he was lying there, quite calm, smiling. When Edwyn patted his hand and asked him how he was he must have thought it was you, *ffrind*. He kept staring at Edwyn and calling him Si-las. I think the *Meistr* was a little…' he pauses to place his child carefully in its cot '…upset. The nurse there said that the old man had been talking about going to the Galenses heaven rather than his own. "Where that good people go must be a happy place," he'd told her. Then, when he saw

Edwyn, when he thought he was talking to you, he told him that he'd wait for you there, and take care of things in the meantime.'

The baby whimpers and Selwyn is quiet. He flops beside the cradle as if the speech has exhausted him and strokes his child's head. 'Edwyn told me to tell you,' he says after a few seconds.

For a few minutes Silas examines his fingers on his lap. Then, when the child cries again, rises to his feet. He squeezes Selwyn's shoulder to thank him and walks mutely out of the house into the night.

When Silas returns home the house is in darkness, and the wind is blowing at the door making it rattle against the catch. He pauses at the threshold. The house is cold, empty. With Yeluc gone from the world he no longer feels safe. The watchful eye, making sure all is well, has gone. Even when he wasn't camped alongside them, Silas felt he was always out there protecting them, and now that he has gone Silas feels exposed and vulnerable. Stupid, he thinks, Yeluc was just an old man. But he'd been saving so many things to tell him: jokes, sayings, questions. And so many questions: whether the striped animal he sometimes saw shuffling through gorse was safe to eat; what was the Tehuelche word for rain; was it normal for the Chubut to rise and fall as much as it did last year; what causes the guanaco to run west year after year? No one will answer them now. A chill passes over him. He longs to touch someone. He calls out quietly but no one answers.

The hearth is cold and the kitchen is empty. Where is everyone? He sits at the table. There is a scribble on the surface with a piece of chalk. Silas smiles, remembering that yesterday Myfanwy had sat where he is sitting now. Then Miriam had asked if tomorrow the two of them could make a short trip in the new buggy. Yes, that's where they'll have gone. Perhaps Megan has gone too. He breathes in and then out again, sucking at the cold wind. Maybe that's what's happened. He feels a little lighter. Maybe at last she is getting better. He lights a small fire in the kitchen and then quickly walks up to the Jones' house.

All three girls are there, sitting around the fire listening to Mary telling them all a story. John is there too, looking as much enthralled as everyone else. For a few minutes no one sees him enter and he listens to the end. It is a well-known story about a girl who dresses up as a sailor so that she can follow her love to sea.

The crew escape from pirates onto a small boat and when they run out of food decide they must turn to cannibalism. Mary is just describing the drawing of lots to decide which one of them should be eaten first when she catches Silas' eye. It is the important part of the tale – the part where they discover that one of the sailors is in fact a woman, meaning, for some reason, that she cannot be eaten after all. However in Mary's version she moves straight on to their rescue.

'So they got married like we did, by hopping over a brush, and lived happily ever after,' she says.

'That's not what happens,' says Miriam indignantly. 'Why have you changed it, Mam?' Then she follows her mother's eyes to Silas and closes her lips.

'Is Megan not with you?' Silas says.

They shake their heads.

His shoulders sink. He should have checked the rest of his house. Megan will be in bed or maybe sitting in the chair by the fire in the dark. He should have gone into the living room. But when he arrives back the chair by the fire is empty and so is their bed. He swallows and hurries to the outhouse and knocks on the door. Nothing.

He realises he is holding his breath. He forces himself to breathe slowly out and then in. He lights a lamp and quickly searches all the nearby outbuildings that are filled with sacks and pieces of equipment, but each one is as dark and as empty of anything living as the next. Where is she? He looks out into his fields and then the wilderness to the north. At least it is not deep winter and the air is not too cold. She'll be all right even if she is caught overnight in the open air. He searches the ground for footprints but the only ones he can see are a mess of his own. Then he remembers the river and the lights. He examines the footprints again with the light and sees some smaller ones leading down towards the riverbank. Perhaps she has decided to go to the village, perhaps at last she feels like some company. At the water he pauses and holds his breath again. But the footsteps do not stop and they don't lead downwards into the river, or eastwards to the village, but to the west, to the mountains and the empty desert.

Forty-eight

Yeluc

Sometimes I dream of Elal's great white swan. I dream I am between her feathers and I am warm and safe. Sometimes I am in the white man's bed and sometimes beside Seannu. Sometimes I journey into the high place and the low. Sometimes I see Turtuga and he smiles at me and tells me it won't be long. But there is another dream too. A dream I haven't had before. In this dream I travel alone. It is cold and when I spread out my arms I rise up to the stars. The stars are like faces burning in the heavens. Where am I, I ask but the stars don't reply. Instead there is singing, all the voices of the *Galenses* singing out loud. It is all around me, as if I am with them. You are in heaven, they tell me. And I know I am safe.

Forty-nine

It is John Jones who finds her. He has set out with Silas at first light. Words fail him completely this time. He comes running back to where Silas is swiping at reed beds with a stick and for a minute he just stands in front of him swallowing loudly. When Silas loses patience and shoves past him John grabs his arm and blurts out, 'Megan!'

'What? Have you found her? Tell me.'

He nods, gestures for him to follow and runs along the path beside the river.

From a distance it looks like a clump of old rags caught up on some roots by the side of the river. Closer he notices her feet. They are bare, her boots either kicked or dropped away. It is these that he notices, these he keeps watching, the way the toes curl inwards, dark pink, each toe edged by the half shell of nail, small now that the swelling has gone. Her body is partly hidden by reeds, and her face is hidden by her hair. Around her are pieces of driftwood, an old bottle and the charred remains of some animal. She has obviously been washed up there, a small quiet eddy in the river, a part of the bank that overhangs with small red willows and gorse. John looks at him and then back to Megan. 'What shall we do?'

Silas doesn't answer. He keeps looking at her feet. She is half submerged in the water but her feet are clear. He goes up to her and hooks his hands under her arms and pulls. A wet cold weight. She is caught on something. John pulls away roots and wood, and Silas pulls again. Slowly she comes. He grunts with effort. She is wearing her best clothes: a long woollen skirt and petticoats, a chemise and stays, her good new blouse and two shawls, one tied over the other, each layer saturated with water holding her down. He lifts her hair. He can't remember the last time he saw it hanging down like this. A long time ago, but he remembers it soft on his fingers, halfway between feathers and silk, and then that time she smiled, that time she dived forward and kissed him hard on the lips, and that time he held her properly, the first time, warm where they touched, fitting together then drawing apart. He draws back now. It is her face, then not her face. The curve of her eyebrow, but not her mouth. Too still. Slouched. Not her. Purple in this early light, dark against the white foam of the river. Half-open eyes. Nothing behind them. Too still. Not her. Coldness on his fingertips when he tries to shut them.

Asleep. He shakes her. Megan, Megan, Megan.

Another time. Another place. Megan! Megan, Megan, Megan. At the window. That smile. Her head on her pillow just like this. Her eyes half closed. Soon they will open. Soon they will look into his and smile. Yes, she will smile. 'I always get what I want.' You don't want this. You don't want this coldness, darkness, and loneliness. Wake.

'No.' He steps back. She falls from him. 'No.' He starts to run. She will wake now. She will come after him, laugh and tell him she's joking. It's all a dream, stupid man. Mine forever, don't you remember?

He sees himself run, out of his body, one step ahead, just as he used to run to her and she'd always be there. Laughing, smiling. Silas! Climb up. It'll be just us. Wake! Come out of your window just this once. Take my hand. It's your turn.

'Silas!'

'No.' Walking now. He sees his feet on the mud, one and then the next. She'll be after him soon. She'll wake and laugh. Megan as she was. Hair shining. Waiting. Hand in his.

'Silas, come back.'

'No.'

'You've got to help. We can't leave her here.'

He turns, watches himself turn back, walk back to the river while John struggles with the weeds, chops at the roots so that Silas can take her in his arms. A dead weight. Not as she was. Not this rigid unyielding, not this chill. He staggers up the bank, until he falls. His face next to hers. Megan. Enough now. Wake.

'Come on, Silas.' John stands there awkwardly. 'We'd best get the cart.'

There is a small bird pecking at something near the grave. A worm. Silas watches as the bird pulls, and the worm grows longer and thinner until it breaks and the bird flies away over the heads of the people in front of him, smaller and smaller, a speck and then part of the sky. Real. It is real. Just the bird and the sky. Nothing else. Not this singing or the mass of people or the hole in the ground or the box.

'The Lord be with you, brother.'

He nods.

'You must be brave now, my son.'

He blinks but there are no tears.

'The Lord watches over you.'

He nods. He wants to believe – in God, in someone who loves him.

'She is in heaven now, with her Saviour.'

No.

Sand. Scattering on the box. Hard, small grains bouncing, springing off. She is here. In there. No. He forces himself to think of it. Inside. Skin drawn back, teeth exposed. Bone. Flesh. Her legs. Those feet. Her face. Cold. Set into place. A doll's. Not her. Not really her.

He draws away, steps back, watches himself. Shaking hands. This is not real. Smiling, nodding. He is not here. Earth to earth. The lid rattling. The box being covered. One small corner left. Dust to dust. Yellow-brown. Dry. The corner gone.

'Come, Silas, time to go.'

A pit slowly filling.

'Silas!'

The slow steady movement of the spade. 'Come on, man.'

Then the wind.

Mary Jones has been baking. Myfanwy and the younger children are both confused and happy. They stuff their mouths full of dark cake and bread spread with the honey Ieuan found last week. They laugh, chase each other out of the room until Mary warns them to be quiet. Silas sits. He looks earnestly at each new face that comes forward as if he is begging them to tell him it isn't true. Clasps hands. Mutters words. 'Sorry.'

She is…

'If we can help.'

She is. She was… she was, she was, she was.

They have gone. He can't remember how or when. They were talking about ships: the *Denby*, then the one Edwyn Lloyd must have taken, but he can't remember now what was said. He tried to listen but his mind kept making journeys of its own: onto the *Mimosa* and then on the *Denby's* small lifeboat. With Megan. Then without her. She is. No. She was.

The room is in darkness but someone comes in, lights a lamp, then the fire. That girl. The strange tall one with the dreams and visions. She comes over and pats his hands. 'She's safe now,' she says. 'Happy. I fancy I saw her smiling.'

A back of a skirt, a blouse, that way of walking she has: 'Megan!' She turns around, her finger to her lips. 'Be quiet now,' she swishes away, her hair drawn up, one lock, one short tendril, where the baby has pulled. 'I wanted to tell you…'

'Later now,' she smiles. Oh, she smiles. Then she turns around again and walks away.

'Megan!'

She is gone.

'Come back.'

But she won't.

'Mam said for me to stay. In case you need help. With Myfanwy, in here.' She stops in front of him waiting for him to move.

'You must go to bed now.' Myfanwy. Little Megan. Her mother in miniature. 'Miriam says so.'

'Shh.' The strange girl looks at his daughter and then anxiously back at his face again. Not Megan. Miriam. Her name is Miriam. He smiles slightly. Wearily he runs his fingers through his hair. 'It's all right. I should thank you.' But he stays where he is. In case she comes back. In case she sits in that chair.

'You should sleep.'

He shakes his head. 'I can't.'

'You should try.'

'Please leave me, I can't.'

The bed is too cold, large and empty. It sags where she was. When he wakes it is too quiet. He reaches out and feels the cold dent where she was, then burles his head in her scent.

He sees her ahead of him, by the river, on her rock. He hears her laugh, though she didn't laugh here.

'A girl, is it?' A voice from long ago. Powell the tailor catching him once more unpicking a seam. 'Beware, *bachgen*. Once they trap you you're like a fly in a spider's web. A spider with a tongue, *mab*. Just think of that. Never any peace. Yak, yak, yak – all the day long.' Powell had laughed at his joke. 'You need to concentrate, *bachgen*, if you want to be a tailor.'

But the shine of her hair was in every fibre that he sewed, and the smallest scrap of velvet was enough to remind him of her touch. Megan. Her voice was like birds singing, he told his mother, and she'd laughed. And her face was like an angel's, and she'd laughed some more. All day it shimmered in front of him and he could spend an hour just thinking about it and not doing much else at all. He knew each part, each feature; the angle of her nose, the space between her eyes, the way her upper lip touched the lower one, and the way her eyebrow disappeared to nothing above the corners of her eyes.

Sometimes Powell would catch him in this reverie and tut. 'No hope,' he said, 'I feel sorry for you, *bachgen*. Love is like poison, an illness; one day you'll wake up and find out the fool you've been, but it'll be too late by then.'

But at last he'd let him go each evening, shrugging and telling him that he couldn't say he hadn't been warned, and Silas would run: down the street to the outskirts of town where her father's business took up half a street, up the small path to one of the windows at the side, and then stand, call, softly and then more urgently: Megan, Megan, Megan.

Then there'd be that face at the window. That smile like

sunshine on her face and then that bird – fluttering in his chest, rising up to his throat, taking away his breath, twittering and chirping and not making sense. 'Are you ready? Shall I come up? Where shall we go?' Then the window flying open and her voice floating out: 'Silas! Wait! I'll be down directly.' Then that laugh, oh, such a sweet sound. Or sometimes, better: 'They think I'm asleep. Can you climb up?' And so he would scramble onto the roof of the outhouse and then up to her window, scratching his legs, tearing his clothes but then into her arms. Her arms. Then the smell of her bed – ah, the sweetness of hay and the sweeter smell of her – and then Megan: in his arms, laughing, covering him with kisses. My love, never let me go, always be mine, forever and ever and ever. Until the world ends. Or we do.

'Eat.'

He shakes his head.

'Mam says…'

He looks at her. Miriam. He should be grateful. He should try to talk. 'And what does your Mam say this time?'

'That you should eat. That I should try and make things you'd like. Bacon, bread, cheese…'

'I'm sorry. I can't. Tell your Mam that.'

But she continues to watch him so he starts to slowly eat his bread. When she goes he returns the crust to his plate.

Why did he not stop her, why did he leave her alone, why did he bring her here, why didn't he talk to her more, why didn't he explain, why didn't he save Richard, Gwyneth, why did he let her go?

'I'm taking Myfanwy to my mother's.'

He says nothing.

'Did you hear me, Silas?'

She turns, walks out. After they have gone a boot follows her out of the doorway. 'Go away!' He bellows. 'Leave me alone.'

No one helped her. No one tried. No one cared.

He stands and starts to kick everything he can find: his chair, the bench, the table, the pans on the fire. A slug of boiling water soaks the fabric of his shirt and sends him roaring into the parlour. He struggles at his shirt sobbing with pain that hits him again and again: red wave then black wave then red again. His eyes are closed. It is as if he can see the pain inside his chest. He touches it where the water hit him with a finger and roars again. Red: scarlet, vibrant, bloody. And with it a sound: discordant like people shrieking. He crumples onto the floor. The red darkens. The shrieks become yelps and then sobs. He rests his head against the settle and listens. There is someone there. Someone sitting in her chair. If he doesn't open his eyes maybe she will stay there.

'And why didn't you try?' he tells her. He knows what she is doing. Without opening his eyes he can feel what she does. She looks up from where she is sitting and smiles back. Smiles, at last she smiles.

'Too late now,' he says, and takes the shirt he is holding and throws it at her. Something falls. He opens his eyes. Her favourite vase smashes against the floor

'That wasn't *y Tylwyth Teg*, Megan, that was me!'

She is still there. Still smiling. As if she can't hear him. As if she doesn't know what he's done. As if she doesn't know what she's done. He gets up, stamps on the pieces and looks back at her. 'Too late now,' he says again, and scoops up the broken pieces with his hands, curling his fingers tightly around them until his thoughts become quiet.

When he looks again she is gone: just a cushion where her smile was, just a seam, curling upwards, grinning at him, until he hits that away too.

'What have you done with your hands?'

Mary tuts, makes him sit and washes them with clean rags and water.

'And your chest!'

He sits without moving while she looks for the butter.

'It's like looking after another child,' she says, then stops. He has lifted his bandaged hands to cover his head. 'Oh *cariad*!' she says and she holds both his shoulders until they stop shaking.

Fifty

Edwyn is talking about Jacob. 'The man is happy in Buenos Aires; I thought it better to leave him there,' he says, glancing at Silas. 'He is making influential friends, and getting quite a reputation. I think to have Jacob a little longer in Buenos Aires will be of benefit to everyone.'

Edwyn stops. His eyes flick over to Silas again. He reaches over and touches his hand. 'I'm sorry, *brawd*.' He's said it before but Silas hasn't heard. He doesn't hear it now. He sits without responding, looking blankly ahead, rocking slightly. She is gone. He tries to hate her but he can't. If he could hate her he thinks it might make him feel better.

Edwyn sighs and looks around. 'Anything else?'

Everyone is subdued. It is hard to concentrate on what is being said.

'Has there been any word about the *Denby*?' Selwyn says at last.

Edwyn inspects his hands on his lap and for a few seconds everyone waits.

'The *Denby*, Edwyn, have you heard anything?'

He shakes his head, his beard that has become more grey and grizzled, brushes against his jacket – one sweep to the right, another to the left. 'No. I'm sorry. There's been no word from either Patagones or Buenos Aires. All anyone can tell me is she left Patagones on 16 February. There were strong winds the next day, they tell me. And as we all know the condition of the ship was not… good.'

Silas looks up. The *Denby*. Her feet. The things she said. Misery overwhelms him like a wave.

'I am very much afraid we are going to have to assume the worst.'

At the back of the room someone gasps.

For several minutes it is silent.

'All those men!' Selwyn's voice cracks. 'Dewi, Gareth… so many of them.'

It is quiet again. Towards the back someone sniffs.

'We can't give up, not yet. There's still a chance – look what happened to the *Maria Theresa*!'

'It's been longer than that, man – much longer.'

They are silent again. Everyone is looking at the floor remembering faces.

'*Jiw, jiw.*'

'What a waste.'

'It is going to be difficult without them,' Edwyn says eventually.

'It's a punishment!' Silas stands. Suddenly everything is clear. 'That's what it is.' His voice is high, taut, trembling. 'Don't you see? We're not meant to be here and we're being punished. A flood and then a famine – it's like the bible. Like when Moses leads them away. We have to go too – maybe back to Wales or Santa Fe.'

'But the crops, Silas, they're growing strongly now, surely that's a sign to stay,' Selwyn says quietly.

'No, we should go.'

Everyone waits in silence. Eyes stare at Silas and then at Selwyn and then at Edwyn. The *Meistr* is trembling. For a few seconds Edwyn's face twists as if a sequence of emotions is being played out in his mind and banished one by one: anger, sorrow, fear, then nothing – as if someone has wiped it clean. Edwyn stands and pulls Silas to him, hugs him close and pats him on the back while Silas stays as he is, his arms stiff and outstretched. Then, still holding him by each shoulder, he looks into his face. 'I'm sorry, *brawd*. You are suffering, I know that. You've lost her and it is hard to bear. But she is with the Lord now, happy.' He smiles sadly. 'We can't know His ways, *ffrind*, we must just accept them.' He lets him go. 'Come now, go with Selwyn and rest. You are tired and God needs you well.'

But Silas stays where he is. 'How do you know what God wants?' he asks quietly. 'What gives you the right to say?'

Edwyn looks at him calmly. 'I can't know, *brawd*, all I can tell you is what I feel in my heart.'

Silas rides. He has taken his strongest stallion, the one which doesn't have to be encouraged too much to gallop. He grips with his knees and forces him faster, along the valley and out of it, into the desert where there is nothing. Then he shouts – cries without words. There is no one to hear him. He shouts until his throat hurts, then he crumples on his saddle and allows the horse to walk until it is darker and the wind has risen. The evening is clear. Around him the wind is blowing a haze of dust, making the ground seem higher. Above it is something like a small bush, the branches tangled around each other as if they are locked in a complicated embrace, and it is rolling above the haze as if it is floating on water. Silas watches it until it stops, caught on a cleft of rocks. Then he watches it as the wind tugs and it edges slowly around, floating there like leaves on water, like rags no one cares about, like Megan. 'I loved you,' he screams but there is no reply. He looks back at the bush and sobs until he is thirsty and has run out of water.

'If there are too many women then maybe some of us are going to learn how to be men,' says Miriam; she throws down her sewing and stands. Her eyes are level with Silas'. 'Looks like I'm halfway there anyway,' she says. When he just looks back at her blankly she punches him hard on the arm. He winces back. 'Well, what do you think? I am just as strong as my brothers, I think. I can even beat Ieuan at running.'

He looks at her slowly, trying to take her in. He finds it difficult to concentrate, difficult to follow what is being said. He looks at her trying not to see Megan. She is as strong and tall as Megan but Megan's strength had a softness about it, something that yielded and welcomed him to her – sometimes in spite of herself. Now, while she knows his eyes are on her, Miriam touches her nest of black hair with the tips of her long fingers. They seem to curve backwards slightly as if the tendons inside pull too hard. 'Will I do, do you think?' She holds her head to one side and blinks at him slowly like a young calf, then laughs at herself.

'Yes, I think you will do very well,' he says.

She looks a little surprised, struggles to control a smile that is more triumphant than demure and then says, 'You were supposed to disagree, Silas. You were supposed to say you couldn't imagine how I could be mistaken for a man.'

He is still looking at her fingers. She follows his gaze, turns her hands over and inspects them herself then shrugs. 'Come on, Myf,' she says and marches out.

The fields are more impressive this year than last. They started sowing earlier and each acre is showing much promise, the stems of wheat growing high and strong. Silas rarely looks. Each time he does he sees the ghost of Megan standing there, her hands on her hips, gazing out at the irrigation ditches then looking back reproachfully at him. My idea, she seems to be telling him. Without me there would be nothing. Without me you would be gone.

Then her ghost follows him inside. Each time it is the same. He catches her in the twilight sitting on her chair with Arianwen on her lap. You killed me, she says calmly. Once he catches himself replying. Once he finds himself weeping by her chair, his head on its empty seat, clutching the arms. No, Megan you did it to yourself. But she shakes her head.

Then there is a touch at an elbow, and there is Miriam, darker and leaner than she was, her mouth slightly open, looking into the place where the voice had been.

'Can you see her?' he asks.

'No,' she says, shaking her head.

'Did you hear her?'

Another shake, but she keeps peering into the gloom, squinting a little until Silas has dried his eyes.

'Sometimes I think I see angels,' she says. 'They are trapped here you know. They can't go to heaven and they don't fall to hell. All they want is to be with God, but something stops them.'

For a few seconds he sits while she stands next to him in silence. Then he sighs, brushes himself down and stands next to her. There is just the room, empty except for a man and a girl. He smiles at her. 'You've not made tea, have you?'

Myfanwy has put her favourite doll – which is just a stick she has clothed with scraps of cloth – onto her mother's chair. Silas catches her talking to it – though whether she is talking to the doll, the chair or her mother's ghost is difficult to tell. 'I have a new Mam now,' she says and smiles contentedly in front of her.

He smiles at her and pats her on the head then returns to his mending. Yesterday one of the stools he made for the kitchen broke and mending it is turning out to be more difficult than he thought. He has mended this stool before – whittled at this same piece of wood until it fitted into the hole. He remembers the kitchen, the warmth of Megan behind him, the faint odour of her milk, her blouse wet as Gwyneth whimpered to be fed.

He stops his work. Tears are dripping on the wood and it is difficult to see. He looks around. It is getting dark, time for him to light some lanterns. Miriam has gone somewhere. He had been tired yesterday and remembers now that he had been a little irritable with her. She had been tidying things away and he had been unable to find his chisel. When she'd told him that she hadn't touched it he hadn't believed her and had stamped around the place cursing and tutting until he had found it where he had left it. He had gone back into the kitchen with an embarrassed grin replacing his frown but she had gone and had not come back that night. Today when he had gone to her mother's house to find out where she was he was told she had gone off on an errand for her father. Mary had been a little short with him, he realises now. Maybe he ought to go and talk to her, offer an excuse for his irritability, maybe take her some flour.

He looks up. Everything has gone quiet. The room is empty. Myfanwy is probably in the kitchen. He picks up the stick and whittles at it again. This time it fits. He stands the stool on the floor and presses down. It is steady on its three legs. He sits back, listens. There is not a sound anywhere. He stands. He has been sitting so long in the same position the whole of his left leg is numb. He stamps on it as he goes out to the kitchen and the blood returns painfully. They are not there. The door is open. He is sure he shut it behind him, maybe Myfanwy managed to let herself out. He runs into their small yard but there is no sign of them.

'Myfanwy?' he calls.

There is no reply.

The sun is setting, the scene is lit in yellows – a mustard field, shimmering gold river, lemon cliffs. He looks around for movement but it is quite still, the wheat in the field upright and silent. How quickly can a child move? He looks around him inspecting the sand, then sees a shuffling track leading between bushes.

'Myfanwy?'

He lights his lantern and follows the path to the river. The ghosts follow him, whispering things he cannot quite hear. He bats them away, shakes his head. 'Go, leave me, you've done enough.'

Then, in the silence following his call is a tiny sound.

'Myfanwy?'

The sound comes again.

He runs forward towards the river and stops. There is the small willow with its overhanging branches and there is the child. He tastes bile in his throat and forces the burning mixture back down to his stomach. 'Myfanwy!' he whispers. The child is near the edge of the water where the current is strong and the water deep. She stops, looks around. 'I'm looking for Mam's ghost.' She smiles, turns around, reaches towards him but her foot slips on the wet mud. He lurches forward but she slithers away from him. She cries out and this time it is as if he is answering her. 'Myfanwy!' She is going, disappearing from view. He scrambles after her, reaches out, calls her name. Gone. The surface of the water undisturbed as if there is nothing there. She must have sunk quickly. He reaches in but he can feel nothing but cold. 'Myfanwy.'

There is no hope. The child will have been carried away by now. He slips heavily on the mud. There is a chuckle behind him. She is caught on the bole of the willow, nestling in a hollow there. He touches her to make sure she is real. Then, as he clutches her to him something moves above his head, as if some great bird had departed from the branch and now is leaving them alone together.

Fifty-one

There are many women and not many men so the women marry young and the men take whom they please. It is a small obvious step for Silas to marry Miriam. She doesn't even have to move homes, merely rooms.

It is Mary Jones who suggests it as he returns weeping with Myfanwy in his arms. 'It looks to me, Silas, as if the sooner you get yourself a wife, the better.'

He follows her gaze to Miriam who is pretending not to listen as she reads her book by the lamplight at the table. 'Well, what about it, girl?'

'What?'

'He's asking you to marry him.'

Her eyes are small, but her eyelids long with dark skin. She looks at him and blinks once slowly. It reminds him so much of a fawn that something inside him weakens. With the entire Jones family and Myfanwy watching, he bends down on one knee.

'Miriam Jones, I would be greatly honoured if you would agree to become my wife.'

Her hair is loose around her face. The dense tight curls look a little like wool. She tips her head so her face is sheltered.

'Miriam?'

Her shoulders are shaking. He thinks she is laughing but she is not. He steps forward and parts her hair. It feels like a coarse version of Myfanwy's. 'What do you say?'

Her long-fingered hands leap to her face. 'It's not how I thought.'

'Miriam? Are you going to answer Silas?'

She looks up. He has never seen her cry before. 'What do you say, Mam? Yes?'

'I think it would be a good choice.'

'Well I don't.'

'Why?'

'Isn't it obvious?'

'Am I too old, is that it?' Silas shifts on his knees.

'No.' She has stopped crying now, but her eyes are still glinting. 'There is something you've forgotten. Something everyone's forgotten.'

'What's that, *cariad*?'

'That! Love. Just some mention of it.'

'Love you? Well of course I love you.' His knees are aching. Something rasps inside one of them as he rises again, levering himself to standing with the help of the table.

'And I love you, too,' Myfanwy says. 'Please say yes.'

Miriam looks at her and gives her a small, tight grin. 'Seems like I have no choice then.'

Caradoc Llewellyn is not even pretending to be happy. He has arrived at Silas' house without warning, striding through Silas' open door and now pacing up and down the short length of the kitchen without taking off his hat. 'It's too early,' he says. 'Megan is barely cold in her grave.'

Silas is sitting alone at the kitchen table; Myfanwy is with Mary Jones' brood. 'My child needs a mother, Caradoc, and I need a wife.'

'Could she not just continue to help you for a while? Wouldn't that be better?'

'Why?'

'Think of your reputation, man. Think of the reputation of the colony. How old are you now? Forty?'

'Thirty-nine.'

'More than twenty years older than her then. She is still a young girl. It is indecent...'

'Indecent? All I am doing is trying to survive in this place, and help my child survive. Don't you care about that?'

'But it is wrong, Silas. If I could, I would forbid it. A mature man like you should not take such a young girl. Especially a man so recently widowed.' Caradoc stops pacing and stands before him. 'Cancel it, man, for the sake of all of us. Say you've been a little hasty. Everyone will understand.'

'No.'

Caradoc sighs. 'I just want you to consider what you're doing. You are ruining not just your life but hers too.'

'Miriam knows her own mind. Surely you know that.'

'Yes, I know she is a strong girl, in will as well as body. But I also know she must dream like all women of her age do – of flowers, of courtship...' Caradoc raises his head and looks at him. '...of love.'

'Love? Of course I love her. She is like a daughter to me.'

'A daughter?'

'Yes. And that, brawd, will have to do for now.'

'This match is wrong. I shall pray for you to come to your senses.' Then, without another word, he disappears out of the door into the early morning sun.

Mary Jones arranges the wedding with her customary efficiency. For days Silas is tormented by smells of cakes baking and he gives her several bags of flour and sugar, and every egg his hens produce. Their diet, in consequence, consists mainly of meat but Myfanwy assures him that Miriam has told her it will be worth it in the end.

Megan, of course, does not approve. In fact Silas thinks that she has disappeared in disgust. One night he comes home and finds that Miriam has rearranged the furniture and added small items of her own. It gives the place a warmer feel: several brightly coloured rag rugs on the floor, cushions tied onto some of the chairs, a few more books on the window sill, and a new cloth over the table. She stands at the bedroom door watching his face as he enters, smiling as his eyebrows rise and he looks around with his mouth slightly open.

'What do you think, Dadda?' says Myfanwy hopping up and down. 'Miriam thinks it looks more homely, and so do I.'

'Well,' he says, seriously, then smiles, 'yes, it is welcoming, quite a transformation.'

After that she adds pictures to the walls, drawings by Myfanwy of animals they have seen, and replaces the plain brown curtains with a red print. She uses the same cloth to pad the chair that used to be Megan's so that it becomes something entirely different, and covers the blankets in the bedroom with quilts of her own.

They have built a chapel in Rawson now. It is made of bricks and has small windows made from rhea gut. Inside there are a series of crude benches, each one owned by a family, and a small platform and table at the front. It is well used: Sunday school, morning and evening services, prayer meetings, choir rehearsals, bible study as well the council and court and Jacob's school – which Caradoc reluctantly attempts to continue.

Although it is John who is officially on the council, it is invariably Mary who speaks – a situation which is acceptable to everyone, especially John.

'This chapel needs more benches,' she says. 'If we hurry we can build them in time for Silas' wedding.'

Only Caradoc and the two Baptist members sitting next to him do not agree. Caradoc sits with his arms folded. 'We don't think it's right,' the man next to him says. 'It's unbecoming. Too hasty.'

Silas opens his mouth, but Edwyn is there before him. 'But it's really not your business, though, is it?'

'Well, Edwyn, I'm afraid it is,' says Caradoc. 'It's the business of us all. She's too young. It gives the whole colony a bad name. What will the people back home say when they hear? We're allowing child brides?'

'She's hardly that.'

'Well, we think it should not be allowed.'

'And I don't think we should condemn.'

'He needs help,' points out Mary, 'he can't look after a house and child on his own.'

Silas is opening his mouth and closing it again like a goldfish. Every time he goes to speak someone butts in for him. He sits back.

'Yes,' says Edwyn. 'His child needs a mother. We have to be practical, *brodyr a chwiorydd,* this is Patagonia, not Ceredigion. It is a harsh place, wild, and there are not many of us here. A man needs a woman.' He sighs. 'And a man with a child needs a woman more than most. Love, romance, courtship – all those – have to be forgotten, what we have to do now at the moment is survive.'

There is silence. Silas is looking at Edwyn. He has forgotten entirely about closing his mouth.

'Are you saying we should not love, *brawd?*' Caradoc says.

'Of course not. I am just saying we need to adapt to where we are and make sacrifices. After all that is what the Lord expects from us, is it not?'

'Yes, *brawd.*'

'So I think we should all offer our congratulations and look forward to the day. And Caradoc?'

'Yes?'

'I expect it to be the shortest sermon you have ever written.'

'But...'

'And your most amusing.'

'But I can't...'

Edwyn sits back and smiles. 'I know. Just do your best.'

The morning before their wedding Miriam opens the windows of Silas' cottage wide. He has replaced the rhea gut now. It is crude stuff for windows, thick and in some places almost opaque, but at least it is sturdy, doesn't rattle in the wind and, for the moment, has little smell.

'There,' she says, 'the old replaced with the new.' It is September and one of the last winds of winter blows in. It rushes around the room whistling to itself, displacing the heavy warm air that was there. Silas fancies he hears moans and faint cries, creaks and curses as if something is being shifted and doesn't want to move. He looks at Miriam to see if she feels it too, but if she does she makes no sign.

When she closes the window again the house feels different. It is not just the smell of the fields outside but a different charge in the air. He sits in the chair that was Megan's and for once feels relaxed and comfortable. Everything is well. He reaches out for Miriam's hand. '*Diolch.*'

Fifty-two

In spite of everything he has slept. He wakes surprised, then becomes dimly conscious of a noise at the window.

'Silas! Get up! Come on you old dog. Get up. Now. Hurry.'

Joseph. My brother-in-law now, he thinks numbly, and then looks at his new wife. She has propped herself up on her arms and is swivelling her head to look, first at the window and then at Silas.

He had just stripped off to his underwear to sleep. He leaps out of bed and immediately wants to cover himself. He sees her swiftly examine him; her eyes passing down his jerkin and then his long johns – neither item scrupulously white any more. He sees what she sees – his thin small shoulders, his small paunch stretching the fabric of his vest, and his legs, obviously thin even though they are covered. Caradoc's words come back to him. Maybe she would have preferred someone her own age. Perhaps she is already a little disgusted. He remembers too well how the middle aged appeared to him in his youth. He has never had time to consider his age before. Middle aged. He gives an indiscernible shrug. At least he's alive. At least he's made it through this long. So many don't. Megan. At the thought of her something vital seems to drop from him. That wedding night had been so different from this one. His shoulders slump. He knows she had been expecting something from him, more than a dry kiss on the cheeks and her own side of a cold home-made mattress.

'Silas!' The voice is in their kitchen now.

He hurries into his trousers, pulls a shirt around him and yanking at his belt lurches into the living room and then the kitchen.

'What?'

'It's Jacob. He's back. Mam told me to come and tell you. She said you'd want to know, just in case.' He stops. Miriam has come into the kitchen behind Silas. She stops at the doorway in her nightclothes, a blanket around her. Her face is flushed and the skin around her eyes swollen and not just because of sleep. 'Are you all right, Mim?' Joseph asks and steps towards her, but she hangs her head, steps back into the living room and then retreats to their bedroom again and closes the door. Joseph looks at Silas, as if he is waiting for him to say something. But Silas looks away. 'Everything's fine,' he says, 'or it will be. It's all taking a bit of getting used to, that's all.'

Joseph nods curtly and goes to the door, then stops. 'Mam said that if there's any trouble to call on us. We're your family too now. She told me to tell you.' He seems to think for a while and then looks up again. 'I think that's all she said.'

'How did you hear he was back?'

'Ieuan said. He went into the village early and saw the ship there, and Jacob coming.'

In the living room Miriam is sitting on Megan's chair examining her hands. She looks up as he enters. 'What have I done, Silas? Or is it something I haven't done?'

He sits down beside her and presses her head to his chest and strokes her hair. 'It's not your fault,' he says gently. 'I've been on my own too long. Even before Megan died I was on my own.'

She forces her head away. 'How?'

'She didn't speak. You must have seen it. She'd drawn away. She was too sad, too full of grief. She couldn't bear it. Some people can't. You must have noticed. They go inside themselves where nothing can hurt them.'

She nods.

'But...'

He is interrupted by the thudding of horse's hooves and then a neighing, loud and close. He stiffens. 'Get into the bedroom. I'll deal with this alone.'

'But I want to be with you.'

'Later. I promise. Now get yourself dressed.'

Someone hammers on the back door. Whoever it is must know there is no need. He opens the door and the wind catches it and throws it wide. It is Jacob – holding on to his hat so it is low on his face, his great black coat loose and flapping like a cloak around him.

'You!' he says, prodding Silas in the chest. 'What have you to say for yourself?'

Silas steps back.

'I've heard it all from Caradoc.' He steps forward, releases his hat so it rises away from his head. His watery-blue eyes are rimmed with red and flooding.

'I'm sorry, Jacob. It just happened. I did everything I could.'

'You killed her.' Jacob is breathing heavily, two dark red patches in the paleness of his cheeks. His years in Buenos Aires have made him look drawn and ill, and he has allowed his beard, now grey rather than gingery-brown, to grow in odd tufted clumps all over his cheeks.

He prods Silas again, a finger hard in his stomach, and Silas grabs hold of his hand. Even though Silas is smaller he is stronger. Jacob tries to pull his hand back but Silas keeps hold, his hand tightening. 'She did it to herself, Jacob. Are you listening? There was nothing anyone could do...' A sob erupts from him. 'I tried, Jacob. I tried everything. Listen to me. She was my wife, for God's sake. My life. I loved her more than I could ever love anyone else.'

Jacob opens his mouth to reply but then looks over Silas' shoulder into the house and closes it again.

Silas glances behind him. Miriam. How could he have forgotten? He can't take the words back. They are true but it does her no good to know them. His hands have relaxed and Jacob snatches his own free.

'Look at her. A child. How could you, Silas? What did you say to her? What lies? That you would look after her like you looked after Megan?' He draws back his lips into the grimace of a smile. 'God sees what you do. Taking a young girl like this. You disgust me.'

'Go away Jacob, you've said enough.'

'I've not started yet.' His voice is close to a sneer, and his smile widens to a grin. It reminds Silas of another grin – the private one that used to belong to Edwyn.

Jacob brings his face closer. 'What are you going to do about it, eh?'

Silas' fist smacks forward. There is a crack and Jacob staggers back, his legs stiff like broom handles, holding his hand to his nose and then drawing his hand away again so he can inspect it. Blood is escaping freely from each nostril.

'Your answer to everything, it seems,' Jacob gasps. The rest of his face is drawn and white. He staggers back then forward again.

'Is it guilt, I wonder,' he says, panting, 'which makes you answer everything I say with a fist?'

'Leave me in peace,' Silas hisses through his teeth.

Jacob holds a handkerchief to his nose and steps closer again, his chin jutting upwards, his beard lifted from his chest.

'He said he wants you to go,' Miriam says loudly. She is beside them now, holding onto Silas' arm. 'He married me because he's fond of me, Mr Griffiths. That's the truth of it. He loved Megan, but now he's fond of me as well. And I love him. And maybe he'll never love anyone as much as he loved your sister, but I know he'll try. He's a good man, he just wants the best for everyone. You should leave us alone.'

Jacob has started at her words, his mouth changing from grimace to open-mouthed astonishment.

'Silas? Miriam? Is everything all right here?' John has arrived with Joseph and Ieuan beside him, their faces set, as if ready for battle.

'I think so.'

Jacob slowly turns. 'I was just giving Mr James my congratulations,' he says, pointedly dabbing at his nose and wincing. 'He's a lucky man.' Then, unwilling to turn his back on them, Jacob walks backwards to where his horse is tethered. 'Shall I see you on Sunday?' he says as if he has just come across them in the village, 'I am looking forward to giving my first sermon in the new chapel.'

'Perhaps, Mr Griffiths. We shall see.'

They sleep side by side as if there is a cold barrier of bed they mustn't cross. During the day she clutches him when anyone sees them, holds his hand or his arm, and leans her head on his shoulder, but never kisses him. And he is aware of her as he would be of an adoring child: another Myfanwy but older and bigger, her body heavy on his, but sometimes too close, sometimes pulling him and weighing him down.

The summer is coming and the wheat is ripening. For an hour Silas and Miriam work side by side almost in silence, intent on their work even though it requires little concentration. Then, abruptly, she pauses and looks at him. 'What must I do for you to love me, Silas?'

'I do love you.'

'Not as a friend. You know how I mean.'

He doesn't answer. His face is burning. He snatches at the weeds, counting them as he pulls them from the ground.

'Look at me.'

He stops. Stands upright.

'What is wrong? My hair? My legs? My face? What is it that repulses you?'

All of these things he thinks guiltily – and yet none of them. 'You are perfect. The fault is mine.'

She strides next to him. 'Hold me.' He touches her on the shoulders.

'Properly.'

'I can't.' He whips his hands away and she stares at him – eyes round and full of tears.

'Is that what's wrong? I want children of my own, Silas. Your children. Our children. How can I have them if you can't even bear to touch me?'

He looks away, kneels down again to dig at the weeds and her shadow stays there, across the ground in front of him unmoving.

'Won't you even talk to me?'

'I can't,' he cries out. 'I can't tell you what I think. Everything is confused. You, me, Megan, Jacob, Edwyn... I'm sorry. I didn't know it would be like this. I'm sorry.'

'Why did you marry me, Silas?'

He doesn't answer. He is close to sobbing and breaking down. The smell of the earth, the sound of the river close by, even the tugging of the wind is reminding him of so many things he would rather forget.

'I think you just wanted a slave. Because that is what I am now. Promised to you before God... but then you made a promise too, Silas, and as far as I can see you have no intention at all of keeping it.'

Fifty-three

It is January and the sun shines down with a hard dry heat. The ground bakes. The ears of wheat are turning yellow, becoming ready to bloom. Every day Silas inspects them and then goes into the village. The same question is asked again and again – in small groups outside each house, inside the warehouse where they all meet to buy supplies, outside the chapel – is it time yet? Shall we wait another day?

Edwyn calls an informal meeting for everyone who is around. Only Jacob is missing, but Jacob doesn't need to know; he has chosen to plant vegetables rather than wheat and can often be seen tending them alone in his field.

'I think we should harvest now,' says Caradoc, and Selwyn agrees. 'Wait another week and everything will blossom and be ruined.'

The American, David Parry, nods. 'The weather is so hot here and things happen quickly in the heat.'

'I agree we should be vigilant,' says Edwyn, 'but if the Lord has given us the sun, surely we should make the most of it. Every day the ears become more golden and fuller. Surely we should wait for as long as possible.'

'There is a danger of being too greedy,' says Silas quietly from the back, and everyone turns to look. The people around him agree. 'At the moment a harvest would be easy, the weather ideal and we all know how quickly things can change.'

'Just another day, *brodyr*, then. Let us make a compromise. Another day and we start the harvest – agreed?' Edwyn's face slowly rotates on his neck. It is like a light, illuminating each nodding head in turn.

Silas goes back to his house and waits. It is cool in the living room and Miriam and the children have gone in their to get out of the sun. Miriam and Myfanwy are absorbed in the book and he enters so quietly they do not look up. The place has begun to smell of Wales, he realises. The perfume of a damper, greener place rises from everything here like a memory from all the pieces of furniture, books and blankets that Miriam has begged or borrowed from friends or family.

When he sits on Megan's old chair it creaks, and the two of them look coolly at him. How alike in their ways they are he thinks. Although Myfanwy looks like a paler, plumper and smaller version of Megan, in mannerisms she mimics Miriam: the way they hold their head slightly to one side, and the way a smile always has to be earned, and then is only given so grudgingly. Miriam stands and smoothes down her skirt. She is plumper than she was he notices – her hips have broadened, and she seems to have done something to her bodice so her chest swells like a rooster's. He smiles.

'What are you smiling about, Dadda?' Myfanwy asks.

'I was admiring what I see.'

Miriam walks from the room into the kitchen and returns with a basket of washing. 'The sky is getting heavy out there. I think it is going to rain.'

He frowns and rushes out. There are clouds building up in the east, a fine even-coloured layer, dividing the sky into two unequal sections. But apart from that the wind has changed direction and lessened. She is right. There is a heaviness. And he fancies the air is not quite as dry. He goes to his horse. The stallion seems restless as if he knows something is about to happen. Silas swings himself into the saddle and yells over to Miriam.

'I'm going to tell them in the village. You go and tell your father. Maybe no one else has realised. Then get the sickle ready. We're going to have to move quickly, I think.'

The rest of the villagers do not take long to persuade. Edwyn organises them, tells each farmer to tell someone else, but most of them have realised already and as he returns to his farm Silas can see them out in their fields, small shapes frantically sweeping the air with their scythes. Miriam is waiting for him, her shorter work clothes on, her sleeves rolled up and a scarf and hat on her head.

The sky has become darker now, the layer to the west larger and more grey. It is a smooth bank of cloud, the line between it and the clear sky to the east straight and perfect. It creeps across the sky towards them and below it the climate gradually changes from the heat of a dry summer day to a colder and more humid autumn. They work quickly and efficiently, side by side, Ieuan coming to join them once he can be spared from his father's plot. Silas cuts and Miriam ties the wheat into sheaves. It is something she only learnt to do last year and he is surprised and pleased at how well she does it. The wind has picked up now, buffeting all of them, picking up the wheat as he cuts it so that she sometimes has to run after it. She is lean and strong, grabbing the wheat like a boy, then tucking it under her arm like a woman picks up a wilful child, and tying it with such an expression of serious concentration that he smiles.

They stop just once for the food she has brought for them both – a couple of hard-boiled eggs and some bread – and finish just as the sun is about to set behind the mountains. Then the rain that has been threatening for the last two hours finally falls – heavy cold drops on the hot land, and they run to the house exclaiming and laughing. Beside the house they pause. It seems like the rest of the valley has succeeded too. All the plots that they can see each have their collection of sheaves. They will have a fine time collecting them all together in the warehouse. There should be a celebration. At last the entire valley has proved itself to be fertile.

'Mam says she is keeping Myfanwy with her for tea so we can have a rest,' Miriam says, slipping in through the door. He face is still flushed and glistening with sweat. Silas pours water from the kettle onto some yerba leaves in two mugs. They have sometimes taken to having their tea the native way, in a mug with a straw.

'You did well today,' he tells her, bringing the two mugs into the living room. She is sitting on their newest piece of furniture – a long settle he has made which she has padded well with cushions. She wedges herself into the corner, sighing, stretching out her legs and arms Her stockings have holes, and her arms are scratched up to where her sleeves end. He says nothing but comes back with a little soap and water, then sits beside her to dab her skin clean. She laughs and cries out, pretending that it hurts her more than it does, then, when he has finished, demands that she returns the compliment.

There is a tear in his trousers, and the material around it is matted with blood. 'I should see to that,' she says, and tries to roll up his trouser leg. 'This isn't working,' she grumbles, then smiles suddenly and grabs at his belt.

'Hey!'

'I'm your wife, Silas, remember. Don't you think I've seen you plenty of times already?'

Mumbling disapprovingly he allows her to peel them from him. The wound is not deep, in fact he cannot remember it happening, but it spreads across the whole of his thigh. She kneels before him with the bowl of water and he watches as her slim fingers squeeze out the cloth and then firmly apply it to the outer edges of his wound, working inwards as she would if she was treating a stain. He leans back, his eyes closed, tries to pretend her hands are not there, but he can feel them, travelling over that part of him that used to belong exclusively to Megan, claiming it for herself with every wipe, every dab. When she reaches the wound he gasps. The pain is close to pleasure.

'Sorry, shall I stop?'

'No, it's all right, carry on.' He hears his own voice, soft, low, like that of a cat being stroked.

She pauses as if registering it. He can feel her looking at him, can hear that she smiles – the almost silent snaps as the strands of saliva drawn apart by her lips break. Then she starts again. Her motions are wider now and her hand more gentle. When the wound is clear she discards the cloth and continues with her hands, one each side of his leg, kneading his flesh – cold but becoming warmer.

'Silas?'

'Yes?' He doesn't open his eyes. He doesn't want to see. He just wants to imagine what is there.

'Don't ever leave me,' she says. 'Promise me.'

His eyes open. Not Megan. He attempts to keep his face steady. He reaches out to touch her hair as he would stroke Myfanwy's. Her smile broadens and he leans over to kiss her lightly on her head. 'I promise,' he says.

Fifty-four

It is still raining. In fact it has not stopped for hours. Just a few steps outside and they are immediately soaked, their clothes and boots heavy. Each step is hard work. The short journey to the Jones' house and back makes Silas feel tired and old.

'You're not old, husband,' Miriam tells him later as they peel away their saturated clothes and put them on the rack to dry in front of the fire. Myfanwy is asleep already. Silas and Miriam sit on the settle and listen to the rain. It drums on the roof, the window, the track, the cart outside, then they hear it hissing along gullies, gurgling around the house and finding places to escape to the river. Miriam shivers. 'Too hot to move just a few hours ago,' she says, 'and now this!'

All night it rains and the day after that. And the day after that. On and on.

'Fine summer this is,' Selwyn says to each person that passes. He is the proud father of two boys now, each one resembling him in face and their mother in build. The neighbours smile back and then look wistfully at their fields; the sheaves of wheat are drenched in rain and there is no chance of winnowing yet.

Jacob delivers sermons on the flood, emphasising the fact that God had found it necessary to start again because of mankind's wickedness. 'We should take this as a lesson,' he says darkly. 'It is our Lord's way of telling us to look to ourselves, and examine our consciousnesses. Have any of us done anything of which we are ashamed and not yet asked the Lord for forgiveness?' He looks around the chapel picking out faces and settling on those he seems to think are transgressors. The colonists shift uneasily in their pews.

'What about the other flood, brother?' says one member of the congregation during the afternoon tea that follows. 'Was that God punishing us too? What had we done?'

Jacob doesn't answer. He smiles his tight smile and moves on. Now that he is settled back in Patagonia he has re-established his ridiculous beard. It stands out stiffly from his face like the mane of an old lion, the rest of his face scrupulously shorn. He socialises with no one but Edwyn and Caradoc. He delivers his sermon, supervises prayer meetings and takes lessons in his school, but mainly he is alone, often seen tending the grave of his sister, an isolated figure, rarely meeting the eyes of anyone in his lone walks through the village.

After the service he catches Miriam alone and asks her if her husband has made his peace with the Lord.

'And what did you say?' asks Silas when she returns home.

'I said that you didn't need to. You had done nothing wrong.' She pauses, and looks at her hands. 'I think he has gone a little mad, Silas – and I think he hates you.'

They sit quietly. The rain beats down against the glass. There is something dripping somewhere out in the kitchen. It beats as steadily as the clock ticks.

'It's bad to hate,' Miriam says suddenly. 'Yeluc told me. He told me that it was bad for the soul.'

'I sometimes think Yeluc knew more than anyone.'

'Once he told me that one day all the Tehuelche will die and all that will be remembered of them are the pictures they drew.'

'Why?'

'I don't know. He said he could see things, he could travel into another place and in one of these places there were no Tehuelches at all. Their tongue was forgotten and no one could remember who they were. Then he travelled a little further and all the Galenses were gone too, and the Cristianos, and all anyone spoke was one tongue which he didn't know.'

'Did he mind?'

'No, he said all that mattered was that Elal knew where everyone was so that he could take them on his white swan to live with their ancestors in the stars. He said that it didn't matter what tongue anyone used, that Elal understood them all.'

'Did you speak to him a lot?'

'Yes, when he came to Mam's kitchen. He used to like to watch her cook. I think he liked the scraps she used to feed him.'

For a few minutes she leans against him. Outside the rain spatters against the new glass in the window.

'One day, I told him about the angels in the clouds, and he said they were like Elal's birds and that it was good to see such things. It helped you to remember that the world belongs to Elal and that we are only here because he lets us stay.'

Something blows against the window making it rattle in its frame.

'Sometimes I think Elal and God are the same thing.'

Silas smiles and nods. 'Sometimes I think that too.'

The window rattles again and she huddles against him. 'It's getting fierce,' she says.

A crack of lightning illuminates the room with a sudden blue-white light, then almost immediately a roar of thunder answers it. The rain smashes at the glass with a new intensity. Silas hurries to the window and looks out, but of course the moon is hidden by clouds. He squints through the glass and the rain but it is too dark to see. All he hears is the rain, falling into water.

In the morning he reaches out but there is no one there – just Myfanwy standing by his bed with a doll.

'Where's Miriam?' he asks.

'Gone out to look at the water. She said not to worry. It's drowned the field but it won't drown us.'

Miriam is standing behind the house just looking. It is something they have seen before. Instead of a river in its valley there is a wide lake, rain still splashing down into it, the heads of the stacks of wheat just poking through.

'It can still be saved, can't it, Silas?' She seems to know he is there beside her without looking at him. 'Dadda says maybe we can fish it out, and it will dry when the sun returns.'

He slips his hand into hers. 'Yes, my love, all will be well.'

Fifty-five

Someone is watching. Silas turns around. Edwyn is standing at the open door to the kitchen silently watching them. Silas wonders how long he has been there and what he has seen: Silas helping Myfanwy to dress in front of the fire then taking the kettle from the stove; Miriam smiling at him when he gives her some tea, and that small kiss he gave her, just a touch on the cheek.

'What do you want?' Why does the man just stand there at the doorway just watching them?

'Your help, Silas. Everyone's help. Did you hear the cows?'

Silas glances at Miriam and they both shake their heads. 'Well, they're getting restless. They don't like the water coming close and I don't think the pen will hold them.'

'What do you want from me, Edwyn?'

'To help me shore up the pen.'

'In this weather?'

It is still raining. A sudden gust of wind causes Edwyn to pull up his collar. Silas has not asked him in.

'Well, there's no use waiting until it stops, is there? They'll all be gone by then.'

Silas glances at Miriam. She tells him with a brief nod of her head to go.

Silas hears it now: the distant lowing of cattle beneath the patter of the rain on mud and the moaning wind.

He considers telling him he has too much to do, but Edwyn looks at him so appreciatively when he puts on his jacket that he changes his mind.

In the end there are just the two of them – everyone else is too busy rescuing what they can from the flood.

The wind is picking up as their horses reach the village. Water has covered the fields, but the wheat sheaves are still intact. There are little waves on the surface of the water and for a few seconds Silas is fooled into thinking it is flowing backwards inland, but then the wind changes direction again and the waves head out to sea. It is cold. Even though it is still January and midsummer it is cold. Yet just a week ago Silas felt too hot to work even in his shirtsleeves and Miriam had stripped down to her chemise and complained that decency did not allow her to go further. The thought of her peaceful presence makes him yearn for home. 'Just a couple of hours, mind, then I'll have to be heading back.'

Edwyn nods his head once, then after a few minutes adds, 'Thank you, Silas.'

The cows are east of the village on a patch of land that is a little higher than the rest. Silas can hear their lowing clearly now he and Edwyn have gone beyond Rawson – a continuous mournful groan – grey like the sky, depressing his spirit, making him long for the warmth of his living room. Maybe the cows can smell the river as it creeps towards them. They are milling around at the end of their pen opposite the river, as far away as they can get from the water. The flooding has churned up new black silt smelling of sulphur and airless decay. They snort at the air, beat up new mud, and then one or two of them lower their heads like bulls and charge at the earth wall that holds them.

'Look,' says Edwyn, 'it's crumbling.'

The mud is slippery in the rain, and the ground is waterlogged. The horses are slithering so the two men dismount and, armed with spades, walk the rest of the way on foot. After a couple of steps Edwyn grunts and falls to the ground. Silas starts to help him then falls flat himself. He struggles upwards then looks at Edwyn and then down at himself and laughs. 'Look at us – we're like two brown, fat elephant sea lions – all we can do is shuffle forwards on our stomachs.'

For a minute Edwyn just looks at him, then a large broad smile erupts on his face. He throws back his head and falls back into the mud, snorting like one of the pigs the colony slaughtered at Port Madryn four years ago. He sounds so much like an animal that Silas laughs back.

They stagger to their feet, still laughing. 'I knew I should find a good companion in you, Silas.'

'You did?'

'Yes. Last night I...' He stops, reaches out and presses his hand down on Silas' sleeve. 'We're too late,' he says.

The cows are now bellowing in triumph. One of them has managed to demolish a piece of the earth wall and is forcing her way through to the outside. Behind her the cows are milling about, pushing and mounting each other in their anxiety to escape. Silas and Edwyn wade as quickly as they can but progress is difficult. They keep slipping over, struggling to get up and then falling over again. At last Silas manages to find a piece of ground more solid than the rest and staggers forward. A few of them have escaped and are making for the northwest where the ground is higher and firmer, but the rest are slower and more timorous. He shouts at them and they back away, then with his spade he begins to dig, one small plunge and then another. The mud is wet and heavy; it is as much as he can do to lift each small spadeful. Soon Edwyn joins him and they work together silently, repairing one section of the wall and then the next.

At last they rest, straighten their backs and groan.

'Good. We've done well, Silas. That should keep them safe for now.'

'But we'd better keep a watch.'

Edwyn looks back at their work. 'No, it'll hold – better to give chase to the rest.'

Silas shakes his head. 'I'm telling you, we'd better keep a watch. Better to keep an eye on what we've still got.'

Edwyn regards him steadily.

'It's easy to lose track of them if you can't see them.' Damn the man, why does he just keep staring, making him talk, making him give excuses. 'You think it's all right, but it's not.'

'The sheep?' Edwyn smiles.

Silas nods.

'Those damned sheep, eh? Nothing but trouble. In the end they didn't matter, did they?'

But they did. He didn't look after them. He let them go. He let everyone down. A sob rises so suddenly to his throat he can't hold it in.

'Do you think anyone cares about a few sheep now, Silas?'

He can't answer.

'No. It's not the sheep that matters, *ffrind,* but this.' He spreads his arms. 'This country, this place, our new Wales.'

'But without the sheep we almost lost everything. Everything!'

'No, without *you* all would have been lost. *You,* Silas. Don't you see?'

Silas shakes his head. And Edwyn smiles. 'Come, *brawd.'*

Their horses are sinking into the mud. Silas and Edwyn pull at their reins but their struggling just sends them deeper. Eventually they find some stones and slowly make a path for the horses to clamber out, neighing and snorting, onto firmer ground to the north. The cows are long gone. There are distant bellows but nothing close. After he has allowed his horse to drink, Edwyn eases himself onto its back.

'What are you doing?'

'Going after them, of course. If we're quick we might get to them before the Indians do.' He looks down at Silas. 'Are you coming? It won't take long, I promise.' He holds out his arm, smiles and then trots away. It is too cold and wet to think. Silas mounts his horse and allows it to follow.

The horses' backs are laced with rain. It dribbles down their necks and onto the blanket underneath the saddle. Silas sniffs. He has always liked the smell of a wet animal. He pats the horse and whispers into the animal's ear, 'Good boy'. They follow the mess of footprints up onto the higher ground and then out of the valley into the barren plain above. It is raining here too but more gently. The horses' hooves make a ringing sound on the ground as if they are treading on the skin of a taut drum. Silas has the impression that they are treading on something hollow and he leans forward, urging the horse to be careful. The cows' tracks peter out and soon they have to get down from their horses to examine the ground. Edwyn puts his ear to the ground as they have seen the Indians do but reports that he can hear nothing.

'Maybe we should be getting back,' Silas says, looking around them. The rain has stopped and it is getting dark, the sun close to setting, and it is still very cold with the wind whipping their faces.

'Just a little longer. Look, I think I see something moving over there.' Edwyn points to where there is a clump of pale-coloured rock and shadows moving around them. They carefully move a little closer but the shadows turn out to be just the branches of an old dead bush moving in the wind.

It is dusk now and they have had little to eat since breakfast, just a couple of old crusts Edwyn found in his saddlebag. Silas climbs to the top of the rocks and looks around. It is the highest thing for miles. Towards the west he can see some dark dots moving together across the plains – and around them some other dots, browner and more widely spaced, stealthily circling around them. He motions to Edwyn who scrambles up beside him.

'Indians.'

Edwyn nods.

'Is it worth going after them?'

Edwyn shakes his head slowly. 'Up here they'll be seen as fair game, belonging to no one.'

'But they know they're ours.'

'I don't think that will matter, *ffrind*, not if they are Gallatt's men.'

Closer to them something is moving through the undergrowth, tail twitching.

'What's that?'

'Shh.'

It is a cat, too big to be one of the small wild cats. This one is a sandy yellow and moving quickly. A puma. Silas has heard stories from the Indians of course, and even seen distant small fast movements, but this is the first one he has ever seen close and it terrifies him. Edwyn motions for them to sink onto the rock and they do so quietly. Only a couple of small pebbles grind against each other as they crouch but it is enough for the animal to stop and for his ears to swivel. His head turns and his eyes glare at them – oddly uninterested and antagonistic at the same time. Arrogant, Silas thinks, and coldly vicious. For a few seconds the animal doesn't move, but then he comes slightly closer. He is silent, his soft paws seem to know exactly where to go not to make a sound – each movement slow and powerful. Silas thinks he can hear the animal's breath. Just the wind, he tells himself, just the wind. Beside him Edwyn is rigidly still. The puma's head disappears. Silas moves slightly, craning to see if he has moved closer towards them or further away. A branch of gorse immediately in front of him shifts. He breathes out. It is a small armadillo carelessly dislodging gravel as it makes its way though the undergrowth.

'It's going.' Edwyn's voice is barely discernible above the wind. But still they do not dare move. It is becoming rapidly darker now the sun has set, and the wind is howling. Shadows are turning into faces and the ends of twigs into twitching tails. Silas has lost feeling in his legs. He shifts a little then falls to one side.

'Hush!' Edwyn hisses and Silas stays where he is, awkwardly supporting himself with a forearm on the ground.

At last Edwyn indicates with his hand that they can move. It is almost night now and they can see only as far as the nearest bush. Silas thinks of the puma creeping around them, biding his time.

Edwyn stands and briskly starts to gather twigs.

'What are you doing?'

'There's no point in trying to return now. We'd only get lost. The best thing we can do is try to light a fire and wait until daylight.'

He's right, of course he's right. Silas thinks about Miriam waiting for him and worrying.

'We shouldn't have gone after them,' he says, not moving, 'we had no chance of catching them.'

'You didn't have to come.'

Silas feels a strong compulsion to hit him. 'Why do you never apologise? Never admit you're wrong?'

'I wasn't wrong, it was the right thing to do – there was a chance we might catch them.'

But Silas isn't listening. 'Why do you lie? Do you enjoy deceiving and tricking people?'

'I do not lie.'

'The meadows, the tall trees – why did you say they were here? Why did you pretend we were coming to a paradise, when this was all there this?'

'I do not believe I mentioned trees. Those were the words of Captain Fitzroy, and I saw no reason to doubt them.'

'But you'd been here, man. You'd seen this place for yourself.'

Edwyn stands and looks at their collection of twigs and then stoops to rearrange it. 'Yes, our land, a new Wales.'

'But it's a desert!' His voice is too loud. His words will travel even in this wet wind.

'No, Silas, not a desert. You, *ffrind,* have shown that it is not a desert.'

Edwyn kneels by the heap of twigs and dry kindling they have managed to find and strikes at flints, but it takes him several minutes to produce smoke and then a small flame. They pull blankets from the horses over their shoulders and sit beside it. Silas takes a twig and begins to trace pictures on the ground. He thinks of Myfanwy's pictures and the way Miriam has hung them so carefully on the walls of their house, and a small thrill of pleasure makes him want to hug himself. When he gets back he will try to make some paint. Next time the Indians visit he will ask them what they use to daub on their cloaks. Megan used to admire those cloaks. She said that one day she would like to own one for their walls. The thought of her is not so raw now. Sometimes he feels guilty that he can prod at the wound where she was and not feel pain but just a poignant gladness that at least he knew her once, at least they shared time together and were happy. Then he remembers Edwyn's woman: her pale small face, and her indignant anger on behalf of her husband. She had seemed so much more vulnerable than Megan, as brittle and as fragile as a doll, and yet Cecilia Lloyd still lives. He looks up at Edwyn wondering how he can bear to continue to live here without her. It must be a strange existence – as if he is married and widowed at the same time. Or maybe he welcomes her absence.

Edwyn is looking at him. For a few minutes he does just that. His face is the palest thing that Silas can see: an oval with the bottom part eclipsed by the crescent of his beard. The crescent moves: 'I'm sorry.'

Silas waits for more but nothing comes.

'For what?'

Silas needs him to say.

'My exaggeration.'

'But why, man, why do it?'

Silence. Edwyn tips his head and his face disappears beneath the brim of his hat.

'Aren't you going to tell me?'

He shakes his head. 'It's too difficult.'

'Please tell me,' Silas says more gently, 'I would like to know. How did it start?'

'It was after my mother died.'

Silas waits again. When Edwyn speaks his voice is small,

strained and so unlike his usual voice that it's as though someone else is speaking. 'After her English landlord killed her.'

Fifty-six

'We don't know what happened.' His voice has returned to its normal timbre. 'Perhaps she had a note, but if she did it would have been in English, not that she could read much, anyway. My mother missed out on school, no one much saw the point in educating a girl like her, I suppose. They still don't – do they?' Edwyn looks up briefly, smiles sadly to himself, and then looks back towards the fire. He pokes it and sparks fly up. Silas wonders if there are any Indians around to see it.

'Anyway, if she had a note she didn't mention it to me. The first we knew was a knock on the door and one of the landlord's henchmen was standing there, pushing her through the doorway as soon as my sister opened it.'

He pauses, swallows, then looks up at Silas. His eyes are reflecting the fire and seem to be burning too. 'They'd beaten her, my friend. She was an old woman and they'd beaten her. She could hardly see, and we'd begged her to come and live with one of us, but she had been so fond of her house and her memories. She'd been determined to die in it, but she didn't in the end, of course.

'He was greedy, he had plenty of land already but he wanted more and the government let him take it. He campaigned for an enclosure act and there was no one to stop him, no one to stand against him. So he had his way. He extended his empire and unfortunately my mother's house was in the middle of it. It was on the common land, one of those houses built in the night. She was so proud of it. Built overnight with smoke rising through the chimney before the morning. She thought no one could ever claim it from her but she was wrong.

'I hated him, Silas.' For a full five seconds Edwyn glares at Silas without blinking. 'I had hated him before but afterwards, after I'd seen what he could do, I hated him more.'

Edwyn looks down again. 'Of course hate is an evil, wicked

thing, but I didn't know that then. At the time I thought of it as revenge – something pure, something righteous. An eye for an eye, it says in the Good Book, in three different places, did you know that? Exodus, Leviticus and Deuteronomy. But that is the Old Testament. Our Lord has given us new commands, since then.' He glances at Silas again. 'How well do you know His words, or the words of the disciples? "But I say unto you, That ye resist not evil: but whoever shall smite thee on they right cheek, turn to him the other also." Matthew, *ffrind*: the tax collector, a wealthy, educated man. He knew the sacrifices a man needs to make. It took me some time to realise the meaning of his words, some more to take them into my heart. It is always necessary to forgive, *fy ffrind*. It brings comfort.'

Silas stabs at the ground with a stick. He had been expecting another tale – one in which Edwyn's great worth is shown through his heroic and selfless actions – not this self-effacing tale of mistakes and wrong thinking.

'Ah, my mother was so fond of that house. I was born there; all my brothers and sisters were born there. It was a simple place; just two rooms. It makes what we have here seem like palaces. But it was a fine place to her, all she ever needed, she said.'

Edwyn is carrying on, almost as if he is talking to himself.

'A house in pieces.' He smiles and shakes his head. 'Surely you have heard of such a thing. For months it was waiting in parts around the village, she said – behind her parents' cottage there would be a door, in the cowshed a window frame, their settle was waiting for them in the pub. There were pieces everywhere – beneath barns, on top of the pigsty, even in the chapel hall...'

A fragment of wood tumbles from the flames and Silas stares at where it has been.

'I often imagine how it must have been. Everything had to be done in secret, she said – single words passed along the pew in chapel before services, spread around during market: all that whispering... then a wink perhaps, or a nudge, and a couple of words exchanged over a pint of ale. Then the night...'

How the man loves the sound of his own voice. Silas leans to one side and allows his body to collapse against the ground. He feels as if he is a child again, being told a fairy story.

'It was autumn and there had been no rain for days, she told me. The moon was full...'

Edwyn's voice drifts away to somewhere distant and Silas shuts his eyes. He sees the men meeting in front of the *tafarn*. The dusk is gathering and their voices are too loud and quick. Anyone passing would wonder at them. They laugh pointedly at any slight joke and there is something strange in the way they each reassure the rest as they go – that they will see them tomorrow, the same time as usual. Silas smiles and turns and Edwyn's voice drifts over to him again.

'When my mother arrived she was cross with herself – the house was already half-finished, you see, she'd missed some of it. She'd had no idea they would get on with the business so quickly. There were a dozen men tapping with their hammerheads covered in rags to muffle them, and some more constructing frames and building walls. Then, very soon, there were walls with two windows and a door and the chimney.

'Then my father carried her over the threshold – laughing so hard he almost dropped her. And then, still laughing, she'd struggled to make the fire light, but then the tinder caught, just as the sun rose, and everything was all right, something she'd never forget, she said, something she told me again and again – how a small thread of grey smoke rose into a sky full of reds and purples and everyone clapped, cheered, and banged the new corrugated iron of the roof. It was done then, you see, too late for anyone to do anything about it. Smoke coming up the chimney before eight o'clock, Silas. "*Tŷ Unnos.*" The house built overnight.' His voice fades.

'But they were wrong, though, weren't they?' Silas says drowsily

'Yes, *brawd*, they were.'

For a few minutes there is silence. The fire is dying down. Edwyn reaches out to gather some more twigs and drops them on top. Silas opens an eye – new fiery houses are lying on top of the old. He remembers seeing houses before, remembers feeling Megan beside him looking too. She'd been happy then, he thinks – or if not exactly happy, content.

Edwyn sighs and then his voice starts again. 'After they evicted her they burnt it down. Didn't even allow us in to clear the place. It was all over before anyone could do anything. A easy target, see. Just an old woman, almost blind, no danger to anyone. All she had left were her memories and they destroyed even those – every little knickknack, every little treasure, went with that house – up in smoke.' His voice has grown hard. He sighs – a long breath out – and when he speaks again it is softer. 'It is so hard not to hate.'

Silas is awake, now, remembering tales of his own: the dogs in their sacks; Melrose on his horse, that little fat lawyer Dewi Roberts not listening: lazy, stupid. He stabs at the ground again. He is nothing of the kind, he reminds himself. There was nothing he could do then and nothing he could do later either. Then he thinks of Megan. He let her down. She expected him to do miracles and was disappointed when he did not. Sometimes he thinks she withdrew into her silent world just to spite him.

'She didn't talk again.' Edwyn is still talking. It is as if someone has broken into the bottom of a full barrel of his words. 'Something seemed to snap inside her. I went to the Englishman's house and demanded to see him but they wouldn't let me. When she died I swore I would pay him back, but of course there was nothing I could do. I hurt, *brawd*, it was as if someone had pierced me with a knife and then run away. I wanted so much to wound them back, but that sort of revenge never heals your own cut, it just makes it burn worse.'

'I started writing a magazine making fun of everything I could find – the chapel, the church, all the people I thought could have helped her but didn't – and, of course, the English. But it didn't make things better. What ever I did I just hurt more.'

Silas is sitting up now, staring at the man and listening. No one in the colony knows very much about Edwyn Lloyd, he realises now. As far as everyone is concerned he is just the *Meistr*, the one who brought them here, the one who went to Patagonia before them and came back again babbling lies. The man obsessed and possessed by the idea of this promised land. He says little else about himself. Yet once he must have been a child, once he must have fallen in love.

'It is as the Good Lord says, but I was too young and hot-headed to listen. I had a good brain, you see, and I'd been lucky, I'd been to school and I thought I knew everything. I trained as a printer then became a publisher. Oh, I had fun, *ffrind*. If the English could do that to my mother then I would hurt them back with my pen. I was cruel, I realise that, now. Eventually I didn't care if what I was writing was true or false, all that mattered is it should hurt those that hurt me. It obsessed me. It was all I could think about.'

Silas says nothing. He needs to hear more. He shifts slightly on his haunches.

'But it didn't work. I never felt satisfied. After all, the people I wanted to hurt didn't even read my paper. And then, after that report, that travesty of a report, *ffrind*, by those inspectors of the schools, the Blue Book...'

Silas nods.

'I realised I could not continue. Welsh was becoming a language of ridicule, "unsuitable for modern life" they said, incapable of explaining complex ideas of law or science...' he laughs derisively.

'It was going to die out, I realised. People were beginning not to teach it in schools. There is something called the Welsh Not, have you heard of it? They pass it round in the classroom, one child betraying the next if they hear another using the language, until the last one at the end of the day is whipped. *Jiw, jiw...*' he shakes his head.

'As if it's dirty! As if it is something to be ashamed of, as if we really are uncivilised, just peasants, backwards – both morally and intellectually.'

He pauses. 'I'm sorry, I've always felt rather strongly.' He looks into the fire again. 'I despaired. I gave up my business. It was then that I met Cecilia. Ah, she is such a gentle, considerate woman...' he pauses for a few seconds and rubs his eyes. 'I don't think I should have lived without her... and it was through her and her father that I met Gabriel Thomas.' He looks at Silas. 'Have you met him?'

He waits for Silas to shake his head. 'What a man, so intent on how things should be done and what needs to be done. He made me see what I could do. If things went on as they were, he told me, if we let the English come in, if we let them close the chapels and open churches instead, make fun of our language, call us dirty and obscene, then we would lose everything, just like my mother had. Our culture and our tongue would be gone within a generation. The only answer was to escape.

'He'd already been to North America – but that was no good, he had seen that. He had gone there as a young minister. Within a generation everyone had forgotten who they were. Ask Selwyn. So we had to find somewhere else. Somewhere clean, uncorrupted, empty of people who could contaminate us. When he heard of

Patagonia he knew it was the place. He called me to him and we prayed together. It was then that I saw.'

He shudders, shuts his eyes. 'Patagonia. The promised land. Kept for the Welsh. All I had to do was go there and see for myself. He warned me it would not be easy to make others see. He said there would be those with blinkers but with time these blinkers would drop away.'

Silas looks up. Edwyn's face is close, glowing in the fire. 'Is that why you lied?'

'I saw what I knew would be,' he says quietly.

'But they were not there.'

'It doesn't matter. I knew what would be; how it is now; what *you* have changed it into, *brawd*!'

'And what about the Indians? It seems to me you saw exactly what you wanted to see.'

'I believe I saw what the Lord wanted me to see.'

Silas watches him. He really seems to believe in what he says. It doesn't matter any more what is true, what is real, all that matters is this place, what it is, and what it will become.

'What about Cecilia?' Silas says coldly. 'Did she see it too?'

At last his face changes. It sags, and then drops from sight. 'No. I was hoping so much that she would. All she ever saw when she came is what the rest of you seemed to see. At first she tried to support me, but then we argued. She said I was mad, ill, obsessed. Even in Buenos Aires she refused to listen. In the end she said she couldn't stand it any more.'

'So she went.'

'Yes. Home. I'm still hoping...'

'Do you miss her?'

'Of course.' His voice snaps like one of the twigs in the fire. 'I had such dreams, but without her...'

'They won't all come true.'

A twig snaps again.

'No.'

Silas wakes with the wind still blowing past his ears. He is cold and stiff, the blankets around him sodden. He doesn't know how he has slept but he has. Then it comes: the despair that overwhelms him each time he wakes. Another day without Megan, another day

Richard won't see. Her face. His voice. He allows himself to think of them for a few minutes before resolving, as usual, to set them aside. Then he looks at Edwyn. He watches his eyelids twitch as the eyes beneath follow a dream. Then, without warning, they open. For a few seconds they meet Silas' eyes. Neither of them speaks. Then, abruptly, Edwyn smiles and rises swiftly to his feet.

'Time to go,' he says. 'If we move now we will be back in time for lunch.'

Fifty-seven

Everything is as grey as the ashes in front of him, but at least now it is possible to see the direction. If they just go to where the sun is dimly rising it should be quite easy to make their way back to the coast. Their horses trudge with heads bowed against the wind. At the edge of each small incline Silas and Edwyn strain to see ahead but they have to rise and fall three times before they can make out the river glinting in the distance. At last they come to the edge of the valley. The drop in front of them is steep and almost cliff-like, but Edwyn walks to the edge, where the ground is crumbling, and stares across – while Silas keeps a little way back.

The rain is falling again – across the sky like slanted spears. The sun appears briefly from behind a thick bank of cloud and sends out a shaft of light. It picks out the river that is now spread across much of the valley in a rippling lake. It is littered with objects – precious pieces of wood, bodies of animals, branches of trees and items of clothing, some of them are being dragged away into the body of the river.

For a few minutes Edwyn stands silently, his toes at the edge of the precipice, then he closes his eyes and raises his arms to the sky.

'Edwyn?' Silas says. He wonders if the man has finally lost all his sense. Beneath his feet pebbles fall away – a few seconds' silence and then a soft chink as they hit the ground far below them. But Edwyn's feet don't move. They stay exactly where they are. Then, with his eyes still closed, he begins to mouth words.

Silas shifts beside him. Just one step forward, that's all it would take. Or the merest push. No one would ever know. Silas holds his breath. It is as if someone is testing him.

There is a renewed burst of rain, so intense that Silas staggers back, he pulls the blanket from his saddlebag and covers his head. But Edwyn stays where he is. It is as if he doesn't feel the rain touching him at all. He looks relaxed and he smiles as if he is listening to a pleasant secret. Water is flowing off him now in rivulets. He slowly brings the palms of his hands together and his lips start moving again. Silas moves closer. Praying. Of course. The only thing left.

Silas shuts his eyes and ties a little prayer of his own. 'Make it stop,' he prays. 'Make the wind still, dry up the riverbank and let me go home.' But when he opens his eyes everything is just the same except that Edwyn is now looking at him, smiling. And even through the rain he can see that smile beneath the *Meistr*'s beard, and hear it too in his voice: 'Did He speak to you too?'

Edwyn is still standing at the edge, still slightly swaying. Silas slowly moves one foot and then the next. 'Of course not. Did he speak to you?'

Edwyn smiles and nods. 'I think that He did. He told me that we should stay where we are and He will make sure that the storm will subside.'

Silas looks around him – if anything the wind is picking up and the sky is darkening.

Another small step: close enough now to feel the man's breath, close enough to hear it rasping from his lungs.

'Did He happen to say when?'

'No, but it doesn't matter. We will be safe. I know that now.'

Silas feels his muscles tense. One small push, that's all it would take, just one touch of his fingers...

'All this...' Edwyn sweeps the air in front of him, '...is part of the plan.'

Silas shuffles forward a little more. Almost close enough to touch him now without meaning to. 'What plan is that? Which stupid plan is that?'

'The Lord's plan. He has everything in hand.'

Just the slightest movement, anyone would believe it was an accident, but it's not, just the flat of his hand, slowly, slowly, slowly...

Edwyn closes his eyes and smiles tightly again. 'All will be well. The Lord has shown us that the wheat will grow through you. You, *brawd*! Don't you see?'

Silas' arm drops slightly.

'Why you? It seems so undeserved. It was you that doubted, you that questioned everything that I did.'

Edwyn sways with his eyes still closed, over the precipice and back again.

'You protested, turned the others against me and I almost came to hate you as much as I hated the English. You were a demon sent to try me, I thought. My test, my temptation in the wilderness.'

His face twists with such an expression of anguish that Silas feels some of it too.

Edwyn throws up his arms again, gasps in a lungful of air and cries out: 'Why? Hadn't I done enough? Hadn't I done all I was told? Hadn't I sacrificed everything? Why did I need to be punished again and again?' He opens his eyes, turns to Silas and grips him by the jacket, his eyes wild. 'Do you know? Did the Lord tell you?'

Silas shakes his head carefully. Beside him a foot-sized piece of the ground breaks away and falls. He tries to shift himself backwards.

'But surely...'

Suddenly Edwyn stops, looks down at his hands and lets go. 'I'm sorry, *brawd*... sometimes I...'

Another clod breaks away, closer to Edwyn this time. Silas watches the ground. Watches while a crack forms close to where the last sod broke away.

'But then, when your crops succeeded, I realised. Not a demon but chosen – by God – to show me the way.'

The crack grows, creeps forward.

'Why, Silas? It doesn't seem right. You don't pray, you don't study His word, you don't even try to listen – and yet He talks to you even though you don't know you are hearing Him.'

Edwyn waits for an answer, but Silas doesn't speak. He is watching the crack, watching it grow. Edwyn sighs and turns again to look at the lake below them. His eyes widen. 'Silas, look! Down there!'

Now that the sun has risen a little more Silas can see that the water has spread farther than he thought and as he watches a fresh surge of water washes down as if something upstream has given way. As it sweeps out towards the sea it picks up hundreds of sheaves of wheat.

'Our crop!' Silas stands transfixed. Not just his crop, but everyone else's crop as well, all of it disappearing in front of them in the current and the wind.

'All those fields of wheat! All gone!' Edwyn turns back to look at the sky, his arms outspread. 'Why, Lord?' he wails, 'why this test?' Suddenly he stops and looks at Silas again. 'Do you know?'

Silas shakes his head, says nothing, waits.

The *Meistr* lowers his voice and arms. He takes a few paces along the cliff and back again. Then he holds his arms out to Silas as if to draw him close. 'But what comes next, *ffrind*? You must know. Tell me.'

The place where Edwyn had been standing falls away. Silas watches it tumble, break and then settle. He breathes out. The *Meistr* is still there in front of him: walking back and forth shaking his head, making strange little flapping movements with his arms, muttering, then making little cries as another surge of water carries yet more of their crop towards the sea.

When Edwyn speaks again his voice is as plaintive as a sheep's 'What must we do next?'

Silas smiles. Yeluc was right. There is no need for a knife. No need to push. No need to run. All a man has to do is wait.

Below them the sheaves are now floating past the spit, being thrashed by the waves and there is a distant shout as someone below wakes and sees what is happening. A couple of men start to wade through the water. The *Meistr's* eyes swivel wildly. He staggers to the cliff edge and then back again. Then he stands in front of Silas with his mouth half open and his eyes oddly empty. 'Silas!' Both a wail and a question.

Silas takes a breath, reaches up to wrap his arm around his shoulder and steers him gently away from the edge. 'You need to do what you did before, *brawd*. The wheat grew. You need to go back to Wales. You need to tell Gabriel Thomas of our good news and persuade more to join us. Then you must bring them all... and you must fetch Cecilia.'

Edwyn subsides a little. 'Ah yes, my own dear wife...'

'You must tell them to come at once. We cannot wait.'

Silas removes his arm and turns to look again at the valley. The sheaves are in the open sea now. Silas watches them sink and float, float and then sink. 'And you must show Dr Rawson that his faith in us has been well founded. You can tell him about our yield, how this is just the start. Tell him to imagine what we can do next year and the year after that.'

'Yes,' Edwyn murmurs, 'yes...'

He looks dreamily to the sky behind Silas' head then stops and points at the sky. 'Look, look over there!'

Silas turns, nods and smiles at the rainbow. 'Yes, *fy ffrind*, it's what comes next. After every storm – a promise.'

Epilogue

Buenos Aires State 1879 (10 years later)

Seannu wakes, remembers where she is and shuts her eyes again.

'*Señora?* Are you here?'

The door bangs shut. Footsteps come over to the bed. From where she is hiding beneath the overhanging covers Seannu can see a black gown and then two sandalled feet peeping out below. The feet pause and then a face frowns at her. Then a hand reaches in and grabs her arm.

'You have to lie on top of the bed, old woman, not underneath.'

She is the only one left. Tezza and Mareea died of the Cristianos' flux as soon as they came here – one and then the next. Like Yeluc. Yeluc. She sits on the floor in the corner of the room letting her thoughts drift. Sometimes she thinks her mind is like a forest in the mountains with each tree a person that she knew. When she stops by Yeluc's tree she always looks up. It is tall and straight. One day she will start to climb, she thinks, and maybe he will see her and pull her close to him. But for now she walks alone.

The rest of them here are young; a mixture of tribes, they talk their own dialects and stick to their own kind. When the Cristianos come close she closes her lips. There is one that smiles and begs her to talk but it does no good to speak. Sometimes she feels she has no words left. Sometimes, in the night, she practises her numbers quietly in her mouth the way Yeluc taught her; one to five in Tehuelche and then one to five in Welsh: *chuche, houke, aäs, carge, ktsin… un, dau, tri, pedwar, pump.*

She smiles. How Yeluc loved the Galenses. Go to them, Seannu, he told her once, if you ever find yourself alone, go to the Galenses. They will help you, the Galenses are our friends. And she had tried. When the news came back that her Yeluc was dead, the three of them had tried to get back to the Chubut but the Gallatts had stopped them. 'You're safer with us,' Gallatt had told them, no doubt he'd believed it.

Seannu shuts her eyes. She had been dreaming when the soldiers had come, sitting by the fire and dreaming as she is now. There'd been a skin in her hand but she hadn't been sewing. She'd thought the sound of galloping horses were the Gallatts returning. It was only when Mareea screamed that Seannu had opened her eyes and seen them. The soldiers had taken her arm too, just like they'd taken Mareea's and Tezza's; squeezed it too tight, then kicked her so that she had fallen, and when she had screamed hit her in the face until she'd become quiet.

It is better to be quiet. That's what she learned. Better not to say a word. *Un, dau, tri, pedwar, pump*. Sometimes she says the Galenses' words quietly to herself as if they are a spell. Mareea had thought the words would protect them if they said them. They are special words, Seannu. They chase away evil spirits. It is what Elal speaks in that place where the ancestors live. She used to know more: *bara, cawl, bach, cacen*. She smiles. She likes to roll them around the tongue. She rocks quietly back and forth: Welsh then Tehuelche. *Mam, yanna; dadda, yank;* Silas, Si-las; Megan, Me-gan; Mi-ri-am. Miriam.

Mother, *yanna*. That is what Miriam had called out the last time Seannu had seen her – a rare trip to the Chubut with Gallatts. She'd come running up to her and opened her loose outer mantle to show the stretched one beneath. '*Yanna*! That's what you say, isn't it?'

Yanna. She wonders how it was for her, and whether the child lived. Then she thinks of the ravine where they buried one and then another child of their own. How Yeluc had wept. How it had pulled at them both each time they'd passed. A place of just rocks, no grass, not even a single *calafate*. But it is better not to stay there. She shifts her mind away. Better to go somewhere else.

Each time Gallatt had gone close to the Chubut valley she had begged for news, but he would tell her nothing – except long tales about the things that men care about but women do not: the roads, the crowds of people, the way the ground was changing colour: from grey mud to great yellow glistening plants that rattled in the wind. Wheat to make bread, she'd said smugly, and Gallatt had opened his mouth a little at her knowledge. They have a mill now, he tells her. They make flour but they put it in bags for the Cristianos in Buenos Aires.

'The Gallenses give the Cristianos their wheat?' she'd asked Gallatt, checking to make sure she had understood correctly, and when he had nodded had thought again about the things she thought she knew.

Gallatt has gone now too. A single shot and he had flown backwards. A good way to die, she'd thought, but wished that Yeluc had been there to tell her what to do for his soul.

'They are taking our land, Seannu,' Gallatt had told her once. 'They're stealing it from us. They want us to stay in one place, not hunt, not speak our own tongue. We have to fight.'

She rocks on the floor and thinks about the forest in the hills and Yeluc's tree.

'Un, dau, tri, pedwar, pump,' she counts in Welsh, and waits for his approval.

'Chuche, houke, aäs, carge, ktsin,' he replies in their own tongue.

'No one speaks our words any more,' she tells him.

The tree sighs, bends down and touches her head with its lowest branches. 'Just words, Seannu, that's all they are. There's no need to fight over words. It's what they mean that's important – and anyway, ysher, in heaven I have found, there is no need to speak at all.'

No need to speak at all. She nods and rocks, nods and then rocks again.

WELSH TERMS

WELSH	ENGLISH
ar frys	immediately
bach	dear
bachgen	boy
bara	bread
bechgyn	boys
brawd	brother
brodyr	brothers
cacen	cake
cach	shit
cariad	love
cawl	soup
chwaer	sister
chwiorydd	sisters
diolch yn fawr	thank you very much
ffrind	friend
ffrindiau	friends
fy	my
gwrach	witch
gwraig	wife
heddiw	today
hiraeth	homesickness
iawn diolch	fine, thanks
llaca	mud
mab	son
meistr	master
mêl	honey
merch	daughter
moch	pigs
on'd yw hi?	isn't it?
taid	grandfather (northern Welsh)
Y Wladfa	colony
wrth gwrs	of course
y tylwyth teg	the fairies
ych-a-fi	expression of disgust

TEHUELCHE TERMS

(from 'At Home With The Patagonians' by George Chaworth Musters, 1871)

TEHUELCHE	ENGLISH
ááskren	stars
aix	council
bola	ball (usually of stone) threaded onto a lead and used as a weapon
cacique	chief
calafate	Berberis heterophylla Jussieu. A common plant similar to a mulberry. (It is said that if you eat a calafate berry in Patagonia you will always return).
chume	two-bola weapon
charcao	The Yuyo moro (Senecio filaginoides de Candolle). A common species of shrub in Patagonia
coquetra	children
Cristiano	Argentine Christian
háchish	Christian man
hogel	piebald
ketz	good
kow	expression of triumph on catching game
mara	type of long-legged rabbit related to the guinea pig
mikkeoush	ostrich (or rhea)
molle	Schinus johnstonii Barkley – a small tree or shrub native to Patagonia and used by the Tehuelches for medicine
pespesh	sit down
rou	guanaco, relative of the lama
showan	moon
tchonik	Indian people
toldo	awning or dwelling of the Tehuelches (Spanish)
wati, wati, wati	expression of surprise
wéen	march
zorrino	skunk (spanish)
zorro	fox

Author's Note

A Place of Meadows and Tall Trees is a work of fiction. I have taken the bare bones of the lives of various people that were part of that first, courageous settlement, and invented their flesh. Silas James is based on a man called Aaron Jenkins (Jenkins was my maiden name). Records from the colony showed that he lost his son, James, and a fortnight later gained a daughter, Rachel, on that dreadful voyage on the *Mimosa*. Rachel died in Patagonia a few months after they arrived, and a year or so later another child arrived, who also died a month later. The mother, also called Rachel Jenkins, was the woman who was truly a saviour of the colony since she suggested irrigation to her husband. She died a month after her last daughter died – of dropsy. I have invented her depression. Aaron Jenkins then married a seventeen-year-old girl, Margaret Jones, and had several more children. This was usual in the early colonists; the girls were married young, and men with children remarried quickly since children needed a mother, as much as a man needed a wife. That is all I found out about Aaron Jenkins, except I read that he had not been happy in Patagonia, and one other important detail: the end of his life was heroic. In 1878 several bandits escaped from a penal colony near Tierra del Fuego in the frozen south and one was captured near Gaiman. Aaron Jenkins volunteered to take the captive, alone, to Rawson but he was overpowered by the bandit who had managed to hide a knife. He cut out Jenkins' tongue and 'left his body to the birds'. Jenkins was buried on his farm, and the bandit later recaptured and killed. All the colonists fired bullets into the convict's body so none – or all – would be accused of his murder. I met one of the descendents of Aaron and Margaret Jenkins in Patagonia. She told me there had been a family interest in medicine sustained throughout the generations – initiated by Margaret (Miriam in the book) who had learnt a lot about local medical plants from the Tehuelches.

Edwyn Lloyd is based, extremely loosely, on the leader of the expedition, Lewis Jones. Again I have used the merest basic details of his life and have not attempted to base 'the flesh' on any accounts of the man himself. I know that his mother was persecuted by the English and evicted from her cottage. I know he was a publisher of a satirical magazine, and that he was instrumental in persuading the colonists to come to Patagonia. He and Sir Love Jones-Parry made a reconnoitre of the area before the colonists came and he did his best to prepare for them (with his wife Ellen and an American colonist, Edwyn Cynrig Roberts – Selwyn Williams in the book). Lewis Jones, by some accounts, exaggerated the fertility of the area. He was later sent to Buenos Aires by the colonists to negotiate with Dr Guillermo Rawson, the Argentine minister for internal affairs. His wife then returned to Wales, but a couple of years later Jones went back to Wales to perhaps encourage more settlers, and Ellen returned to Patagonia with him, giving birth to a daughter on the voyage over. This daughter, Eluned Morgan, wrote an account of her travels in Patagonia which is till in print today: *Dringo'r Andes a Gwymon y Mor*.

Three ministers accompanied the colony to Patagonia, but the characters of Jacob Griffiths and Caradoc Llewellyn are made up and not based on any one of them.

The encounters with the Tehuelches are, as far as I could glean, pretty much as they happened. Their first contact was with an old chief, who helped them and saved them from starvation, and later they were surrounded by the members of three other tribes. They traded successfully, and the two peoples lived harmoniously with each other, even inventing a Welsh-Tehuelche hybrid language. Although I researched the Tehuelche culture as much as I could – including the folk-lore, myths and lifestyle – the character of Yeluc is my invention

The incident with the dog bringing game is recorded, although this may be myth. The natural disasters – flooding, storms on the *Maria Theresa*, the loss of livestock, the drought and the eventual irrigation – are all recorded.

The main part of the book ends in approximately 1869. In subsequent years the Welsh obtained a bumper harvest, and they were soon winning prizes for their wheat. The colony grew, spread west to the Andes and today there are five towns with a significant Welsh character and population – Trevelin and Esquel in the

Andes, and Gaiman, Trelew and Rawson towards the Atlantic coast. On satellite pictures from space the eastern towns are green patches in a yellow-brown landscape. They still hold *Eisteddfodau* and are proud of their Welsh heritage. The Welsh language spoken in Patagonia is a unique blend of both north and south Welsh. Their other language is Spanish, and they consider themselves to be Welsh-Argentines. Gaiman is the most Welsh-looking of the towns, but the eastern valley is littered with Welsh chapels and tea rooms, only differing from their counterparts in Wales in that the roofs tend to be corrugated iron rather than slate, offering greater resistance to the strong and frequent winds.

Thanks to a campaign by the Argentines started in the 1870s to rid Patagonia of its indigenous nomadic population ('The Conquest of the Desert') there are few Tehuelches left in South America, and the Tehuelche language is now an endangered one.

Acknowledgements

Thank you to the North West Arts Council and the Authors' Foundation for grants which enabled me to go to Patagonia in 2004 and interview the descendants of the colonists.

Thank you also to the many people of Patagonia I interviewed, especially Luned Gonzales de Roberts (descendant of Michael D Jones), her sister Tegai Roberts (curator of the museum at Gaiman) and Erie James (Auron Jenkins' descendant) and also Albina de Zampini, Rachel Davies-Butrick, Rhiannon Gough, Dougie Berwyn and Lizzie Lloyd. Many thanks also to Gwyn and Mónica Jones who arranged my trip to Patagonia, Susan Wilkinson, author of *Mimosa*, for useful discussions, Elvey MacDonald, author of *Yr Hirdaith*, who was most helpful in giving me a list of people to see and places to visit, Harold W. Carr-Rollitt and Rini Griffiths, my guides in Patagonia, Fernando Coronato of the Centro Nacional Patagónico, and Robert Owen Jones (professor of Welsh at the university of Cardiff). I would also like to thank Morina Lloyd who taught me Welsh at Lampeter University, Howard and Elsa Malpas who gave me some shamanic training and the staff of the National Library of Wales, the British Library and the British Museum. Thank you also to the authors of the following books which I recommend for further reading: *Mimosa* by Susan Wilkinson, *The Desert and the Dream* by Glyn Williams, *Hope and Heartbreak* by Russell Davies, *Shamanism* by Mircia Eliade, *The Language of the Blue Books* by Gwyneth Tyson Roberts, *The Epic of South America* by John A Crow, *Yr Hirdaith* by Elvey MacDonald, *Crónica de la Colonia Galesa de la Patagonia* by Abraham Matthews, *Patagonia Un Jardín Natural* by María Elena Arce and Silvia Adriana Gonzales, *La Patagonia que Canta* by William C Rhys and *Una Frontera Lejana* by Bill Jones et al and *The Great Adventure* by Aled Lloyd Davies, *At Home with the Patagonians* by George Musters.

The following people read this work in its various drafts and I am grateful to them for support and advice: my editor at Seren, Penny Thomas; Stuart Clark; Natasha Fairweather and her assistants

Naomi Leon and Judy-Meg Kennedy at A.P. Watt; Carole Welch; Helen Garnons-Williams; my mother Nancy Jenkins; and my husband Christopher Dudman.

Thank you also to my friends in Chester and on-line for your support and encouragement.